ALSO BY ARTHUR JEON

City Dharma: Keeping Your Cool in the Chaos

Sex, Love, and Dharma: Finding Love Without Losing Your Way

SNOWFLAKE

Arthur Jeon

Global Animal

SNOWFLAKE

www.globalanimal.org

Cover Design: Julian Whatley

Snowflake / Arthur Jeon

PAPERBACK ISBN: 978-1-7340935-0-6

First published in the United States by Global Animal

AUTHOR'S NOTE

Although *Snowflake* is set against the present-day destruction of our planet, it is a work of fiction. But the attacks on the environment Ben chronicles are real. The media headlines, tweets, and quotes are authentic. And, as of 2020, the facts he lists about our accelerating climate emergency are accurate.

– Arthur Jeon

Comfort Suites – Youngstown, Ohio

Mom, Dad, June –

By the time you read this, I'm probably dead.

Middle of the night and I'm writing you this awful note in a motel room that smells like an empty swimming pool. Here's my latest journal, which I started right after the fires – it will explain everything.

Hate myself for lying nonstop for weeks, but it describes what's at stake. Why I had no choice. Don't blame yourselves, there's no way you could have known my secret.

Hands calm and cold as a corpse. Is it really happening in less than 24-hours? Guess one step at a time gets you here.

Please be careful – everything will happen. Keep Gigi close. When the cops bust in, they'll shoot her for sure. They always kill pit bulls in no-knock raids.

Need sleep. Need to function tomorrow. Journal will explain everything.

What an unforgivable letter. Hope someday you can forgive me.

Love you always. And I'm sorry beyond all words.

—Ben

New Journal #9/5

I gazed inside the gates of hell today. They flanked the 405 Freeway.

And not "hell" in the way people complain about driving in LA, inching along in traffic, wondering, how did my life go so wrong? It's always a parking lot after school, but today's hell was no metaphor...

Embers skitter across ten lanes. Trees in the Sepulveda Pass crack and explode in tornadoes of fire –

"Mom! Take the Getty exit so we don't get trapped." June, five years away from a driver's permit, is backseat driving as usual. "We can cut up into the Valley."

Mom swerves onto Getty Drive. Above us, the museum, crapped onto a beheaded mountain by a billion dollars, squats behind a burka of smoke. June wheezes and takes out her inhaler for a hit. I shut the fans. Futile. The car smells like a chimney.

"There's fire everywhere." Mom hesitates at the intersection, squinting.

"Turn right. If it jumps the freeway, we'll be better off on the other side," I try to sound calm. But is this how it happens – everything normal, running errands, living your stupid life, and then some horror shows up out of nowhere like a school shooter? And you die in a mudslide? Flood? Inferno? Happening every day now in the Golden State.

Mom cuts right, away from home, and floors the car. The roaring Santa Ana winds disappear everything in smoke as afternoon becomes midnight –

"Look out!" June yelps. Two men carrying trash bags emerge like ghosts. Mom slams the brakes, and the men scurry into the brush. Did they start the fire? It happens. Homeless in encampments light cooking fires that get away from them, what with everything so dry and –

"There's fire right there." June points to an exploding tree, each leaf spectacularly aflame. I'm momentarily mesmerized, like a guy jumping off a building, thinking as he falls: This is intense. This is life! Splat.

A Mercedes slings by us, forcing an oncoming car into a gully. Mom swerves into the breakdown lane, scraping the concrete barrier.

"Mom!" I'm shouting as if I can control any of it. "Take it easy."

"You just tore off the mirror. Badass!" June sounds thrilled, suddenly the star of one of the *Fast and Furious* movies she drags me to. Mom barrels up the breakdown lane, ignoring the fire truck blaring behind us. That's when I know she's losing it. Mom always obeys the law.

"There! Open sky," June declares as we crest the hill that overlooks the valley, slumbering in its usual blanket of smog, unaware that behind us it's pure movie destruction – like Godzilla belched up from the depths of the ocean to scorch the world.

"Will we get to evacuate?" June asks, picturing a vacation from fifth grade.

"Depends on the wind." I roll down a window, take a deep breath, and exhale in a rattle.

Turns out, we do have to evacuate. It's a nightmare because they won't even let us up to get Gigi, no matter how much we beg the cops at the canyon barricades. Only one way in and out, and they don't want to risk it for a dog, the heartless bastards. So now Gigi's stuck up there by herself with fire everywhere, left behind like the pets after Fukushima melted down from the earthquake/tsunami.

Left to starve or die of thirst. Or burn to death. Christ!

I'm trying not to bug out, downloading this horrible day in a damn Kimpton Boutique Hotel in Westwood because Dad had some points on a credit card. The hotel advertises "Wilshire Chic," and I'm up on the roof deck with a tiny pool, watching fires rim the distant hills under a nuclear bomb of smoke. Couples drink twenty-dollar "craft cocktails," like somebody spent a year woodworking them into existence. Like nothing is wrong. And for now, for them, I guess nothing is.

But so far, ten houses have burned just two streets away from ours. I'd pray if I thought it'd help. Pray our house is spared. Pray Gigi's not burned alive. Is useless prayer all that's left?

The sun goes down blood red over West LA.

The merciless wind shifts.

This is good news. Now pluto mansions in Bel Air will burn instead of Gigi. It's terrible, but you can replace houses.

At least that media mogul's estate gets torched. Love that his compound burns as his lie factory for the adult diaper crowd denies Climate Chaos. What do you say to an old bloodsucker spreading fake news and poison around the world? Grasping all that fear money?

Do you shout, "Go to hell!"?

No, that would be redundant.

Godzilla just broke the gates of hell and banged on our front door.

Today's Headline

"Over 5% of California Burned in Last Five Years." And fires alone produced nine times more emissions than got reduced here last year. We're full speed in reverse.

– LATimes.com

Typical

I'm sitting outside Nichols' office waiting for the tiny light to go off so I can enter "the sanctum," as she calls it. As if therapy will help me deal with what's happening. Hell, even my writing isn't helping today.

At least they let us back in the house, soot covering everything...

Gigi's hiding in my bedroom closet. When she bolts out, body wriggling like she's about to explode, eighty-five pounds of pure muscle hip-checks me down, and then she's scraping my face with her tongue. We all gather around hugging her and everybody gets teary except Dad.

"I'm sorry. I'm so sorry, Gigi." I kiss her blockhead and can't stop apologizing. It's amazing dogs don't hold it against you, no matter what you do or how you let them down. And we did screw it up. It was pure luck the wind blew into Bel Air, roaring through brush as dry as matchsticks – and still burning in distant hills. We dodged a bullet. For now.

But I can't dodge damn therapy. Can't cancel Nichols – it's under 24 hours and she's strict about these things, apocalypse be damned. At least Gigi's here. Don't ever want to leave her alone in that house again during fire season, which just gets longer every year. So, we wait together, ready for the session that Mom thinks I need.

Gigi, mute, and calm as Buddha, sure doesn't need therapy.

And even though I'm anxious, I don't want to be here either, with Nichols nodding and furiously scribbling notes.

She always denies it, but I just know Nichols is writing a damn book. She still thinks my memory is cool, no matter how much I tell her it's a curse to remember everything I've ever read and everything that ever happens to me. She still doesn't believe I envy "neurotypicals" their amnesia – they get to forget their horrors. Not me. I'm stuck scrawling every detail in journals just to stay sane. Usually, that's okay. Writing is way better than Nichols for my mental health. But now, the more everybody lies and denies the state of the world, the more the stats flowing through my brain churn my guts. Today's log just makes me feel sick.

I'm sure Nichols thinks it's gross to be complaining about my gift. She's right. But gifts are a two-way street, like the oil that heats our homes and suffocates the planet.

Christ... Feeling scrambled today. A crack in my shell? Hope not.

Guess after getting evacuated and nearly losing Gigi, I'm just not in the mood for Nichols pointing out how my lists and stats and obsesso climate spirals are "borderline OCD."

Okay, Old. Don't tell it to me...

Tell it to the clueless rich people whose houses just burned down. Tell it to the heart-broken kid whose ancient tortoise died in the fire because he was too panicked to grab him. Tell it to Greta Thunberg, pleading the truth like an environmental Joan of Arc, nobody listening. She's not "neurotypical" either. But just because you slap a label and dole out drugs doesn't make us Zoomers wrong. Or crazy.

I think I'll quit Nichols. I don't want to listen to her BS anymore. I don't need a paid friend. I'm 18 now and don't need –

Damn. The light just went off.

Today's Headline

"How Scientists Got Climate Change So Wrong." Misunderestimated, as another terrible president would say. Our country could use a dose of my "OCD" just to pay attention.

– NYTimes.com

Molly

I'm sitting on the bathroom floor with my journal, staring at a tile that looks like an etching of our halfwit president. Starting to come down from a life-changing night...

It starts randomly, with Tim texting me. Best friend since kindergarten and now he's a stoner who hasn't returned my texts in a year. And won't again after tonight. But he surprise pings me, asking if I want to go to a party. And he's got some Molly. Fires be damned, life blasts on...

Tim knows I hate parties and never get invited anyway, but I've always wanted to try Molly. And I'd like to see him. So, I emoji thumbs up and he picks me up in his dad's Lexus.

"Dude, you really off Snap?" He asks. No preamble. No talk of the fires still burning in not so distant hills. Yesterday's news, I guess.

"Snap-Shit?" I smile, hitting the ball back.

"Insta?" He grins as we fall right back into our ping-pong routine.

"You mean Insta-Lie? Fakebook's evil daughter?"

"Twitter?"

"Twister – 280 characters of presidential BS?" I respond. Tim laughs his wild laugh, blue eyes blazing like the day we met so long ago. Makes me realize how much I miss him.

"Seriously, dude, why'd you unplug?" Tim unplugs the game, which used to go on for minutes.

"Just feel more human off it." I shrug. Tim nods, and we drive a bit in silence.

"Not gonna help with your social life," he says, as he pulls up in front of some Bitterwood McMansion. "Cutting cords."

"From the Reactosphere? Whatever. Never helped much, anyway."

Tim laughs and shakes out two little white pills from a full plastic bag, passing me one.

"See you on the other side." He pops his pill with a swig of water. I do the same.

"How long before it hits?" I'm suddenly nervous.

"About half an hour. You might feel a bit sick. But it passes fast."

"Now you tell me," I try to smile. He hits a vape – no more old school blunts for Tim – and offers it to me. I shake my head. Still can't hang with pot, how it speeds my brain and slows my tongue until I'm verbally disarmed, trapped inside myself like Lou Gehrig's disease. Has Tim drifted away on a cloud of weed or is our distance my fault? Probably me...

"Wanna go in?" Tim asks. I'd rather just hang in the car and catch up, but I know that's not what he wants. He wants to rave it up in a McMansion. So, I nod and in we go.

Before I know it, I'm standing in the corner of a colossal living room, blitzed by sweaty faces and pounding EDM. Tim has disappeared. I'm not feeling anything except the sickly anxiety I get in crowds, but more intense. Is that the Molly?

And then in walks SG. Her thick hair falls on shoulders toasted golden in some Indian/Wasp combo of perfection. She's given me no sign I exist at Harvard Westbridge, even though she's in my Gov class and I heard is also vegan. I should say hi. Introduce myself. Act like a Normie. But I suddenly feel Mt. Vesuvius sick and holy shit it's coming NOW and the closest door is the front door SG just came in, so I bolt for it.

I don't make it.

I turn my head to avoid vomiting on SG and spew all over some pretty Insta-Feeder. I feel better and then, strangely, magically FANTASTIC.

"I'm so sorry," I shout at the poor screaming girl who won't be Insta-Lying this. I try to wipe the vomit off her. I just want to hug her and make it okay because I LOVE her and it's so awful what I've done. Some guy, her boyfriend I guess, pulls me off. He thinks I'm pawing her. People are laughing and pointing – their jeers are needles on my skin. SG's smiling but trying to hide it and looks sympathetic and so maybe laughing with me instead of at me? I don't stick around to find out. I surf the wave of contempt rising behind me and barrel out the front door –

WOW! Feels so good to jump into the fresh silence, with the scent of burning wood perfuming the air.

How can I feel the world through every cell in my body!?

I wander canyon streets flowing past me like a movie, all the houses gone dark from their endless ambition. I lie on a lawn so perfect it's like the plastic grass people now use – oil to save water. I stare up at the moon and make angel wings as a thousand blades massage me. For hours, days, years, I am Earth itself, connecting from this meadow to the entire planet.

Then I just disappear – every thought, hope, fear. Me. I'm gone.

Wow. Wow! WOW! Empty. Free...

When I finally stand, I leave the ghost of an angel in the grass, ash from the fire instead of snow. Somebody's house? Car? Tortoise? Surely. The stuff of stars and the dead. Like me.

As dawn breaks, a family of raccoons – mother, father, and three rascals – trundle by with their bank robber masks and trilling voices. I'm not hallucinating, I can see every bristle on their faces. I ramble and meld with them as they ransack alleys, raiding garbage cans for all the food we toss, the little ones learning and playing and herded along. I am a fourth child, clumsy and not cute, but tolerated. We eat overripe apples out of a cardboard box next to trash bins and they taste <u>amazing</u>.

When the raccoons climb a fence, the mother turns and looks at me, wizened, knowing something about me I don't know about myself – a stillness that lasts a lifetime. It's as if she's trying to tell me something important. Something I have to be. And then she's gone, over a fence to wash her too human hands in a swimming pool. I end up on a curb weeping about that little raccoon family, so innocent, who I love so much, like the whole damn world. Love – I am it!

Guess that's Molly for you.

Roger, the old hippie at Face the Wave where Mom drags me for my "executive functioning" always says, "No time like the present to wake up." That meditation isn't just a stupid productivity tool, but a way to wake up from the illusions of our conditioned personality. Now I finally know what he's talking about. Nobody home. No separation. Empty.

Note to future self: don't do it again.

Might get addicted to that melting sense of oneness and love until I just want to drop Molly all day, every day. I'll become a Molly version of Tim, high all the time. How is he? I'm sure he'd ghost me forever if I tell him the raccoon story. Final straw, I guess, eating garbage with raccoons. And for sure, that was my last party – puking on that girl was the nail in my social coffin. No doubt it's already all over social.

And SG? She was the only one not laughing at me. I think. But that chance is gone too. I don't care. I felt something huge and beautiful –

"Benji?" June is at the door in her Thor PJs. "Why are you lying on the bathroom floor?"

"Just trying to see something." I point to the tile. "Does this look like the president?"

"You're such a dork." But June, ever game, comes over and squints. "Yeah. I guess he does look like that Demento."

"Thanks. Thought I was losing it for a sec."

"Can you get out of here? I have to pee." She takes a hit off her asthma inhaler.

"Oh, sure." I stand, close my journal, and shuffle out.

What was that raccoon trying to tell me?

Today's Headline

"Humans Speeding Extinction, Altering Natural World at Unprecedented Pace." That's just sad. Maybe the whole world needs to take some Molly and wake up.

– NYTimes.com

Porno World

Monday lunch in the Harvard-Wanna-Be cafeteria, quiet as a church with everybody praying over iPhones and I overhear this from two newbies who sit down next to me...

"Then she took her jeans off," whisper-talks this frosh, who looks about 12, grinning a mouthful of green braces at his buddy, the same kind I've got for a couple more weeks. "She had hair down there."

"Yeah, so?" His friend is wolfing down a sandwich. "She's a Junior."

"I just, wasn't expecting it. Bugged me out."

"Was it a big old bush?"

"No. I just... never seen it before. In porn."

"Me neither, but I know it exists. I'm getting hair down there. Aren't you?"

"Yeah. Not really." Braces hesitates. Is this kid for real? Or trolling his friend? "I just freaked and couldn't go through with it."

"Big mood, dude," his pal says, all sympathetic. Braces suddenly sees me eavesdropping and abruptly stands, drawing up his five feet.

"You ear hustling me, bitch?" This just gets better and better – is that prison lingo from an HWB newbie? Ha. No doubt a big gangsta rap fan. "What you looking at?"

"I'm just wondering if you're for real," I say, surprised into honesty. "I can't tell."

"Why don't you just mind your own business, freak?" Braces is practically shouting.

"You're right next to me," I protest. "You think I want to hear all that?"

"He's that doofus who puked on that hot senior," his friend chimes in helpfully. "TikTok loser."

Damn Socials – guess it'll be a month of eating shit. I want to explain it was the Molly but they've already grabbed their lunch trays and are striding away. And what's the point? He's a kid – who's only seen porn stars shaved dolphin smooth his whole life and is too inexperienced or dumb or <u>something</u> to know pubic hair even exists. Really?

But I guess it makes sense. Braces isn't the only one who's never seen a real girl's hair – me too. Only half of American high school seniors went on a date last year. Nobody's hooking up in meat-world, everybody just fapping in the safety of their bedrooms, growing soft as human veal.

Guess you can't put IRL sex on your college applications, so why bother? Ha. Truth is, #AllPornAllTheTime should be the hashtag for us net native dudes. But in getting your reality from the web, you can forget you're an animal, with hair, living in a network of life that's collapsing around us. I mean, you can see the whole world online and still be totally lost. Like what Hale says – the map is not the territory.

High tech debases to our lowest self – that's my new theory. The web distorts reality, serving up extreme versions of life to our darkest desires until we're cowering under our damn beds, "entertained" to death.

I think quitting porn is helping me see reality more clearly. Hope so. Going cold turkey like a damn alcoholic still sucks. Especially vanilla – I mean everybody watches vanilla. Miss how it froze my anxiety numb as Novocain. But that dark web porn was so snuff – Bukkake and Rule 34 just wore me down. The hard-core stuff always ended in violence. And not fake pain – they hurt those girls for real. Guess numb always needs more. Christ, what a world.

Hope I'm not permanently scarred from watching all that DW porn.

Like porn PTSD.

I still miss the distraction – guess I could use a hit right now the way I'm going on about it. But I don't want to go back to imagining girls gagged and bound and clamped in a snuff film sling with every hole stuffed and pretending to enjoy it. There's some mental freedom in not running that spiral. All those big dicks and dominant dudes who last forever – too much of that going around these days.

Maybe, I was hiding in all the fake tits and horse dicks – living in Voltaire's world of illusion. Porn illusion.

But I want to know the truth at this perilous moment. To see reality unfiltered. Not disillusioned – unillusioned. Like the Molly helped me <u>know</u> the raccoons and how connected all life is. Like the 405 fire made it clear I'm an animal fighting to survive the burning of my habitat by bloodsuckers, the same as all the animals of the world. Like all we humans are, even though people don't see themselves as animals.

But doesn't everybody have to wake up to that truth?

No time like the present to wake up. Ha.

That pube story is funny/sad, my favorite kind.

Today's Headline

"The Average Age Kids First See Porn is Eleven." And 35% of all Internet downloads are porn. I get it, jerking off as the world burns. Hell, I did it.

– HuffingtonPost.com

Today's Tyler Tyranny

Is Molly still kicking around in my brain? Feels like it. I had another intense animal encounter on a field trip to Animal Acres Farm Sanctuary.

And I finally talked to SG! Even though Tyler messed it up…

So, I'm standing in front of this cow they rescued after she fell off a slaughterhouse truck. I'm petting her and she nuzzles me and looks up with these liquid brown eyes filled with trust. Her warm breath ruffles the hair on my arm and her lungs sound like bellows and she smells like hay and something inside me just melts. I get tears in my eyes – like a religious experience, like a <u>communion</u>. But it isn't religious, that's man-made BS. It feels bigger, a mystical merging with nature – animal to animal. Like with the raccoons. So close to some primal innocent force my brain spin halts. That never happens. And now, I become stillness itself…

Is it the Molly? Has it changed me forever?

But I feel normal, and it's been three days and –

"Beautiful, isn't she?" It's SG, glowing and smiling at me with the almond eyes of a Bollywood star. And I'm standing here with tears in my eyes for a cow. Lame.

"Yeah." I turn away and wipe my face. But SG doesn't notice or pretends not to as she scratches the cow's jowls and makes cute cooing sounds.

"Is your stomach better?" She asks, I guess referring to my puke-fest, now viral.

"Um. Yeah. That was un malo burrito. Gets you every time."

"Yes." She smiles kindly. "I felt bad for her but glad you missed me."

"Split-second reflexes."

SG laughs, like music. I've got no idea what to say to her, so I just smile and we're in a sweet silence with the cow when Tyler crashes in and destroys the moment.

"Then I took the shot," he says. WTF? Turns out, Tyler is bragging to his pals Dim and Dimmer about flying on the private jet to a weekend hunting trip at the family ranch in Idaho. Libertarian Central for his billionaire Daddy, who wants to build floating city-states in international waters off California to keep out the government – but also brown people. SG quietly steps away like a deer sensing danger.

"You trying to hit that, Puke Boy?" Tyler nods at SG, now gliding toward the barn. "Too bad you got no game."

"No." I hate the way he looks at her, a combo of contempt and leering appraisal.

"Right." As usual, Tyler's bullying knack for sniffing any vulnerability is on point. "You know, Soy Boy, your dick won't work after you go tranny from all the tofu you eat."

Dim and Dimmer laugh at Tyler's comedic genius. I want to follow Soy Girl, my fellow vegan, but don't want to draw their attention to her. Or leave the mystical cow alone with this sociopath, as he rhapsodizes about killing bighorn sheep while visiting a damn animal sanctuary. So, I stand listening to Tyler talk about "blowing its brains out" because – I have no idea why. I picture the sheep tumbling, horns clanging down a cliff, scraped tufts of hair pinched in the rock, wondering WTF? I mean, if you can kill them as they're grazing as peaceful as can be, why bother? Take a picture. Paint-ball or shoot them with a dart. Anything.

"You don't eat them, so why call it hunting? It's just slaughter." Why do I blurt this out? Revenge for the tranny insult. Or pure masochism –

"What?" Tyler's face flips a switch. He looks like he wants to punch me in the face, but he hasn't done that since ninth grade. "What d'you say?"

"What's the point of killing sheep? It's not like they can fight back."

"It's fun. Don't expect you to get it," Tyler scoffs. I glance at the cow, staring at us with wide innocent eyes, staying out of it, smarter than me.

"Yeah, I don't eat cows like this because I couldn't kill her myself.

Seems fair enough."

"Retarded," Tyler pronounces. He prides himself on being anti-PC but is really just an A-hole. "I could kill it no problem. But the whole idea is somebody else kills it. Capitalism. Separation of labor. Factory farms."

"Cowschwitz? Standing in their own shit getting pumped full of antibiotics – 70% of all made? So now they're not working on humans because we eat all those drugs?" Got to stop. Tyler's going to call me a virtue-signaling snowflake again. But what if there's real virtue in what I say? Like Americans not eating 222 pounds of meat a year is a no-brainer for our planet and our hearts? Our dead hearts...

Have I lost my sense of humor? Gone full preacher? Hope not.

"Gotta fatten them up, Snowflake," Tyler says. There it is. He flashes teeth as small and even as corn kernels. Sociopath would probably love to live in a world where you can die of an infected cut on your finger.

"So, boil the planet for a burger." I take a last stab, simplifying it down to a meme. We're never going to change each other's minds, but I still can't let it go. How stupid and futile is that?

"Bear burgers. President's gonna allow hunting them while they hibernate." That's terribly true, but Tyler's just trolling now, so I walk.

Am I ever going to crack his Carnism? Nope. Tyler's been given everything except the ability to feel for another creature. Or too afraid to feel – that would be Emo. What's manly is you kill everything in sight without a thought. You like your life, little animal? Too bad. I'll eat you even if the CO2 produced burns down my own house. But not before I chop you up so you can't stare at me and remind me of your spirit.

Guess after the Molly I'm feeling it all more than usual, sympathy for the nonhuman animals, living in agony their whole lives to be our food.

"Good luck at the woke Olympics," Tyler calls after me.

"Sleep tight, Prager Bro," I retort, looking back at him.

Tyler just gives me the finger, popping his muscles. Last week he declared himself "swole AF" to his lacrosse pals Dim and Dimmer, who just watched this whole exchange, mouths open, fellow gym gerbils on the same wheel. Tyler doesn't get that you don't exactly have to be "woke" to know Meat World creates 20% of greenhouse gases, the same as all the cars on the planet. So, meat really is murder. Or more accurately, suicide. And endless torture for billions of animals like chickens, social birds debeaked into wire coffins, driven mad before being deep-fried into a bucket of McNuggets, perfectly teeing up an avian flu to wipe half the humans off the planet – Christ, we're idiots, so cruel and hopeless!

So much for avoiding my "obsessive climate spirals."

Nichols wouldn't approve.

And fighting with Tyler – what a waste of time. As if he'll ever drop the green pill and see all the suffering. It never occurs to Tyler that he'll be an overlord of a scorched planet filled with starving people. Because life is good at Harvard-Wanna-Be – what fires? Ha. Supposed to be the best high school in LA, with robotics and even an electron microscope, but HWB is full of legacy morons like Tyler. Guess it goes with putting Harvard in your name to attract the pluto crowd – pure lux branding.

Whatever. Tyler will never change. That psycho's funny and popular, but as cruel as the Aryan youth we're studying, with the same blond hair. If Tyler saw me crying about the cow, he'd laugh in my face. He's got no idea Hindus revere cows as a sacred symbol of life. He'd say what he always says, "You know, Soy Boy, Hitler was veg. 'Sup with that?"

It's a good troll, I'll give him that. The first time he rolled it out.

But it's all so old school toxic – Christ, Benji! Stop!

Let it go before you can't. Got to watch myself...

Least I had that moment with SG. Wish I said something interesting.

Today's Weird Fact

On its first birthday, a human baby engineered to grow as fast as a Frankenchicken would weigh 650 pounds and be unable to stand. How horror-movie-sick is that?

– Science.com

June

My world is upside down. I've got to write this out or I'll explode.

It came out of nowhere – just a typical day. Well, not totally typical. Smoke from the new fires in Malibu has turned Bitterwood air Beijing brown again. So bad it's setting off indoor fire alarms, the sound screeching through the canyon like deranged birds.

And June has a black eye and a bruised knee, launching into a story about a fistfight with some school bully. She's so exuberant in her description of the brawl, Gigi opens her one eye to listen. Then she goes back to snoring like a drunken sailor, chipped bowling ball head hanging off her bed, jowls spreading like spilled milk on the floor.

"So, this jerk Alex comes up on Olivia and me and says girls suck at Fortnite. Then he shoves Olivia!" June can't believe this unfortunate boy gave her a green light to go all Wonder Woman on his ass.

"June, language." This is the second time Mom's heard the story, so she's only got one ear on it while she makes dinner, saving enough for Dad, who's working late again.

"It's his language." June flips her pigtails, ready for a fight.

"Don't stoop. Go high." Mom stoops to put a sheet of veggies in the oven.

"Can you believe it, Benji?" June turns to me, reveling in her recount of the fight.

"You rumbling on the playground? Yeah."

"You should have seen it." June laughs. "You will see it – somebody took a video. Me and Olivia are gonna TikTok it. It'll be hilarious!

"So, what happened after Alex shoves Kelly?" I'm trying not to think about viral videos.

"I kick him in the nuts and down he goes. That's what's going on TikTok. Gonna be epic, the kick to his balls over and over." June grins wickedly. "Crush your lame puke video."

"Language," Mom says, glancing at me. I shrug like I don't know what video June's talking about.

"Sorry, Mom. So, I snap-kick him in the groin and start with the ground and pound."

"Ground and pound?" I ask, steering the conversation away from the video of me puking on that poor girl. Don't need Mom's questions. "Sounds like a cheap burger joint."

"No, Benji." June laughs her hearty laugh. "MMA. It's when you take somebody down, get on top, and beat the crap out of them."

"Right. Makes total sense." I'm not surprised June knows all the lingo. She still has a poster of Conor McGregor in her room. He looks like an insane leprechaun with his green tattoos and popping muscles like his whole rooster body is shouting as loud as it can. When June showed me a fight she sneak-streamed on Reddit, it looked like a two-man riot with interludes of rough sex –

"Then I twist Alex's arm and make him apologize, and he starts crying like a baby." June claps her hands. "That's when his friend jumps me from behind and pins me down and punches me in the eye. See why Karate's not enough and I need BJJ, like, right now?"

She directs this at Mom, who ignores her. June never misses a chance to make the case for Brazilian Jiu Jitsu, saying it's the only way a smaller person can defend against a bigger one. Might be a smart idea to learn it, given her love of a good fight. She's still always trying to demonstrate the counter-punches and arm locks of "the hurt business" on me. June insists it's like chess, only you choke people out instead of moving a piece. It's her idea of a party.

"Then Markel rushes in and breaks it up. I pity the fool if I catch him alone." June is all "I pity the fool" about everybody after she finds a meme of that old A-team show.

"You better not. I don't want you fighting," Mom warns.

"Mom. Bullies only understand power." Out of the mouths of babes.

"Then, I'm going to have a talk with dad about your karate lessons."

"You better not because –"

Then June can't catch her breath, suddenly gasping like a fish flopping on a dock. Gigi knows this is bad and pops up from her croc doze on the floor and starts licking June's bare legs. I grab her Vin Diesel backpack and rip it open.

"You have an inhaler in here?"

June nods, eyes bulging and watery as I tear through the pack. But Mom already has one out and hands it to June, who takes two big blasts of Albuterol.

"Easy June," Mom instructs. "Slow your breath down."

"Just try to stay calm," I add, more for me than June.

"You okay, honey?" Mom asks, rubbing June's back. We're waiting for her breathing to normalize and her freckles to reappear, surfacing like toasted islands in a sea of crimson skin. Waiting for her to launch right back into her story like she always does because a little thing like suffocation never slows June down.

But today June isn't okay. Her lungs are whistling and she's turning red as Vin Diesel's car on her backpack.

"Grab the meter," Mom directs. But I've already got the Peak Flow Meter out and am holding it to June's lips.

"Do your best," I encourage. June tries to blow air into it but the needle doesn't move. Nothing.

"Call 911." Mom's eyes are wide with fright.

I grab my cell as Mom holds the inhaler for June, saying, "Lean over and take another hit."

June tries to inhale as I'm on with 911, shouting my response to, "what's your emergency?" But June can't take another hit because she can't breathe. She sinks to the floor like a skyscraper detonated from within. Her lungs take wheezing sips. Her lips and fingernails turn blue. Then she passes out and stops breathing.

She's dying right on the kitchen floor and I totally lose it.

"June! JUNE!" I'm shaking her and Mom jumps in and starts CPR, and the EMTs are banging on the door, and I'm rushing to let them in, and they're zapping her – CLEAR! – and the rest is a whirl of professional focus until here I am with Mom and Dad in the hospital, waiting for June to wake up, my whole life feeling out of control for the second time this week. FUCK!

Thirteen minutes. That's how quick the EMTs showed.

But Mom and I couldn't keep June alive because wildfire soot hangs in the air like tear gas. As if normal LA pollution wasn't enough to kill asthmatics. The doctors have sedated June and they say she'll be okay, but she died for a minute and –

"You want something to eat?" Dad peers at me through glasses so strong his eyes look like blue marbles. He seems so shambling and exhausted these days, with his shoulders stooped from editing TV shows over a body like a rotting pear.

"I'm good. Thanks."

"You should eat something, Benji," Mom chimes in, her face tight with worry.

"I said I'm good," I snap. But seeing June intubated and surrounded by beeping machines fills me with a sudden rage. I just want to kill the bloodsuckers who pollute everything and swim in a sea of blood money. As more people get asthma from a pandemic of air pollution – 300 million worldwide. And over 250,000 of them suffocate every year, most of them children because now more people die from tail-pipe exhaust than from car crashes and – June. She too, reduced to a lifeless blue body, today's fire and fumes adding her to the incomprehensible numbers endlessly flowing through my brain –

"It's going to be okay," Dad interrupts my spiral, seeing it on my face.

"Sorry." I wince at him. "I'm just –"

"It's understandable." Dad tries to smile. "Just take care of yourself."

He means write it out, but today it feels useless. My notes. Little essays and stories. The daily record. It's so messy and slow, throwing up my insides and parsing the chunks of my literary logorrhea. Wish I didn't have to examine every idea and feeling and experience for the truth. It's a chore. But I do. Processing my unforgettable thought tsunami in this journal keeps me sane. Today, it's just not working. Right now, seeing June collapsed in the hospital bed looking so tiny, my brain goes biblical.

"Blessed is he, who in the name of charity and goodwill shepherds the weak through the valley of darkness, for he is truly his brother's keeper and the finder of lost children."

Could that be me? My sister's keeper? Ezekiel 25:17?

Watching June die on the floor feels like a breaking point. But not in the name of charity and goodwill. Anger. Fury.

Samuel Jackson in *Pulp Fiction* righteously ENRAGED.

The valley of darkness calls to me. What does it want?

Today's Headline

"Worldwide, 7 Million People A Year Die from Air Pollution." Holy Christ, a Holocaust a year! Why does everybody ignore it? If anything else killed this many people the world would come to a standstill fighting it.

– ScienceDaily.org

Sheeple

*I*t's way past midnight and June is still unconscious.

That's what they're calling it now, hours after she was supposed to wake up from sedation. They moved her to ICU, where Mom and Dad finally doze in chairs, leaning on each other in a pyramid of support. The doctors say the brain scans are fine and that she'll wake up soon.

So, we wait.

Can't sleep. Instead, I watch June. And try to distract myself by reading *Escape from Freedom* on my phone. Out-of-body combo for sure, but today's homework feels relevant. Erich Fromm, a Holocaust survivor, writes about Germans stuck in the relentless capitalist machine shoved on them after WWI. They feel isolated and yearn to be part of something, <u>anything</u>. Fromm says belonging fulfills a deep psychological need, way more than democracy. Scary thought –

Because here's Adolph! Hacking at humanity's door like Jack Nicholson in *The Shining*. Fromm called Hitler a grandiose Malignant Narcissist – an antisocial mix of aggression, paranoia, and sadism. Adolf promised Germans freedom from having to think – he'll do it for them. He pledged purpose and belonging and to <u>make Germany great again</u>.

Wow. Groundhog Day. What else explains what's going on?

"That millions of people share the same forms of mental pathology does not make these people sane." Fromm sure got that right. Half our damn country is now in the same delusion, marching like lemmings off a cliff, clinging to their disbelief the cliff even exists. Like a death cult.

After seeing June die, can I watch the world end like a sheep herded to slaughter? Which is an insult to sheep, BTW, who stay together for protection because they know they're prey. Little use it does them when men come swinging blades to turn their kids into racks of lamb...

But am I too just a Good German sheeple, desperate to turn over my brain keys to be part of a group? Like the frat pledges on my college tour who bragged about ass branding and rolling in shit to join? They don't mention the guys who drink themselves to death just trying to belong.

People do stuff in a tribe they don't dream of doing alone, like rioting and looting. Or religious violence – a flock of sheeple! Or watching their Frat Brother choke to death on his own vomit. Christ.

Is this why I enjoy being alone? Or with nonhuman animals? That's a pack you can trust – in the animal kingdom, there's no such thing as a Malignant Narcissist. I won't kill myself to join any pack, that's for sure. Or is that just a self-serving delusion and not my first? I'm American, so I'm already in this messed-up mob, even if I didn't choose it.

What about watching your own sister die?

I glance at June, a machine breathing for her. If I do nothing, aren't I just a sheeple? A bystander watching the world burn? Yes. But what the hell can one person do? Civil disobedience? Go Greta? What's changed from children screaming and scolding adults, trying to save the future's lost children? Absolutely nothing.

No time for that. Children are dying now.

June, she died on the damn kitchen floor.

Today's Headline

"The US is the Biggest Carbon Polluter in History." Only 4.4% of the planet's population, America has put 33% of the total CO_2 in the atmosphere. Go USA!

– NYTimes.com

Conscious

June woke up at dawn.

As I'm writing, I glance over, and her eyes are open wide in a panicked WTF? And like magic, doctors and nurses crowd the room. They tell June to take it easy, that they're running ventilator-weaning tests. And then, after forever, they're gently pulling the tube out.

With a gasp, June's suddenly free of the tentacles invading her lungs. We hover, impatiently waiting for the doctors who ask questions like, "do you know your name?"

June ignores them and locks eyes with me standing behind a doctor.

"Benji?" The oxygen mask they put on muffles her voice.

"You had a bad asthma attack and passed out," I say before a nurse herds us out of the room. They run protocols that go on forever until the neurologist comes out and grins, announcing that June will fully recover. After many questions and appreciations, we're allowed back in with June.

"How long was I choked out?" June asks, her voice a hoarse whisper behind an oxygen mask.

"Overnight," Mom says. "We called an ambulance."

"Cool," June croaks, and we laugh with relief because we know she'll be okay, especially after what she does next.

"Benji, listen to this." June presses the oxygen mask against her face and breaths like Darth Vader. "Luke, you are my son."

That's so June. And Dad, the movie buff, totally loses it and starts crying. He's such a stoic, but like all stoics, when he breaks, he breaks hard. It's contagious as we huddle around June, a lost sheep now back in the flock, and I suddenly start sobbing.

That's how close it felt to losing June.

But my tears aren't just relief. They are tears that come when words fail. Tears of fury and vengeance and impotence – an internal howl beyond rationality. RAGE!

June isn't the only one who just woke up. I feel changed forever.

How can I tune out the reality that something primordial is unraveling my life? That Gaia, everything animate and inanimate on Earth, is delivering humans an epic smack-down. Purging us for her own survival.

It's not coming, it's here.

Can a sheep become a wolf?

Today's Quote

"America, if eligible at all to downfall and ruin, is eligible from within herself, not without." No shit. And taking the rest of the world with us.

– Walt Whitman

Pity the Fool

June got out of the hospital after a day of observation and shrugged off dying...

Getting ready for school today, she doesn't even talk about it, doesn't even want us to mention the asthma attack to her teachers. But she's right back into her vendetta.

"If I see that little jerk, Alex – I pity the fool, right, Gigi?" She hugs Gigi's broad chest and gets a kiss in return. I do not want to get on the wrong side of June. She's got mafia memory.

"You almost ended up a vegetable," I point out. "Why not let it go?"

"Let it go?" June is indignant. "You can't let this stuff go or it never ends!"

"No. It never ends if you don't let it go."

"Don't be a victim, Benji." Ouch. That one stings.

"June," Mom says. "Remember. Calm."

"I'm calm, I'm calm." June grabs her Vin Diesel bag. "Let's roll."

And off they go. I imagine it'll become a whole thing at Turning Point, where Mom chauffeurs June every morning like a little mogul past the crumbling public schools of Los Angeles with their packed classes and teachers who have to buy school supplies themselves.

Meanwhile, Turning Point is an oasis that grows pale kids like little heirloom tomatoes in a greenhouse of art, music, and attention. In eighth grade, June will go to Venice if it's not entirely underwater. Some might call that care and privilege excessive – June needs it for her ADHD – but what if every baby born won that life lottery? Imagine that world.

No doubt it'll be quite a "turning point" after two boys ganged up on a girl. There will be many meetings as they ratchet up the anti-bullying campaign. But June will be a hero to all the other kids tortured by Alex, and not because of the adults, but because she's no bystander to bullying. Every time she sees Alex, she'll sink into her karate stance and motion four fingers in a "bring it" gesture like Keanu Reeves in *The Matrix.*

And Alex will avoid her like the plague.

June seems indestructible, but I'll never forget how she sank to the floor, felled by forces she didn't create. Will she even be able to take a deep breathe when she's my age? From all the climate science I'm reading and the gigatons of pollution coming – NO.

Nichols always says, to avoid "unpleasant arousal," I should stop obsessing over obscure scientific journals until it's morning and I'm staring at the ceiling with acid in my stomach. Like I should stop reading way off syllabus about Hitler.

She's finally, maybe, possibly, right about something. I know it's not good for me, but it's a horror movie I can't turn off.

But what's the point if I'm just a victim bystander? Don't I need to act?

If you keep letting something go, it never ends.

Today's Stats

The year I was born, we could have decarbonized at a rate of 3% a year. Today, we need 10%. In 2030, we will need 30% a year. OCD me. But isn't the whole world kidding itself?

– Nature.org

Normal?

I'm writing this in my usual spot at the top of the quad stairs, but I'm in a parallel universe.

Kids hang, laughing and talking in the sun. Holding their phones like fussy babies, checking and stroking them. Selfying – look at me! And anxiously watching how many Insta-Hearts it gets.

They call us Gen Z – hard to believe marketers made money on that – everybody acting like nothing is wrong. As if our air wasn't, for days during the freeway fire the worst in the world, causing June's deadly asthma attack.

Gen Z – so right, mankind's last fucking letter.

I'm suddenly furious. I want to jump up and shout, "Why aren't you angry about inheriting a planet in flames? Why aren't you like the rabid bat I once saw hissing and frothing on a sidewalk? Why aren't you tearing your clothes and gnashing your teeth? This world isn't normal just because it's all you know. Get off your phones! My sister almost died!!"

Of course, I don't. Somebody would call the school nurse. They already think I've had my sense of humor surgically removed since I gave up on meme culture and SM. And the video of me puking on that girl has turned me into a joke. But that's all just BS.

What the hell am I going to do about what happened to June?

Her words ring in my ears: Don't be a victim, Benji!

Bloodsuckers

The crazy dangerous idea popped into my head in AP Gov.

We're still studying Hitler and I'm officially obsessed. Maybe it's because Mom's Jewish, which makes me Jewish, even though we never go to Synagogue. I don't feel Jewish, whatever that means. But try telling it to the 1488 mob that shouted all that "Jews Will Not Replace Us" crap awhile back. I don't want to replace anybody with a POC. I'm just trying to understand how a viral madness turned an entire country of people who loved art and music and architecture into savages.

Searching for a reason it can't happen again. Not finding it these days.

So, when I first hear the question it grabs me by the throat: If I had a time machine and could kill Hitler when he's a baby, do I? Like, I'm holding an infant, all cute and helpless, can I be so heartless, even to save the world? Doubt it – Baby Hitler was innocent. But if I can't do it, how can I live with all the death and destruction I don't prevent? I can't.

And then the kernel of the Idea pops in my head.

A different killing to stop a different system of death and destruction.

But who am I kidding? I've never killed anything bigger than a mosquito. And silverfish in the bathroom – those squiggly creatures with two long antennae reaching out like a blind guy with canes. They sleep curled up in a ball like miniature armadillos, their shimmering backs facing the world, hoping it'll protect them. Something heartbreaking and human about that hope. And if I miss them the first time, they run away frantic. They think they're hauling ass.

They want to live, too. Like Mom, June, and me fleeing that fire.

But silverfish don't have any <u>perspective</u> and end up a smudge on a piece of toilet paper I flush, feeling a terrible shame. Like, what right do I have to kill a little creature who values his life so much?

Guess everything ends up that way, dust-to-dust, and all that. But I hate punching down. Better to punch up and get your ass kicked.

Another reason to "live and let live" is all the invertebrates have declined 75% from pesticides. I read that today. It's called the "clear windshield phenomenon," where bugs don't splat cars like before I was born. So now 49% of the birds in parts of Europe have vanished because they're starving. How freaky is that?

And if insects die – 90% of all life on Earth – then everything up the food chain dies. Holy shit! And what are we doing?

Sitting at the top like Humpty-Dumpty, obsessed with amusements.

Maybe I won't kill silverfish anymore. Just got to stop thinking about one curling up in my nose to dream his little armadillo dreams. But they're harmless. Not like mosquitoes. Sorry, too many of you bloodsuckers around these days. You've killed half the humans who've ever lived, so if you little vampires hunt me – no mercy. It's self-defense, as Zika virus moves north from Climate Chaos, creating brain dead babies with empty doll heads – real live zombies.

We live in strange days getting stranger. Like, going viral strange.

Anyway, swatting an occasional mosquito is a long way from killing a baby Hitler. I would need to become more cold-blooded and patient, like the spiders spinning their world into existence and waiting for some bloodsucker to buzz in. Are spiders starving like the birds from a lack of bugs to eat? Hope not – I like how you can't see a spider web in the woods straight on. You need <u>perspective</u> to spot it shimmering in the sunlight between trees like a miracle. And if you don't see it, if you're not paying attention, if you don't have <u>perspective</u> like the whole human race doesn't have these days, you end up eating a cotton candy web spun from a spider's ass.

Tough luck for zombie-walking your phone like a grown-up Zika baby.

I don't know... Mom and Dad taught me to be non-violent, which doesn't add up to killing Hitler, baby or otherwise.

But I guess there's some hope for me because I'm not a Jain. That sect in India kills nothing, not even a mosquito as it sucks their blood. That's so radical, like the civil rights protesters we studied who sat there and let the cops cudgel them. Talk about courage. My best self aspires to have that kind of love, compassion, and self-control.

But I don't. June's death and resurrection destroyed all that.

If you come for my blood, I'll swat you.

That's the Idea.

Today's headline

"Insects Experience Chronic Pain After Serious Injury." Really? Wow. Jains have the right non-violent idea, but isn't it bringing a flyswatter to a firefight? As cyclones, floods, and fires now displace three times more people than war?

— Sci-News.com

Gigi

Something kind of crazy happened today. Gigi barked...
"ROW, ROW, ROW."

June and I run outside to see a guy looking over the low fence.

"Did she just bark at you?" June asks the man.

"Oh, yeah. She barked," he says, keeping his distance. "I'm here for the sink."

"Good girl! Gigi. Good girl." June and I shower Gigi with hugs and kisses. The plumber looks at us like we're crazy. So does Gigi.

"She's been mute for five years," I explain as Gigi wags her tail, not sure what all the fuss is about. "We thought the dogfighting scum who pulled her teeth also cut her vocal cords."

"She okay? She gonna bite me?" The plumber eyes Gigi skeptically.

"Like he just said, she can't bite, she's missing two incisors," June informs him, managing to keep her patience. "Might gum ya."

"Huh." The man hesitates as Gigi keeps a wary eye on him. Stand-off.

"She's a bit scared of men," June tells the plumber. "They tried to make her fight because she's so big and strong. But she's gentle as a lamb, even after they turned her into a bait dog."

"Yeah, I get it. But would you mind holding her while I come in?" the man says, still not getting it. "I've had my fill of dogs like that."

"Whatever," June sighs, hugging Gigi, who's massive and limps and looks scary depending on who you are, like a canine Rorschach test. But as the plumber rushes past us, Gigi just gives him a side-eye and doesn't move in June's hug. Like a poor trained elephant unaware of her strength.

"Idiot." June shakes her head, turning to me. "Remember when we got her? She was the one afraid of everything?"

"Yeah." Luckily, it was Mom who saw Gigi lurking under a table at an Angel City Pits adoption event.

"Remember Dad? What the hell?" June huffs, impersonating Dad when he first saw Gigi. "I thought we were getting a Labrador. A puppy."

"Nobody should buy puppies when half the dogs on the planet are strays." I pick up the game, imitating Mom lecturing Dad. I agree – hell, I feel the same way about kids. "There's a rescue for every breed."

"Then why not rescue a Lab?" June continues her damn good impersonation of Dad when he gets flustered.

"Because people think Labs are sweet. They don't need it as much as pit bulls," I mimic Mom's zeal. "But pit bulls are as gentle as labs. Just look at her."

We both crack up and can't keep it going. Back then Gigi looked like a super-max prisoner, raw scars instead of tats. Sure, she has one good eye as warm as the stained-glass saints in the HWB chapel. But the other is a puckered socket. Still, June, ever fearless, on Gigi's first day, marches up and hugs her beer-keg chest. And Gigi relaxes her huge head in June's lap.

"We're keeping her, daddy," June announces. Dad just shakes his head and shrugs. No use fighting the lovers of animals and underdogs in this house. I've been bringing home injured strays – dogs, cats, snakes, lizards – since I can walk.

Scratching Gigi's blockhead now, it's hard to believe it took me three hours of coaxing before she finally came out from under the kitchen table to take the treat in my hand. It was such a moment of trust, an actual decision she made to give me – just another guy out of all the guys who tortured her – a chance. Now, we're inseparable. And today, Gigi finds her voice!

Feels like the whole animal kingdom is talking to me lately.

What are they saying? Don't be a sheeple. Do something. Don't forget! Your sister almost died and you're lucky to be able to goof around with her on this sunny afternoon.

I look at June and am filled with an overwhelming rush of love. It could have gone so badly. Brain damage. Paralysis. Death.

I can't let this go.

No sheeple would ever contemplate my desperate Idea. It just wouldn't occur to a clone, only a freak. Is that a plus or a minus for me? Can't tell. I've opened a can of worms in my head and I can't wriggle my way out of it. Feel like it's making me crazy.

The idea that killing Hitler at any age is a no-brainer.

Today's Headline

"More Evidence That Pets Benefit Mental Health." No-duh. But with me these days, Gigi's got her therapy work cut out for her.

— MedicalNewsToday.com

The Real Terrorist

Didn't sleep again last night. The Idea.

Brain skittering and sick of school today.

And not just because of all the Tyler types running the place, everybody humble bragging like their parents how "buried" they are, as if it's a cool thing and not a sickness. It's just AP test-test-test – learn nothing – then vape weed for the stress. All battling for an Ivy, as if that'll save them from what's coming. Makes me sick to be in this bubble of privilege and ambition, stuck on a hamster wheel of busywork, everybody putting on training wheels for Dante's fourth circle of hell – Greed. Even with the photog memory grinding it out, it's all so meaningless and boring.

But what's the alternative to this Darwinian mess? Live like a cop, monotony punctuated by violence in an LASD classroom? No thanks.

Still, here it's pure ennui – some damn disorder might spice things up.

Christ, I feel itchy and impatient, not myself. No sleep. Or maybe it's the endless eye rolls today after somebody leaked my ACT score. How does that even happen? I'm so sick of the hate for being Mega-Millions-winner-lucky, as if I'm cheating or something. It's all so stupid. Born into another family, with different nature/nurture, I'd have a different IQ and no photog memory. Free will is such a joke once you really look at it.

Even now in Gov, as I write this, I'm getting jealous side-eye from some thirsty Insta-Feeder. But I didn't brag about my score or even tell a soul. Just doing my time on independent study and writing out these never-ending thoughts, trying to keep myself sane.

Is it working? Not today.

I glance at SG across the room. So beautiful and gentle, like from another planet. So different from the other girls at HWB, who look tight around the mouth. Could SG ever be interested in me? We haven't spoken since Animal Acres, so that's probably a stretch...

Baxter drones on about the planes hitting the towers. War on terror, blah, blah, blah.

I'm not listening. The lifetime odds of a foreign terrorist killing an American are one in 45,000. From refugee terrorists, it's one in 46 million. From illegal immigrant terrorists, it's one in 138 million. Meanwhile, the lifetime odds of dying by car accident are one in 113. Walking down the street, one in 672. Choking to death on dinner, one in 3,409.

Stat Man!

But we spend trillions and overreact to all the wrong stuff. We should worry about Mother Nature going haywire – little things like extinctions, plagues, and Climate Chaos. Instead, everybody's bugging out about BS terrorists – not an existential threat! – as the real terrorist gets a pass.

Not from me. I still can't get the ear-worm Idea out of my head...

Am I going to kill the tantrum toddler, the ignorant ogre, the speed-addicted conman spewing gibberish, the know-nothing leader of mobs, the vile appeaser of dictators, the sadistic mind-fucker, the deluded crusher of dreamers, the vain insecure bully, the lazy aspiring fascist, the shameless racist-racist-racist media whore, the small-dick sexual predator, the syphilitic grandiose liar looting the planet and destroying Truth, Justice, and the American Way?

Am I really the only one willing to stop him by any means necessary? Stop the demon holding us prisoner in all nine levels of Dante's Hell, including his specialties of Fraud, Violence, and Betrayal?

Am I really thinking about killing the president and –

Toddler Torturer

Whoa! Baxter walked up on me as I was writing that screed.

Got to be careful with the Idea. Even if it's just a thought experiment, getting caught writing about killing the president is an epic shit storm. On 9/11! Doesn't matter if I don't look it, I'm 18 now.

They can arrest me as an adult.

Still, it feels good to vomit up all that Ad Hominem, Ad Nauseum. Reaction "to the man." Damn right. Because that man is a money-hungry Malignant Narcissist who's drunk-driving the planet and killing us all, stuck in the backseat of his madness. And if you're in a car with a drunk, you grab the wheel. You don't ask permission, you stop him.

I stop him?

Nobody has ever stopped him. Not from when he was a ten-year-old bed-wetter caught throwing rocks at a toddler in the yard next to his. Not even now, as he puts toddler refugees in cages. <u>Malignant Narcissist</u>!

That's a mouthful, Fromm's description of Hitler. Need a better name for this pouting haze of cotton candy hair and self-tanner, with eyes too close and a fake squint he practices every day. What word sums him up? Pig? No. They're smart as two-year-olds, play games, plan, and show empathy – like whales and elephants...

Dick? Asshole? Loser? Idiot? Moron? Vandal? Con? Crook? Cretin?

Cretin is such a great word. So satisfying to crunch out with a "k" sound, like a swear word – CRETIN YOU!

Webster says a Cretin is, *"a stupid, vulgar, and insensitive person."*

Perfect. The president's all three, plus the ultimate bloodsucker.

Can I be his spider?

What else will stop him? Protest and politics? Too slow, and he cheats and has all those sheeple. Art, movies, TV? Just distractions. Religion? They're handing him toilet paper while he craps on the world. Books? I've heard of them – they're made of paper, right? Ha. Nobody reads anymore and writing can't even deal with every awful fact stabbed in my head. How long before blood gurgles out my ears?

No, somebody's got to shuffle Cretin off his mortal coil. But could I be a murderer? I hate that idea. I'm not even a delinquent like one of the 850,000 traumatized teenagers we toss in jail every year. Wish I could forget that stat, but it'll get worse. Autocracies need their gulags.

Got to think this through, my reasons why – the stuff keeping me up at night. Start a list and make my case that I've got a good enough motive to kill him. I think I do.

"And I will strike down upon thee with great vengeance and furious anger those who would attempt to poison and destroy my brothers."

Amen, *Pulp Fiction*! Just watched it again to deal with my biblical brain. Shooting somebody in the head sure is gross.

Am I serious? Deluded? Or just enjoying the fantasy? I'm so unprepared – how would I do it? Should I, even if I could? Am I going crazy?

Good questions.

Guess there's no harm in mind-tripping if it stays locked in my head.

It's got to – I really don't want to blow up my life.

I'm not a natural-born killer. But I am killer-curious.

Today's Fact

When Earth reaches 2.0C hotter, now our best-case scenario, 153 million people worldwide will die. That's 25 Holocausts. Hitler's rolling in his grave with envy for Cretin.

– Phys.org

The Only Thing That Matters

It's late. Can't sleep again. Nightmares about June dying. Obsessing about the Idea. Got to start writing it out. Get it straight in my head...

I hate Cretin. But does he deserve to die?

Sure, he sucks dictator dick and dreams of being one, using ICE like his personal Gestapo. Yesterday, they went all "show me your papers" and snatched Luis's mom right off the street as she was dropping him off at SAMO High. Guess because he's a Dreamer activist.

Sure, Cretin's a conman who starts his smash and grab of America right away, selling access to foreign leaders who spend money at his hotels. Paying himself the hundreds of millions of our tax dollars he wastes golfing his own resorts! Adding two trillion to the deficit and handing my generation the bill. He'll bankrupt and steal us blind – it's who he is.

Sure, Cretin is a racist who baits every day – about black NFL players or Obama or the poor brown refugees washing up on our shores. They like to say not all Cretin voters are racist, some voted for Obama. But 33% of them use the N-word. And 77% think a president can use it and still be a good president. So, all racists are Cretin voters.

Sure, Cretin tantrums every day at the press, courts, and institutions that make our country a country. He dreams of crushing them. And holding Banana Republic military parades.

And sure, Cretin gets a cruel little hard-on when he hurts people, cheats, or trolls. But all a troll wants is attention, good or bad. So, we give Cretin exactly what he wants by squirreling after every turn of his gross unreality show. Nobody can keep up with his nonstop fog of disinformation and distraction – he only tells the truth by accident.

But all this Cretin Crap is no accident. He wants us <u>disinforstracted</u>.

So sure, the list why I hate him is endless, all of it true.

But <u>NONE</u> of it matters.

What matters is <u>every day</u> Cretin does something against us having a livable future. And by livable, I mean a planet we can all live on without being burnt alive running errands. Or our little sisters dying from wildfire smoke and air pollution. Every other messed up thing Cretin does is deck chairs on the Titanic. Except if he drops a nuke, then we're screwed. Might happen because he actually said, *"what's the point of having them if you can't use em?"* Ha. Such a troll.

But Cretin's not a troll or a Baby Hitler to the environment.

He's <u>Gas-Chamber Hitler</u>, building the ovens to kill us all.

The UN's Emissions Gap Report says the difference between the reductions needed to avoid catastrophe and what countries pledge is "alarmingly high." That's a euphemism for "we're screwed." That's the truth. They finally admitted it. Along with the 11,000 climate scientists who signed a decree that says we're already in a full-blown climate emergency.

So, unless humans are cockroaches, with a few surviving like when we got down to 7,000 people during Earth's last greenhouse gas meltdown, we better focus on human <u>EXTINCTION</u>. That's what's at stake. Stopping Cretin from triggering it is the <u>only</u> thing that matters now.

Nothing else is an existential threat.

Every other disaster mankind faces is a mere warm-up. Or a symptom.

Because you can't have an autocracy, militocracy, or plutocracy if you don't exist. You can't have a civil war, race war, nuclear war, or Cyber war if humankind goes extinct. But we'll have all those wars on the way to extinction, once a billion starving people from global crop failure flee failing, burning, and drowning states. Soon, we'll be too crippled by apocalyptic storms to do anything more than butcher each other.

Holy Christ! I'm bugging myself out.

But why don't people see all the fear, hatred, and violence Cretin promotes is just the cartoon before the main attraction? The death rattle before humanity expires, as he accelerates the catastrophe every day, supported by his Clown Cult Congress of planet killers.

I sound insane. But am I? Even pandemics won't kill everybody!

But the climate can relentlessly bake us off the planet.

I mean, <u>is baking us now</u>, because every year I've been alive has been hotter than the last, with this year being the hottest ever. And come hell or high water – both are already here – next year will be hotter still.

So, I'm not crazy. And it's not "climate change." That's a joke.

It's <u>CLIMATE CHAOS</u>. Here. Now. My sister almost died!

While Cretin calls it a hoax – wasting precious time, blood on his hands – Earth is already a different planet, prepping our extinction. Cretin sadistically punishes Mother Nature like a wife beater, enjoying watching her unravel. But if you mess with her, she will mess you up in ways you can't imagine and can't stop. Mess us all up. It's happening...

Like, today, I read about the Pine Beetle, who feasts on millions of acres in the Pacific NW, killing trees dry as toothpicks. Our winters don't get cold enough to kill the beetles anymore. So, now mega-fires disappear Seattle's Space Needle in clouds of smoke, dumping billions of tons of CO2. And these fires are quaint compared to what's coming, as Cretin does all he can to make the world hotter while we stay "entertained" by his noise pollution. Disinforstracted!

Not me. I've got to focus down and write some lists about how dire everything is. First up? An extinction list. Christ... That's bleak.

Would killing Cretin even change anything or is it already too late? Good chance all this writing is the captain's log on a sinking ship.

At least I'll punch up and go down with a fight.

Today's Headline

"A Species Goes Extinct Every 20 Minutes, Over 26,000 A Year." Soon, humans will be left in a staggering silence. What will we say?

– *Biologicaldiversity.org*

Henry David on the Quad

"*The question is not what you look at, but what you see.*"
I was minding my business on the quad stairs today, reading Thoreau, and that line jumped out at me. America's first environmentalist, Thoreau built a cabin the size of a jail cell on Walden Pond so he could immerse in nature, write, and really see the world. I get it – this writing helps me really see it too. Probably saves my life, if I'm honest...

I look up and spot Tim strolling across the lawn. He pretends not to see me. Christ. What a sad state of –

"Head's up, Soy Boy."

Tyler sweeps down the stairs with Dim and Dimmer and knocks *Walden* out of my hands, cartwheeling Thoreau down the stairs. Guess I can't really call Tyler a bully anymore because he's too subtle. Now that we're seniors, he never gets physical. He just says mean stuff you can interpret in different ways, like, "I really love your car, so retro." Translation, "your car is a POS." Or he does quasi-physical "accidents" like knock books out of your hands. So moronic –

"I'm sure you gentlemen want to treat Henry David with a little more respect than that." It's Hale, our new STEM teacher. He always calls students, 'ladies and gentlemen.' Aspirational or ironic, I can't tell. "Why don't you hand him back to Mr. Wallace?"

"Wha-u-say?" Tyler suddenly blurs his words, blank and slack-jawed, as if Hale is too beneath him to articulate, like the hired help. He squints up the stairs at Hale, who's not muscle-bound like Tyler. He's wiry, like a triathlete, with ropy forearms and hands popping with veins and missing half his pinky finger. How did I not notice that before? From the second knuckle down, it's just gone.

"The book, Mr. Kincaid."

A long moment as Tyler tries to stare down Hale, who's hardcore no BS and doesn't care who's your daddy. He's some kind of tech security consultant out of the military. Rumor is Hale was a Navy Seal – probably got his finger cut off in a knife fight or something more intense than I can imagine. How he ends up at an elitist cesspool like HWB is a mystery –

"Wha-ever-u-say." Tyler shows his belly, but is still contemptuous. To save face he picks up the book by one cover, dangling it like a dead rat, and hands it to me. "Jus-a-ccident."

"Yeah, sure," I retort. Tyler leaps down the stairs, throwing his arms around Dim and Dimmer, all bursting into laughter as they look over their shoulders.

"Assholes," I mutter.

"'For an impenetrable shield, stand inside yourself.'" Hale is suddenly squatting next to me, quiet as a ninja. "That's my favorite Henry David."

"Different drummer and all that," I bounce the ball back. "Hard to do when rich bloodsuckers think they own you."

"Is it? Thoreau said, 'I make myself rich by making my wants few.'"

I look at Hale. Is he a poet warrior? A fellow traveler? Maybe.

"I agree. And I do stand inside myself. But like John Donne said, no man is an island. We're all connected by nature. To nature."

"I'm glad to hear you say that, Ben. No man is an island. I heard you quit all your social media." Hale looks at me, more curious than concerned... calling me Ben. I shrug.

"'Men have become the tools of their tools.' Guess I'm going full Thoreau today."

"You could do worse."

"I doubt he would be on Insta, that's for sure," I joke. Hale laughs, his lean face creasing around his eyes.

"Why'd you quit?" He's not judging, just... truly interested?

"'What is the use of a house if you haven't got a tolerable planet to put it on?'" Christ, I'm a fountain of Thoreau today. "That's what's got me up at night. Everything else feels like a distraction."

"I get it." Hale nods. "So, what are you going to do to make the planet more tolerable?"

"It's all I think about." The Idea embedded in my head. Couldn't dig it out if I tried.

"I'm sure with all your gifts, you'll be a part of the solution and not part of the problem."

Hale uncoils from his squat like he's done it a thousand times, looking out over some desert battlefield. He just paraphrased Eldridge Cleaver, that Black Panther who saw the rape of white women as a revolt against white men's control. How sick is that? I'm sure it's not what Hale meant, even though being a former soldier, he must know extreme. Is extreme action the only thing left against suicidal extremists? Damn right –

"Ben?" Hale's voice reins in my wandering mind.

"I don't know about solutions. It seems futile here," I blurt this out, suddenly wanting to be honest with him. "Swimming upstream into a waterfall."

Hale appraises me like an empty glass, as if figuring out how much I can hold.

"Yeah, it's a challenge, our culture," Hale says, finishing some internal calculation. "I spent some time in India. The ashram trail. People used to ask me about the culture shock, what with all the poverty over there. But the shock was returning stateside, with its cold comfort cleanliness and people who live in their bodies like hungry ghosts. Nothing ever enough."

His sincerity is surprising – he meets me right where I am.

"I think I know what you mean," I say. "But, super poor there, right? Was it hard to witness?"

"Yeah, there's heartbreaking poverty, but somehow, not as much separation or desire. It feels like everybody's flowing in the same stream, in it together."

"Must be nice to swim with the tide." I suddenly yearn for it, that Molly sense of love and connection. But is it against my nature?

"Got to jump in the water first." Hale smiles as if reading my mind. Did he go to India after the military? To decompress? Meditate? Cool.

"I want to." Weirdly, I'm nodding. Hale makes me want to be on his team, which is another surprise. How did he do that? "I want to dive in."

"Good. Got to run, but my door's always open if you feel like talking."

"Thanks, Mr. Hale."

He nods and strides his springy stride across the Quad.

Who is this guy?

Today's Headline

"Ocean Fish Numbers Cut in Half Since 1970." Great. If I jump in and swim with the tide, it'll be in a dead sea.

— ScientificAmerican.com

Unabomber

Tonight, Dad and I watched a documentary about the Unabomber living in a shed in the woods with a hermit beard and how they finally caught him. Gigi heaved her rhino body onto the couch between us and snored through the whole thing, but it riveted me.

The Unabomber is like an anti-Thoreau. Am I starting to become him?

No. I won't kill innocent people with bombs through the mail because they "represent" the system. <u>Cretin is the system now</u>. And a real threat.

But Ted got the problem right, way back in the 70s. Hard to argue with the first sentence of his manifesto, *"The Industrial Revolution and its consequences have been a disaster for the human race."*

Yeah. And since Ted wrote those words, an existential disaster.

I'm just trying to figure it out here. Not only what's real, but what's right. To SEE, like Thoreau did, through the maze of disinforstraction and get to the truth.

Ted K. is a certified genius, 168 IQ, but so what? He goes to Harvard at sixteen – a big mistake because he wasn't emotionally ready. Mom and Dad were wise enough to make sure I didn't skip grades like Ted. They didn't want me bullied and alone – best laid plans and all that...

After the show, Dad and I talked about the Unabomber and how he fixated on the wrong murderous solution. Had to watch myself, discussing it with Dad, which felt weird – we're always so honest with each other. But I didn't say Ted was right and his genius allowed him to sound an early alarm before Earth was too far gone. I tried to keep it philosophical.

"Do you think it's ever okay to kill somebody for a higher good? Not random people like the Unabomber did, but if you really know some-body's evil?"

"Does the end justify the means?" Dad looks at me. Even his eyebrows are going gray.

"Yeah."

"I don't think so. Because if your means are unethical, you corrupt yourself by the time you reach the end." Dad sighs. "There's lots of hor-rible history behind that fallacy. The road to hell is paved with good intentions."

"But what if it's important and it doesn't matter if you're changed for the worse? Like, saving the world or something?"

Dad looks at me with a tinge of concern. Got to be careful, not so absolutist. Can't get him worried I'll throw fake blood somewhere, like when I was June's age and obsessed by all the dead animals in the window of Bel Campo butchery. Especially the pig's head, one of 100 million killed a year in America, with 18 million piglets crushed or dying of star-vation because they're too small to feed while their mom, crammed into a metal gestation crate, can't even turn her head to see why one in five of her babies is whimpering in agony –

"I thought the Marvel movies bore you now." Dad distracts me from those straitjacket days – stop spiraling! – when I was PETA before Greta. Now I'm not tossing blood, I'm going to spill it. Big leap –

"Ben?"

"They do bore me," I say, trying to focus.

"So then you know things aren't black and white. Everything is more *Casablanca* than *Captain America*."

"Not everything, right? Not Hitler."

"No. Not Hitler."

"And as Burke said, 'The only thing necessary for the triumph of evil is for good men to do nothing.'" Am I doing nothing beyond thinking about the Idea? Hope so, the rest is too scary.

"But Ben, everybody has both sides in them. Good and evil. Exceedingly rare to be all one way." Dad is eyeballing me again. Got to slow my roll. "And you know most behavior is contextual. Even being a Good Samaritan depends on whether you're in a hurry."

"Yeah. I know that study about the seminarian students late for class who don't stop to help somebody. But what if people are hypnotized? And you're the only one who sees the truth."

"The truth? You can't handle the truth!" Dad smiles as he air-quotes this. I have no idea what he's talking about. "I've got the perfect movie."

Love how Dad still does this, has conversations with me through movies. It's easier for him and I don't mind, it's easier for me too. I'm glad he's obsessed and not just about the new stuff, we love old comedies like *Dumb and Dumber* and old westerns like *High Noon*. The townspeople turn away from Gary Cooper and his desperate search for help against the gang riding into town. Dad says it's about McCarthyism, which is like the time we're in now. Truth. Nobody's grabbing a gun and standing up to Cretin. They've all become cowering townsfolk.

Dad pulls out *A Few Good Men*. Guess it's the frugal TV editor in him that won't toss any of the free screeners he gets for being in "The Industry." Thousands – every good old movie made. No matter how much Mom bugs him about making room and streaming and Netflix, Dad's old- school. He likes the quality and the interviews with cast and crew.

We watch the movie as Gigi snores through Jack Nicholson shouting, *"You can't handle the truth!"* Defending the killing of an incompetent soldier to keep the country safe. Does the end justify the means? Not in Tom Cruise's world. Justice triumphs. Jack goes to jail.

"See?" Dad pronounces. "Jack Nicholson's character was wrong, even though he thought he was serving a higher good."

"I guess."

"You guess?" Gigi picks up on Dad's tone and opens her one eye. Dad's concern is in both eyes. "Remember, you can't sell out your humanity for a future ideal. Every step must be humane, for you and the other person."

"I get it." I've got to shut this down before Dad gets worried. He grew up Catholic and even though he gave it up, he still has clear lines of good and evil. "I agree with you."

"Good," Dad says, looking a bit relieved.

But I lie. Ted also said no revolution starts without the "application of violence." Hasn't violence been the ultimate authority since time began, including our own country's war for independence? Isn't violence the only answer to those violently killing the planet?

Guess time will tell if I'm the Unabomber or Paul Revere.

Or just a sheeple bystander.

Today's Headline

"The US Now Leads in Energy Waste – 71% of the Energy Generated is Wasted." No wonder Ted started making bombs.

— EnergyCentral.com

Five Alarm Fire

$\int$ itting on the quad stairs again, struggling with my end-of-the-world-extinction list.

This heartless catalog drags me back into my parallel universe, so far from daily reality. Could be no sleep after my "does the end justify the means" conversation with Dad, but writing out this list has got me more than just alarmed. I'm terrified. And lonely.

Guess staring at extinction all day can do that to a person.

When the bell rings, kids shuffle by, heads down like I'm invisible. If my alarm went public, would they even look up? Or would they call me alarmist? But when the facts are scary, isn't it good to be scared? Fear can save your life. It can save all our lives.

This list, it's making my palms sweat. It's changing me. Into what?

If I act on it, will they call me a psycho loner? What a joke – I'm only lonely half the time... Will they spin it as insanity from a "disturbed personality?" They'd be right. I am deeply disturbo by what I'm researching. Heart-broken. Enraged. Deranged –

Why isn't everybody?

"The world, we are told, was made especially for man – a presumption not supported by all the facts." John Muir said that in 1867. Try telling that to the kids at HWB. They think the world was handmade for their pleasure. Talk about alternative facts!

But this list shows I'm not crazy. The last words of every crazy person ever. Ha. Truth is, it makes me feel helpless, like when Dad hit ice last year at Big Bear, and we slid across the road and bounced off a guardrail...

A smartphone suspends in front of my nose in zero gravity, useless in the silent eye of the storm. We smash into the other guardrail and the windshield explodes into pebbles. The airbag punches me in the nose and the seatbelt garrotes me back like an assassin. Metal screeches as the car flips and slides across the road, all the sound of the world BLASTING IN – Dad and me amazingly unhurt in the chaos.

For sure, we're in the first impact – between guardrails. But we won't survive the second collision – the climate crash. We've got no seat belts. Except for me. Maybe I'm the seat belt, if it's not too late, like putting one on after a pileup. Because the planet's skidding out of –

Christ. Researching this extinction list has got me feeling unfocused and itchy again. Irritated. So alarmed I'm the alarm clock. An air-raid siren – RAGE! RAGE! RAGE! Wailing about the man-made asteroid hitting Earth. Why do people think life will just go on as usual?

Denial. Anger. Bargaining. Depression. Acceptance.

Guess I'm stuck in ANGER, Dante's fifth circle. But humanity needs to find the kind of anger that saves lives in an emergency – like moms who rip open car-crashed doors to save their babies. We're in a planetary crisis. Don't we need a Jaws of Life emergency response?

And anger beats denial. I just read that Hurricane Harvey flooded the houses of oil execs in Houston's third "500-year storm" in three years. But the execs still deny the reality they created with all their fossil fuel – five feet of rain falling on them in two days.

When alligators move into your living room and caskets from the cemetery float in your driveway, you might want to snap out of it. Ha!

Hippie Roger's right: No time like the present to wake up. And not in some stupid "woke Olympics" way. Screw alarm bells. I need to buy bullets. Don't I? How can I know for sure? The list –

"Hi, Benji." SG appears in front of me, as startling as an apparition. Where did she come from? "What are you writing so furiously?"

"Notes for list of how humanity goes extinct," I blurt this out and SG laughs, revealing perfect teeth. I smile to hide my stupid braces.

"Keeping it light, huh?"

"As always." Weirdly, I do feel lighter, SG yanking me out of my dark thoughts. But I don't want this. I don't want to be distracted out of my parallel universe. Too much is at stake.

"Is it for a class?" She asks. I want to resist, but she is the sun, pulling me into her orbit.

"Yeah, um. Sort of an independent project." It's hard not to feel like everything's okay looking at her, wearing jeans and an off-the-shoulder white top that reveals a sliver of her belly as she shifts from sandal to sandal. She makes the end of the world feel pretty damn abstract.

"Cool. Well, I've got Latin." She smiles again. "Have a beautiful day."

"Carpe diem." I smile back. Guess this is the way it happens. You're standing on a green quad with a pretty girl in perfect California sunshine and you just live your life. Until you don't.

Wait, she called me by my name. Cool.

Focus. Facts. Finish list!

Today's Headline

"Hot and Bothered: Experts Say Violent Crime Rates Increase with Heat." I guess that includes me now. But isn't the murder of the planet a violent crime? Damn right it is.

— CBS.com

Ten Ways We're Going Extinct

"*Illusion is the first of all pleasures.*" Voltaire again.

Do I have illusions? Or worse, delusions of grandeur? Maybe. Okay, probably. But not about our climate reality. That 405 fire could have easily snuffed out Mom, June, and me. And some version is going on everywhere, with people drowning or burning or starving to death every second. Like June was almost snuffed out!

That's just reality these days – facts, not alternative.

My list shows most signals are blinking red for human extinction:

1. WE'RE OUT OF TIME AND WAY BEHIND THE CURVE.

The head of the United Nations says we have two years before we pass tipping points taking us to "Hothouse Earth." This is when our planet's systems switch from neutral to harmful, <u>spewing more CO2 than all human activity combined</u>. One scientist calls it "an extinction-level event where all life on Earth will end." That's a long way of saying, we die. I believe it because <u>every predicted worst-case scenario</u> has come true. Like, our oceans capture 93% of the CO2 but are reaching saturation and warming 40% faster than forecast. The International Panel on Climate Change finally admitted our "threshold for irreversibility" is a rise of 1.5 Celsius and it requires "rapid, far-reaching, and unprecedented changes in all aspects of society." We need to cut global emissions in half by 2030. Does anybody see that happening? At our current burn rate, we will eventually hit 5C (9F) hotter! But Senegal is already a dust-bowl at 2.0C, with no men left to farm the land – they've all migrated, canaries in the coalmine.

2. OUR RATE OF INJECTION OF CO2 INTO THE ATMOSPHERE IS TEN TIMES FASTER THAN THE PERMIAN EXTINCTION.

Earth has been here before and rebooted. During the Permian extinction 252 million years ago, runaway greenhouse gases killed almost everything on land and sea. Back then, it took awhile. But now, most of our planet's 1.1 degrees of warming has happened in only the last 35 years. And the concentration of CO2 in the atmosphere, already the highest in 800,000 years, jumped a record 2.7% last year. We're on the same path that brought us the "Great Dying," only ten times faster. Not only can we tip into hothouse Earth, but we can become Venus, a planet that used to have plenty of water before CO2 hot-boxed it into a desert.

3. WE CREATED THE FIRST MAN-MADE EPOCH.

In just the time Cretin's been alive, his generation has crash-created a new epoch. We're in the Anthropocene right now, not created by huge forces like time, asteroids, or volcanoes, but by grandma and grandpa. Humans are the asteroid! I'm terrified that what we do in the next 10 years will decide the next 10,000. Thanks, Boomer! Can you blame my generation for trying to stay hypnotized by video games and Socials?

4. IN THE LAST 30 YEARS WE'VE EMITTED MORE CO2 THAN ALL THE PREVIOUS YEARS COMBINED.

An epoch of change in decades. And the CO2 we've dumped in the past 30 years hasn't even hit the atmosphere yet. When it does, the climate bullet will blow our heads off. Scientists predict a 4C temperature rise just from what's already baked into the system. Christ, are we already dead?

5. WE CREATED THE SIXTH EXTINCTION.

Our habitat destruction and mega-fauna murder are 1,000 times the natural "background" extinction rate. We're up to 200 species a day. Polar bears and gorillas and rhino and tigers and everybody's favorite, giant pandas – all heading towards extinction. The Northern White Rhino's not going anymore, it's GONE. Our distant relatives, the orangutans in the rainforests of Borneo are getting choked out by palm oil plantations. This global extinction rate is higher than anything since the Chicxulub asteroid impact 65 million years ago. It killed the dinosaurs and most other life on Earth. How's that for a warning something is terribly wrong?

6. OVER 75% OF THE CARBON THAT HITS THE ATMOSPHERE LASTS THOUSANDS OF YEARS.

The other 25% lasts forever. The damage we've done in a few decades will last longer than the entire history of human civilization. Our total emissions are at 415 ppm of CO2, up 1.5% every year for the past decade. Humankind has never lived on the planet when CO2 levels are this high or Mother Earth was this hot. There's probably a damn good reason for that. And so now the IPCC says we must lower emissions by 7.6% a year between 2020 and 2030 to avoid disaster.

With Cretin in charge? Ha!

He's the pestilence we brought on ourselves.

Christ... Up to number six and I need a break.

Do we human cockroaches even deserve to survive? Why don't we just put ourselves on the extinction list and be done with it?

Guess now I'm depressed. I've skipped bargaining – can't bargain with reality. It's all too overwhelming and devastating.

But it's the opposite of illusion, this never-ending river of facts flowing in my brain. I don't want to believe, but like Heraclitus, every time I walk into that river, I drown in the new and escalating evidence we're committing ecocide. Every day, the river is different and deeper.

Gigi's looking at me. Time for a walk and to forget it all for awhile.

The damn list can wait.

Nichols

Today was huge! I officially quit Nichols.

Then, I bumped into SG on the street and we talked. I think I was even a bit witty, flying high from dumping therapy. But Nichols was a drag, as usual.

"I'm surprised. Have you considered this carefully, Benji?" Nichols never stops taking notes, even as she looks over her glasses at me after I make the big announcement. It's weird, like her hands, bare of rings and always moving, belong to another body.

"Yeah, I have," I say. Only came in as a courtesy and want to keep it short, ripping the Band-Aid off quickly, like breaking up with a girl. As if I knew what that's like.

"Well, we've been working together for many years. Do you want to talk about it?"

"Nothing to talk about. I just don't need it anymore." I shrug, feeling numb, watching myself cross another threshold, this one here since the bloody Bel Campo days.

"How do you feel right now? Quitting therapy?" Oh, here we go. How do I feel? Like I need to get out of here before the full hour goes by and I reveal too much or let slip something about the Idea. I stand abruptly.

"Benji?" Nichols looks startled. I can see white roots along the part of her thinning brown hair. It makes me sad. Doesn't she have anybody in her life to tell her stuff like that?

"I don't want to be rude. And I appreciate everything you've done for me, but I've made my decision." This is from a little speech I thought up, but now when I say it out loud it sounds stilted and formal, like HWB's rendition of *Our Town*. "I'm just going to go."

"Really?" Now Nichols looks alarmed. "Have you told your parents?"

"Not yet. But it's not their decision." I'm getting annoyed. I don't want to be managed anymore. My list proves I'm not the crazy one. "Goodbye, Miss Nichols. Thanks for everything."

And with that cruel bit of casualness, I walk out. How else do you quit therapy? You can spend months just processing getting out the damn door. I don't have time for that now.

As I exit onto the Santa Monica street, I feel skittering and free and a bit afraid, a bird released from a cage. Got to fend for myself now and –

"Benji?" It's SG, carrying a big Uniqlo bag. Shopping on the prom.

"Are you stalking me now?" I tease, feeling loose, like anything can happen.

"I think you're stalking me." She smiles. "What are you up to?"

"I just quit therapy." It seems I can't lie to SG about anything.

"You were in therapy?" SG sounds surprised. "Is it your end of the world list?"

"It's definitely not helping my other issues. OCD. Manic depression. Psychosis." I laugh and she laughs with me, in perfect harmony. "What are you doing downtown?"

"Shopping." She checks her watch. "Dinner with my parents, like, ten minutes ago."

I nod and we stand like that, neither of us wanting to move as a bus pulls up with a groan and disgorges its passengers. For a second, it's like a movie where a crowd of people separates the lovers. We lock eyes, smiling. Is she thinking the same thing? You wish, Benji.

"I'll see you at school," she calls out, turning with the crowd.

"If you keep stalking me!" She grins over her shoulder and waves.

Amazing girl!

Four More Ways We're Going Extinct
(ugh, just get it done)

7. IT WILL DESTROY US ECONOMICALLY AND SOCIALLY.

As we sleepwalk our way to human extinction, we'll go broke. Utilities will go bankrupt. Cities like Bangkok, Mumbai, and Shanghai will drown, putting a billion on the move. Crop failures, fishery collapses, crime, and storms will take us back to the barbarism of the Dark Ages. Last year's CA fires alone did 4 billion dollars of damage. So "1.5 to stay alive" is a joke. We're already in the crash at 1.1C above preindustrial levels. At 2.0C, the carrying capacity for Earth could drop to a billion people. That's 7 billion not staying alive. And America's not changing. SUV sales are surging, wiping out all the oil and CO2 our electric cars save. Faster than sleepwalking, we're sleep-driving to our own funeral!

8. THE GULF STREAM IS SLOWING DOWN.

Earth's regulator isn't permanent. We've gotten lucky during 10,000 years of habitable climate that's allowed humans to stop being nomads, plant crops, and thrive. But it's already weakened 15% from warming oceans, the most in 1600 years. The Atlantic Meridional Overturning Circulation (A.M.O.C.) could run AMOK tomorrow and go berserk – droughts, floods, and "polar vortexes" all over the place. Oh, wait, those are already happening because –

9. CLIMATE CHAOS IS HERE.

Indonesia is moving its capital Jakarta inland. Mexico City is sinking from tapped-out aquifers, as 21 of the world's 37 aquifers are on the verge of collapse. They take 20,000 years to form, but Big Ag drains them to grow corn – cow feed – in deserts. So now 3.6 billion people are at risk of water scarcity. Meanwhile, industrial cities in China drown in the rain and super hurricanes wipe out the Caribbean. Mega-fire vortexes burn from Australia to our West, creating their own weather systems – right now in British Columbia 600 fires burn! In the Middle East, temperatures reach 134 Fahrenheit. In El Salvador, 20% of the people have chronic kidney disease from harvesting sugarcane. Worldwide, outside labor has dropped 10% due to lethal heat waves. As wheat harvests in Germany die, quadruple famines in Somalia, Sudan, Nigeria, and Yemen kill 20 million this year alone from drought – a taste of famines to come. Christ, Stat Man – Dante's inferno is already here. Now!

10. NOTHING WE DO IS NEARLY ENOUGH.

The Paris Accord is eating kale while shooting heroin. Ratcheting down to zero net emissions by 2050 is a bad joke – like saying you'll chain-smoke cigarettes for 30 years and then quit. Ha. And no country is close to hitting its five-year Paris goals, but even if they did, we'd still go to 3.5 Celsius and catastrophe. We tell ourselves comforting stories and nudge the oil tanker when we should blow it up. We think we can overshoot our lame CO_2 goals and catch up later, as if our withering planet has a thermostat we can regulate! It's all BS. The world's biggest polluters increase their emissions every year. As the glaciers in Antarctica silently melt three trillion tons of ice between 1992 and 2017, enough to fill Lake Erie 12 times over. And more every year. No surprise – it was 70 degrees there last week, the hottest in the continent's recorded history, just another example of global weirding and –

Thank Christ! Finally made it through this damn list. Horrible.

I wish they would just tell the truth: a "draw down" is happy talk. We need a slam down to <u>negative</u> CO_2 emissions. We need to create massive carbon capture technology that nobody's imagined, never mind invented. Unprecedented and unified world government action!

Because aiming to be "carbon neutral" decades from now is like treading water – doing the same thing that got us here. Half measures, inching into solar, feeling good about driving electric – it won't stop Earth from melting until she reaches a new stable state that kills us. I mean, even if we totally decarbonized the planet, everything electric <u>today</u>, just the current machines aging out will get us to 1.5C. Fact.

So, yeah, we're blasting past "1.5 to stay alive" no matter what we do.

No wonder I can't sleep at night, my brain looping the same infinity eight, trying to comprehend this reality. Buckle up, we need to CHANGE EVERYTHING NOW to survive.

That's the Truth. Can't argue with it. And it already might be too late.

Because the scary thing about tipping points is you don't know when you're in one. Unaware, like during the incubation period for a virus. Unaware, like when you brush a glass of milk and don't notice it's falling until – WHAM! Suddenly there's spilled milk everywhere. Contained to uncontained in an instant. Unaware, that's where we are – in the fall.

No use crying over spilled milk. We'll be too busy dying. And not just other countries we watch on TV winking out from starvation, drought, and war. They'll be watching us back, as our trucks stop delivering food and the riots start. As everything perishes everywhere – omnicide!

Will we remember this moment, when we watched and did nothing, while Cretin played Russian roulette with humanity, every chamber loaded? Christ. We'll end up fighting each other for a gun just to perform our own merciful murder-suicides.

What thoughts – I'm totally losing it on planet freak-out.

But Oscar Wilde was right – everything in moderation including moderation – because the time for moderation is over!

And I'm not the one living in Voltaire's illusion. Even though I've unearthed nothing hidden, it's obvious we're about to unearth ourselves. The enemy is us – I blame myself too. But at least I'm trying to wake up from my delusion, forcing myself to see it, even though pondering human extinction is like staring at the sun.

What can I do to wake up the world? One person?

Be the solution, not the problem.

The idea. Take out the one person who's making everything worse, who's stopping anything from changing. Kill the Kamikaze flying the plane into the ground. Kill Cretin.

I already wish I could forget this horrible list, even though I never will.

The nightmares. As we slumber through our incubation.

Death to come.

Today's Cretin Tweet

"They changed the name global warming to climate change because the concept of global warming just wasn't working!" How about Climageddon? As the Aussie inferno burns a billion animals alive. Wow. Our fires became quaint much quicker than I thought.

Closing Doors

They did my locker again today – every damn year on the anniversary of Alphabet inviting me to their "open doors" program. Guess in a school so competitive, once they hate you from the get-go, they'll never stop. So, the locker got glued shut because of "open doors" – Dim and Dimmer's version of witty. As if he doesn't have enough to do, Hector cranked it open again...

"The locker. That time of the year already, huh?" Hector's eyes crinkle when he smiles, making his salt and pepper stubble stick out. There's just something about Hector that's peaceful. I always feel calmer around him.

"Yeah. Like a sign of winter." I'm joking, but also sick of it.

"You don't want to report it this year?" Hector pulls a box-cutter out of his toolkit. He knows everything that goes on in the school, even that Dim and Dimmer are the culprits.

"Nah. It'll just make it worse." As if being a tall, pale, ginger with braces who gave up on anti-social media and pukes on girls could get worse.

"It'll pass." Hector smiles again. "My son went through the same thing."

"He did?" It never occurs to me Hector has a son, a family, a life. The problem with my end-of-the-world self-absorption. "How's he doing now? Did he get through it all?"

"Graduated college. Got a job. Didn't boomerang home." Hector smiles. "Success."

"That's cool. Good to know it's still possible." That's sort of a joke.

"Nobody gets through high school without some ugly." Hector pops the locker. "Especially if you've got a 4.7 GPA. Just take care of yourself. Stay close to your family."

"Yeah." Is that what I'm going through? Extreme high school ugliness? And my family, I will lose them forever. Christ.

"I'll keep it on the down-low again," Hector says.

"Thanks, Hector. I appreciate it."

"You got it, Benji." Hector would be a great therapist. So much better than Nichols or Klein, who always looks at me like I'm a specimen when I get my prescription. Not anymore!

Hector's supposed to report any bullying, but everybody gives a 4.7 a lot of slack. They assume I've got my shit handled. But I don't have my shit handled. Not at all. I'm feeling disjointed – my mind careening like a penny tossed in a sink. Wish I could take an Adderall like the kids at HWB who eat it like candy. But then I'd just mono-focus even more down the Climate Chaos drain. Obsession. I hate it.

Is it my mental problem or justifiable terror?

The Idea. The lists. This shit is getting real.

Today's Headline

"Largest King Penguin Colony Shrinks 90% In 30 Years." Bullied off the damn planet by a stronger species – us. Dim and Dimmer would approve.

– BBC.com

Feedback Loops

I was trying to explain that old milkshake duck meme to Mom today.

"It's a reality tunnel that isn't real," I tell her. "Like, a duck is drinking a milkshake – so cute, until you find out the duck's a racist."

"So, it's a surprise?" She looks at me quizzically.

"A reality flip. Like that old pull-your-pants-up comedian in jail now. All cuddly and selling Jell-O and wearing sweaters, until you find out America's Dad is a lifelong pervert."

"Boys will be boys," Mom says whenever she thinks I'm being immature about meme culture. It makes me want to tell her the <u>big reality</u> everybody swallows isn't real. The climate appears one way but is really another. Each year we plod along getting warmer, CO_2 levels rising bit-by-bit – linear. But the hidden reality is any minute it can start lurching unpredictably – exponential. Surprise!

Imminent extinction, that's our milkshake duck meme.

But I don't tell Mom. I'm afraid I won't stop talking until I tell her everything. Then it's back to therapy for sure – inpatient lock-down like after throwing blood at Bel Campo. But I need to stress this on my list.

As much as I hate to go back into it, I need one damn addendum:

11. IT'S ALL HAPPENING IMMINENTLY.

Hale says we live in a time when "velocity crushes veracity," when BS speeds around the world before Truth gets out of bed. But imminently is no BS. Sea level rise has <u>doubled</u> 2013 forecasts. The IPCC undershot the Arctic ice melt, which <u>tripled</u> predictions. Science has underestimated every climate prediction they've ever made – being cautious is the nature of science as they try to capture the ever-changing flood of data to reach consensus.

But it's not the <u>nature of Nature</u>, which just HAPPENS, and not on our puny schedule. The latest paleoclimate records show Earth has already had "planetary transformation" within mere years. And now, can again.

Everybody talks about CO2 feedback loops. Like the melting Arctic sea ice, a bald spot cooling our planetary head because ice reflects 95% of the sun's heat. But now our sweaty planet is growing hair, creating dark ocean that absorbs 95%. This makes our planet hotter, which melts away more ice, which makes it hotter – the albedo effect. So, all the Arctic sea ice will permanently disappear in four years. Peter Wadhams, an eminent climate scientist, predicts this alone will increase warming by 50%.

Boom. Just from one "Hothouse Earth" feedback loop.

But CO2 feedback loops are part of our planet's slow endgame. Like forests dying from heat, fires, and deforestation – especially in the Amazon, as they clear-cut it for cows and gold. The more trees die, the less CO2 they extract, the hotter it gets, the more trees die, round and round – another amplifying feedback loop. But still linear. Slow. Polite.

What nobody talks about is exponential. Fast. Rude.

Nobody talks about what happens when Earth goes from friend to mortal enemy – as out of control as a viral infection. Like with Methane, which creates a feedback loop on steroids, a hundred times worse than CO2. But unlike CO2, methane has an instantaneous greenhouse effect.

This is terrible for our survival.

Because 25% of the Northern Hemisphere is permafrost – from Siberia to Alaska – frozen dirt where <u>1.8 trillion tons</u> of methane lives. And that frost isn't so perma anymore. It's already melting, releasing all that methane, along with the Arctic lakes bubbling it. Plus, there are <u>gigatons</u> of frozen methane hydrates in the oceans. As they thaw from warming oceans, the methane will vent in oceanic Godzilla burps. Lightning can ignite these methane pulses and create primordial plumes of fire!

That's EXPONENTIAL.

When our terminal cancer becomes a bullet to the brain.

Nobody wants to talk seriously about human extinction, even though a million species now don't have enough habitat left to ensure their survival. We're next. By 2030, in India, scientists predict heat waves so lethal they'll kill people sitting outside in only four hours, even in shade!

Christ, what else do we need?

The planet's dog whistle has become a foghorn as we pass tipping points every day. And you don't have to "believe" the world is melting. You can pick up ancient Pliocene seashells 200 feet above current sea level. This is the map of where Earth was when it had the <u>same CO2 levels as right now</u>: water halfway up the Statue of Liberty.

As you hold that seashell, Cretin demands: Do you believe that lying shell or me? Ha. I'm joking, but not really. What if he wins again? What will Cretin be saying for the next four years? And doing? What will any of them do?

At best, not enough. At worst, Cretin. Who's methane gas for us all.

I need to cold turkey the apocalypse porn like I did the sex porn. Don't need to research anymore – I can just watch the news about today's mega-fire, hurricane, drought, or polar vortex. As our sick planet reboots, going from paradise to hell, immune to "incremental fixes," revealing its dark side in the ultimate milkshake duck meme.

Imminently. No fucking joke.

This is stressing me out. Need to sit in the garden with Gigi.

Christ, what an addendum.

Today's Headline

"President Cuts Regulation on Big Oil's Methane Leaks and Intentional Flaring." That's a third of this super pollutant produced. Why not? It's been two days since Cretin gave Big Oil a gift.

– NPR.org

Gigi in the Garden

Another night of crap sleep, working on my second list – why I need to kill Cretin. That's terrifying. No wonder I can't sleep...

Plus, the more I think about the end of the world, the more I can't stop. Christ... Need a break from all the death and destruction.

The garden helps – skipping morning classes and sitting outside our mid-century modern home built by A. Quincy Jones. He specialized in houses for artists and writers, which made him a communist in Bitterwood back in the 50s. They're kind of like tract housing – cheaply made, but with cool architecture – and tiny compared to houses in our neighborhood that have garages bigger than our home.

Right now, it's empty. Wish my mind was as quiet.

Gigi shuffles into the little yard and with a groan of contentment, flops down in the sun. Panting in the heat, I can see gum where her incisors should be. Must have been hell, deranged dogs attacking her while she was chained up and with only a few teeth for defense. Every time I think about it – RAGE! I want to John Wick her torturers, shoot or slice them open and let dogs eat them alive. The only way you can get dogs to fight is to torture them, so torture is the right punishment. But I can't hunt them down – they sealed Gigi's records.

So much for getting away from all the death and destruction.

"Guess I'm becoming one of those people who like animals more than humans, eh girl?" Gigi snuffles in agreement. "People are too cruel. But you know that, don't you?"

I stare at Gigi's scarred head and clipped ears, abused her whole life until cops busted up the fighting ring. How could I ever say goodbye to her, my spirit animal, voiceless as the rest? But she's the only one I can be honest with about leaving on this mission. If I go.

"You never judge and never tell, do you, girl?" Gigi grunts, as innocent as all nature. In the silent garden, I feel a moment of peace from my horrible lists. Nothing but me, Gigi, and my journal.

I try to meditate like they taught me at FTW. Mindful. Not easy with this mind. My eyes pop open.

"They say meditation can melt your mind like Molly, but mine sure hasn't melted, eh girl?" Gigi, a born meditator, gazes at me calmly with her one eye – like, what's the big deal?

Watching my thoughts is more natural in nature. My best glimpses come sitting in the garden with Gigi for hours of magical do-nothingness. I try to stop – right now! – and pay attention to the moment. And my grim thoughts fade as the garden comes alive...

Hummingbirds dart to full stops at buds on the orange tree. One divebombs and thrums my ears. Another flies backward, iridescent colors shimmering as she hovers – delicate, beautiful, and vibrant. I love them. And today, I feel real envy for their incredible lightness of being.

"This is okay, ha girl?" I stare at Gigi dozing in the sun. After about ten seconds, she opens her eye. How does she know I'm watching her? She ambles over to the dappled shade next to me and flops, all four legs in the air, like a baby looking up from its crib, wriggling, scratching her back on the grass. Her crocodile mouth opens in a grin missing every other tooth.

"You're a real therapy dog, eh, girl? Way better than Nichols." My face is low, next to her mighty jaws, and as I scratch her belly she slips me a lick on the cheek. "Kisses, huh?"

It's a pure moment of connection, in the puddle of sun, and I feel the anxiety drain out of me. I'm less tethered to the Idea. The world isn't ending. Not here. Not right now. Gigi pulls me into the moment, the gift of all animals. I grab the Zoom Groom and start brushing her.

The meditators at FTW always ask, "What else is there but this moment?"

Good question. Even facing the end of the world tomorrow, you can walk out the door and get hit by a bus today. So, what else can I do but enjoy every moment, now being the only livable one and maybe my last?

I try – sinking into the smell of fresh-cut grass down at Gigi's level. The sound of her grunts as I brush her. The heat of her breath on my cheek. Her eye glazing down to half-mast in a massage coma.

Finally, I simply am.

A fluorescent green caterpillar climbs a twig beside Gigi, hairy legs inching along, with no idea it will soon float over the same terrain, a flying god for a few weeks. Are we caterpillars, unaware of what we can become, unaware of a different way of being in the world? Can we evolve to the next level and save ourselves? Do it or die...

What am I transforming into? When will I reach the point of no return? From Idea to Plan to Action to Death? Now I'm just a horrible monster, trapped, mid-metamorphosis –

But the garden! Without my phone and with trees and flowers and buzzing with life, it makes me feel better. Untethered, unreachable – like I imagine it was before the web. Simple. Just me, Gigi, and my journal...

A rare Monarch lazes by, floating from flower to flower. Congratulations! You made it from caterpillar to god. Pollinating. For now, and –

An unwelcome thought from my colonized mind flitters into view. A CNN headline: *"Beetles, Butterflies, and Bees, Oh My!"*

Today, news that 40% of pollinators face extinction from pesticides because man has altered or destroyed 75% of Earth's land. Oh, my, CNN!

How about a side of cutesiness with your extinction sandwich?

"Why can't we save our garden from the Exxons and Monsantos of the world?" I ask Gigi as I brush her. She just licks my arm. Perfect response, really. Comforting, as always.

The Chinese already hand-pollinate because they've got the people. The Japanese supposedly invented a drone to pollinate flowers. So you can sit in a garden and listen to the plastic clatter-clacks of a contraption, hoping for techno-fixes that suck energy, never scale, and totally miss the point. Privatizing the environment – like the companies plotting to build millions of carbon-capture machines, eye on the money.

Christ, we're as stupid as the drones Amazon plans to land in our gardens, making it easier for people to consume more and more, choking the planet to death as we all end up as mindless as Wall-E – fat, isolated, and depressed. Like a poor Frankenchicken.

"Maybe that's how I kill Cretin, eh, girl?" Gigi opens her eye, questioning me. I would too, if I was her. "Make a drone tiny as a silverfish to crawl up his nostrils when he's sleeping. Eat what's left of his syphilitic brain. I'm sure after raw-dogging his whole life with porn stars, his brain is Swiss cheese."

Gigi yawns, a sign of stress in dogs. It's not working today. Even in the garden my mind skitters into Cretin obsession. I've started tracking his movements. He's in Arizona today, jabbering more BS about the wall.

He's close, and it's got me on high alert.

"Okay, girl. How about a biscuit?" That's a word Gigi knows and she pops up, tail wagging. Might as well go to school. Can't lose myself in the moment.

Can't get extinction out of my head. Or the Idea.

Today's Headline

"Monarch Butterfly Population Plummets 90% In One Year." A death spiral for 900 million beauties, gone forever. Guess the garden with Gigi will be way less magical.

– CNN.com

Harvard-Wanna-Be Sucks for Real

School is no better. They took another girl today.

Sounds like a horror movie, but I guess the last straw was her seeing friends partying on Insta-Lie without her. She ends up silently crying during our AP calculus test, while pulling her hair out strand-by-strand.

Trichotillomania – whew, what a word.

"She's crying. Look," a dude says as Chen gently takes her hand, off to the school nurse. I feel so bad and want to say something but she's already gone. Everybody just grabs their phones to post it. Will it knock my puke video down a notch on their feeds? Christ, what a heartless thought.

The kids at HWB try to ignore the anxiety infecting the place like the plague. Still, no matter how rah-rah everybody is, kids keep browning out, off to some psych rehab. Parents go from worrying if Junior will get into an Ivy to worrying about if Junior's going to live to be a senior.

I think it's because kids these days spend less time outside than prisoners. That's messed up. Cut off from nature, of course we get depressed. Like that San Quentin study, where prisoners looking out at concrete get 23% more depressed than the ones on the other side of the prison with a view of grass. Even a glimpse of Mother Earth heals our sadness.

Instead, we get meds.

Wish I could have told that girl to just quit all Socials – that they're gasoline to every spark of sorrow. That the truth no tech company tells is all screen time makes you less happy, and all non-screen time makes you more, no exceptions. That there's a reason it's called the web and keeping us ensnared is "stickiness," caught by spiders we can't see. And not the cool eight-legged ones – the greedy bloodsucking two-leggers. No wonder suicide is the second leading cause of death for kids my age, up 70% this year. Depressed, alone in the glow of our screens, gulping the lies of Insta-Lie as our future dies, we kill ourselves at record rates.

How sad is that?

But the more I talk about going cold turkey on Socials, the faster kids like Tricho-girl stride away. Even Tim thinks I'm a freak for quitting. But why give them your whole life so they can scrape your soul and sell you off to some Black Mirror company control? All Socials are in the extraction and mining business, just like Exxon. I don't want to be oil for a bloodsucker like Zuck, who actually said, *"Privacy? Get over it."*

Good one, Zuck!

After lurking on feeds, quitting was like waking up from a trance. At least I never got goosed into doing thirsty stuff like eating detergent. Or snorting condoms. Or whatever else kids will do next that can kill you – all Exhibit A for good old natural selection.

Now I'm feeling anxious. Free-floating infected. Is it the Idea? Or my second list? Reasons Cretin deserves to die! J'accuse!

Working on this list is giving the Idea dangerous life. It's mutating in me, taking over my world – opening this Pandora's box. No wonder I'm anxious. What do I expect from a list of everything Cretin's doing to kill us? And why I need to kill him.

At least if I act on it, I'll never see HWB again.

Put one in the plus column.

Today's Fact

America, 4.4% of the world's population, has 25% of the world's prisoners. Isn't that a sign we might be doing something wrong?

– Wikipedia.org

Ten Reasons Cretin Deserves to Die

"*Be the change you wish to see in the world.*"

That Gandhi quote is everywhere at HWB. Ha. I'm the change all right – from silverfish pardoner to assassin-in-waiting. Not what Gandhi had in mind, but he was living in less critical times.

But I'm not insane like John Hinckley, trying to kill a president to impress an actress. I've got reasons, a million facts why Cretin should die, as he erases hundreds of planet-saving regulations and cuts enforcement to the bone. I've finally narrowed it down to another list of ten...

1. HE GETS PAID OFF BY THE COMPANIES KILLING US.

Cretin, who owns Dante's fourth circle of Greed, will do anything for money. <u>Anything</u>.

Like, after Big Oil heavily donated to elect him, Cretin yanked the new drilling rules put in after Deepwater Horizon exploded, killing 11 people and a million seabirds in the worst oil spill in U.S. history. Yanking rules for mandatory Blowout Preventers that avert oil spills will save Big Oil a measly $228 million over ten years – the salary of one CEO a year. Meanwhile, Deepwater cost BP 62 <u>billion</u> dollars, so it's not even good business. It's madness. But Cretin got paid off, so what does he care? When it happens again, Cretin won't make BP pay a dime in fines.

2. HE IS ACTIVELY KILLING US YOUNG PEOPLE.

Every day, Cretin pours gasoline on the fire, as if he resents young people our youth, refusing to meet with even one environmental group or climate scientist. Ever. His assaults on our inheritance are endless. Off the top of my head, in one month he:

- Repealed emissions standards on cars. He wants them to pollute more, releasing billions more tons of CO2!

- Ended regulations on coal ash pools filled with arsenic, lead, and mercury that leak into our drinking water. Same for our air.

- Permanently handed millions of acres of our public lands to the mining industry.

3. HE SUPPORTS OTHER CLIMATE DENIERS.

Sure, Paris is way too little, way too late, and nobody's close to their goals. Just a Band-Aid to pat ourselves on the back so we don't have to make real sacrifices. Still, it's better than saying "drop dead" to the kids of the world. But even worse, Cretin's greedy denial makes it easier for Mini-Cretins around the world to lie – from Climate Chaos is a hoax, to humans don't cause it, to it costs too much to fix, to it's too late to do anything. Ha. Might be right about the last one.

4. HE REPEALS THE CLEAN POWER PLAN.

Cretin creates billions of tons more emissions – 12 times more just for coal plants – by repealing the law controlling CO2 from smokestacks. In the U.S., this single act will kill thousands more people every year from air pollution alone for people like June. So, Cretin just green-lit mass murder as a warm-up for extinction. The WHO says 90% of humanity is already choking on dangerous levels of pollutants that weaken our lungs, inhaling fine particle poisons, chemicals, and mercury that create asthma and disease. Cretin doesn't care. Big Coal gave 97% and Big Oil gave 88% of their blood money to Republicans. So, Cretin got his cash.

5. HE IS CRIMINALLY INSANE OR DEMENTED.

What else can you call him? That psychopath not only has zero empathy, like the Joker, he gets off on the mayhem. Doesn't matter if he causes it. Look at his response to Hurricane survivors – tossing paper towels to people who've lost everything says it all. Of course, he might just be demented.

6. HE'S TRYING TO CHEAT HIS WAY TO RE-ELECTION.

Rules are for suckers, says Cretin, who's such a loser, he can't win fair at anything. He's already cheating, trying to steal the next election. And if he loses, he'll call it rigged, incite riots, and torch our democracy. His Clown Senators won't help – 73% don't believe in climate change! They'll just service their wealthy overlords and stay loyal to Cretin, even as he says wind turbines cause cancer. Insane! Criminally.

7. HE OPENS ALL U.S. WATERS TO DRILLING.

Except Florida. He doesn't want oil sloshing on his cheesy resort. But Florida is already sinking – Atlantis for real – with the ocean burbling up from the manholes of Miami in "sunny day flooding." Such a happy name for the beginning of the end. Sorry Cretin, no matter what you say, sea-level rise from that "Chinese hoax" will swamp your cheesy hotel. Rains will flood you. Just ask Houston or New Orleans or farmers delaying crops because of 12-foot floods in Iowa. Food shortages to follow.

8. HE DOESN'T CARE.

Living over 70 years during the best time to be on the planet, Cretin leads his generation in turning Earth into a garbage dump. They've emitted 85% of the CO2 humankind has produced in its entire history! Gassing his fat ass around in a jumbo jet his whole life, Cretin doesn't care about destroying a planet that took millions of years to reboot from the last CO2 extinction. And instead of leading the fight to save us now, he fights tooth and nail for the companies killing humanity. Four more years of Cretin will put us past catastrophic tipping points.

9. HE BURIES THE CLIMATE SCIENCE.

"Science is not something that should be just thrown about to try to dictate policy in Washington, D.C." So says Cretin's latest criminal at the EPA, as he fires scientists, hires climate deniers to gut it from the inside, and "loses" climate and pollution reports that tell us how our health is affected. It's still called the EPA, but the oil and coal companies own it now, pumping disinformation as bad as the BP green-wash commercials. They

show workers on gleaming equipment while liar slogans roll out, *"Because safety is never being satisfied."* Ha. Like Blowout Preventers to protect our oceans – safety is never being satisfied!

"Our brand is doubt," is Big Oil's real slogan, as they bribe Cretin to kill the science and won't even acknowledge Earth is getting warmer.

10. THE BEST SIGN OF FUTURE BEHAVIOR IS PAST BEHAVIOR.

Nichols always says that when she shrinks my head. Pretty neg, but true. Except for me, my behavior's definitely changing! But Cretin and his Clown Cult of old bloodsuckers won't stop slurping the marrow from the planet. They love picking their teeth with our bones. They've already enjoyed clean skies and oceans full of fish and Earth's abundance and are lucky dead by the time the coming wave crashes. A natural death for the old screw-you-I've-got-mine crowd rationalizing that if they don't get theirs somebody else will. Meanwhile, our breadbaskets drown and our children starve. Our wild spaces are drilled and paved over. What is it with these rich bloodsuckers? And all the Olds killing us? When is enough? What about some empathy for us young people –

Christ! Got to stop. I feel sweaty on the inside. Weird. Not normal.

But isn't it <u>abnormal</u> to feel normal now?

Shouldn't a species destroying its own habitat be anxious? For teenagers like me, not even born as the Olds pollute Earth beyond hope, we won't get to die of natural causes. Our death will be highly unnatural, from a nature gone as crazy as a bull stabbed with lances to cripple it in a bullfight. Soon we are at the part where nature, the mighty beast, is killed for no reason beyond Cretin's sick pleasure – are you not <u>amused</u>?

But in the end, Nature will gore us all. Life itself is a china shop that will shatter in a geologic instant. It's happening. The climate bullet is speeding toward us right now. You can't negotiate with the science – it's not interested in compromise. It will do what it will do.

Writing out my two lists has helped me SEE. Cretin needs to die.

I need to stop him from leading mankind's murder of the natural world. And our own suicide, as nature keeps us alive to the tune of 24 trillion dollars a year. Little things like wetlands purifying drinking water, and rain forests absorbing CO2, and coral reefs sustaining fisheries. Bees pollinating our food! Instead of gratitude, we kill them all.

We give Gaia no choice but to exterminate us right off her surface.

Enough! No more lists. The more I write about the science of what's happening – just nausea. Like a cabal of bean counters is living in my head, computing our actuarial end date. No wonder nobody wants to talk about it. Or give up their lux life for my desert headspace. They'd rather ignore it, like the Aussie government subsidizing 53 new coal mines as their own scientists wonder if the entire continent could become uninhabitable.

Olds killing Youngs, all day long. Mother-Earth-fuckers!

What the hell did she ever do to you?

I've got my answer. It might be too late, but if I do nothing – good men doing nothing so evil prevails – Cretin's death cult will turn Earth into a spinning coffin.

This is terrifying, but when I boil my lists down...

HERE'S WHAT I KNOW

    – Climate chaos is hurtling our planet toward mass extinction.

    – Every day, Cretin accelerates the devastation.

    – To save my generation and defend our planet, Cretin must die.

HERE'S WHAT I DON'T KNOW (YET)

    – How to kill Cretin.

Today's Cretin Tweet

"There is no reason for these massive and costly forest fires in California except that forest management is so poor. Remedy now, or no more Fed payments!" A threat before they even bury the burnt bodies in Northern California. Another reason to kill him, as if I needed it.

Mall Rats

Today I was with Mom and June at the Galleria Mall in the valley, shopping for a Halloween costume for June.

This was depressing for too many reasons, but mainly because if I don't give up the Idea, I'll be dead before Halloween. Christ. Felt so blasted all day, like melted lead has replaced the blood in my veins. Is it my lists that have mono-focused me down into such a dark place? Fear.

But then, at the mall, of all places, the universe sent me a message...

In front of The European Wax Center, a woman yanks a toddler along like a roller bag, his feet barely touching the ground. Then she stops and just slaps him across the face. I've never seen anything like that in my life, but everybody looks away. Something I see every day in these toxic times. Nobody wants to do anything –

"I'll call child services if you hit him again."

It's Mom. Don't be a bystander is something Mom drills into June and me. Guess I over-learned that one.

"Just stop and look at him," Mom pleads, pointing at the kid.

Weirdly, the woman does stop and look at her wailing child, snot running down his face, heaving tears like a sprinkler. But her eyes narrow into a pair of sneers.

"Mind your business." She's drunk. "He's no goddamn snowflake."

"You abusing your child is everybody's business." Mom stands in front of the hulking woman, feet planted. "Just look at him. You're holding him so tight his fingers are blue."

The child stops bawling, just sobbing a bit now, watching the interaction between the tiny woman and his mother, who's glaring at Mom like she's from another planet, a really annoying one. Mom stares up at her, holding her phone in one hand, moving it slightly, ready to call, as if to say, all flinty Clint Eastwood, *You feel lucky, punk?*

That's mom. The family hatred of bullies, the strong torturing the weak, originates with her. Don't be a bystander – why does she expect June to be different? Or me, if she knew about my planned political violence? Bullies like Cretin depend on us all hating violence to get away with it – like we're too good for it. But don't we need to get over our fear and distaste when we see abuse in the world? <u>Abuse of the world?</u>

"He'll never forget the trauma of being slapped," Mom urgently whispers to the woman so the little boy can't hear. "Even after he forgets this day, it will live in him and his children. And his children's children. All he knows is his love for you and all he needs is patience. He's a <u>child</u>."

Children's children – I pity them, the world we leave if we make it.

They got crappy ancestors.

The stunned woman lets go of her son's hand as Mom squats and whispers something into the wide-eyed boy's ear. Then Mom stands, curtly nods at the woman, and strides away. We rush to follow her.

"That was badass," June declares. "What did you say to that kid?"

"If I told you, I'd have to kill you," Mom repeats the family joke to avoid telling us.

"I'm curious too, Mom." I give June the look we share when trying to talk Mom and Dad into something. Like, jump in, pull your weight here –

"Yeah. Let's hear your words of wisdom to other people's kids," June chimes in with more than a little sarcasm, not exactly following the script. "Maybe I can learn something."

"I doubt I can teach you anything, June," Mom volleys back.

"You're not going to tell us?" I suddenly want to know what comfort she gave the little boy trapped in that family. Is it because my world is disintegrating? Do I just need to hear some compassion and wisdom, both in such short supply these days –

"Okay, okay. I told him no two snowflakes are alike," Mom says in a rare surrender. "Alone they are weak, but when they stick together, they can become a powerful avalanche. And that someday he will find his friends."

June and I look at each other and shrug-nod. Damn good name and reclaim. Doesn't an avalanche start when one last snowflake falls and gets the whole thing rolling? Could my grand individual act trigger a collective political avalanche and –

"Not bad, Mom," June grudges. "If he's ever seen a snowflake."

"High praise from you, my dear." Mom arches an eyebrow, making us laugh. She is a steel hand wrapped in a velvet glove. She has zero fear, except of cops – that family story. But around everything else? None.

Reality check: no matter what Tyler calls me, nobody in our family insta-melts like a snowflake. Nobody's a fragile PC Nazi. Sensitive, sure. But me killing Cretin is about as far from being a snowflake as it gets.

Was this horrible encounter at the mall some sort of sign? Step up? Don't be a bystander? I'm going to say yes.

I don't need a trigger warning. I am the trigger warning.

Today's headline

"Birds Are Vanishing from North America." Thirty percent over the last fifty years, as Cretin revokes the Migratory Bird Treaty Act. So now Europe and America can share the same silent spring, as Rachel Carson dies another death.

– NYTimes.com

Rapist by the Numbers

Today Cretin said we can emit CO2 at current levels through 2050 – a planetary death sentence! When will the last snowflake finally fall, setting off my avalanche of rage and action?

I don't know... Today I feel like Cassandra, that teenager from Greek mythology. She visions Greeks hidden in their wooden horse and races to Troy to warn them. But the guards don't believe her and the Greeks overrun the city. Turns out, Apollo only gave Cassandra the power to see the future to seduce her. And when she says no means NO, he spits in her mouth and inflicts a curse that nobody will ever believe her prophesies.

That's so gross, spitting in her mouth – talk about sexual harassment. Turns out liars silencing the truth go way back, even to the Greeks.

But I feel exactly like her. Impotent.

It's not what you look at that matters, it's what you <u>see</u>.

Thoreau was so right. I see the danger. I see how Cretin rapes the planet – it's the entire M.O. of him and his Cult. They gang-rape Mother Earth behind closed doors and nobody stops it. The whole damn world is suffering from the bystander effect, just watching the desecration, doing NOTHING.

Me too. I'm just stalled out being a do-nothing Stat Head.

As today, Cretin's EPA guy, Climate Criminal #1, signed off on a gold and copper mine in Bristol Bay, Alaska. Big as Manhattan and deep as the Grand Canyon, they'll slash it in pristine wilderness, killing the world's most valuable salmon fishery and over 14,000 jobs. He decides this an hour after he meets with the mining company CEO. An hour! That's how fast money changes hands in the once proud EPA that Cretin hollowed out. All in a day's rape...

"It is difficult to get a man to understand something when his salary depends on his not understanding it." In *The Jungle*, Upton Sinclair exposes the savagery in slaughterhouses, to both animal and man.

True then, true now.

Meanwhile, today's news says humans released a record 80 quadrillion pounds of CO_2 last year. A quadrillion is a thousand trillion. A meaningless number. For <u>perspective</u>, I found this meme:

- A million seconds is 12 days.

- A trillion seconds is 29,000 years.

- A quadrillion seconds is 29 million years.

Now multiply that by eighty and you get 80 quadrillion pounds of CO_2 dumped into our atmosphere every year. Makes my head hurt. My heart? It just breaks.

And next in command is Climate Criminal #2, a coal lobbyist who's dedicated his life to fossil fuel crimes against humanity. What an endless conga line of A-holes. I feel helpless, doing nothing but reading, writing, thinking. What about some action, Stat Head? Fuck!

Cretin, the naked emperor, is spitting in my mouth.

Today's Headline

"Administration Rolls Back Clean Water Protections." They like to say Cretin's "malevolence is tempered by his incompetence." I call BS. Seems damn competent at one thing.

— NYTimes.com

Hitler Rant

Stuck. Not moving on the Idea, not chucking it.

Limbo – Dante's first circle. Super frustrating. STUCK!

Still, the Idea grows in me like a tumor. Even as I'm sitting in class watching SG and half-listening to Baxter saying, "history makes the man." What BS! If it wasn't Hitler it would have been another madman who has the crazy charisma to turn ordinary people into mass murderers? Another Cretin teeing up Earth like a golf ball to smash it? No way.

"'Nothing is more frightful than to see ignorance in action,'" Baxter is quoting Goethe, who sure got that right. Isn't that the definition of our time, ignorance in action?

I know I'm obsessive – on the OCD spectrum, whatever that is.

And I know if you bring up Hitler, you've supposedly lost the argument – Godwin's law, "reductio ad Hitler" and all that. And I know Cretin's not Hitler, not yet. But even Hitler didn't start out as HITLER. There are many steps to get to all caps. But every genocide in history has started with the hate-filled words Cretin now spews. To pretend his constant scapegoating is "just clowning" is like saying a toddler playing with matches in a puddle of gasoline is just "having fun."

A Cretin wife said he kept a book of Hitler's speeches beside his bed. While it's hard to believe Cretin's actually read a book, it's obvious he's studied Hitler. He calls reporters enemy of the people. He uses simple words anybody can understand, pounding the same slogans. He's capricious, constantly contradicting himself, crushing logic. He's infallible to his cult. He buries us in disinformation, a master at manipulating fear and hate. And there are rumors that he's a speed freak, like Hitler was.

So, I'm sure Cretin knows Hitler loved the Confederacy and copied its Jim Crow laws. And I'm sure Cretin would kiss Hitler's jackboots, like he does with dictators now, copying their humiliation of any politician who opposes him. Not that any in his cult ever do, their deal with the devil has colonized their minds. I just learned it's called an "authoritarian bargain."

"Every age has its own fascism." Wrote this Auschwitz survivor, Primo Levi. What a thought. But it only matters because Cretin's fascism equals extinction. So, at least our fascism will be humanity's last. Ha. Grim...

But Cretin hides his authoritarianism under smirking meme jokes. Like, I'm a WWE "heel" playing out a fake conflict and if you don't "get it" you're a snowflake. But the joke's on us – Cretin isn't trolling. His wrestling arena is the planet, which he pile-drives every damn day.

Meanwhile, our corrupt congress thinks they can use Cretin like the German parliament thought they could use Hitler. And at first, Cretin obliges, selling off our planet and cutting taxes for billionaires. But now, Cretin has made Republicans his bitches and does whatever he wants and "jokes" about being president for life, getting us used to the idea.

So, what the hell am I waiting for? Why can't I take the next step?

Will I just talk and do <u>nothing</u> as fascism clown-rides in on the back of corruption and a total lack of values where only MORE matters? Will I just watch until we all feel nothing, high on the drug of hate, our compassion crushed and corrupted, numb to our own impending death? Will I not even protect our precious planet from the sociopaths destroying it, standing by while corporations marry governments in fascist shotgun weddings – marital rape to follow? Christ!

So, do something, Benji!! Or this will never end.

Because Cretin's father lived until 93, and his mother until 88. Even though he's a fat, sweaty blob, Cretin thinks he's got 20 more years in him. Fueled by hate, he might. And while it's true Cretin could only crawl out of the toxic sludge of a dysfunctional society, he's the demented maypole his sheeple dance around. Like Hitler, it's Cretin's dark magnetism that destroys the world. So, I'll worry about the next one history produces when it happens. Got to deal with this emergency now.

Am I the only one who thinks this way? I don't care.

I'm sticking with kill Cretin, kill Cretinism, save the planet.

I've just got to stop sitting on my ass, all BS, no action. Truly, pathetic.

But I feel so alone, everybody bullied or fooled by Cretin.

Why can't they see what Cicero saw?

"The traitor appears not a traitor; he speaks in accents familiar to his victims, and he wears their face and their arguments, he appeals to the baseness that lies deep in the hearts of all men. He rots the soul of a nation ... he infects the body politic so that it can no longer resist. A murderer is less to fear."

Wow, perfect description. Cretin's all that and a mass murderer too.

Will I also become a murderer? I hate that idea. There's no way I want to become an executioner, but doesn't a higher moral code allow for it in this situation? It's all so confusing. I'm stuck!

I don't know... What if it's too late? And if it is, does it matter Cretin today refused to sign the Kigali treaty to phase out HFCs, a greenhouse gas packing 1,000 times the punch of CO2? Endless, endless blows.

Is Mother Earth already mortally wounded, bleeding out? And Cretin, who denies the difference between climate and weather, just pulling the plug on a species in hospice? Maybe.

But even if we're already dead planet spinning, I've got to stop Cretin from fucking our cadaver like a depraved necrophiliac. At least if I defend Earth, I'll die with my boots on.

If not me, who? If not now, when?

I need to unstuck myself!

Worst Prediction Ever

"Within two months, we will have pushed Hitler so far into a corner that he'll squeal." So said Chancellor Franz Von Papen in 1933 after they elected Hitler. Ha. Good one, Franz. You've reincarnated as a Republican.

– Historyplace.com

Revolting

It's 3 AM after my Hitler rant. I'm wide awake listening to Gigi snore.

I've got to move from Idea to Plan, enough is enough.

No matter what – tonight! <u>NOW</u>! How? Guns, of course.

But just the idea of guns brings me back to Dad asking, "does the end justify the means?" What if the end is a revolution? And not just in thinking, we need that for sure, but a real guns-in-the-street rebellion?

"Whenever any Form of Government becomes destructive of these Ends, it is the Right of the people to alter or to abolish it ... to effect their Safety and Happiness." Amen, Declaration of Independence.

Time to <u>alter and abolish</u>, starting with Cretin. Because nothing is an existential threat to our "safety and happiness" more than Climate Chaos, as we sink up to our noses in it like quicksand.

But what if killing Cretin just creates rivers of blood?

"The tree of liberty must be refreshed from time to time with the blood of patriots and tyrants." Jefferson again, sounding damn glib about bloody revolution. What would he say now, when his tree of liberty is on fire? Isn't that reason enough for a bloody civil war? If I could resurrect him, I'm sure Thomas would say yes.

Half the country loves our tyrant's climate lies. The other half detests him as much as John Wilkes Booth hated Lincoln. But we're stuck together like neighbors sharing a fence.

As he shot Lincoln, Booth shouted, *"Sic Semper Tyrannis! The South is avenged!"*

Ever thus to tyrants. Ha. Guess every assassin thinks he's a hero.

Christ, is that me? Have I changed that much?

In Gov class, we're reading this military guy, Clausewitz, who said, *"War is merely the continuation of policy by other means."*

Yeah. When the policy is just corruption, what else is there to do but revolt and go to war? I go to war? What a weird thing to write! But with human extinction at stake, does it matter if the country goes up in the flames of revolution?

Nope.

Because as Cretin lies and cheats to stay on the Iron Throne, he ignores the White Walkers at the gate. Winter is coming, except it's going to be hot. And all of nature is howling like a Dire wolf with a leg caught in an steel trap, slowly dying. We too, are that nature – our leg is in the trap. To survive, we need to chew through our own flesh. And it will hurt like hell. It might even hurt like a revolution. Doesn't matter. The stakes are that high. We'll either deal with it by decision or die by disaster.

Will I be the Nature that fights for life by any means necessary? So Earth Day can have real meaning – the day we saved ourselves from the bloodsuckers? Humanity First! Survival?

Will I finally get off my ass and do something? Yes.

Guns. First thing in the morning. Decision or disaster...

Maybe it turns out horrible, but it's going to anyway. And if I fail, at least I'm no bystander listening to nature's dying screams. I'll put my flesh on the line and can die in peace. Or like Sophocles said, *"Rather fail with honor than succeed by fraud."*

Sophocles was the opposite of Cretin, who <u>only</u> succeeds by fraud – a hungry ghost blood-sucking the body of an exhausted planet, destroying all that's innocent and pure in the world.

If a life of endless craving is your idea of success.

Maybe I shouldn't have gone off my meds. Feels like my hatred of Cretin is going OCD. Can't help it. We need an amicable divorce, break the country up in a way that nobody gets shot in the head, but it's too late for that. And so, war as the continuation of politics by other means.

Enough dithering. Obsession. Inaction. If it must be me, I will end it.

When darkness falls, even light as young and weak as myself must flicker on. Christ. Bad Batman dialogue. So tired. Wish I could sleep. Stop this endless fomenting.

Time to go from Idea to Plan. Time to get a gun, see where it takes me.

Booth said, as he lay dying, shot in the neck, *Tell my mother I died for my country.*

Me too, but for Mother Earth.

What else can I do with my grief for her?

Today's Headline

"No One Threatens the Environment Like the President." No shit. MSM finally catching on, as Cretin removes pollution controls on streams and wetlands, allowing cities to dump raw sewage in our rivers. Okay, maybe a lot of shit!

— NYTimes.com

Guy with A Gun

I've always sort of wanted to fire a gun, but never have.

Don't think I can train to become John Wick, much as I sympathize with Keanu Reeves as he mercilessly hunts the A-holes that kill his dog. But a gun is still the best way to kill somebody, and there's a gun show coming up this weekend out in Ontario that looks perfect – like you can get any gun ever made. At least I can check my options, get some ideas.

Their site boasts, *"During the last year, Crossroads of the West Gun Shows attracted more than half a million guests, more than any other gun show in America. Crossroads of the West gun shows are America's <u>best</u> gun shows."*

Right above this lame sales pitch is, *"Join the Fight, Join the NRA."*

That cracks me up. Join the fight? For guns in America? I think you won, partner. We have more guns than people. Right now, it's more dangerous to go to school here than serve in our military. Americans love to kill each other with guns! You might even call it our national sport, with over 125,000 people killed or wounded by firearms every year.

Good thing, because I need a damn gun!

The Crossroad's logo is a boot and stirrups. Not the jumper boots the dressage kids at HWB wear on their 50K horses. These are old-timey cowboy boots. Guess the gun nuts see themselves as cowboys riding the range and handing out rough justice. They sure don't see themselves as the real Old West, filled with genocidal maniacs killing Natives and slaughtering millions of innocent buffalo for the hell of it. Shooting them from trains and letting them rot untouched in the sun, wantonly destroying Earth's bounty for no reason. Natives must have thought they were insane.

Crazy is as crazy does in the forming of America.

And the patient gets worse every day.

But we've always enjoyed killing in the U-S-of-A. Last night, Dad showed me *Unforgiven*, my new favorite Western. Loved what Clint tells the Kid who cries after shooting his first man, a guy taking a crap in an outhouse. The Kid tries to justify it by saying, *"He had it coming."*

And Clint, dry and tired of killing, says, *"We all have it coming, kid."*

What a line. And we all do, sooner than we think.

Cretin has it coming for sure.

But if I'm honest, I'm just like the gun nuts who see themselves as Clint Eastwood – a good guy with a gun making things right against a bad guy. Or maybe I'm a bad guy with a grudge and a gun, depending on your tribe. Either way, I don't think I'll enjoy it...

Christ, hope I don't get all bathetic like the Kid after I kill Cretin, surprised how bad it feels. I know it will be terrible. Even if Cretin's a psychopath or sociopath or just our crazy path to extinction, some part of him is human. Even if it's all the worst traits rolled up into one person, a rabid pile of junk DNA, I'm still going to be assassinating a person.

That's terrifying.

"I do not like assassins or men of low character," Gene Hackman says in *Unforgiven.*

Even if Cretin is the lowest of characters, I still hate the idea of murder.

But at least I know where I can gun up. Progress!

Today's Terrible Stat

A full 58% of Americans report that they or somebody they know has been on the wrong end of a gun. And 108 people a day die. Holy Christ! We need to put ourselves into straitjackets.

– EveryTown.org

Makers and Takers

Me and SG ganged up on Tyler in Gov today. It was awesome!

"Homelessness is just the price of freedom," Tyler intones.

We're studying Reagan and Tyler's defending the guy who first said MAGA – yeah, Cretin stole that line – while emptying our madhouses in the name of "freedom." Reagan was the first to shovel money up to oligarchs instead of spending it on the helpless. Or investments in our future – he blew up the first international attempt to nip Climate Chaos in the bud. Because government is the problem! Or so said Reagan and his Republican PR campaign, as they cut the EPA 40%. Climate would have been a minor course correction back then –

"It's the American way. Makers and takers. And I don't give a damn about the takers," Tyler is spouting like a one-man Cretin State News vomitorium as Baxter lets us debate it out.

"Sorry them dying on the street is harshing your Ayn Rand buzz," I counter. That shit-writer-fraud with books full of fake-ass people is a hero to dim bulbs like Tyler and Cretin. They love to comfort the comfortable and afflict the afflicted. After Cretin's tax cut shoveled two trillion up to his pluto masters, his leader in the Clown Cult Congress tweeted, *"A secretary at a public school said she was pleasantly surprised her pay went up a dollar fifty a week."*

Wish that was a joke. But Cretin's Malignant Boy Scout, now on the board of Cretin State News, believes a $1.50 a week helps with all his "Christian" heart. Ha! He can't even see the working poor or middle class. He only considers the 400 families who own 61% of America's wealth. As for planet Earth, he claims to be "no scientist" when questioned about using all that tax cut money to fight Climate Chaos —

"Nothing's gonna harsh my buzz, Ginj," Tyler scatters my thoughts. Spiraling today. No sleep, no meds — gun show on the horizon. "Everybody's free to make their own choices."

"Free to starve, you mean." I try to focus. "Half the country can't cough up 400 bucks in an emergency and 25% of American kids live in poverty. We have the money to help."

"Nanny state," Tyler smirks. "What about personal responsibility? People need to work for self-worth and freedom. What about pulling yourself up by your bootstraps?"

"MLK said you've got to have boots first." It's SG, piping up in her lilting voice. "Or a boot factory, like your hero, who was given 400 million dollars and still went bankrupt six times."

She smiles at me, nodding support. Cool!

"She's right. He even lost money in the casino business, where it's like printing it," I assert, still stabbing at Tyler. But what will penetrate? "And why's your wanna-be-billionaire business genius too afraid to show his taxes? Daddy's boy is probably broke."

"Why should he show them?" Tyler sputters. "Taxes are theft."

"The ultra-rich pay a lesser tax rate than their maids," I retort. "The terrors are coming, Tyler. Lots of these huge fires start in homeless encampments. Even Bel Air isn't safe."

"You're proving my point!" Tyler's triumphant. "Takers be taking from the makers, who pay all the taxes!"

SG laughs out loud at that. Scoffs, really, and says, "To privileged people, equality always feels like oppression."

The class goes momentarily silent as they digest that nugget. Then Baxter breaks it up. Tyler gives SG a look of pure hatred, but she's right. Tyler's happy to let the jaws of capitalism chew up the less lucky. As his techno-Utopian heroes talk about how great humanity is doing compared to history, giving billionaires like his daddy an excuse not to spread the wealth, sacrifice, or change a damn thing. Oblivious!

What about the fact we can <u>see our own extinction on the horizon</u>?

WTF? Talk about ignoring the burning elephant in the room!

And what a joke, Tyler spouting *"Work Sets You Free"* Nazi slogans without working a day in his life. Does he even know *"Arbeit Macht Frei"* is on the gates of Auschwitz? Nope.

In Lit, we're reading *A Tale of Two Cities* about the French Revolution. The famous opening sentence is us, only it's the best of times for a few and the worst for the rest...

All part of the plan – hungry men don't make waves. If you take any time to rock the boat, to fight for our planet, you will get shoved out and drown. There are so many people in the water now, as slumlord Cretin and his cruel Clowns make it all more brutal – here's $1.50!

Do they really think things will stay normal as they dine in fancy restaurants blocks from families in tents surviving on cat food? Pure decadence while the hills burn and 240,000 people die of poverty in America every year?

Tyler certainly does, the heartless A-hole.

But maybe I need to learn something from him, a guy who's been torturing and killing animals his whole life. Maybe a hefty dose of Tyler will help me become an assassin. How else can I get that cold-blooded? I've got no idea. I've never really thought about it in my thought experiment.

Could SG be an ally? She's cool, but no. Can't tell her about the Idea. Or the gun show. I like her too much to get her killed.

Guess I'll write up "Makers and Takers" for my Gov essay homework.

Greed. It writes itself.

Today's headline

"America's Top 1% Own as Much Wealth as the Bottom 90%." Do they really think their money will save them from all disasters? They sure do.

– Politifact.com

Mental Health

I haven't slept since I decided to go to the gun show. Feeling... disjointed.

Three days left and I'm sitting at the kitchen table while Mom makes dinner. Writing as usual on paper with a pen, the only real air-gapping. Write "kill the president" on your "air-gapped" computer and get online once and just wait for every acronym of the surveillance state to knock on your door. Not that Google doesn't spy and read everybody's Gmail. Don't be evil. Ha. How's that going? Oh, yeah, they dropped it as a mission statement.

So, pen and paper to unclog my head, the daily drain of an overflowing sink. What harm can come of it? Just everything. Ideas have thrown every bomb in history, for good and bad –

"So, I got a call from Nichols today," Mom interrupts me, which is rare when I'm writing. She's trying to sound casual. "You told her you're quitting therapy?"

"Oh, yeah," I also try to sound casual. "Not really getting anything out of it."

"Really?" Mom dries her hands on a dishtowel and sits across from me. I close my journal. Got to be careful here. "Do you think that's wise?"

"Yeah. I'm ready. Sorry I didn't tell you. Just feel like I've outgrown it."

"She was concerned. I'm concerned you didn't discuss it with us."

"It's my decision, right?" Got to play on Mom and Dad's belief in giving us a lot of responsibility, willing to let us learn what we need to and make mistakes if we must. Ha. Mistakes don't get bigger than this –

"Yes. I just wish you had told me, so I didn't have to hear it from

Nichols. And you seem a bit preoccupied. How're you doing? Are you still taking your meds?"

"Of course." Lying my ass off. "I'm fine, Mom. Sorry I didn't tell you."

"Okay." Mom looks at me closely but opts to keep it light. "Just don't disappear on us."

"Don't worry, can't get rid of me that easily," I say. She stands, tussling my hair. I smile, happy she's going to let it go. And sad, too.

I'm stripping down. Quit porn. Quit therapy. Quit Socials. The damn Dark Web. And the drugs! So satisfying to flush the pills for that BS diagnosis – OCD my ass. I'm just beginning to see reality. I don't want happy pills and therapy to hide it.

Don't want to smile through the damn apocalypse.

Am I preparing and purifying myself like a warrior monk? I sure don't have a monk's focus. But so what if I sometimes corkscrew into the darkest part of my brain? I'm still trying to SEE everything. And it's not like I'm fixated on a ritual or counting or a complete germophobe like Cretin. I get obsessed – Hitler, climate, politics – but I'm not incapacitated. Am I? No. Just interested in lots of different stuff. Important stuff I can't forget. That nobody should.

Maybe I'm just a teenager growing up in these crazy times. Maybe having to write everything down is sad. Maybe my daily tally of misery is making me depressed. A murderer.

Or maybe it's my way of getting through the ugly.

Today's Headline

"President's Daily Lies Triple His Last Year's Average." When deep fakes can make anybody say anything, Cretin will claim every pussy-grabbing tape is fake. Or maybe not – he's our national shame, but totally shameless, so what does he care?

– TheWeek.com

Reality

"Objective reality doesn't care what you believe," Hale said in class today. "You can have your own opinion, but not your own facts."

"But who supplies the facts?" Tyler demands.

"Science," Hale responds. "Remember, I don't care what you think. I care _how_ you think."

"But science is always getting things wrong, making mistakes," Tyler persists. "Biased."

"Fake news, Tyler?" Hale has that amused look on his face again, as if seeing himself when he was young. "Anybody have an answer for Tyler?"

"Is it replicable?" I chime in. "If other scientists can't replicate it, then a good scientist goes back to the drawing board. A paid-off quack with an agenda doesn't."

"Good." Hale continues to look at me. "What else?"

"Science constantly evolves as we develop better tools to observe the natural world." As if we need tools these days beyond opening our eyes. "So, results will change."

"Good. What else?" I shrug, unsure, so he moves on. "Tyler?"

"It can't tell you what to do about it?" Tyler takes a stab.

"Good," Hale says. "Science describes how the world is but it doesn't make moral judgments about whether it's good or bad. That's up to you."

After class, I approach Hale.

"If science can't provide a road-map to what's right and wrong, what can?"

"Moral philosophy, ethics." He's swiftly packing his bag, but smiles. "Reading Thoreau."

"But science can point the way. The scientific method."

"Yes. It will save you from living in a demon-haunted world if you believe it. But it can't tell you how to use its knowledge. It can only help you see reality."

"That's not nothing." I hustle to keep up with Hale as he strides into the hallway. "Being rational. It helps you make hard decisions. Life and death decisions."

"Yes. But it takes intellectual honesty." Hale smiles. "I've got to run. Pick this up again?"

"Sure." He nods like a comrade, disappearing in the swirl of students.

What do I want from Hale? Permission? Why? Mother Earth has a deadly fever. We should all stop and give her our love and attention. But instead, we waste the last 100 seconds on the doomsday clock, closer than it's ever been to midnight, and watch Cretin auction her off. As he says to people, who know Climate Chaos is real because they're dying from it – tough shit.

And so it goes, faster and faster, the whole world a tilt-a-whirl where the evil Carny won't let us off no matter how much we puke and beg.

I'll never get permission for this.

I've got to figure out how to stop the carny ride.

Alone. That's the reality.

Today's Headline

"Greenland's Ice Sheet Is Melting Faster Than Scientists Previously Thought." Science, behind the curve again. It's the fastest melt rate in 350 years of recording it. Never mind building boats, we better build Arcs.

— TheGuardian.com.

The Defense Rests

*N*ews! Today I found a legal reason killing Cretin isn't murder. Not even a crime!

It was staring at me the whole time – Cretin's a crazy suicide bomber, so we have a right to protect ourselves. And I'm not talking about the Declaration of Independence and our right <u>to alter or abolish a destructive government.</u> I'm just talking basic self-defense, like what all those open-carry Gundamentalists worry about.

What a relief; I hated the idea of being a murderer, going to war with my core self. I think it was stalling me out. But now, GREEN LIGHT!

Because the law says you can't be guilty of a violent crime to protect yourself if your conduct is "reasonable under the circumstances." You just need to have:

"Reasonably believed that you were in imminent danger of being killed, injured, or touched unlawfully."

Check. Cretin is taking a crap on the last bit of green grass, killing the planet every day. Methane and the latest science about tipping points we're passing handles "imminently." As for "touched unlawfully" – grabbing Mother Earth by the pussy says it all.

"Reasonably believed that you needed to use force to prevent that from happening."

Check. What else stops Cretin and his Clowns? Politics? Even if it worked, it's too little, too late. Nation-state California, with 40 million people and the fifth-largest economy in the world, gets the same number of senators as Kentucky, population 4 million and a welfare state taking

100 billion a year from the Feds they hate. Never going to change. Old hicks attached like babies to the flabby tits of their Dear Liar, holding America hostage!

"Used no more force than was necessary to prevent that from happening."

Check. Nothing short of elimination stops this guy. The tiny group of old men killing us in the CCC won't stop him. Half the country off the rails in a fantasy-land of demented beliefs won't stop him. They love getting riled up by Cretin and told he's the only one who can save them. It's called a cult of personality. Maximum force is the only solution.

"Because of stand your ground laws, you are under no obligation to retreat — that is, to run away or try to escape — before you use self-defense to protect yourself."

Check. Not that there's any place to go because there's only one planet we can live on, no matter what techno-babble Elon Musk spouts about living on Mars.

Wow. This brings me full circle to when I first got the Idea — if you come for my blood, you will get swatted. Well, Cretin's not just coming for our blood, he's already clamped on and sucking us dry.

So, I have the legal right to swat him as an act of planetary self-defense!

Call me Cassandra with a damn gun or Chicken Little screaming the sky is falling. Call me sick in an even sicker country. Or sane in a world gone crazy.

Whatever you call me, you can't call me a murderer.

Any more than you can call a sheriff or a soldier one.

Today's headline

"Pentagon Calls Climate Change A National Security Threat." Look at the world's largest institutional greenhouse gas emitter getting right with reality. Hooah!

— NRDC.org

Traffic Stop

I can't believe it. SG asked me out today! But I totally blew it with my endless obsession. It was after some visiting lecturer pitched a bunch of environmental happy talk at HWB...

"What did you think, Mr. End-of-the-world-list?" SG falls in with me afterward.

"Way too optimistic. Half a billion Chinese already lose five years off their lives because of pollution. And their pollution, a third of what the world produces, goes up every year."

Way to be a player, dude. Bore her to death with death.

"Really? How terrible." She's so close I can smell her sandalwood smell.

"Yeah. But you can't just blame the Chinese. We put the most CO2 in the atmosphere. So, Climate Chaos has a made-in-America sticker on its pickup bumper." Christ, Benji, just stop.

"Is it weird to remember everything?" SG smiles, gold bracelets tinkling on her arm as she pulls her hair down one shoulder – an onyx waterfall I can only dream of swimming under.

"It's no picnic." I smile back. Is she flirting? I wouldn't know.

"We pollute less than China," Tyler breaks in from behind us. Christ! Ubiquitous A-hole. Why can't this guy just disappear?

"Maybe now, but it doesn't matter," I say, turning to look at him. "Theirs ends up here. In San Fran, 29% of pollution is now Chinese."

"Maybe we should send them our wildfire smoke." Tyler smirks. "It's only fair."

It's funny and I laugh, but Tyler just coldly stares at SG and me, like he's measuring us for coffins. Such a creep. Is he into her? Cock-blocking?

"Smile," he says to SG like a threat. "Can't you take a joke?"

"Because you're so hilarious, making jokes about people dying in wildfires?" SG is feisty. Tyler looks at her like a bug he wants to squash. He might be into her, but she'd never go for it. Maybe I can get rid of him if I spray him with some facts, like a pesky mosquito.

"Americans blow off double the CO2 – 19 tons a year – of a Chinese person," I squirt out this droplet from the river of my brain. "What happens when they catch up? What about our historical responsibility? Or taking the lead in solving it?"

"Everything's our fault, right Soy Boy?" Can't believe he used that insult in front of SG, who just stares at him. Does she have any clue she's Soy Girl in my head?

"Tyler, you know why the Chinese don't riot in the streets in protest?" I ask, trying to get the upper hand. Pure ego – all so stupid.

"Cuz they're commies in a surveillance state." Tyler strides away.

"There's no room, they have traffic jams that last three days," I raise my voice, calling after him. Mission accomplished. He's leaving – just stop!

But I can't.

"Villagers sell food and water to trapped motorists. They're crushing themselves trying to follow our example!" I practically shout after him.

"You worry too much, Soy Boy," Tyler dismisses me, catching up to Dim and Dimmer.

"That was such fun." SG grins, cute and mischievous. "Why bother?"

"Can't help myself." I laugh like an idiot, but I can't. Billions of people want to live large like Americans, as the climate bullet from a gun we fired slams them in the head.

"'We don't see the world as it is, we see it as we are,'" SG quotes. "Do you believe that?"

"Anais Nin? Yeah. Mostly." Why is she asking this? Do I see it clearly?

I think so but how would I know? I can only see it as me. Maybe I'm just hysterical and not in a funny way – but anxious and catastrophizing. Way to blow it with SG. Christ –

"You okay, Benji?" SG looks at me, concerned. "Don't let Tyler get to you with that Soy Boy stuff. I'm vegan too."

"Yeah, no. I'm fine. Sorry for the downer deluge." I try to smile. "The mind is its own place and all that Milton stuff. Making a heaven of hell, a hell of heaven. That's me."

"You're just keeping it real." SG flips her hair. "Want to get a coffee sometime?"

"Um." I can't believe she just asked me out. But I'm going to the gun show tomorrow. I can't get anything going with SG as I start the mission. "You know, it's not the best time."

"Oh. Are you seeing someone?" SG gazes at me, more present than I could ever dream of being. I look down and try not to drown in her eyes.

"Me? No. Ha. I'm just not fit for human consumption these days." Have I ever been? Can't remember. Maybe a long time ago...

"Oh." She smiles again. "Rotten fruit, eh?"

"Rotten to the core." I smile back, but it's a bummer I've got to shut this down to protect her feelings. Protect her life from the Idea. Protect her from the world after I do it. "I'm just going through some stuff."

"I understand," SG says a bit sadly. "Let me know if I can help make a heaven of hell."

"If anybody could, it's you," I say, unable to play it cool. "Bye."

She nods and walks away. If anybody told me last week that I'd ever turn her down, I'd say they're crazy. Now it's me.

Today's Headline

"Homeless Americans use twice the energy of the average non-American." Christ, even our homeless – on what? How?

– Science.org

Cartoon Man

A cartoon imbecile lands on Earth and kills everything in sight...

Sees a couple snakes, pulls them on as boots. Clubs a seal, makes a coat, and marches onward like a king. Waves a wand at an elephant and turns it into a piano he sits at, playing a mad march. Jumps on a boat and dumps toxins into the ocean, killing the seas. Shoots a bear and chops its head onto a plaque, chaining its cub for entertainment. Stomps a lion into a rug. Taps forests into stacks of wood. The cartoon man dances a dervish of destruction, consumption, and torture, with a mad grin and dead eyes that don't twinkle, same as Cretin. Finally, he climbs a trash peak, and we can see the whole world is now garbage – a dead planet. He struts over to a gold throne, puts on a gold crown, and lights a gold cigar, king of Turd Mountain, supremely satisfied with the destruction.

Until a couple aliens show up and stomp him into a welcome mat.

Even though it's the middle of the night before the gun show, it's not another horrific nightmare. It's an old animated piece called *"Man"* by a guy named Steve Cutts. Over 40 million views, plus five more by me, that's how brilliant it is.

Will I ever sleep? Nervous about the gun show tomorrow. First concrete action. I can't help watching the video again. Getting obsessed. But Christ – it's a damn biography of Cretin.

We're all cartoon cretins – stupid, vulgar, and insensitive thrusters. We all drive and fly in planes and live our oh-so-important and clueless lives, Earth be damned. But Cretin <u>is this cartoon man</u>, right down to his pathetic need to paint the world gold. Like a toxic patient zero, Cretin stuffs his face on our planet and spews his virus values, everything greedy and vile. He's not just living life like a normal person. Like the Cartoon man, he delights in destroying life, killing all he touches.

A-hole! Every time I see his resting bitch face, I want to punch it.

Maybe I feel too much, worry too much. It's just a nightmare cartoon, not real. Mankind isn't this bad. But looking at animal videos today, I stumbled on the National Wildlife Property Repository in Denver.

Wildlife "Property?" WTF?

It's stuffed with millions of dead animals seized from smugglers at American airports. A holocaust warehouse bursting with stuffed monkeys, snow leopard coats, and lion heads open in a silent roar. Foot tools made from elephant feet. Trophies. Like what the Nazis did with human remains, turning them into soap and lampshades of skin. A nightmare.

It's true most people just live their lives. But not the toxic men who fill this monument of misery. The assholes fast-tracking us to an ecological Dark Age do it on purpose. They are, like John Muir said, *"Astonished whenever they find anything, living or dead, in all God's universe, which they cannot eat or render useful to themselves."*

Their leaders are climate deniers, from America to Australia to Brazil. Or simply short-sighted, like the Japanese, now building 22 new coal-burning plants. This, after a thousand Japanese died last year from heatstroke during record heat waves.

But the worst are the type who tortured Gigi for entertainment. Baby Cretins. They killed 27,000 African Elephants this year, out of 400,000 left. And Cretin is their ringleader, erasing Obama's ban on importing their heads as trophies so little dicks like his sons can hang them on walls.

These men will never change – we must stop them. Because next up? Cretin gutted the Endangered Species Act, the law that saved the eagle and grizzly from extinction. Wildlife the world over is in the way of pipelines and hunting and money and rape, rape, rape – Christ!

I'm so sick of people calling the lowest human murderers "animals." What an insult to animals, as man tortures 74 billion to death every year in the name of food. As man decimates nearly extinct pangolin anteaters because they're a "delicacy," even as they curl up in protection like the poor silverfish. As man slaughters the last rhinos and sells their tusks — now more valuable than gold — to Chinese idiots who think it gets their dick hard instead of a dollar dose of Viagra that actually works.

Because, hey, you're 90 and still sure women want to see your junk rising from the ashes of your saggy balls!

Those cretins torturing the planet are the worst of us. But the rest of us are guilty too. We're all so clueless maybe we deserve the climate death coming for us. Damn...

I'm so wrung out exhausted. Tortured. Like I'm losing my mind.

I need to completely unplug from the web and stop OCDing about the parade of human-inflicted suffering. I wanted to see it. Feel it. Prepare. I never want to be ignorant of the world's pain. That feels like death, living in a mental gated community.

But enough is enough.

Nietzsche said if you stare into the abyss, it stares back. And the abyss is all the misery I've written about since the fire. It haunts me. I keep rolling it around in my mind, staring at it from every angle, looking for a reason not to believe. Looking for a way to escape the Idea. But that abyss, it keeps staring back, implacable as death. I can't unsee it.

Nietzsche also said if you fight with monsters, you become a monster.

I hope so. Because it's the only way I can kill Cretin, the cartoon president. So happy not to be just recording it all.

Tomorrow — gun show.

Action! Thank Christ.

Today's Headline

"Humankind Has Wiped Out 60% of Animals Since 1970." This annihilation started 30 years before I was even born. The cartoon man is dancing his mad gig.

— TheGuardian.com

Lies

Finally – today, Crossroads of the West Gun Show. Whew, made it!

I'm nerve-wracked, like the time I froze on a ten-meter platform trying to jump, and June rushed past me and leaped first – fearless as ever.

"Bock. Bock. BOCK!" June chicken called as she treaded water, getting pool laughs until I shut my eyes and forced myself to jump.

Is going to a gun show like that jump? Irreversible? I hope not.

I'm up early and tell Mom I'm going to the robotics lab for the day.

"That's nice honey," Mom says. "Have a super creative time."

And that's that. She's off to morning yoga after a long week of selling hats on Amazon. That's Mom for you, putting a Happy Hat on the gig economy as the world melts. Battling Octopus Jeff, who keeps a big chunk of her sales each month to "cover" potential returns. Hey Octo, what's the interest you make on billions of dollars of free money withheld from sellers? It's so unfair, but Mom just keeps going. Monopoly, the only game in town.

"Hey, kiddo." Dad walks in from an all-nighter as I gulp granola and cheerios. He pats me on the back, kisses Mom on her neck, and plods off to collapse into bed.

"Hey dad." I know he needs sleep, but if I want to talk, he'll hang, so I don't say more. Even June follows our unwritten rule to let him sleep. I gather my backpack and am almost out the door when she bounces in, twirling the tween rage Slime.

"Why you up so early?" June immediately starts grilling me. "Where you going?"

"School." I'm mesmerized by the Slime, perfect for Cretin's America.

"On a Saturday?" June scoffs, the only morning person in the house, her ponytail bouncing perky as an Olympic gymnast. "Yeah, right."

"Right. Some people actually like to learn." June always knows when I'm lying. Sometimes I catch her looking at me like she's read all my journals –

"Nerd." June turns toward the kitchen. "Mom, Benji's lying to me. He said he's going to schoooooool. Like, why would anybody do that on a Saturday? Except Neeeeerds?"

June hangs off me like a chimp. The cute babies before they tear off your face.

"June." I try to pry her off, but she's got chimp grip as she tries to wrap me in the rubbery Slime.

"June, leave your brother alone."

"But he's lying, Mom. I know it. I can tell."

And she can. Because I am. Don't know how, but I'm glad it's June. Because she's just a kid and can scream the truth from treetops and no-body will believe her. Such is the fate of kids.

June unzips my backpack where I've got seven hundred dollars stowed. All the money I have from every birthday my whole life. I put the Spock grip on her. Same old routine as I clench the ropy muscle connecting her neck to her shoulder, using my height to keep her away.

"Not the Vulcan death grip!" June laughs wildly, the gap between her front teeth flashing black. Then I squeeze and her eyes widen and she shrieks like a banshee. Same sequence every time – laughter, eyes wide, shrieking. Christ, I love her.

"June! Get off your brother and eat your breakfast. Dad's sleeping."

But I've got it handled. June grabs my Vulcan hand and tries to put an arm-lock on it, but I shove her on the couch and run, ducking a ball of slime that splats the wall by the front door.

"You liar, Benji. I know you're lying!" She shouts as I slam the door.

I am a liar, but only about the Idea. Everybody lies sometimes, but

Cretin lies all the time. Like *Hello, He Lied,* that book Dad has about Hollywood, Cretin lies even as he greets you.

"Satan is a liar and the father of lies," Jesus said. Is Cretin Satan? Not that I believe in Satan, but if I did, Cretin sure fits – a slippery deceiver bringing Armageddon. Like a true porno sadist, Cretin lives to mount power players, getting off on making them lie, bringing them down to his low level. Extreme bullying!

And Cretin's sheeple love it because he trolls the Libtards. He's authentic! Doesn't matter if he's an authentic liar. They don't care, living in conspiracy theories without even a theory. Like, Cretin finished the border wall. And Cretin never plays golf. And Cretin never lies. Ever!

Just pure delusion, leaving the rest of us trapped like kids in a family abused by a drunk stepdad.

"Every age has its own fascism."

Can't get Primo Levi's line out of my head. Truth decay, like tooth decay, destroys from within. Until Cretin can lazily yank democracy out by the roots.

Easier now, as only 12% of Americans read beyond a middle school level. Read like a child, think like one. So, they believe whatever the BS-in-chief says as he dismantles the very idea of objective reality.

Nothing is legitimate! Scapegoat anybody! Truth is so 2015.

Mounted.

Can't wait to get that gun. Put his head on my wall.

Today's Quote

"Everybody is somebody's Jew." Primo Levi again. Cretin sure loves his scapegoats – a word from Leviticus about casting a poor goat into the desert to carry away the community's sins. And to die of thirst. Christ, we'll all be the goat eventually, living in Leviticus.

Seeds in Shit

I stride down the hill after I hide my unneeded alibi, some robotics research, in the carport under Dad's car.

Poor guy, pulling another all-nighter because his latest job just cut down to two editors. Some producer needs more money and that's how the "below the line" guys get it in the neck. So gross, what they call the people who do the physical work of making a show, brick-by-brick, as opposed to the writers, producers, and directors, who are "above the line."

How obvious can you get with your contempt?

But that's America now, above and below the line.

Guess I'm thinking about this because I finished *A Tale of Two Cities*. And I've got revolution on my mind, off to buy a gun!

I hate Cretin but get why he got elected. The bloodsucker .01% living way above, while the workers grind it out below. They know they haven't had a raise in 40 years. They know 90% of the money since the crash of '08 has gone to the top .01%. They know three people own more wealth than the bottom half of the country. Maybe they don't know the exact stats rushing through my brain all day, but they know things are insanely unfair. They feel it. And so, elect Cretin in a shotgun rage.

Plus, of course, the racism.

But surprise! Cretin doesn't drain the swamp. He stocks it with alligators and feeds his followers to them for his own deranged amusement. He trolls his fanatics by hiring a Wall Street cabinet of clowns to go full throttle on trickle-down economics – Robin Hood in reverse!

I didn't know trickle-down theory was first called "horse and sparrow" economics. As in, the rich horses get the oats, while all the poor little birds pick through horseshit for any undigested seeds. Going on as long as time itself. Christ. Isn't it time for a massive REVOLT by the have-nots?

Bet Cretin <u>loves</u> that idea, making people eat shit to survive. Makers and takers... Ha. The tax bill Cretin signed cut his own taxes in half. But power is no fun unless you can make people eat shit! Make them accept the unacceptable. Make your followers deny that you punch them in the face <u>as you punch them in the face</u>.

Don't you Cretin Cultists know Cretin wants you miserable, so he can manipulate your misery? Simmering in a racist stew, so he can goad your grievance? Afraid of losing what you have, so he can accuse others of stealing it? Nope. You've got no clue the only lifeline Cretin will ever toss you has a noose on the end.

But whining about Cretin picking our pockets and stealing our wallets is dumb. Sure, he rigs the system against the poor and middle class, but who cares if the rich can buy a better view of Armageddon? Pointless!

Christ. Are we all corrupt? Complicit? A country of grifters unable to spot Cretin's con? Whatever. The environmental Ponzi scheme has gone bust. Mother Nature is collecting and we're all going to pay.

Even now, as I walk past a massive gate built to protect the riches within, the house is a crater of gray ash. You'd think they'd figure out fences won't save them from embers flying around like viruses. Sure, we might start out in different boats in the same storm – you might be in a yacht, I might be in a dingy. But eventually, we'll all end up shipwrecked, even though the poor around the world will drown first and quickly – same old, same old.

But I think the plutos will have it worse. They will die last in the terrified agony of anticipation, wondering when starving cannibals will climb their gates and claw into their bunkers, even the ones buried in converted nuclear silos. Sorry guys, your own guards will kill you and eat your stockpile. Then eat the rats, like what happened during medieval sieges.

Then eat your remains. Then each other.

Christ, that's dark, even for me.

But all the food we now waste – a third of what we grow, creating billions of tons of additional CO2 – someday we'll dream about it like a song from a country picnic.

In the end, we'll all be hunting for seeds in shit because there's no food, no matter how rich you are. We've eaten our seed corn and money will be meaningless as we enter humanity's final hour.

There's grim fairness to that, the climate equalizing everything out on our way to End Days, everybody shuffling there like in *The Road.*

Holy Christ! Is this going to be one of those endless days, on my own obsessive road? I hope not. Got to watch my thoughts.

Can't crack up, taking my first step to kill Cretin.

Today's Headline

"Majority of Americans Unwilling to Spend $10 A Month to Address Climate Change." What a bunch of cheap asses. Sounds like a bargain to me.

– Newsweek.com

Dumb Ideas

I pass my old elementary school, perched in the twisty canyon, where they auction parking spots to keep the arts program alive.

"A hundo large," Tyler bragged about the $100,000 Daddy paid for the top parking spot the family driver dropped him in, down from their five-acre estate. At ten years old, sure of his money and status, Tyler was already a mini version of what Bitterwood is about, filled with people at the top of the food chain, but still anxious and unhappy about all the wrong things.

They should hang with more dogs – no pockets, no problems. Ha.

We all should. Wish I was hanging with Gigi right now.

I walk past multimillion dollar homes set back from the street, standing stately in the dappled sun under old oaks. This world, such a long way from the gun show.

I hear Canyon before I see it – kids shrieking, a bullhorn bulling, and music that sounds like a clown's first day of accordion lessons. Round the bend in the road and there's the Canyon Elementary School FUN-raiser.

The parking lot is full. And preening in the primo spot is the black Bentley Tyler's dad drives, probably at the fundraiser with Tyler's younger brothers. You can say so much with that car. But mostly I live a life you can't even dream exists because my car costs ten times the average American's yearly income.

Why does he need to rub it in? Like father, like son...

Last week Tyler bragged his dad bought seats for them on Elon Musk's Starship. They will be in the first group of tourist passengers to orbit the moon! No joke. The plutos think they'll fly away to a magic future like that movie *Elysium*, where Earth is a dung heap of people scraping by on garbage, while rich people live in a floating blimp that's green and beautiful. Ha.

Musky is a sad obsesso, which I like, but I'm not a total fanboy. Sure, the cars are cool if they're not coal powered. And the solar does it if we spread a Nigeria-sized solar build for the planet's electrical needs – RIGHT NOW. But the dude is out of his Musky mind about Mars missions and techno happy talk about colonizing the universe to survive as a species. The idea we spend trillions to try and live in a can, on an airless planet, is an example of a smart person being Ben Carson stupid – brilliant in one area and a moron in others.

Carbon Dioxide, the very thing that's killing us, is 95% of Mars' atmosphere. The average temperature is 80 degrees below zero. At night it goes to minus 195 degrees. And in the year it takes to get to Mars, you get irradiated and your IQ plummets. You become a moron.

So, in the real world, Matt Damon dies on Mars. If he doesn't die getting there. And we don't have time to wait while Musky boots up Mar's atmosphere with nuclear bombs, another one of his great ideas. Haven't you heard of nuclear winter? You'll make it colder! If you're even serious.

Meanwhile, no mention of the 99.999% of the people left on our garden planet we've turned into a dumpster fire. What about us?

There is no planet B, Musky.

Scream about what little time we have left on planet A. Put every dollar into surviving this crucial moment. Shout about how we need to spend trillions to <u>stop our planet from becoming Mars</u>, which also once had oceans of water. Instead of trillions on the fantasy of a few people living underground on a planet with no air.

To get stupid. To go mad. To die.

Christ, I hate all the big dick fantasies about blasting rockets into space – don't have to be Freud to figure that one out.

If we radically change the systems we live under, our blue planet is a life raft with enough supplies for every living being... If we learn to see nature has intrinsic value and isn't just an opportunity for rape, and if we cherish our brothers and sisters as something beyond customers, and if we wake up to see pulling millions of years of carbon stored in coal and oil and instantly shoving it into our atmosphere is SUICIDE and –

Shit. Suddenly skittering. Feeling so anxious – must be the gun show.

Got to settle down. But how do I stop thinking about our endless destruction of Earth, as we kill a million species, destroying the very biodiversity keeping us alive? How can anybody?

Christ – I'm feeling the pure panic of that desecration.

Our life raft is sinking. We greedily gobbled all our food and water. We think we'll somehow survive and make it to shore, but we won't.

Every living creature depends on Earth's bounty, an oasis twinkling in the cold silence of an indifferent universe. Every innocent nonhuman animal is dependent on us to keep their habitat alive. And we're failing them and ourselves. We're the citizens of Pompeii who died ignoring the erupting volcano, thinking they had time and could ride it out. Until it was too late.

So, terraforming Mars is a cool fantasy, Musky, but keep it to yourself. It's like daydreaming on the Hindenburg. Our planet's not a used tissue we can toss and then tech-pull a new one out of a box. If we keep blowing holes in our life raft, no technology will save us.

We'll all be dead way before anybody can get to Mars.

Tell that fucking truth.

Today's Terrible Stat

Fly round trip from LA to NYC, and you mainline 6.5 tons of CO2 directly into the upper atmosphere. It's three times that for business class.

– Nature.org

God Free

walk by Canyon without looking in. Too depressing, all those kids running around without a care in the world, doomed because we have crazy new ideas on top of dumb old ones. Makes me jittery.

Still thinking about Musky, who also warned about a coming population implosion. Like that's our problem and not extinction level Climate Chaos caused by overpopulation. What about the fact we've blown way past Earth's carrying capacity? We're at 7.7 billion people and about to add a billion more in ten years. They will all want to live and consume and pollute just like us. Holy shit! Why are we sitting around waiting for mass die-offs or forced sterilizations before we change our values? Idiots!

And then there's Octopus Jeff, trying to become immortal without thinking about the hell on Earth he'll create if nobody dies. Just can't get over the obscene ego of that. We're already dope-sick and depressed now. What happens when Cretin, who wants to stay in power forever, gets to live forever? What happens when we live life as a never-ending-sentence without the meaning and relief death provides because the greediest want to gorge on the bounty of our planet and escape the one thing equalizing life no matter how rich or poor you are?

I've got to stop freaking myself out! But how come nobody just tells the truth? The planet is crashing with too many humans, breeding like rats overrunning a ship, goaded by religious craziness that says gay marriage, birth control, and abortion is the problem. Really?

How about mass extinction? That's worse.

"Go forth and multiply." Ha. Done and done. We need to stop.

Forcing women to have unwanted kids is part of Cretin's creepy misogyny. Why else end funding for women's health centers worldwide? No sex Ed. No birth control. More people. Extinction! Supported by wackos who believe a book written when people thought the world was flat. Some still do, as flat-Earth societies pop up like mushrooms of morons. WTF?

"If I can get you to believe in absurdity, I can get you to commit an atrocity." Voltaire says in a sentence the violence of religion is it destroys critical thinking. If you really believe Jesus walked on water and Mary was a virgin, then you're marinated and ready for mounting. After surrendering your mind to those old whoppers, believing Cretin's boast that he's a self-made man after he inherited 400 million dollars is easy. Or Earth is flat! Or 6000 years old! Or it doesn't matter if Armageddon comes because the Rapture will save the truly devout!

And once you believe the absurdity, bring on the atrocity – like letting our planet die. Like believing your god gave you a divine right to Earth – both absurd and atrocious. Humanity needs a whole new story!

But if you must believe fairy tales, why not live Genesis One, as a steward for, *"Every living thing that moves on the face of Earth"*?

From the Bible itself. Boom – drop the mic.

Believe that part, you crazy fundamentalists. Or Revelations 11:18, which promises god will *"destroy them which destroy the Earth."*

Amen! That's a good one if you need a threat to do the right thing. But Armageddon is a feature, not a bug – the crazy Christians can't wait! They refuse to see we're doing fine ending the world without supernatural help. Just today, Cretin hired another Christian Climate Criminal who said, *"our air is too clean for optimum health."*

Ha! Exact quote. Orwell would be proud.

Annihilation, coming to a theater near –

Benji! Stop tripping! But I'm so stressed by these moral midgets in a moral fog, obsessed about sex and gay marriage and abortion as the world crashes. These religious fanatics ignore Cretin as he vandalizes our planet like the Catholic Church ignores rapist priests. Christ would be crying!

Hey, all you "persecuted" religious zealots who are pro-birth but not at all pro-life, will your god forgive you for what you've done to his creation by unleashing Cretin? Nope – wrath to come for totally fucking his paradise. And all those innocent children. But unfortunately, God won't cosmically punish the fundamentalists. Or save us in some Deus Ex Machina. We're on our own and –

Whew, take a damn breath, Benji! Your hands are shaking. Don't go down this rabbit hole yet again. It's pointless. People like Theocrat, Cretin's VP, aren't going to take down their favorite bible quote from their office walls, *"For I know the plans I have for you, plans to prosper you and not to harm you, plans to give you hope and a future."*

What a bunch of prosperity preaching BS. On our public property!

Hey Theo, what about my generation's hope and future? Ashes!

What about humanity's future unborn, a million years of future life lost if we destroy ourselves? Aborted!

Since Zeus, mankind has invented gods to explain the mysteries of life, but why not just love the mystery? Religion be damned, the planet needs protection and fewer people. Grow up and be good without god!

Good without god. Not that hard, really.

The Golden Rule is enough – now that rule's a master principle.

"Do unto others as you would have them do unto you." Sure.

Or even better – the Platinum Rule.

"Do unto others as they'd like done unto them." Imagine that world.

Today, crawling with anxiety, I can't. Got to stop thinking about it!

I'm going to do unto Cretin what I never want done unto me.

Old Testament all the way.

Today's bible quote

"There will be terrible times in the last days. People will be lovers of themselves … of money, boastful, proud, abusive … ungrateful, without love, unforgiving, slanderous, without self-control, brutal, not lovers of the good, treacherous, rash, conceited, lovers of pleasure." Wow, Timothy 3:1-4 nails Cretin!

Nature Is Salvation?

Got to get a grip. Gun show day just started and I'm already losing it.

My attention is too mono-spiral – I hate how much the Idea is colonizing me. I'm so sick of Cretin, this spoiled toddler holding my brain hostage with all his tantrums. But what do I expect on the way to a gun show? No wonder I'm bugging out.

Still, what's happening right now as I walk down the sun-dappled street and the shrieks of the children fade? Nothing bad.

The poet Mary Oliver says attention is devotion. Have we forgotten how to be devoted to our beautiful planet? Have we ever been? Not if you look at our actions. We never consider Earth, assuming she'll always be there for us. I barely spend time in the garden with Gigi, even though I need it to stay sane. Need it to stay happy. When was I last happy?

Everything today is death and darkness. Cretin's crowd at the top, rancid and corrupt, seeps into my brain like mold in the walls of a house, rotting my world from within, nonstop grim. But what if Cretin's just a symptom and killing his noise won't stop the bedlam –

Short of breath. Got to sit for a sec. Calm down. What's with me?

The sun lobs shafts of Michelangelo light on the road. I drink it up, the quiet punctuated by chirping birds. My dark thoughts, they fade a bit. What a relief to watch them go.

A finch flits through sprinklers just for the joy of it, his yellow breast shocking the green lawn and waking me up to the moment. He spies a curled leaf filled with water and splashes down, improvising a bath. He dunks his head and fluffs his feathers, spraying a kaleidoscope of rainbow drops and suddenly it's all so magical...

I just don't understand the idea of heaven – I mean, it's right here.

Nature is paradise, more awesome than anything humans can dream in imagination or factory. It's in the local park or pond or even the ant that scouts the kitchen floor – how wild and improbable a creature is he – one of 20,000 types of ants? Heaven on Earth isn't just peak experiences at World Heritage Sites, like the animals of the Serengeti in Africa – RIP. Or the Great Barrier Reef – RIP. Over 25 million years old and we kill half of it in the last two years, bleaching it into bone-yards, as ocean acidification happens 10 times faster than anything in the previous 300 million years, creating dead zones choking marine life from the Gulf of Mexico to Namibia –

BENJI! Stop the endless dark factoids. Please!

Mind is too manic from all the man-made horror and miserable lies. Need to clear my head or I'll never make it through the day. Need to be present and observant as I see a guy about a gun, not asleep in some OCD mono-spiral and –

Just pay attention, Benji, to <u>this</u> moment on <u>this</u> leafy road.

Life stripped-down simple and quiet. Remember this neat trick and give yourself a break from all the thinking and anxiety. Like Roger says at Face the Wave, save yourself from your self. No time like the present!

I kill my phone – having it on leeches my attention.

Just sit on this stone wall and pay attention to <u>this</u> giant oak in front of me. I slowly become absorbed in the tree. My thoughts fade...

I stare and stare at the ancient oak. Guess this makes me a tree-hugger, but so what? It actually feels good to hug a tree. And studies show trees emit a signal when machetes hack them and another when the hacker returns. Wow! So much of Gaia is unknowable, like trees leaning toward just the recorded <u>sound</u> of water. I love that. It's not that the natural world isn't also tooth and claw violent – it is, but only for survival. Like me? A purging force of nature –

Come on, Benji. Pay attention. Focus. Right here, right now.

I watch the tree dance in the breeze, cheerfully waving as it calls out with a soft rustle, light shimmering leaf to leaf.

I get as quiet as possible and really absorb the simple soulfulness of this oak, the trustworthiness of its deep roots, the joy of it breaching the Earth and stretching for the sky, the hope in its tender greens, and the death in its yellow leaves – the entire life-cycle in one being. I take a deep breath and bask in its quiet company and exhale and –

Disappear. For a second, it's like being on Molly.

Whoa! Such a relief from ME. And the madness of my mind.

If I really pay attention, can I breeze right by devotion and into a momentary taste of nothingness? If I am fully awake for even an instant to the natural world can my mind dissolve? Pure freedom? Oneness with the world? Why not?

This Goldilocks planet – not too hot, not too cold – is heaven. It's a glorious gift. It soothes me. It heals me. The idea that when we die, we go somewhere better if we're good and to the pits of hell if we're bad – that's the saddest lie I've ever heard. This beautiful planet, right in front of us, winking and waving, this is "god." And we kiss it goodbye without even considering what we destroy. That's not just terrifying, it's the sorriest thing ever –

Stop, Benji! Please. Just concentrate!

It's hard. Thoughts and judgment going wild today.

Right now, with every fiber of my being, I pay attention to the tree blazing with aliveness. Blazing in all its glory right in front of me, offering itself, talking to me – here, now. I just need to listen and really see it. Right now, this tree saves my life, it saves me from me –

And I disappear again. Wow. Wow! WOW!

And now I'm back. Damn. Skittering in thought. Okay. Fall asleep a thousand times, wake up a thousand and one. Pay attention to a single breath. Listen to the tree, Benji...

But look around, my ricochet-mind protests. Heaven is here on Earth and it desperately needs help. It's calling us to stop – just please stop.

You stop, Benji. Right here. Right now.

Like Eric Garner, that big guy the cops choked to death, Earth is saying, "I can't breathe." There are too many of you piling on. Eleven times Eric says it, dying under the weight of them.

You breathe, Benji. Pay attention. Watch.

But Eric Garner's daughter just died of an asthma-induced heart attack. Asthma! What's the point of meditation when the world is on fire? I can't stop, I need to act!

Benji, see the deeper in the deep.

I want to stop and see the deeper in the deep, but –

Then stop. Right here. Right now.

Wish I could... But it's impossible with the horror on the horizon. And all the fear in my head today. The Molly sense of oneness and love just won't stick.

But I had it for a second. Until my mind stole the moment from me.

And now my tears roll for the merrily waving tree.

The deeper in the deep is we are dying.

Do I see the world as it is or as I am?

Today's Headline

"Half the World's Coral Reefs Destroyed in The Last 30 Years." I guess it will just be one of those days – too much sadness at the madness.

– Inhabit.org

Homeless

The sun is higher as I cross Sunset Boulevard, cars flying by. It's going to be a sizzler. California just gets hotter, with actual "firenados" burning people alive – there's the real hell of our own making. A biblical reckoning. A never-ending fire season of horrors –

Whew, my mind. What a grind. Wouldn't wish it on anybody.

I catch a Big Blue Bus with the other poor bastards who don't have a car in LA. We pass the Brentwood Country Club behind a chain-link fence gussied up with Bougainvillea. But flowers can't hide the barbed wire on top cordoning off the only park in Bitterwood. Nobody is even golfing its lush acres greened by tons of water, as joggers shuffle the dusty path outside the fence trying to catch a bit of fresh air to balance the four-lane highway that's San Vicente. *Elysium*, already here –

Was it a mistake to stop meds and therapy?

It's so bad in my head right now I wish I didn't.

But it's impossible to escape Cretin. Like, on the bus seat is a news-paper – an actual <u>paper</u> paper. Cretin is on the cover, looking like one of those Rose Bowl Parade balloons, all bloated cheese-doodle face and polyester hair. He's everywhere, nonstop with his Barnum style circus huckstering, "Planet here. Get yer planet for sale!"

A sucker born every second. Us.

I get off the bus and walk through Santa Monica, home of the home-less, a rise of 25% just this year – a thousand people sleeping on the streets in a city of 92,000. Christ. I truly hate my brain today.

I pass renovated Reed Park, with its new slogan: *Meet Me At Reed.*

But only drug addicts nod off on the new exercise stations. Who wants to catch Hep C, now an epidemic? A dozen bodies with backpacks dead-fall the lawn. Meet me at Reed? Addicts got the message. Wow! One takes a crap in the bushes ten yards away. Gross. I hustle by him, poor bastard.

Across the park, Repent Guy, a regular, drags his big cross. "Repent!"

Ha. The world mocks me. But don't we all have to repent?

Santa Monica is the theory of multiverses come to life. In one, it's a tourist town the world visits. It's got wide beaches and a pier with rides and a closed-off fake street for shopping. It has a sunny buzz with tourists speaking Italian and eating thirty dollar "pizzas" at cafes. It's rich and booming with so many tech companies they call it Silicon Beach. But in another universe, it's shrinking. There are commons you can't use because the human misery is so bad – the library and parks and even parts of the beach. I'm counting the homeless as I walk. Nine in two blocks – 117 per square mile. Humans lying on the street – once babies – who smell so bad I hold my breath as I stride by every category of the abandoned:

- Toothless-shouting-at-shrubbery.

- Bike-stealing-meth-punk.

- Dazed-old-lady-what-the-hell-happened.

- Drunk-drifters-my-age-begging-with-dog-on-twine.

- Zombie-crackhead-mugger.

- Couple-hauling-whatever-in-grocery-cart.

- Camo-wearing-face-like-a-beaten-dog-veteran.

It's a disgrace. It pains my heart and makes me angry at the same time.

And here comes one now, the saddest kind. Tyler would approve – an old schizophrenic wizard Ronald Reagan "freed." His shoe-less feet are swollen black like he's got a flesh-eating disease. His hair is a gray nest, cradling a mind of rolling marbles. His eyes glint, shards of glass, seeing nothing or everything. Chuckling, he stumbles past me and I catch a smell so rancid – shit meets rotting rat carcass – that puke rises in the back of my throat.

Everybody ghosts him like he's a pane of glass.

My chest tightens. What can I do? Have to steel myself to keep walking – to help would take over my world. I'm ashamed of my disgust, ashamed of my country. As life gets harder in our individual bubbles, we all get harder-hearted.

Makes me so anxious. The homeless feel like the dawn of a new reality.

Can I do it? Forage on the streets after civilization collapses? What happens when millions live this way? It's coming. Even to Canada, where they don't have a bloated military to suck up their dollars. Instead of tossing you on the street, they give you free healthcare and college. But 37 million Canadians are no match for 327 million boiling Americans with a steroidal army. And under us, 130 million Mexicans dying of thirst. People won't just quietly croak as rich nations live it up in gated countries. Borders will disappear. And after the refugees start moving, what will stop them? For psychos like Cretin, it'll be nuclear bombs and the nuclear winter that comes with them. Try hiding from that in New Zealand, you old plutos –

Christ, I'm in a total grim cycle today. Crazy negative mono mind. Feeling so desperate! But the homeless crisis always make me feel like the end of the world is already here –

A Lamborghini blows past me with a loud whine. Makes me wish I already had my gun. Did I really just think that? I'm losing it!

But SaMo is turning into Bev Hills, with gas-guzzling douche-mobiles jerking from light to light. Tyler says the "Lambros" are "totally balling it." Where does he get his dumb lingo, always destructive, like crushing or killing? What kind of person drives a $400,000 gas guzzler past people dying on the streets? A vulture capitalist. But that's an insult to vultures. They never harm a living creature. They eat carcasses infected with lethal diseases like cholera. They're good for the environment.

Can we say the same? No, we're the damn infection. Viruses and humans, the only two species that destroy their own ecosystem.

So, those Tech Bros aren't like vultures making the world a better place. They're vampire capitalists who want every living interaction to pass through their filters, spying on everybody with everything – even our damn refrigerators. They destroy human connection and call it connection. They distort reality and sever us from nature as if their games can replace it. These shallow sociopaths, Tyler's heroes, charge their "Lambos" headlong into a dystopia without a thought to the consequences.

So now, only 14% of American children can tell fact from fiction. So now, kids surf their slot machine crack pipes six hours a day, spending less and less time outside. So now, we're numbed out and manipulated by dudes with all the humanity of robots, who say stuff like "move fast and break things." Ha. Mission accomplished, Zuck.

What about mend and attend?

What about Tikkun Olam – repair the world?

Instead, we're permanently distracted as we try not to notice the homeless living on the streets. Try not to see Mother Earth is in a rear-naked choke like the one June showed me. Try to hide inside as we kill our one and only home.

Homeless.

Today's Headline

"One in Six Americans Go to Bed Hungry." But 50% of kids have a cellphone by age eleven. Big Tech likes to addict kids early, getting us hooked on the dopamine hits of fear, lies, and outrage.

– TheGuardian.org

Wrong in My Head

I'm in a foul mood, my dance with the tree long gone.

What the hell am I even doing, going to get a gun? What good is a Hail Mary pass when you're down 30 points with 100 seconds on the doomsday clock? But what else can I do? Even if it's futile against a mountain of planetary inertia and human denial, I need to do something.

Can't just lie down and die – that's not me.

I board the new train from Santa Monica to downtown LA. Locals call it the Crime Train Express because it shuttles transients into the small town, as serious crime in Santa Monica went up 30% in the last three years. Soon, the goose that lays all the golden tourist eggs will be cooked. Who will want to visit, when 94% of American cities, big and small, are safer?

Skipping into every damn stat today. I'm so worked up.

Got to calm down. STOP!

The train pulls into downtown LA at the Seventh Street Metro station. I transfer to the purple line for six minutes. As the train goes underground, I feel a vomiting dread. Earthquakes – 388 in Southern Cal this month alone. When the San Andreas unzips, let the hunger games begin, Cretin presiding, as lurid and corrupt as President Snow in the movies –

Christ. My brain is so bad today it should be funny. But it's hell. No perspective. Like Tyler says, no sense of humor. Feeling suddenly sick.

Vertigo – am I making myself nauseous?

Benji. Chill! Just get to the damn gun show – mission of the day.

The train pulls into Union Station and I rush into the old deco building, an echo of a beautiful past, and echoing as I run through it, panting and clammy. I'm no athlete, but this feels weird – out of breath, like a kind of panic.

I stumble outside to a bench and sit, trying to calm down. But the day just started and it's gone so wrong in my head. Disoriented, I can't concentrate. Like I've got the flu. Is it fear of the gun show? Of taking the first step to kill Cretin? Should I just go home?

I wander in circles, letting the baking heat set me straight. Walking until I catch my breath and my pulse slows and I stop sweating. Maybe I'm okay. That was just too much obsesso-head. Got to just be here now. But isn't that terrible advice if you want to see what's coming around the corner and –

JUST TURN IT OFF BENJI.

March forward. Stop tormenting yourself.

I get on the Riverside line and write the endless morning out, passing warehouses baking in the sun, not a solar panel in sight. Then take a bus for the last leg down streets with one mini-mall after another offering fast food and payday loans – all of it in the dictionary under UGLY.

The morning already feels like a lifetime in my anxious mind.

I'm ready to buy a gun just to put myself out of my misery.

Today's Terrible Fact

It took four hours to get to the Ontario convention center by public transpo. By car, it's an hour. No wonder every single American melts 10,000 tons of Arctic ice a year. What choice do we have?

– Phys.org

Clenched Fists

The Ontario Convention center is a gleaming oasis of glass surrounded by palm trees. I'm here! Feel better. Back in my body...

From a distance, the center could be the palace of a Saudi prince, with columns jutting skyward and limp flags adorning a long promenade. It's hot enough to be the Middle East, where MIT predicts, "many major cities in the region could exceed a tipping point for human survival." No kidding – it's 129 degrees in Saudi Arabia today. Deserts they'll be deserting, done in by the oil that made them rich – if they don't rubble themselves first like Syria...

At least today in Ontario, California, it's a cool 109 degrees. Ha.

Parched, I stagger in under a three-story glass wall, the blast of air-con tingling my skin. The mission starts. Focus!

Any illusion of Middle Eastern exotics evaporates in the crowd of balding men wearing dad jeans cinched below disemboweled guts. All white, with gray hair and a gray vibe, it's like some Westworld factory mass-produced them. A few young dudes wear dull Harley T-shirts and fatigues – just off a tour from some war, real or imagined.

I walk under a Crossroads of the West Gun Show banner with all the "Os" done up like sniper cross-hairs. Cool! I pay 18 bucks to get in and am overwhelmed by the smell of oil and – I don't know, a smell I don't recognize. Gunpowder? Gunmetal? I stop in front of a sign:

"We respectfully ask that you not carry loaded at the gun show. We are proud supporters of the right to carry and have lobbied extensively to extend that right to all. Our request is motivated solely by concern for your safety and the safety of everyone at the show."

That's funny! They want loaded guns in bars, colleges, grade schools –
but their own gun show? Too dangerous. Even in a room full of gun nut
experts. Same with the politicians bought by the NRA – they don't allow
guns in their hallowed halls. They don't want a "Second Amendment"
solution like Cretin suggested if he lost the last election.

Wonder if Cretin has any idea half the country contemplates one now?

It can't only be me that dreams of it. Can it?

At least I'm not outsourcing my violence like Cretin. His Second
Amendment "gun solution" isn't just his usual BS. Baxter said it's called
"delegation of violence." Hitler did it using the Brown Shirts. Putin does
it now. And Cretin does it all the time, giving permission to "rough up"
protesters, he'll pay the legal bills. Yeah, right, check's in the mail.

All in good fun until a Nazi runs over some poor girl.

I look around but nobody even glances at the banner. They're focused
on the guns – which we Americans love. But it's mostly gun nuts who
love guns – 3% hoard half of them. Four out of five Americans don't even
own a firearm.

But the gun nuts who hoard guns like squirrels prepping for winter
are in heaven here, surrounded by an acre of them. Hunting rifles stand
at attention. Handguns lie packed with their comrades. Assault rifles recline, black and deadly. Antique collectibles retire with fellow members of
the American Legion. An army's worth of ammo, gun safes, and holsters.
Plus, tables of knives and Samurai swords, in case your gun jams and you
need to go old-school *Kill Bill*.

"This will stop any school shooter in his tracks," a gun seller is saying.

Ha. A kid going school shooter doesn't care – suicide is part of his mission. He's taking notes during the "active shooter" drills that terrify first
graders, as effective as the old "duck and cover" drills protecting kids from
nuclear bombs. A school shooter does the drills while saying to himself,
"Oh, this is your plan? Thanks for the tip. See you soon!"

"You can keep it in an ankle holster." The seller is eying me now, giving
me a rush of paranoia. Can he tell I don't belong here? But I'm no tourist.
I'm planning to use my gun exactly as intended – to take a life. Not as a

school shooter. Nope. This tall, pale ginger is going to kill your hero.

I shake it off and head over to the sniper rifles, taking in the men stooped over tables of death. Is the Idea turning me into them? Hope not. These aren't the dads of Bitterwood, who don't get fat or lose their salesman sheen of success. These men look permanently tired.

I pass a table of bumper stickers:

Black Guns Matter

Gun Control, The Ability to Drop A Liberal At 500 Yards

I Like My Gun the Way Obama Likes His Voters – Unregistered

I Love Animals, They're Delicious

Save The Male

Look What Illegal Immigration Did to The White House

NRA commercials on wide screens show panic, with Obama looking way darker than he is. Shots of the Rodney King riots flash by – burning buildings and cars – blacks misbehaving. They might as well say society <u>will</u> break down and the blackest blacks <u>will</u> skullfuck your family. Get a gun and save yourselves before Big Gov takes them! More likely, they shoot themselves or a family member by accident or on purpose.

It's weird to see the Obama slamming going on, like they're as obsessed by him as Cretin – can't let him go. I mean, isn't the dude on permanent vacation now, kite surfing and writing books? I'm sure the gun sellers miss Obama – the browning of America is good for gun sales.

No browning going on here at Crossroads. Looking at this gun-thirsty crowd, it's hard to believe new polls say 89% of all Americans are for strict gun licenses. In fact, 79% already thought we had them. Ha.

When was the last time we had taxation without representation?

Oh, yeah. Revolution.

A crowd gathers around a large screen. It's a new NRA ad. The TV spokeswoman bites out her words with pure contempt.

"They use their media to assassinate real news."

Shots of the NY Times building, I guess ground zero of Fake News for this crowd. That's better, Obama is so 2015.

"They use schools to teach children their president is another Hitler."

What BS. I'm a self-taught Hitler obsessive.

"They use their ex-president to endorse the resistance. To make them march, make them scream racism and sexism and xenophobia and homophobia."

Hey, if the shoe fits... Gun Whore also still can't seem to let go of Obama. She hocks the words out like bile as black rage plays on the screen. No Nazi white rage –

"To bully and terrorize the law-abiding until the only option left is for the police to stop the madness."

Cue police and demonstrators clashing. But police often let A-holes beat up or run over peaceful protesters with cars. They have all the power and do nothing –

"The only way we save our country and our freedom is to fight this violence of lies with the clenched fist of truth."

Gun Whore scornfully taunts the camera. Guess I've got that in common with them too. What am I if not a clenched fist of truth fighting the violence of lies?

"I'm the National Rifle Association of America. And I'm freedom's safest place."

Really? Freedom needs a safe space? Ha! There's no safe space in today's world. We are one people who live or die in one ecosystem. And if my generation doesn't abandon our bedrooms, stand OUR ground and fight for our lives, then we're Gen Last. How's that for some marketing?

Gen Last. Fuck.

The ad ends with the NRA logo, a group started for hunters but is now just paranoids selling guns to other paranoiacs. A guy in a USMC cap shakes his head, but the crowd loves it.

"That's right," a graybeard with a MAGA cap says as the ad starts again. "They use their media to assassinate real news."

I wonder what you think is the "real news" getting assassinated? The drivel scrawling down your Old Fakebook feed where computational propaganda spreads ads like this? Or a tweet written by one guy with ten followers in his Red State basement getting bot-herded around the world? Or Russia and Republicans creating rage-bait Fakebook pages to intoxicate us all with hatred – pure information warfare?

Hey, it dumbed people down enough to elect Cretin.

Fakebook's response? Just keep talking about "cracking down" on bad actors, as Zuck okays fake election ads. And sticks to his yearly apology, promising to create more community. Oh, you're creating it, Alt-Right. Can't wait to see what crawls out of your new private groups, Zuck!

I want to shout at this MAGA graybeard about the forces stocking his feed with fear and shoving him into his gun tribe. How propaganda creates his unreality. How Cretin's already got people ripping immigrant kids from parents in the name of "security," a move right out of the fascist playbook. But this Old wouldn't care – 91% of Cretin disciples trust only him for the truth. Like he was Moses with tablets and a fake tan. Only 11% of them even watch MSM anymore.

"What you're seeing and what you're reading is not what's happening," megaphones Cretin. That's a direct quote, as he pushes the meme that nothing is true except him. Because Cretin knows you can't speak truth to power once you destroy truth. All that's left is raw power, as his clenched fist of Nazi-level propaganda punches us into madness.

Armed to the teeth.

The old master would approve.

Today's Headline

"Americans Own 40% of the World's Guns." And we're only 4.4% of the world's population. No wonder 8 kids a day are shot here in what they call "Family Fire." Ha. Like a game show competition... Go USA!

– Independent.co.uk

MMA Ears

I push down an aisle of beefy guys to a table with sniper rifles. This is what I came for. Can't afford them, not here. But online, used – maybe.

These sniper rifles are so elite there are only two under signs: *"The McMillan TAC-50 Sniper Rifle. Longest Confirmed Kill in Combat!"*

Next to it is the: *"Barrett M82A1, As seen in the movie The Accountant."*

Of course, Dad and I saw it. Ben Affleck plays an Asperger Dude who launders money for criminals and then assassinates them if they break bad. He controls his autism by playing heavy metal and beating his shins with a metal pipe, kind of like "pray the gay away," but for autism. As somebody accused of being aspy myself – isn't everybody these days? – I call BS on that BS. It's a new take on the western, but Affleck is no Clint Eastwood. Still, a man with a gun gonna solve a problem gets me every time, so I liked it. Can't avoid my own culture no matter how much I try. Even though in the real old West they took your gun at the edge of town or the entrance to bars – gun control! Against drunks with pistols...

They knew the simple truth that more guns equal more gun death.

Two men stand behind the sniper rifles on the table. One looks like Clint when he was young, but more grizzled, with a short-cropped beard and tatted Popeye forearms. The other dude is wiry and intense, with the chewed-up MMA ears June always points out to me.

"So cool, Benji," June says after we saw a guy at the mall. "I'm gonna get those ears."

"Why would you want ears that look like a disposal ground them up?"

"Because, Benji," June talks to me like I'm an idiot. "When you have those ears, nobody in their right mind messes with you."

"What about people in their wrong mind? Crazy people?"

"Then you really need the training that creates those ears," June says, laughing. Could she help me? Maybe. June's a born warrior, no doubt...

So are these two – neither looks like the fat asses wandering around. My guess is military. They glance at each other as I stare at the two rifles. They look heavy as hell – I wouldn't even know how to pick one up.

"Both these weapons fire a 50-millimeter bullet. Blow a man apart or stop a car," MMA Ears says helpfully, talking quick and clipped. His pupils are tiny. Is he high? "This Tac-50 has the longest confirmed combat kill in Stan. Mile and a half."

"A mile and a half?" I dumbly repeat. Christ, I sound like a newbie.

"Yep. Sexy, right?"

Not how I'd describe it, but a gun like that sure does the trick. Because a mile and a half is about as close to Cretin as I'll ever get.

"Yeah, cool." I stare at it, not sure what to say.

"Course, you got to have a spotter to plot the wind. And the trajectory of the bullet at that distance takes four seconds. If the target is on the move, you gotta put the bullet where the target's gonna be. Not easy." MMA Ears talks fast using his hands and is certainly informative, calling living humans targets. But what kind of training does it take? A lifetime. And where do I do it? There's no public transportation out to a place you can shoot a gun a mile and a half.

Clint just eyes me, arms crossed, hovering between bored and amused.

"You're not gonna buy this rifle." He spits a stream of tobacco into a red plastic cup.

"I might," I protest, feeling defensive. "Just looking, you know. But I might."

"What you gonna use it for?" Clint's eyes narrow a bit.

"Um. Just, you know. Sport. Target shooting."

"You ever even shoot a gun before?" He's no salesman but can see through this customer.

"Sure, lots of times." I try to represent. Watching online videos of dudes shooting guns is more like it. Including a video of the very McMillan TAC-50 coiled in front of me. They celebrate the rifle's longest confirmed kill on YouTube History Channel clips – how sick is that?

"Really," Clint says in the tone he probably uses to call BS.

"But never a sniper rifle," I hastily add.

"First time for everything," MMA Ears chimes in, giving Clint a look.

"You got eleven grand?" Clint squints at me.

"What? No. Wow." MMA Ears glances at Clint again – something just short of bayonets.

"The Barrett is only eighty-five hundred," MMA Ears says.

"You got eighty-five hundred?" Clint already knows the answer before I shake my head.

"Excuse us a sec." MMA Ears throws an arm around Clint and pulls him away.

"Don't touch those guns." Everything out of Clint's mouth is a growl.

MMA Ears walks Clint a couple steps away and whisper-shouts at him, but Clint just rolls his eyes. I'm not sure what's going on. Are they military? Or part of some Militia like the Oath Keepers – that right-wing gang of military and police who show up to protect free speech at Nazi marches? Where they "keep the peace" in combat gear, carrying assault rifles? Or are these two actual White Supremacists? Racists don't have swastikas on their arms or skinned heads or jackboots anymore – they've learned to evolve and blend in, joining the military and police to get training. Or are they undercover FBI agents trolling the gun show for active shooter nut jobs? Am I paranoid? Is it contagious, the paranoia here?

Clint glances at me, shrugs, and they walk over. Maybe just gun dealers, profiting –

"You want to shoot this rifle?" MMA Ears asks. "We're going out to the desert tomorrow. You can tag along and try it out."

WTF is going on? Does MMA Ears want to recruit me for something? Or do they think I'm a damn school shooter? I always double-VPN my

IP via the Tor browser, but maybe it isn't enough and they've tracked my weird searches, grabbed that puke video from somebody's Snap account – and BAM. Using facial rec-tech as a precaution at gun shows, I'm tagged. Hundreds of billions in homeland security have to go somewhere.

"Um, I can't do that. And I... I can't afford these guns." I've got to ease my way out of here. Clint looks pretty pissed at his intense partner, his way too intense partner.

"We've got payment plans," MMA Ears cheerfully sells away. He stares at me with his chewed-up ears and pinhole pupils and my heart races. He looks like one of those unstable pit bulls. Not like Gigi, but the ones tortured to within an inch of their lives to be vicious. The ones that stare at you, eyes sideways, and suddenly lunge. One thought pops into my head – this guy has killed people. Lots of people. What if he just wants a target to get his kill on? Now that's totally paranoid, but the hair is up on the back of my scalp in pure animal fear. No way in hell do I go out to any desert with these two. I instinctively step back as my mind skitters to movie plots. Maybe they need a patsy to set up for an assassination they plan. They give me the gun, kill somebody, rat me out and –

"What do you think?" MMA Ears snaps me back. I think I already left, that's what I think. But I'm still standing here in a total spiral with my mouth open like a dumb-ass.

"Just looking." I try to focus and stay calm. "Cool guns, but to be honest, I don't know what I'd do with one even if I could afford it."

Clint spits into his cup. MMA Ears looks suspicious as I stride away, suddenly short of breath, feeling clammy and panicked for the third time today. The whole gun show was a bad idea. I don't even know how to shoot a handgun, never mind a gun that kills people over a mile away.

I push through all the dense white guys and the sweaty fear convincing them a gun will buy safety. Past the NRA commercials that brutally binds this tribe together in a gleeful hatred, the same glue cementing Cretin followers to him no matter what he does. A Cretin clan stuck together by despising the same people, goading up the adrenaline of old chimp warfare that ends reason and science and democracy, that results in rage and violence and death, until now it's just a low gathering around the fire grunting at each other – you-me-together-kill. HUH!

Cretin wants a fight to the finish. Sell endless guns and promote man against man, country against country – the exact wrong message as the world gets smaller and smaller. Don't we need a new definition of a clan? Where we take the love for family and cast it as wide as the planet? One people, one precious habitat for all us traumatized global animals?

"E Pluribus Unum." Out of many, one. Cretin doesn't understand our Founding Fathers – that we are one people. That we can, with imagination and courage, expand that idea worldwide. Or is that just a pipe dream? Are we all too far-gone into petty tribalism? I hope not...

If we all don't learn to go from combat to collaboration, we die. If we don't imagine an all-inclusive electric future instead of the 5% who can now afford it, we die. If we don't *"E Pluribus Unum"* our asses in gear and invest in massive change, we die. How's that for a choice?

Cretin doesn't know how to think big. He replaced the Latin phrase of togetherness on the presidential coin with his cheesy MAGA slogan. He put his name in four places and defaced the coin's presidential seal. The eagle now looks right instead of left. Get it?

And, of course, he sprayed it gold.

Christ. He's a small, small man. He's never going from ME to US.

I swim through the roar of men talking over the clatter of metal-on-metal ratcheting – locking and NOT LOADING. Because even gun nuts don't want loaded guns in their gun show. But will happily sell you one to bring into your house, into your school, into a moment of instability you wish you could take back.

But you can't call back a fired bullet, climate or otherwise.

I wobble across the freezing lobby and stagger out into the heat.

Today's Cretin Tweet

"Giving guns to teachers will act as a deterrent. Stop shootings! We need more guns!" Ha. Real tweet. Cretin lives in a world of pure fiction – he should just write some novels and leave us all alone.

Crushed Bug with A Gun

It's a pizza oven outside.

I turn my face up to the sun, giver and taker of life. As the heat seeps into my bones, I'm grateful for its raw power – bring it.

I feel dizzy and open my eyes, looking down. A black stinkbug trudges in front of me. As my shadow looms, the little bug comically sticks his ass in the air, ready to spray, about as useful as his black armor against the indifferent feet falling around him. As if to prove it, when I kneel to rescue the little lowrider, a worn brown shoe with frayed laces squashes him.

"Want to buy a Glock?" A soft voice startles me into standing. A bald guy with gold wire-rim glasses and a basketball belly stands too close, with no idea he just mushed a little creature going about his business. "No paperwork. No ID."

I stare at him and want to tell him to watch where he's going. Watch what he's doing. Be a little mindful, for Christ's sake, there's <u>living</u> going on here. But what's the point? He wouldn't know what the hell I'm talking about. And wouldn't care. He wants to sell me a gun. In his dad jeans and plaid shirt, he doesn't look like a Fed or a cop but now I'm so freaked and paranoid from MMA Ears I can't think straight. Hope I never see his chewed-up ears again.

"No. I'm good." I take a step back from Bug Crusher.

"How old are you?" He asks genially. "You look about twelve."

"I'm eighteen." Why do I feel defensive?

"Then they won't sell you a handgun in Cali. Got to be twenty-one." He lights a cigarette and tosses the match like the whole state wasn't on fire. "They'll sell you a rifle, not an assault rifle, gotta get out of Cali for that. But a hunting rifle, sure."

I know all this – I've done my research. There's this little thing called the Internet I want to snottily say. But I'm silent. My original idea was to research what kind of gun I want and then maybe buy it out in the parking lot. But now that Bug Crusher offers to sell me one, I don't know what to think.

"You look like you might be looking for protection. The Glock is tried and true." He inhales his cigarette, looking like an insurance salesman on a smoking break. "Either you're a sheep, a sheepdog, or a wolf. Now, you'll never be a wolf, but you can be a sheepdog – protect yourself and the herd from being sheep. Wanna look?"

Sheep again. Christ. But being a sheepdog is cool. Isn't that the essence of the Idea more than me becoming a wolf? A dog protecting the planetary flock – I like it. Bug Crusher doesn't seem dangerous, and it'd be good to at least hold a damn gun, maybe learn something, even if it's useless for my plan.

"Okay," I say. We walk in silence through the baking parking lot to a battered minivan. He remotely clicks the sliding back door.

"Hop in." He points and heaves himself in the driver's side. Instead of getting in the back seat I walk around and climb in front to be near a window I can open. Bug Crusher starts the van and turns on air-conditioning, but it's too played out to make a dent on the heat.

He leans over, opens the glove box, and pulls out a handgun. Just sitting in there like a tarantula. He pushes a button and the magazine slides out. With a practiced motion he racks the slide. The chambered round pops and he palms it midair as the slide snaps back, loud as a rat trap.

The insurance salesman is John Wick's fat, bald brother.

"This here's a semiautomatic Glock gen4 G19. Magazine capacity is fifteen bullets." He hands me the unloaded gun as casual as can be.

And in a rush, I suddenly understand everything. It's warm and oily and heavy. It gives me a feeling of god-like power, death in my hand. It surprises and scares me – how strong the gun floods my whole being.

Instantly, I forget when compared to other wealthy nations we are 25 times more likely to be intentionally killed by a gun.

And 6 times more likely to be accidentally killed by a gun.

And 8 times more likely to commit suicide using a gun.

Photographic memory and I can't forget anything but suddenly I do. I forget it all and –

"How's that feel?" Bug Crusher knows how it feels. I crave this gun in an irrational surge, like Gollum quivering with desire in *Lord of the Rings*,

"We wants it, we needs it. Must have the power of my precious."

Am I on the wrong path slippery slope like Dad said? The end not justifying the means? My secrets and lies already starting my moral decay?

As I squeeze the gun, I don't care. Now, I am Zeus and can fire off a thunderbolt and destroy worlds with a flick of my finger. Nobody, <u>no body</u> ever gets the upper hand on me again. I banish the Tylers and the minor Cretins of the world. I am a hero. I save people. I ACT –

"You can kill any turd dead with that," Bug Crusher says as if reading the saddest corner of my mind. I quickly hand back the heavy gun and the spell snaps. Gandalf says to Frodo when he offers him the ring, *"Don't tempt me Frodo ... I would use this ring from a desire to do good. But through me it would wield power too great and terrible to imagine."*

My job is to kill one man who kills the planet. To start a revolution. To wake people up. I will take the ring and become a monster. I will probably die, not even knowing if I've succeeded. That's a sacrifice I'm willing to make. I have no illusions about it. But not with this gun designed for lesser evils, tempting me to right every wrong with its fifteen bullets. Vulnerable to a moment of rage. Or depression – most handgun deaths are suicides – dead before the first twenty minutes it takes for the impulse to pass. No way.

My attention pulls back to see where I am, in a van, with a sweaty stranger who has a gun in his hand. This is fucked up and –

"Four hundred bucks and it's yours," Bug Crusher says.

"I don't think so." I'll have to find another way to kill Cretin.

"Sure? It's a sweet deal." I nod. What was I thinking coming here?

Research the true believer world I'm entering. Put myself in the belly of the beast. Well done! I'm sure here now –

"Okay." Crusher slots the magazine back into the Glock with a loud click. I have a moment of terror, sitting with a stranger holding a loaded gun in the anonymity of a vast parking lot. But he reaches over, drops the gun in the glove box, and snaps the compartment shut. I get a glimpse of a needle. Christ, is he dope-sick? Soon to be one of the 74,000 Americans dead this year from overdoses, more than the entire Vietnam War and mostly from Red states –

"So, what do you want to do now?" On the way back from the glove box I guess his hand got tired and now rests on my knee, its chubby fingers like big caterpillars. But they're not fluorescent green, filled with the promise of new life. They're the color of maggots on a corpse.

"I'll suck your cock," Crusher says, as matter-of-fact as offering to sell me a gun.

I stare at a faded photo of two kids taped to the gray dash. A boy and a girl, arms thrown around each other, gap-toothed smiles awaiting adult teeth. Don't rush it, I randomly think. I didn't see the gay thing coming, but now him asking my age makes more sense – he doesn't want to get arrested cruising a kid. Did he even want to sell me a gun? Did he misinterpret me getting in the front seat? But he's married, with kids, and probably too old to be married to a dude. So, I'm surprised, even though I know gay comes in every shape, size, and marital status –

"What do you say?" Bug Crusher's hand moves up my thigh. I feel strangely frozen. Christ. I've had zero sex beyond jerking off to porn, so the last thing I want to do is lose my cock-sucked virginity to a creeper in a van at the damn Crossroads of the West Gun Show.

I search his face, round and sweaty. Shiny bald. He looks so sad and lonely and out-of-sorts I almost feel sorry for him. Poor old bloodsucker just wants to feed – blood or semen – any precious bodily fluid will do. I should jump out of the blasted mini-van with its faded paint and crusty windows, smelling like an egg-salad sandwich died under the seat. Instead, I find myself saying –

"I'm not gay. And aren't you married?" I nod at the kid photo, frozen in a filmy amber. Bug Crusher yanks his hand off my thigh like he was scalded back into his life. He nods, looking miserable. I exhale, suddenly aware I've been holding my breath.

"My wife, we got an arrangement." He sighs. "A shit sandwich for everybody."

"Why don't you leave?" I lean away a bit. "You're a gay dude. Nobody cares. Leave and go be gay."

What the hell am I doing? What stops this guy from grabbing his gun and taking his blowjob? Nothing. Except I know he doesn't want that, not really. I mean, maybe he wants to forget himself and his sorry life for a minute sucking a stranger's dick. But then what?

"Nobody knows except the wife. I got kids heading into high school." He sighs again, Bug Crusher deflating into Crushed Bug right in front of me. "It's all screwed up. Lost my job and I'm working at Walmart. You want to know the truth? I can't afford to get divorced. The wife's the breadwinner now."

The first note of bitterness enters his voice. He's right about the shit sandwich – his job automated or globalized right out from under him. No doubt, he voted for Cretin, which will automatically lower his life expectancy by four years. That's the price for living in Cretin's fevered fantasy. But I don't mention it. The poor guy just wants to talk to somebody who listens and doesn't give him a hard time. I can do that.

"That sounds tough," I say, feeling real sympathy. I'm understanding the toll a secret life takes – we've got that much in common.

"Sorry." He swallows loudly. His eyes fill and his glasses steam. "You're the second person I've told."

I want to reach over and pat his beefy shoulder, but I don't want to give him any ideas. I suddenly feel so sad for him that I almost start sniffling myself. WTF? But I'm the second person he tells, a total stranger, after he takes, like, 40 years to figure out he's gay. Guess the first person is "the wife" when she finds out. Bet that's not a fun conversation. It's all too terrible.

"Lots of people in your situation right now." I try to think of something sympathetic to say to this messed up Old. "Country's hanging on by a thread."

"You got that right, kid." I'm sure we mean different things, but for a moment the agreement creates a companionable silence. For a moment, we're in the same tribe, just two humans being. Even though I'm a spy, the harmony feels good. I relax a bit and ignore the lie at the center of it.

Can't we all get along, like poor old Rodney King asked?

"The whole world's a mess," Crushed Bug continues. Then he snuffles, snorting like Gigi after she gags from eating grass. He yanks off his glasses and wipes his eyes. This guy's in bad shape. "Sorry."

"Why do you even have a gun?" I try to change the subject. Crushed Bug pulls himself together enough to look at me like it's the stupidest question in the world.

"Protection. For when the shit hits the fan."

By shit, does he mean cruising gone wrong? Ha. No. He means the "turds." But he protects himself with a tool as effective as the stinkbug's gassy ass against an unseeing and indifferent shoe. That's how much good a gun is against a climate that will grind us underfoot, even if it allows you to fight off a few cannibals on the way down. It's all so screwed up, but that's being human for you. That's reality. And like Hale says, reality doesn't care if you believe it or not. Reality just IS. Like this poor blood-sucker is gay, much as he'd like not to be –

"I guess if I'm honest, I just wanted it." Crushed Bug pulls a cigarette from the crumpled pack on the dashboard. "You know what I mean? I like the way I feel when I hold it."

"Yeah." I nod. I do know what he means. Power. Against all enemies, real and imagined. He lights his cigarette, looking a bit more in control.

"And I got a gun lock. I was responsible. I got training. And I practiced that cool move catching the bullet over and over and…" His voice trails off as he stares out the cloudy windshield, maybe realizing how stupid it sounds when he says it out loud.

"Why you selling it?" I already know the answer to this.

"Need the money." He sighs so deeply it sounds like a death rattle –

tired, hopeless, and fed up. I fear for him. I wish I felt nothing for this Old who wants to sell me a gun without asking what for, who comes on to me, who calls people turds. Christ, why do I feel anything for him? But I can't help it. He's just so totally run over by his life.

"I'll buy it from you," I announce. WTF? Why do I say this?

"You'll buy it? Really?" He perks up a bit. "Why?"

"I don't know, just want it." I don't know anything at this moment except this sad sweaty man shouldn't have a gun. White American males, lots of middle-aged Cretin followers, were 70% of suicides this year, almost 24,000 by their own gun – deaths of despair. Someday, he might kill himself. And on a terrible day, maybe he kills others. Maybe his family, maybe the little kids taped like insects to his dash –

"Good enough for me." He reaches over, pops the glove box, and grabs the Glock, suddenly all business, no chubby hands lingering anywhere. "I'll throw in the box of bullets."

He drops the gun and a box in a grimy plastic bag with handles and a Forever 21 logo – the poor guy with a teenage girl to support and has to get all the money from his wife. That's got to be a blow to male pride. He hands me the bag and the one bullet still in his moist palm.

"Four hundred bucks, like we discussed." He says briskly, back to Bug Crusher. "Now I bought that in a parking lot transaction just like this one, so there's no paperwork and no trail to me, we clear?"

His eyes are beady and anxious, eying me with suspicion. Why? Because now I'm holding the loaded gun. I know how he feels – is this why people get them? Mutually assured destruction? To put him at ease, I shove the Glock in my pack and quickly pull out the money, counting out all the small bills.

"I don't know what you got planned. And I don't want to know. Forget you ever met me." He pockets the money. "Just don't shoot your dick off."

Figures he goes there. I just nod and hop out of the minivan into the sunlight glinting off cars. You could sear a steak on their shimmering roofs. With a cough, the van drives off, belching a cloud of shame. I stick the extra bullet in my pocket.

Suddenly, I've got to piss, but there's no way to go back into the convention center with a loaded gun. Ha.

I step behind a pickup. After gingerly putting my backpack on the ground like a damn bomb, I unzip and let loose. It's like I've been holding my breath underwater, swimming and swimming up toward the light for minutes before bursting the surface and gasping for air. What a relief – the whole sad and ugly day's been like being held underwater.

I zip up with shaky hands. I suddenly yearn for home, to sit in the little green garden with Gigi. I pick up the bag and trudge through the parking lot, filled with a thousand cars.

All hot as hell, most packing heat.

Today's Headline

"Bats Fall from The Sky in Australia's Heat Wave." Christ, what's next, Beelzebub himself? Nah, Cretin's already here.

– LiveScience.com

Not Sexy Business

The endless trip in reverse.

Downtown, I walk to avoid going underground and to shake off the depressing day. The gun weighs heavy in my pack and on my conscience.

Illegal. Should I keep it? Do I need it for anything? I could go to jail.

What the hell am I doing?

I hike uphill until I'm on Olvera, the oldest street in LA, settled by the Spaniards after all their conquistadoring of the Aztecs, their version of Cowboy/Indian genocide. All the gold they took out of South America was equal to only one year of the Aztec's potato crop. Talk about not knowing what's valuable – we still don't – you can't eat gold. But that hasn't stopped the current Amazon gold mining rush, using mercury slurry techniques, as we poison Earth's lungs. As the jaguars retreat deeper and deeper until there is no deeper in the deep –

Christ, will we ever learn? Do we humans even deserve to survive?

Funny how I keep returning to that question.

A beautiful old church anchors Olvera. Ralph Waldo Emerson said, *"I like the silent church before service begins better than any preaching."*

Me too! Churches, when they're empty, are man-made gardens best appreciated in silence – pews worn to amber, more responsive than god because at least they glow in reply to years of asses-in-the-seats prayer...

Don't go down that atheist screed rabbit hole again, Benji!

As much as it would do me good to sit in a church's deafening silence, I stride past it – can't wait to sit in the garden with Gigi.

Tourist traps hawk painted puppets and pregnant piñatas. Old-timey Mexican music wafts with the smell of deep-fried churros. For a moment, I'm back when people went to markets to see and be seen. And talk to each other in person before our attention got so hacked and engineered. Back when the country was all possibility and not eating itself alive –

Then a guy zombie-walks his phone into me and I'm yanked back to the here and now. I walk and walk downtown until – am I lost?

A hipster girl, pods in, wearing skinny jeans, suede ankle boots, and a "Hello Kitty" backpack slung over her shoulder, waits for the light. Her face is studiously blank as she ignores the witch from another century hanging off a shopping cart next to her.

I walk west on Seventh and within a minute, I miss that hipster.

"Weed, crank, oxy, smack. Weed, crank, oxy, smack." A burner dude chants as I clench my backpack and rush by him. Santa Monica may be home of the homeless, but LA is the kingdom. Over 36,000 people camping on sidewalks, under bridges, in alleys – up 23% this year – with 1,000 of them dying. Wish I could get those numbers out of my head. Is this what the end of the world –

"Yo, skinny whitey." The pimp half of what looks like a pimp-hooker team calls out to me, his voice raspy.

"Wanna date?" The hooker whispers. She's thin, with a missing tooth, and is meth-scratching her skin, as if trying to arrange a dirty drape hanging over a birdcage. Probably thirty but looks fifty and comically unappealing. It's hard to believe anybody would pay –

"What's the hurry?" He's fat, with a hundred acres of the Amazon around his neck, disappearing and reappearing like streams in his folds of flab. He ignores a guy shooting up right behind him.

"Not interested." I clench my hands into fists until I remember I've got a loaded gun in a Forever 21 bag. I can make you stay Forever 21 with a flick of my finger. Can I get it out in time?

"You talking to me? You talking to me? Then who the hell else are you talking to?" Is that who I am now? Travis Bickle in *Taxi Driver*?

I feel as lonely, peeling away from the world. Am I going crazy? No!

But it's crazy to think of pulling the gun growing heavy in my pack, pregnant with bullets. Can't go to jail for some lesser crime.

June's advice pops into my head.

"If a shit-talker tries to get position on you, the attack is already on. It's a simple rule," she quotes one of her self-defense videos after I tell her about Tyler coming up, looking around, and POP, hitting me in the gut without even slowing down. Only a couple years ago.

"But how do you know their intent?" I ask, getting advice from my little sister. Embarrassing.

"How do you know their intent?" June is incredulous. "You get out of your head and feel the situation. If it feels bad, you rip off your glasses and throw the first punch."

"Really? But what if you're wrong? You just hit an innocent person."

"Better to be judged by twelve than buried by six," June declares.

"Good one." I stare at her. "But who the hell are you?"

"Not a dumb-ass letting some jerk talk his way into my circle and sucker punch me!" June squints like a drill sergeant. "While still asking 'what's the problem?'"

She mimics a dolt for that last bit, but I know she's just upset at Tyler punching me for no reason. I love her for that.

"Okay. Thanks. Appreciate it."

"Don't mention it." June waves it off. "Just remember, once they're in range, it's on. Don't spend any time hoping it isn't."

It helps. I don't let Tyler close again. And I now universally apply the position angle. True for Tyler, and guess it's true for Cretin, who has position and is punching out democracy itself, which is trying to figure out what's going on. I'll tell you what, liberalism small "L." Cretin has shit-talked his way into your circle and you're getting your ass kicked. The fight is on – the prize is the planet. Christ... stop. Focus!

Cretin already has position on me – pitched a damn tent in my head.

I angle, keeping the pimp/hooker combo in sight. But neither moves. The pimp is cemented to the sidewalk and the hooker's lamppost is the only thing holding her up. It's weird how much people look like stereotypes of who they are. Pimps with their bling. Hookers dressed Halloween sexy. Terrorists with beards and wide blank eyes. Pale school shooters, with the same wide eyes. All looking like something out of –

"You a faggot?" Hooker hisses, a viper puncturing my thoughts. It's all gays, guns, and homeless today.

"Yeah, he a faggot," Fatty chimes in helpfully. "Ain't ya?"

"No," I respond without thinking. "Just ruined by porn."

"Gay porn?" She cackles and makes me laugh. Harmless. My Travis Bickle fantasy is ridiculous. Like Bug Crusher's fantasies of self-defense when it's his own life that crushes him. Got to ditch this gun before I do something stupid.

"Ya can't make chicken salad outta chicken shit," Fatty pronounces. "Move along."

But I'm already hustling past rows of filthy camping tents and people collapsed on busted couches. A crusty-eyed dude in a wheelchair, with a Chihuahua in his lap, lights a glass crack pipe. And everywhere piles of garbage – or belongings, who can tell – stinking of urine and hopelessness. Is this the future? Cretin dividing the planet into the have-it-all and the have-nothing?

I hurry through the dystopian world – like Santa Monica, but with reversed ratios – ninety-nine percent homeless. Which means I've suddenly vaulted to the one percent.

How depressing is that?

Today's Headline

"Cattle Ranching Remains Top Threat to the Amazon." With 17% of it already Savannah, if the Amazon loses 3% more jungle, it won't produce enough rain to exist. Take your pick pimps, death by cow or gold mining?

—LATimes.com

Litterbug

I get off the train in Santa Monica after four more hours of lovely public transportation. Gives me lots of time to empty my head and write out the day, I'll grant it that. Maybe Bug Crusher could be a short story...

The sun is low in the sky. The Pacific blows a cool breeze, starting its nightly battle with the baking heat. I trudge to the Santa Monica pier and walk under the famous neon sign. To my right, tank-topped hip-hop dudes dance and flip, pumping a crowd of tourists.

Right after them is Iguana Guy, Snake Guy, and Parrot Guy.

The heat has faded the poor animals, handled all day by tourists, who pay a buck for an animal selfie. It's terrible how the lowest human on the planet can make a slave of any nonhuman animal. A killer whale swimming in circles until his dorsal fin flops and he dies in a Sea World tank. Or a baby elephant ripped from her mom, bound, and shocked with cattle prods to stand on her head. Or a tiger rotting in a rusty cage in some roadside zoo. It doesn't matter – any ignorant human can torture them into slavery. Like, this poor parrot baking in the sun is intelligent and can live over a hundred years in a tropical rain forest. But to parrot guy, she's just a buck from some tourist.

As I walk by, I feel the weight of my Forever 21 bag.

Can't go all Animal Liberation, even if it's where my heart lies. Want to punch the dumb tourists who don't see how exhausted the animals are, but I've got to keep my eye on the bigger picture.

A surge of humanity climbs the incline from the pier, sweaty and stuffing themselves with corn dogs as they huff past. Tank tops and shorts for the guys, crop tops and too-tight jeans for the girls. Flesh spilling over. All climbing, climbing, climbing – to what? Looking for what?

In the middle of the incline, a bony barefoot guy wearing black pants and wrapped in a ratty blanket swoops and whirls, conducting a symphony only he can hear. Everybody ignores him. I try to focus on the setting sun, but all I can think is, as the oceans die, the toxic methane sunsets over them will be beautiful long after we're gone –

Christ. Mind still looping eights, infinitely.

Could it actually be OCD? Not taking the drugs?

A cloud of weed wafts over the packed pier. The crowd undulates around a vendor selling your-name-on-a-grain-of-rice. Caricature artists try to satirize the dazed European tourists jostling gang-bangers with white T-shirts and neck tattoos.

It all feels so random and I just want to go home. But I trudge past Bubba Gump's and the police mini-station and the neon Ferris wheel. Here, at least, couples can lean against the railing and take in the setting sun. I pass the Route 66 Last Stop Shop and then nothing but silent ocean. Last stop is right – all the human loose change has rolled as far as they can, blocked by the Pacific and left spinning endlessly in Santa Monica and Venice.

Fishermen lean on the rails, standing next to five-gallon buckets that entomb small fish. One still flops, green gills opening and closing, scales shimmering in the dying light, unnoticed on top of his dead brothers. I flash on June and her asthma attack. Any other day I would do something – pretend to trip – and knock over the bucket, swiping the little fish back into the ocean where it can swim and be free. Where it can LIVE.

But I've got a loaded gun to toss and can't afford a scene. Ashamed, I walk away until I can't hear his last hollow thumps against the plastic bucket. Why is it all so heartbreaking today?

Shakespeare wrote, *"Hell is empty and all the devils are here."*

For sure. It feels so grim and hopeless, the idea of humanity changing. And that I can start it with one swift slice to the system, if I can even muster it. Christ. Am I depressed? Maybe.

I walk to the left side of the pier and look down at the surfers skimming between the pylons. I feel a little better watching the marine layer roll in, soon to blanket the city. From this angle, with rosy sunbeams bouncing off buildings and the twinkling lights of the amusement park and the vast beach, Santa Monica looks like its postcards. Magical.

I take out the Forever 21 bag and lean on the railing, holding it over the gray sea sloshing below. Don't want to litter, but I can't exactly take out a gun and drop it in the water, the only place I can think to disappear it where it won't be found.

Instead, I just open my hand.

The bag drops sixty feet, plops into the ocean, and vanishes. Instantly, I feel a hundred pounds lighter. I keep the bullets in my backpack, so fish don't eat them and –

"You shouldn't litter, mister."

I turn and look down at a little boy with black hair and round solemn eyes. Smartly dressed in jeans and a Western shirt buttoned up to the top, he eats an ice cream cone and has chocolate smeared on his face. His mother grabs his wrist.

"Louis, leave him be." She wears tight acid-washed jeans and has lots of bangles around her wrists that jangle as she pulls Louis away.

"No. It's okay," I protest. "He's right. I shouldn't litter."

"Sorry he bother you, mister." She marches as quickly as her heels allow down the pier's uneven wood, with Louis hop-skipping alongside while still managing a lick of ice cream. He looks over his shoulder once and I wave, but he doesn't see me. I feel bad because she's so afraid of me, just some kid. And so hard on Louis, who seems like a terrific little boy. But they're brown and may be illegal and can't afford even a minor confrontation with anybody. Not with Cretin's Gestapo arresting Moms in front of their kids at school.

Such is our show-me-your-papers country now.

Suddenly, I'm totally blasted. The day has been too long and dark.

I walk back along the crowded pier, spotting Louis and his mom at "The Owl," an installation that offers a view of Santa Monica Beach. It looks like the salt-pocked telescopes you feed quarters into. But instead it shows how the coast will change from sea-level rise. They predict a two-foot rise by 2050. Ha. So optimistic, this glimpse of Santa Monica's beaches disappearing in thirty years. If only we had that much time.

I trudge up the incline surrounded by another sea, the rising sea of humanity.

Today's Headline

"Administration Cancels Limits on Marine Mammals and Sea Turtles Trapped in Fishing Nets." Good thing fish are high on our flushed anti-depressants – it'll keep them happy about all the plastic in their gut.

– LATimes.com

Stuck Again

I plod home, open the door to a quiet house, and flop on the couch.

Gigi trots over like a miniature rhino, wagging her tail, which wags her entire body. In full wriggle routine, she licks my arm hanging off the couch, greeting me like I've been gone for months. Sure feels like it.

"Hey girl, aren't you a sight for sore eyes." I heave myself up and grab her blockhead and go nose-to-nose while I scratch her jowls. It's our ritual greeting and she grunts in pleasure. I grunt in return, like Dian Fossey communicating with the gorillas. Gigi wants a walk. And it's past dinner-time for her, but no note she's been fed.

"Are you pulling a fast one, girl?" She snorts and trots into the kitchen, doing her best to convince me she's starving. She sometimes scams two dinners this way, taking advantage of our scattered schedules. "What the hell – if you eat twice, so be it."

I feed her kibble and follow her to the door. Trudged a million miles and walking Gigi is the last thing I want to do. But like cowboys take care of their horses before they feed themselves, I take care of Gigi. She deserves nothing less and –

Christ. Who will do this when I'm not here? Abandoned, Gigi won't know what's happened, she will only know GONE. Too sad, betraying all her love. Can't even think about it.

And it might not even happen at the rate I'm going.

We walk out into the minty perfume of eucalyptus trees. I carry Gigi's leash as a formality because she sticks by my side, pausing only to snuffle the smells along the dark road.

The day was a waste, for sure. But like a science experiment that fails, I can still learn something. What's the truth of this messed up day? Getting a gun is a dumb idea. No chance do I get one near Cretin. And MMA Ears' monster gun is out of the question.

What about a knife? The same metal detector problem unless you use a non-metal knife, which isn't a bad idea. Plastic, like a shiv? Ceramic? But who am I kidding? I'm not Rambo, rising out of a river with a knife in my teeth to kill bad guys. Not sure I can even shoot somebody, let alone stab them. And I'm dead way before I get near Cretin.

A car bomb? Ridiculous.

RPG to Air Force One? Ditto. That plane is a tank in the sky.

Poison? Impossible.

A drone? Put a bomb on a cheap one and wait for an outdoor speech? I'm sure they jam all signals. And I don't want to kill anybody else. Except maybe Theocrat and a few Clowns. Ha. Better watch out, I could slide right off Dad's slippery slope and end up like Cretin, a mass murderer with no logic or reason.

"How the hell do I kill the most protected person in the world, Gigi?" She wisely ignores my dark thoughts, squatting for a pee.

I've got to get close. Got to look innocent, which I do. Advantage of being an ectomorph – or if you don't see geek, guess today you see gay. Need to get past metal detectors, which rules out a gun. Unless I plant one inside, way in advance, like Sonny did in *The Godfather*. Hide it in a toilet – but I'm sure the SS sweeps the place with dogs.

My ideas are lame or come from movies, where anything is possible.

"Am I kidding myself, Gigi, David without a slingshot?" Some hero I am. Too blasted to think about it anymore. I feel like a fool on a fool's errand.

Gigi stops at a bush and sniffs the daily news from all the dogs that have peed on it. All so satisfying – snort-snort. After one look at Gigi, the dogist neighbors cross the street with their designer Labradoodles. I swear, when they shun Gigi it makes her sad. Don't they know she's the gentlest dog on the planet? Stable, as the dog trainers say.

But now, occasionally, people don't cross the street. And when their dogs get loud or aggressive, Gigi just stands there, patiently waiting for them to settle down. And they do. She changes them by her mere presence. Wish I could do the same. Be more MLK than Malcolm X. But no time for that. Back in Martin's time, the entire planet wasn't at stake. And if MLK was alive now, he would give up trying to wear them down like water on a stone. He would join radical Malcolm to save Earth, because nothing less than drastic action will work.

But I have no clue how to do it.

Will the Idea be stillborn? Locked in my head forever?

"Gigi, what am I going to do?" Gigi just looks at me and shakes her head, jowls flapping.

Wiser than me, she sniffs a patch of wildflowers.

Today's Fact

A gun was used in all four presidential assassinations and attempts. Damn. If past is prologue, I'm stuck again.

DIY!

Today in Hale's 3D printing class, Tyler wore a polo shirt with a stitched MAGA where the brand logo goes. Do they sell these? Or did he get one made by Daddy's tailor? He's also got a new haircut – buzzed around the sides, the top flopped long like a neo-Nazi.

Christ. The Brown Shirts of today dress like weirdo preppies.

"Too bad you didn't come to my party, Soy Boy. It was a rager." Tyler is talking at me, blue eyes glittering. "You could have puked on somebody."

It's funny and cruel, Tyler's specialty, and Dim and Dimmer titter. But Tyler did sort of invite me to his party. He has open houses all the time and invites everybody, which I guess is cool enough. I wonder if SG went? Haven't seen her all day. Avoiding me?

"So, what d'ya do?" Tyler takes out a piece of jerky and takes a bite, chewing loudly. Goading me. I feel like saying I went to a gun show, but it would get me flagged, instantly creating a bunch of school gossip ignited by the lighter fluid of Socials. Somebody would rat me out to counselors, who will report it to the LA County response team for troubled youth. Then a visit from detectives. Clusterfuck.

"I went down to the pier and hung out," I say. So much easier to lie with a partial truth.

"Really," Tyler draws out the word. "Playing with yourself in the arcade?"

More titters from his goons. This is sub-moronic. WTF am I doing even talking to him?

"Spanking in public?" I retort. "Is that what you're into?"

Why can't I resist his BS? Tyler's an immature sicko, like his hero Cretin. And like Cretin, he's the same leaking bucket into which he pours the entire world, trying to feel full. But you can't fill a bucket with a hole in it. Even I've figured that one out. But I haven't figured out how to avoid Tyler's endless BS and –

"I don't fap at all. I take it for real," Tyler snorts. Take it? Don't even want to know what that means.

"Wow, you're just so dope, dude." It's a lame comeback, but what can I say? I'm sure I've seen whatever he's into on the dark web. It's the reason I gave it up. He's probably a Proud Boy, never masturbating, but watching girls get ATMed for the pure degradation.

"You want a bite?" Tyler shoves the jerky in my face. I step back and stare at him. He's provoking me, but later he can say he was being friendly. <u>Sharing</u>. The strip of meat, wet from his spittle, has a label – Filet Mignon Jerky. Not calling it a cow, or even a body part. Just a BS brand.

"It's expensive," Tyler says, smirking.

"Fuck you." My blood thuds. It's such a casual troll, calling out its cost, with no idea of the suffering in his hand. The A-hole only knows, like Oscar Wilde said, the price of everything and the value of nothing.

"Fuck me? That'll be the day, Soy Boy." Tyler's face hardens. So freakish, that instant transition, like he's left his body. He starts toward me as Dim and Dimmer whoop –

"Listen up people, I've got some news." Hale strolls in. "Gather round."

Hale to the rescue before Tyler reaches me. But even Tyler knows when Hale says "listen up," what he means is shut up. And if you keep talking, you are in for a world of hurt, an interrogation where he quietly asks you why your time is more important than everybody else's. Why is what you have to say more valuable? Maybe we should all hear it if it's so exciting. Until your ears are pink and you want to "duck and cover" under your damn desk.

"We just got the new Stratasys Elite 3-D printer. Faster flow and you can remote access to monitor your projects," Hale announces.

We gather around something the size of a barbecue as Hale lifts the cover and reveals a sleek 3-D printer with a brushed aluminum case. It's bigger than our current 3D printer, which has exposed wires – T2 versus old Arnold.

"Cool," I say it out loud, startling myself. Didn't mean to say that. Meant to just think it. But the only good thing about HWB is the technology – anything for the princelings.

"Cool," Tyler snickers. Guess I'll be paying for that fuck you.

"It is cool," Hale says, eying Tyler. "A commercial machine that students your age rarely get to use. I want to see all your CAD designs before you convert to STL files."

Everybody gathers around for a closer look.

"No unauthorized projects. No sculptures. No weapons. No simple vases. I want projects that are multi-pieced. Extra credit for something that positively impacts mankind's wellbeing –"

I've stopped listening. No weapons? Like what beyond a knife? A gun? Do they exist? Could I make a 3D plastic gun? Undetectable. Cheap. And I can get close. Holy shit, that's it!

The answer sitting right in front of me this whole time.

And it definitely will positively impact mankind's wellbeing.

Today's Headline

"There Are Diseases Hidden in Ice and They Are Waking Up." Bubonic Plague and who knows what else is thawing out of the permafrost. Guess that's an example of Hale's "Known, unknown" – some horrible pandemic that kills us all. Or maybe, Godzilla?

– BBC.com

Jackpot

When class ends, I rush to Munger and sit with my back to a wall of books so nobody can look over my shoulder. I boot my laptop, pick a VPN, and type "3D printer plastic gun."

And there it is, right on the old web, video demonstrations of various weapons assembly. Earnest articles by gun nuts who dream of printing arsenals in their basement. You can even 3D print a metal AR15, but why bother when you can just buy one down the street?

And then, the exact weapon I need, a simple plastic handgun called the "Liberator" that only fires one round. But that's all I'll get to fire anyway before I'm swarmed or dead. And having only one bullet removes the temptation of lesser evils. This gun is perfect!

The Liberator – a ghost gun made from fifteen pieces of 3D printed ABS plastic that uses a small nail for a firing pin. From a CAD design called "Def-cad." Because they're, like, so cool.

The guy who designed it says his goal isn't an undetectable gun, but an "uncensorable digital one." As libertarian Cody Wilson sees it, we can make firearms into a printable file that, *"blurs the line between gun control and information censorship, blending the First and Second Amendment, demonstrating how technology renders government irrelevant."*

Holy libertarian horseshit!

"Call me crazy, but I see a world where contraband will pass underground through the data cables to be printed in our homes as the drones move over-head," Wilson actually says. *"I see a kind of poetry there … I dream of this very weird future and I'd like to be a part of it."*

Okay. I'll call you crazy, same as the Koch brothers, the greedy anti-gov libertarians who've been trashing our planet forever. Wait, now there's just one Koch left – one down, one to go!

And your future, Cody? It includes the Feds kicking down the door of Defense Distributed because an eighteen-year-old kid printed your gun and assassinated the president. With a plastic weapon that looks like a squirt gun.

The hunk of metal in the grip so detectors can spot the gun isn't even mandatory now. Not that you couldn't just take it out, but now you can legally glide through without it. Thanks, NRA!

How do I get the bullet and metal firing pin through a metal detector? I'll have to figure that out.

But this is it. A couple years ago, as an experiment, they sneaked one into a press conference for the Israeli Prime Minister. No problem.

I now have a workable weapon, David with a slingshot!

Suck it, MMA Ears.

Regulations Libertarians Hate That...

End child labor. Put seat-belts in cars. Prevent plane crashes. Eliminate lead in paint and gasoline. Stop Big Tobacco from advertising cancer. Keep bloodsuckers from selling rotten meat. Clean up our air and water. On and on, the laws that keep us from living in hell.

– Wikipedia.org

Bad Hair Boys

An epic day. Finally, getting the braces off!

What a long mess. Like Climate Chaos, procrastination doesn't work with teeth. That's a lesson I learned the hard way, wearing braces at my old age. But today, I'm sitting in the dentist's waiting room where Mom dropped me off, watching CNN on mute.

They're saying Kim Jong Un might be dead. Nobody's seen the guy, who at some point a million years ago called Cretin a Dotard – a person weak-minded from senility. Almost as good a name as Cretin...

What if Cretin is just senile, shitting his pants with the world watching? Should I feel sorry for him? No. Even if the guy driving the car runs you over is demented – like the Old who killed all those people at the Santa Monica Farmers Market – you're still dead. We're still dead.

On TV, they're showing vintage footage of Cretin and Kim – all fatty bluster and bizarre hair. Like two drowning men grabbing each other to say afloat, disinforstracting us from the Kleptocracies they build, the people they torture, the planet they destroy. Threatening each other with nuclear bombs – kids in a schoolyard – neither giving a thought to the borderless climate bomb whistling down on us all.

It's so messed up, nobody separating the signal from the noise.

But Cretin's cruel conduct isn't just noise – it's the ongoing and deliberate murder of nature. Today, he lifted Obama's closure of Arctic waters to drilling. It's home to thousands of Orcas, like the one who just carried her dead calf for two weeks, grieving. Two weeks! They gestate for 17 months and her baby only lived an hour. So, she grieved and suffered like elephants do, more human than some humans.

Why don't we grieve all the animal death we cause? What's wrong with us for destroying their habitat? Nobody owns our planet – we only borrow it from the Universe. Even the richest bloodsuckers are only passing through, mere renters, no matter how much land they buy.

Sorry Octo-Jeff, even you – the richest man in the damn world, with your Amazon logo sneer as the real Amazon burns – will die. No matter how much you spend not to. So why not donate all your money to save the rainforest who's name you stole and is keeping us all alive? Because, I repeat, you will die!

I mean, it even looks like Kim Jong Un has kicked the bucket.

Will Cretin grieve his buddy Kim? Ha. Has he ever grieved anything? How could he? Only a sociopath with a tar pit for a heart intentionally trashes our planet for every future generation. Cretin can't feel a thing.

Why won't Cretin just join his dead frenemy? Save me all this trouble.

I'm not even sure any of it matters. Today, more research showing Cretin's constant attacks might be shooting a planet that's running dead, as insignificant as stabbing a corpse.

Still, it's a vile defile. Not going to just stand around and watch.

I'm so tired of recording that dinosaur's daily desecration. I can't wait to stop thinking these grotesque thoughts. All TV reality shows, even with nukes and creepy hair, get canceled.

With my plastic gun, I'm going to permanently fire his ass.

And smile a brace-less smile.

Proof Cretin's A Sociopath

After thousands died on 9/11, he couldn't resist lying that his building was now the tallest in New York. As if I needed more proof.

– RollingStone.com

Letter to Libertarians

Found the CAD design for the Liberator and downloaded it. So great to actually start concrete action!

Got to love you crazy libertarians who think Gov is the problem and want to make plastic guns in your basements to fight THE MAN. While corporate libertarians fight to make us all see the air we breathe.

Why don't any of you care if our rivers catch fire, like the Cuyahoga in Cleveland in the 60s? Don't you like fresh air and water? Why do you only care about stirring up anti-gov "freedom" trollery?

I call BS on that BS. It's about your greed, not your freedom.

Because everything you do is trying to destroy the one thing powerful enough – We-The-People – to stop you from sodomizing Mother Earth.

But don't you know, Cody Wilson, that you're a puppet? That it's Wall Street hedge fund money that stokes your "don't tread on me" anti-regulation crap? Money that stacks to the moon and back and turns politicians into dancing monkeys controlled by organ grinder plutos?

I'd worry about the blood money that sets the world on fire and watches it burn just to make more money. Worry about the rights of the individual trampled to <u>increase crony corporate power</u>, as they swallow governments whole. Worry about that as you make your plastic gun, Cody.

Which I love, BTW.

And for the working people of Cretinstan who get none of that money, including you old white dudes in some kind of Stockholm Syndrome with Cretin – the big libertarian bloodsuckers aren't your friend. They just want to feed off you, the strong eating the weak, without interference. They want to treat your commons like their personal toilet. If they had their way, they'd go back to diluting your children's milk with formaldehyde like they used to, I kid you not.

You need current proof libertarians don't care if you live or die? Okay. Purdue Pharma, owned by the Sack-of-shit-Sacklers, made billions selling you Oxy. They knew it was addictive, even as they mega-marketed you the plague. So now 174 of you die every day. TODAY. With millions more hooked, like poor old Bug Crusher. Without the Gov you hate as a counterweight to stop them, the killers will keep on killing – YOU.

Koch Industries – one brother left! – are the biggest libertarian killers.

Hey Charles Koch, you're worth 45 billion dollars after inheriting Daddy's company that built oil refineries for Hitler. Christ, Hitler at the bottom of everything again, even Douche Bank, Cretin's favorite place to borrow money and not pay it back –

Stop! I don't want to digress from your crimes, Charles. Because you stack the courts with judges who vote against environmental laws. You break the legs of agencies and jeer at them for not walking. You phony philanthropy a tiny fraction of your fortune to put your name on ballet centers – guess that's how you sleep at night – while raising billions to buy senators who vote to kill the planet. As Cretin disinforstracts everybody, you vampire Mother Earth, stripping her of beauty and bounty.

Hey Charles, you'll die soon. Do you ever consider you have a sickness? That you've won a game nobody else is playing? That with the second largest private company in America, the money you extracted from our commons – oil, gas, timber – could go to preventing human extinction? What's stopping you from pure altruism in your final days??

Don't you have any damn grandchildren?

I think these are fair questions, Charles. You might want to dig deep and answer them instead of supporting Cretin as he destroys the very idea of a common destiny that binds us.

I really don't get you and your type. Does this really bring you joy?

No way – I'm not buying what you're selling. You hide your sickness behind your libertarian philosophy, but I think deep down you know that it's just BS to keep the status quo. If you don't, here's a reality check:

In cementing our inequality, you're as clueless as Marie Antoinette.

She built a farm inside the Palace of Versailles and play-acted being a peasant, still surrounded by the comforts of a royal lifestyle. She even had sweaty laborers on her fantasy farm sprayed with perfume, while the real peasants starved. Let them eat cake!

Ha. That's some old-school trolling – until they decapitated her.

So, Charles, you might want to do some good in your final years, just for your own self-preservation. Spread the money around and stop killing our commons. Maybe even have a Scrooge about-face and become generous for future generations. You'll feel better and be happier, I promise.

But the party's over – what goes around comes around. We-The-People are coming for you with guillotines. And if we don't get you, if you check out before you pay for your sins, that would be a damn shame. Because the Climate Chaos you created will get us. It's everybody's guillotine.

Let them eat cake – Cretin and Koch.

Vivre La Revolucion! – Me and Mother Earth.

I watch a video of a guy shooting the Liberator. With it, I can get close enough to take the law into my own hands.

Now there's some damn libertarianism for you, Charles.

Today's Reality Check

Lots of you anti-Gov jokers made your fortunes off basic Gov research and investment, including radio, telephone, electricity. The Internet. GPS, Google, Siri, Tesla, touchscreens – everything that makes our smart tech smart! It's your dirty little secret... Plus, you depend on the commons. Like roads. And the police so your trucks don't get hijacked. And the military to do the same for the country. Why so cheap and ungrateful?

– History.org

Falling

In the car with Mom and June, coming from Klein for OCD meds I won't take. I'd like to have the satisfaction of quitting him like Nichols, but it'll all be over by my next monthly appointment anyway.

"How's it going?" Klein asks while he writes the prescription, not looking at me.

"All good." I don't want to talk to him any more than he wants to talk to me.

"Super." He hands me the script. What a great doctor, a real healer. He comes highly recommended, which is how Mom and Dad fall for his malpractice – they try so hard to give us the best of everything. And I turn my back on it all... Christ. It's so unfair to them.

Now we're heading to a place called Rockreation, a climbing gym that's June's second home. Mom's joking about being our chauffeur, carting me to shrink appointments and June to karate practice and Rockreation.

"You should put Benji to work now that he's got his license," June needles. "You'd love that, wouldn't you? Driving me all over the place."

"It's my life dream." June laughs and Mom smiles. It makes me sad. Now that I have a blueprint for a weapon, every good moment feels like the last. As the Idea morphs into the Plan...

The climbing gym has rubber floors and fake walls with colorful holds that mimic real rock. It's loud and echoes with oldies songs – *Eye of the Tiger* pumps up the climbers now. Seems weird, so different from how I imagine climbing out in the still wilderness, surrounded by trees and light. The closest this place gets are posters of climbers stuck on the walls of El Cap like bugs on flypaper, the dizzying view of Yosemite Valley below. Everything's a simulacrum these days.

I sit on the floor writing, occasionally glancing at June scampering squirrel-fast up the walls. She's strapped in a rope and a self-belay line that she never needs. Mom's outside on a Happy Hat phone call to Amazon Support. Goodbye, three hours –

"Hey Benji," June calls down to me. "Look. No hands."

She releases her hands for a second and then slips off the top –

"JUUNNNE!" I scream and charge the wall. Her little body tumbles. Got to get under her, got to save –

Then the rope catches. She hangs upside down like damn Spiderman, nose-to-nose with me. She giggles and pats me on the head.

"Gotcha." She spins around and smiles her little gap-toothed smile. I'm so relieved and mad and filled with love, I just grab her and hug her for a long moment.

"Don't ever do that again," I say fiercely. "Ever."

"Aw, Benji, don't cry," she says, hugging me back. "I'm sorry."

But I'm sniffling a bit, more from relief than anything – we already almost lost June. But now, it will be the Plan that will destroy her. She'll never recover, never be the same person, never have a normal life. She'll always be the sister of <u>that</u> guy. It's so unfair – I'm sacrificing the rest of her childhood. But what future do any kids have after Cretin and his Clowns finish murdering the planet? What future do any of us have in the face of such destruction? We'll all be as dead as the climbers thawing on Everest because now even that glacier is melting –

"You look so sad," June says. "Can't ya take a joke?"

"Good one. You got me good." I quickly wipe my eyes and crack a smile. Probably look like Frankenstein's monster trying to grin, but I don't want her to worry.

"What's going on with you?" June tugs on her climbing harness. She's spotted me lying again.

"Nothing," I respond, as nonchalant as I can muster. Maybe I should bring June into the Plan, as her normal life will be over anyway. Could I do that to her? What —

"Really? You're acting so weird lately." She won't let it go without an explanation. But I can't say I'm feeling sad about the impact of the Plan to kill the president on my innocent family.

"Just writing something a bit dark. I'm a little preoccupied."

"Maybe you should give it a break before you go all perma-Eilish."

I laugh and tousle her hair. "Maybe."

Got to be way more careful. June's observant and knows me too well. Better than Mom and Dad and the shrinks, who don't have a clue as I do my thing and crank out the A-plusses.

"What's going on?" Mom or Dad asks occasionally.

"All good." The same standard reply I give to Klein. And they accept it. What can go wrong with a kid like me, who's never been in a bit of trouble? But I've got to watch myself with June.

Especially as I make my plastic gun.

Today's Headline

"Administration Sells Off Drilling and Mining Rights in the Arctic Wildlife Refuge." The rights are not reversible, even after I kill him. But neither is his death.

— NYTimes.com

Theocrat

Theocrat, Cretin's wooden dummy totem pole VP, was in the news to-day for something hilarious he said in 2000: *"Smoking doesn't kill. In fact, two out of every three smokers doesn't die from a smoking-related illness."*

Ha. Bad grammar, bad thinking. On the year I was born.

Theocrat also said stuff like, *"big government disguised as do-gooder healthcare"* is a *"greater scourge than cigarettes."*

So, in Theocrat's Christian morality, it's better to sell cancer than help people live. Christ... Or, more accurately, anti-Christ.

Theo's been a fundamentalist corporate tool forever. He pushed the Koch's "No Climate Tax Pledge" through in 2009, forcing candidates to promise not to spend <u>any</u> tax money on limiting carbon pollution. WTF?

"Have a Koch and a smile," is Theo's motto. He's as responsible for the end of the world as a person can be, helping the GOP – Greed Over People! – push venal to a whole other level. No wonder Cretin felt so comfortable taking over the party and naming Theo VP.

They all made their authoritarian bargain beds and will die in them.

But foot soldier Theo, Big Oil's lapdog, is quietly insane against the planet. Cretin's a carnival of madness. Plus, that toadying toad is just too joyless and weird to get elected after I eliminate Cretin.

It's the raving, rabid top dog I've got to put down.

Sorry dogs, some metaphors are irresistible.

The Plan, Part One

Today I'm nervous, sitting with Gigi in the garden. A strange feeling to have in a normally peaceful refuge from the world.

I stare at the CAD design for the Liberator. So far, it's all been theoretical. Sure, I bought a Glock for five minutes, but I got rid of that just by opening my hand. To build a gun in school under the nose of a guy like Hale – that's dangerous as hell. If I get –

Whoa. A ladybug just landed on my arm. It tucks translucent wings under its red shell. A shiny shellacked jewel, with black dots and a black helmet, it explores the forest of my arm hair. So beautiful that I forget my CAD design – staring, lost.

Seconds? Hours?

Until out go the shells, splitting halves of a Volkswagen Beetle, magically levitating her up into the orange tree. A wink from nature itself saying don't be afraid. Help me. Speak for me.

From bug club in kindergarten, ladybugs, the hummingbirds of insects, have been my favorite. They eat crop-destroying pests like aphids – no Monsanto Roundup cancer needed. Don't see many around, done in by pesticides like chlorpyrifos that Cretin wants to reintroduce. It's a banned nerve gas that inhibits fetus and baby brain development, causing lower IQs. But hey, Cretin likes low IQ voters! So why not start turning embryos into zombies?

Christ, why is Cretin on the dark side of everything?

Because Dow Chemical, the Chlorpyrifos maker who brought the world napalm, gave a million bucks to his crooked inaugural committee. And as long as there's a cheesy party filled with adulation for him, Cretin is happy to sell anything not nailed down, brain-damaged kids be damned. Luckily, California banned it again, which forced Dow to take it off the market. Power of the Nation State – and the world's breadbasket.

Why do I keep creating justifications? I've already made my lists. Taken on the moral duty to revolt against our own extinction. Why keep making my pitch to a hostile world? But new reasons pop up <u>every day</u> –

Make the gun!

I focus on the Liberator's CAD design downloaded from Pirate Bay. Hard to believe it's made from just fifteen printed pieces of plastic, none of which looks like a gun. Or even part of one. So theoretically, I can print them under the nose of somebody as smart as Hale. But what if he wants to check the full design?

Back when we were fellow prisoners in middle school, Tim told me the way he shoplifts expensive crap is he buys something cheap to distract the cashier. Be friendly during checkout and they don't think you're a thief because you're a casual customer. And then he proved it right in CVS with a pack of gum and an electric razor.

Can I apply the same principle? Make something legit and hide the Liberator pieces in the design? Seems risky. How dumb would it be to get busted making a plastic gun in high school to kill the president? Stopped in the starting blocks and spending forever in jail while Cretin keeps on destroying the planet? That would suck. Especially by Hale, who I like.

Guess that's another person I'll betray – the cost of changing the world. Is that even true? Sounds glib. Am I sliding down the slipperiest BS slope, my road to hell paved with good intentions? As true-believer spooky as that Theranos founder with the weird voice and unblinking eyes I met after the science competition? She freaked me out. But am I like her? Obsessing about the mission, truth and ethics be damned?

Christ, I hope not.

Killing Cretin has to be the masterstroke that changes everything.

It's just got to be!

The shoplifting idea is the only one I've got. Need a printing project with lots of pieces to hide the fifteen Liberator bits. Something innocent I can make right out in the open.

A toaster pops into my head. Innocent. Lots of little moving parts – that could work. I can pull my gun pieces as they print and shoplift them past Hale while the toaster gets constructed.

That's how I'll make my gun, hide it in plain sight.

Today's Fact

The chemical industry gives $100,000 a year to every single clown in congress. Meanwhile, the bald eagle can't reproduce because runaway chemical pollution has destroyed their sperm count. Humans to follow.

– ScienceDaily.com

The Zombie Apocalypse

I pitched my toaster idea to Hale today and had an existential setback...

"Is it sublime or ridiculous?" Hale stares at me, his best student. "Ambitious. Lots of moving parts that need to fit together seamlessly. But it's a toaster."

"I know it's not super cool."

"It's a lot of tech to build something frivolous."

"But think about this." I've practiced my pitch. "Someday, you live in a desert and you can't get a toaster because of the zombie apocalypse. All you want is a nice piece of toast to remember bygone days. Now you can build it. It's the little things in life that make it worth living."

I thought up this bit to get a laugh and Hale obliges.

"Good luck downloading toaster STLs during a zombie apocalypse. But if you insist."

"I might need some extra time," I put it there out casually. Have to print a toaster. And a gun.

"You got it." He leans back in his chair. "How's everything else going?"

"Not bad," I say, taking the invitation to linger. "I've been thinking about our discussion after class. Subjective versus objective reality."

"We kind of left that hanging." Hale smiles easily. "Thoughts?"

"Guess I've been wondering if I see the world as it is or as I am." Does SG see me? Do I see her? Moot. Damn...

"'For there is nothing good or bad, but thinking makes it so?'"

"Yeah. Hamlet," I say, surprised. Hale's impressive – who am I if not

Hamlet trying to make a life or death decision? "Exactly."

"What do you think?"

"I think I see the world as I am. How could it be any other way?"

"It can't, not for perceiver dependent reality like color or sounds. Or social constructs like money. But it doesn't mean perceiver <u>independent</u> reality doesn't exist, like say, an ocean. We just have to keep wiping our doors of perception clean to see it in all its infinite glory."

"Blake." He's paraphrasing Blake. "You're like a quote factory."

"We might have a few things in common besides a love of science."

"Yeah. So how do you wipe your doors of perception clean?"

"Science experiments. Meditation. Certain drugs – not for you," he jokes. Ha, too late. "Anything that helps you to see through your conditioning to realization, capital R."

I nod appreciatively – totally know what Hale's talking about. Molly and meditation. Oneness with all. Love. Not the addictive drugs we take to numb all our national trauma. The real thing that gets you THERE.

"Do you believe in free will?" I ask. "Since we can't control that conditioning?"

"Whatever we inherit – biological, familial, societal – is a roll of the dice." Hale shrugs. "But isn't that the journey of life, to see through the bonds of that conditioning?"

"To become free?"

"To wake up." Hale smiles again. "Few can. It's hard to even know you're asleep."

I nod. Reality. Do I see it? Am I the only one willing to act on it?

"Thanks, Mr. Hale," I say, off to build a gun and face the ultimate reality.

"My door is always open."

"Your doors of perception?"

"On good days." He laughs. "Once in a while."

An hour later, Tyler passes me in the hallway with Dim and Dimmer.

"Soy Boy," Tyler sneers. Just seeing him brings me down. I suddenly imagine Tyler in a few years. Like the Kochs, he'll supply the money, manipulating behind the scenes – a business, a government, a think tank – anything that allows him to impose his will on ordinary people.

"Hear about the Libtard that just shot up Congress?" Tyler is saying. I'm off Twitter, so I haven't heard about today's daily mass shooting. Tyler's saying it's on a bunch of the Clown Cult Congress playing baseball in Arlington, Virginia.

"And the guy who did it was a Bernie Bro," Tyler finishes with a grin of satisfaction. Guess he thinks it's more ammunition against his mortal enemy. Me.

"Anybody die?" I try to sound casual, but my stomach is sinking.

"Nah, the loser couldn't even get that right," Tyler says. "Probably never shot a gun before. This is what happens when they allow shitty comedians to hold up a decapitated president's head. Or lame versions of Julius Caesar dressed as our leader. It gives losers ideas."

"Julius Caesar is an anti-assassination play," I retort, trying to hide an onslaught of anxiety. "You'd know that if you read it. Or even read the Spark notes."

"They made the actor look like the president," Tyler hisses. "And then they stabbed him. It shouldn't be allowed."

"Speech isn't violence. Violence is violence." Guess I'll prove that soon enough. "A play about war isn't a war. Even you should know that."

"It's you Libtards who're trying to start a war," Tyler crows. "One you'll lose."

Tyler has no clue he's talking to a revolutionary plotting a revolution even as he speaks. But I can't debate him about *Julius Caesar* or comedians or the fake decapitated heads of Cretin used as fodder in the culture wars. What's happening in the real world of bullets? It's this that affects the Plan. The level of security I'll face. Even the effectiveness of killing Cretin. Everything!

I rush to Munger and pull up CNN. Tyler's right. The guy who shot up the baseball field before Capital police killed him was a Bernie supporter. He was anti-Cretin and anti-Clown and is now dead.

Is this how I end up? My stomach is inside out.

This is a whole new reality.

Today's Definition

Heckler's Veto = Cancel Culture. Guess I'm the ultimate Heckler's Veto to Cretinstan. That sucks. But what choice do I have? I mean, Cretin is already trying to manipulate and suppress this election like he did the last.

Irony Banquet

The guy was angry. He shot across his neighbor's lawn with a gun. He was a violent domestic abuser – still the best predictor of gun violence besides torturing animals. He had foster girls he dragged around by their hair and who knows what else. He was furious about what the Clown Cult Congress does in the dark.

That last one sounds familiar. Is he me? Hope not, but maybe a little?

The right wing Clowns instantly start their BS about how violence isn't the answer and how we all need to come together. Nobody talks about Cretin's policy violence. Or how the Clowns enjoy platinum <u>government</u> health insurance as they try to cut 20 million people with preexisting conditions. They kill at rates mass shooters can only dream about, but they're shocked, *shocked*, when somebody wants to stop them by any means necessary?

Irony must be dead.

Of course, all of them have an A+ rating from the NRA. So, even as the Clowns get shot, their corruption overwhelms their self-preservation. Kind of like how they support Big Oil as Climate Chaos kills us.

That's a damn irony banquet. Almost as good as an anti-gun vegan using the Second Amendment he hates to kill a pro-gun president.

Irony jackpot!

The guy shot worst is a leader of the Clown Cult who rubber stamps Cretin on everything, including climate denial. What does he care? Shot Guy gets personal security, even as he votes to swamp the country with guns. And the policewoman who runs into a hail of bullets from one of those guns to kill the shooter is gay and black. Does Shot Guy give a damn about the gay, black woman who saves his life? Hell no. He had to "apologize" for a speech he gave to David Duke's Nazis back in the day.

And yet she saves him. Oh, the irony.

"You came through for me, I'm gonna come through for you," Cretin promised the NRA after their 30-million-dollar donation in 2016. The Baseball Shooter knew this crooked game. He posted a cartoon of a "Bill" saying, *"Corporations write the bill and then bribe Congress until it becomes law."*

And up next? The Clowns are voting to legalize silencers. Silencers! Can't we just call BS on the Second Amendment, 27 words of pure "huh?"

"A well regulated Militia, being necessary to the security of a free State, the right of the people to keep and bear Arms, shall not be infringed."

What's that even mean in today's world?

Am I dreaming anything ever changes? Or will the swamps always be swamping? Haters hating? Rapists raping? I don't know. Without Cretin cheerleading his Clowns to deeper levels of depravity, will they wake up and stop setting their own world on fire?

I can only hope. Can't kill them all...

Today everybody is saying you shouldn't fight fire with fire, that it just feeds it. But as my state burns from the worst wildfires ever recorded, firefighters set containment blazes all over the place.

Turns out, you <u>do</u> fight fire with fire.

With the Liberator, I've got my match. Do I dare strike it?

Today's headline

"Annually, 45,000 Deaths Linked to Lack of Health Insurance." Did I miss something? Have they made murder legal in America? Guess just for the Clown wing of congress.

— TheGuardian.com

Men on Fire

Working on converting my toaster CAD to STL, hiding the Liberator pieces in it.

And trying not to throw up at CNN, which blanket covers the mass shooting – they make for such good TV. And now comes more fake unity and pretty words. Now the Clown Cult Congress pledges a bunch of Kumbaya BS about "getting along" with the other side. Even Cretin has a momentary lapse and can read a few lines from a teleprompter.

"We are strongest when we are unified and when we work together for the common good." Read like a toddler by the man who does nothing but divide us for evil.

It's total BS, but today, I don't know. Suddenly, I'm plagued by doubt.

Shakespeare's *Julius Caesar* is bugging me out. Brutus assassinated Caesar to save Rome but ended up destroying the Republic. Madness. Civil war. Blood in the streets. Is this what I'll bring? If a leader of the Clown Cult getting shot doesn't change their minds about guns, what does?

Fifty people dead? More kids killing kids? It's coming.

But even if I cut the head off the monster, will people wake up in time to save our planet? Or will we all keep running around like poor decapitated chickens until we drop dead?

Today, I've got no idea. Writing isn't helping me see through it – all so confusing for a formerly peaceful person. But what else can I do?

Can't be like that Buddhist monk Thich Quang Duc, who burned himself alive in downtown Saigon to protest the repression of Buddhists. It worked; he brought down the whole South Vietnamese government.

That picture of him sitting in full lotus position, on fire but not moving a muscle, that rocked me – the sheer internal power of him.

Is that kind of sacrifice the answer? Could I do that?

No. I don't have that monk's courage or power.

And it doesn't always work. During Vietnam, this Quaker guy, Norman Morrison, set himself on fire outside the Pentagon to protest the war. But he made no difference. Nothing changed. Maybe because there was no picture – got to have an image to make it real.

A world of cameras will record Cretin's death. Will it make a difference? Will I bring down a government? Or will I be an ignored footnote because I fail?

"Pollution ravages our planet, oozing inhabitability via air, soil, water, and weather. Most humans on the planet now breathe air made unhealthy by fossil fuels, and many die early deaths as a result — my early death by fossil fuel reflects what we are doing to ourselves."

That's the actual suicide note left by David Buckel, a lawyer who set himself on fire in Brooklyn last year. Talk about commitment. And he got the situation right – but no picture, so no impact.

I don't know. Ben Franklin said impeachment beats assassination, but who will ever convict Cretin? Not his Clown Cult in the senate. So, what else can I do with this tyrant destroying the world?

But will anything, even killing Cretin, have an impact?

I'm having epic doubts.

Today's Headline

"Overfishing Has Wiped Out 96% Of Pacific Bluefin Tuna." What do they expect using mile-wide nets for sushi, tossing billions of dead "by-catch," including 300,00 dolphins a year? Massacre takes no holidays.

– Vox.com.

Dogs of War

"An attack on one of us is an attack on all of us. For all the noise and fury, we are a family. Show the country, show the world that we are one House. The people's House, united in our humanity. It is that humanity which will win the day. It always will."

More fine words from the Republican head of the Clown Cult about the attack on his fellow dinosaurs. I have no idea how he says this with a straight face. He sells his humanity every day.

But to be honest, I really want it to be true – that we learn to swim in the deepest sea of our own humanness. That we all come together. When has violence ever done that? Never.

And what about Newton's Third Law – for every action, there's an equal and opposite reaction? What will be the reaction when I kill Cretin? Martyrdom? War? Antony's speech clangs in my head like Roman armor, *"Infants quartered with the hands of war. Men groaning for burial."*

Christ. Is this what I'll unleash? Can I even risk it?

Should I give up the Plan? I'm bugging out!

Maybe violence isn't the answer. Especially if the climate bullet is in the air. Besides, Cretin's no Julius Caesar, he's the other Italians, like Mussolini or that corrupt "Bunga Bunga" guy – both elected. Or Caligula...

No, he's Nero! Another insecure paranoid who was obsessed with fame. Except Cretin fiddles while the world burns.

But killing him won't wake people up from their tribal trance. It won't stop the bloodsuckers from sucking. Instead, killing him will, *"Cry Havoc and let slip the dogs of war."*

Christ – what a line and an insult to dogs. A pack of humans is way more dangerous. And the clueless planet-killing pack in the CCC is the most dangerous of all. So cowardly, murdering with a pen. At least when you shoot somebody it takes some balls and you're honest about what you're doing. BUT SO WHAT?

If I kill Cretin, I'm no better than the Roman Senators who stabbed Caesar in the back. No better than the Baseball Shooter. And I might have the same impact. <u>Nothing</u>. Except to start a civil war, distracting everybody while Earth dies. Maybe even contributing to her death –

No, no, no. I'm so sick of living with the end of the world.

So sick and so tired.

Besides, half the country voted for Cretin, so isn't he just a symptom of our illness? I mean, that pedophile banned from malls in Alabama for stalking children barely lost his senate race – if we can beat a pedophile by one point, we can do anything! Ha. But the Cretin disciples mainlining Cretin State News are this same tribe of morally depraved Olds. Dumb as turkeys voting for Thanksgiving, but deciding climate policy and if we all live or die. You can say Cretin lost the popular vote by 3 million votes because of a gerrymandered Electoral College against the will of the people – blah, blah, blah. But half the country voted for him! They'll still be here after Cretin is gone. As will the Clown Cult Congress.

Where do you even start with people who don't value Earth?

Is killing Cretin going to change their values? No.

So why ruin my life? And Mom, Dad, and June's? It's not their fault or mine. I'm just a kid. I didn't destroy the planet. And I don't want to kill anything. Even Cretin, with the too-close eyes of an idiot, must have somebody who loves him. Maybe his gold digger wife. Or porn avatar daughter he wants to diddle. Or his boys with their low foreheads and hair slicked back like villains in 80s movies – so small and stupid – with their dreams of riding Daddy's coattails to more power.

But maybe I've got it wrong. Maybe they're all victims, trapped in a family version of the Stockholm syndrome. Maybe growing up with Cretin's abusive craziness makes what's happening seem sane and normal.

And if killing Cretin doesn't change a thing, why mangle myself so I can never again sleep without drugs? Best-case scenario. Most likely, I die. For <u>nothing</u> – too late, or nobody cares, or they care for a minute before moving on to the next disinforstraction.

No, no, no. I'm not doing it.

Somebody else can defend us from Cretin and the Clown's corrupt madness. It's a stable overflowing with shit and I'm no Hercules.

Whew. It feels so good to abort this secret plan growing inside me like a deformed fetus. Sick of it kicking me in the gut all day long – so burnt out I feel crazy. Could sleep for a week if I could just sleep.

No. It's time to pull the plug while there's still time. I'll just ride it out like Slim Pickens going down with that nuke in *Dr. Strangelove*. Just go to college and whoop it up for End Times. Just live in denial like everybody else until the great dying begins.

The climate won't kill me today, so screw it. We have the sociopath we deserve, who reflects us the most. What right do I have to shoot him, no matter how ignorant and greedy he is?

What a relief to go back to being myself, a teenager. Innocent.

"Useless, useless." John Wilkes Booth's last words. Voice of experience.

Over and out, I'm done. No Heckler's Veto.

Not going to kill Cretin.

Today's Headline

"Administration Dooms Future by Gutting National Environmental Policy Act." This will allow Cretin's Gov to approve pipelines and power plants without considering climate change. Not my problem anymore.

—Missoulian.com

Gone to The Dogs

Wow. A full night's rest and I feel transformed. Lucid! Like chemicals aren't corroding my brain. The sleep of the innocent, I guess.

Nice to feel like me again.

Plus, it's Saturday, and we're all in the car going down to Huntington Dog Beach. Mom and Dad are in front, and me and June are in the back, with Gigi dozing between us. June reaches over and tries to tickle my ear as I write this. I give her the hairy eyeball and she laughs. So great not to be alone in my head today. All-day, every day – plotting. Done!

This is a rare family outing, what with Dad working all the time. But yesterday Dad quit his latest TV show. He's an excellent editor and is steady as a coal miner going into the dark rooms, working Herculean hours. So, his latest producer must be a real walking pustule for him to quit – a ball of ego and bad behavior Dad can no long ignore. And he can ignore a lot, keeping his head down, grinding out the shows below the line. Dad never allows himself to get sick or expects life to be fair or easy. He never complains when bloodsuckers renege after promising him directing gigs if he'll edit their all-important first season. Dad went to Cornell – Ivy League, but not a bragging one – and never mentions it. He wrote and directed a super scary short film but isn't enough of a Cretin to turn it into a career before he has me, screwing up his life plan. Dad just doesn't have the BS gene. In middle school, I didn't like him much – he just wasn't fun. But now I respect him. He's humble and talented and stoic as Seneca – the philosopher who said, *"Rest satisfied with what you have, which is sufficient."*

And we do, as Dad mans up so we can have a great life if we watch our dollars. Which we also do.

I stare out the window. As relieved as Dad is to quit his job, that's how relieved I am to quit the Plan, happy not to be betraying everything he stands for and every sacrifice he makes. Thrilled to be heading down to the simple pleasure of the dog beach in Orange County. It's lame that LA. County has endless sand and no dog beaches, but today I'm even enjoying the hour ride with the family. In celebration of Dad quitting, it's Dukes for lunch, so we're all in a good mood. Some famous surfer opened it at the pier and it has a great vibe, despite having nothing vegan except a black bean nacho plate, hold the cheese. Oh, well...

We park and get out.

Not really a beach day, but we're here for Gigi, who wriggles with excitement. Perfect weather for her because it's chilly, and the marine layer hasn't burned off, so the breeze has a bite to it. Short-snouters like Gigi don't do well in the heat. Some airlines won't even ship a boxer or pit down below because if they get stuck on the tarmac they can die quicker than a baby in a hot car. No wonder people stick service vests on their pets to get them into a plane's cabin. Who can blame them? Gigi's a member of the family, not damn luggage!

Everybody loves their dogs – even bloodsuckers.

Except Cretin. He doesn't have a dog or cat in his life. He's got no feeling for the beautiful otherness of our fellow animals. No desire to be stewards of their planet. No kinship from bringing an abandoned dog or cat back to life and feeling their unconditional love, a close and wordless bond. And none of the thrill as they help you discover your own heart.

Cretin's got NOTHING to give because all he does is take, take, take.

Stop obsessing! The Plan is dead, so bury it.

Will I ever get him out of my head? Will I ever be happy again? Is this the depression stage of grief? But I'm not wrong about animals...

"I am in favor of animal rights as well as human rights. That is the way of a whole human being." Abraham Lincoln knew if you don't love animals, you might be an unholy sociopath, a damn Cretin who sees animals and their habitats as objects to exploit.

I mean, aren't other species shouting by their mere presence that the planet isn't just for humans? And so maybe we shouldn't bulldoze their wild spaces to build another stupid golf course? Or cage and disease critters from feedlots in Chicago to wet markets in China – where they eat their cats and dogs and endangered animals because I guess the SARS pandemic wasn't bad enough? FUCK! Zoonosis!

Can't think about it with Gigi dozing and using my leg as a pillow. Too painful, all those dead dogs, millions a year that they eat.

A dog might change Cretin's life. But I wouldn't trust him with one.

Look at how he treats humans.

Today's Headline

"Half of Plant and Animal Species at Risk of Extinction due to Climate Change." Guess I can terminate this list of daily misery. But like all bad habits, it's tough to quit.

– WWF.org

On the Beach

Gigi waggles down the stairs to the beach. Totally over her initial fear of all the loose dogs, she now loves the pure fun of Dog World.

Dad and I wait as June and Mom hit the public bathrooms with their metal prison toilets and shit smears. Gigi knows the routine and sits with us, eying the dogs that stroll by.

"How's it going?" Dad asks. "Bet you're glad to lose the braces."

"Sure am." I'm happy to keep it light with Dad.

"Make any decisions yet? On schools?" Dad tries for casual because he hopes I go to Cornell, even though he'd never say so. But Mom and Dad met at Cornell, before the movie bug bit him, infecting him for life, so he's sentimental. "Don't mean to hound you."

"It's okay, Dad," I say, patting him on the shoulder.

I was leaning toward Princeton for the writing or MIT for the science. But now that I'm not going to die or attend University of Penitentiary, I feel a surge of love and a sudden desire to make Dad happy. What a relief to be an ordinary person, thinking healthy thoughts, with typical plans! And it really doesn't matter to me.

"I'm thinking Cornell after all –"

"No kidding?" Dad grins like a cactus blooming in one of those time-lapse videos. "I think it's perfect for you. The mountains up there are beautiful. And the lake is pristine. Plenty of nature for rambling."

Mom comes out of the bathroom and Dad throws an arm around her.

"Honey, Benji's going to Cornell."

"Really? I think you'll love it. They just got a couple of new novelists teaching next year."

I smile and nod. It feels great not to be lying – I'm going to college! But I also feel weird, like I'm naked without the Plan.

June rockets out the other bathroom.

"Whew, that was sooo gross. I mean, DISGUSTING." She announces to the world. "Smells like something died in there."

June notices me right away, with my fake smile. And Mom and Dad with their real grins.

"What's going on?" June squints at me. "You look like you just came out of that toilet."

"I just told Mom and Dad I'm going to Cornell."

"I thought you liked Princeton." June is always in my business.

"Changed my mind." I turn away, feeling queasy lying to her. "Come on, Gigi."

I walk ahead to avoid June's interrogation. The dog beach is the happiest place on the planet for me, but I suddenly feel like it's the last time I'll be here. Why? I've given up the Plan. What the hell is wrong with me?

But I feel so strange, like… nostalgic for this moment, <u>as it passes</u>.

Is there a term for this weird déjà vu? Probably in German. They have all the great words that boil concepts down – Schadenfreude!

Or is this undertow just a horrible residue of the Plan? Of letting it go? Is this "acceptance?" Christ, it would be terrible if I never came here again with my family. What a gut punch.

Denial, anger, bargaining, depression – give it a break. I'm free! I try to shake it off. I'll be back again. Many times. I stop and wait for my family.

We walk the beach, watching the frolicking dogs do their dog dance. Surfers do the human version, playing on the waves. I inhale the breeze as Mom and Dad hold hands. June does cartwheels and Gigi stands, tail wagging, trying to get something started with other dogs. She has good luck at this beach because it has a lot of Hispanics who love the breed and understand the mock fighting and growling and wrestling she likes –

Whoa – Gigi just bolted down to the water. Little kids are shrieking in the shallows and Gigi jumps around, getting her feet wet, cropped ears pointing toward them, watching. Concerned as a mama bear.

"It's okay, Gigi," I call out and she returns to my side. But she keeps her eye on the kids. Protective. Like when those boxers attacked a puppy here. Gigi hears him yelping and she charges into the middle of the snapping jaws and human limbs and hip-checks one boxer and just stands there. Not aggressive, but formidable. And all the dogs and humans freeze, shocked by this AmStaff with all the scars – alert, hair raised, but calm. It's the craziest thing I've ever seen a dog do, Gigi protecting that puppy. And everybody settles down, especially those two boxers. Teeth or no teeth, they do not want to take it to the next level with Gigi.

Wow, now real nostalgia...

Is it end-of-the-world wistfulness? Like when you have a terminal disease and know your end date? Accepting your helplessness? This sucks. At least the Plan gave me the feeling of doing something. Kept the despair at bay. Might have been an illusion, but now I've just given up on the planet.

I stare out at the ocean. Beyond the surfers are oil rigs, an eyesore reminder that Exxon has known about climate change for fifty years, building their platforms higher to prepare for rising seas. But not a football field higher – ha. Back then, changing course by one degree would have put us in a whole different place. Instead, they told the worst lie the world has ever heard – climate change isn't real. Over and over, they said it. Now, with the speed, scope, and severity of it all, one degree is a joke. We've got to do a complete 180 to prevent a cascading spiral and –

Christ. The Plan is history. So why can't I drop this endless brain loop of bad news? I hate the person I've become, stuck in the prison of my mind. I need to jailbreak my damn brain.

I try to focus on the mighty Pacific as it crashes on the beach.

Enjoy the moment.

But even the ocean's a reminder, connecting to the pristine Chukchi Sea in Alaska that Cretin just opened for drilling – begin habitat destruction – further endangering the polar bears that depend on the disappearing sea ice for survival. That video of a bony polar bear, shambling, close to death and eating plastic from a garbage dump, is one of the saddest things I've ever seen. A starving canary in the coalmine, that mighty beast brought so low – I HATE THIS!

Insignificant against the killing powers. No plan. Impotent.

Again, I try to shake it off and get out of my OCD brain. Pay attention to the sand under my feet and the joy of Gigi as she plays, overcoming her fear of what a pack of dogs can mean. Hell, if Gigi can shake her melancholy terrors then goddamn-it-all why can't I concentrate on the salt spray stinging my face and just STOP?

Wake up, like Hale said. Be free!

But this is no day at the beach. The sadness of the growing loss floods me. What good is McMindfulness when the world is ending? What good is writing if it doesn't even ground me? It's all a waste of time – I feel terrible without my Plan. Shouldn't I finish that gun and kill Cretin before this beach disappears? Shouldn't I act –

"Look at the dolphins, Zombie!" June snaps a wet ball of sand into my chest. And BAM, I'm AWAKE.

I chase her squealing down the beach as Gigi lumbers after us. When I spin, I glimpse Mom and Dad in the distance, amused by their children. And then we stop, laughing and breathless, to watch dolphins jumping beyond the waves, frolicking, just for the hell of it, as the sun burns through the haze, saturating everything –

"Look!" June exclaims. "In the wave."

Seven dolphins surf, suspended in the emerald wall of water as it rolls in. They are in perfect formation, like the pelicans flying overhead.

And then I can just be – not to be is impossible.

I forget my sadness about all the loss and all the loss to come.

I am flooded by the joy only <u>this</u> moment can give.

I am awake.

Earth Last

The beach was great until it wasn't.

Still, what happened after was a game changer for me...

As usual, Gigi stops playing and sits facing the ocean in what we call her "batman pose," cropped ears forward, hulking shoulders brooding, so her shadow on the sand looks like the bat signal. It's her way of saying she's done, so we head back to the car.

"Did you see that German shepherd?" June asks, kicking sand in front of her, pushing an invisible soccer ball. Mom and Dad are ahead, and Gigi is behind, reluctantly crossing the Sahara to the bike path, tongue long. "Gigi really liked him."

"Unfixed male," I say. Ninety percent of dog bites are from unfixed males under the age of two. An aggressive time, along with their human counterparts – no wonder the army and gangs recruit kids my age. Back to Eric Fromm, looking for community and purpose –

"Put that pit bull on a leash!" Shouts a dude riding by on a bike. He's wearing a sparkly red, white, and blue long coat and matching stovepipe hat, like somebody vomited the American flag on an Abe Lincoln impersonator. Gigi isn't even off the dog beach –

"Put yourself on a leash!" June shouts back, fearless as usual. I'm a little too shocked to be that quick, but June's got a real future as an insult comic. Pity any heckler who tries to veto her. The guy, white, middle-aged, and carrying a sign I can't see, doesn't even turn around as he flips us off. June and I look at each other and bust out laughing.

"Put yourself on a leash? Good one."

June grins as I tousle her hair. Gigi lumbers up, panting. Her tail wags to the right in response to our laughter – happy. Dogs always tell you what's going on if you speak their language. I give her some water which she noisily slurps.

We catch up to Mom and Dad, who missed the exchange. Arms around each other's waist, they're just happy to be together. We load Gigi in the Prius. From the ground, she puts her front feet up on the seat and looks back at me. I hoist her ass into the car by grabbing her back legs. Ridiculous – she can get in by herself, but she trains me too well.

We drive toward Dukes, where we will park in the shade with open windows. Dad will tip the valet to keep an eye on Gigi, who will doze, cooled by the ocean breeze. We're all a bit paranoid after seeing a woman find her St. Bernard dead in her SUV at a Vons, windows cracked an inch, smears of blood on the glass from where Bubbles sucked his last breath – her screaming his name over and over. The most heartbreaking thing I've seen IRL. People forget dogs wear fur coats.

But now we're crawling through traffic. As we approach the intersection of Main and PCH, we see the hold-up. Pro-Cretin protesters in MAGA hats clog the sidewalk holding all cap signs:

MAKE ENGLISH AMERICA'S OFFICIAL LANGUAGE

BUILD THAT WALL!

STOP ILLEGAL INFESTATION!

AMERICA FIRST!

GOD BLESS AMERICA

Love the sheer profanity of the last one, as if good old god should bless America only. Meanwhile, this crowd would scream "lock him up" if they ever encountered his son, that migrant with his long hair, brown skin, and dusty sandals – tired, poor, and yearning to be free.

And "America First?" Henry Ford, who hated Jews, created the slogan back when racists opposed WW2. Antisemitism – Built Ford Tough!

Christ, Hitler again.

But now America First also says to global bloodsuckers, feel free to chew up the world because Cretin will do the same in his corner. So, the Cretin Wanna-be in Brazil can keep his vow to pave the Amazon, his extraction plans creating as much pollution as China. Not only is there no interference from America, but Cretin urges him on. Protests? Just kill the environmental activists; four murdered a week around the world –

"Build that wall! Build that wall!" The chant tears up my obsesso mind-scroll. Cars honk in support as we drive by a mob of white people, red-faced with sun and anger. The guy in the stovepipe hat holds a sign, "America is for Americans." But 84% of Americans support a path to citizenship for Dreamers – kids my age. We-The-People ignored again.

It's all so stupid. Are these pale men, who haven't seen their dicks in twenty years under their belly flop, going to stoop 12 hours a day to pick strawberries? Will they stand knee-deep in the blood and guts of slaughterhouses? For minimum wage and below? Ha. They wouldn't last a day in a factory or field. Their backs would break and their skin would boil –

"Keep that dog on a leash!" Stovepipe Hat screams at us.

"Suck it, nut job!" June shouts back.

"Day of the rope, little girl. It's coming!" He almost spits this out at June. Holy shit, that's from the Turner Diaries – the mass murder of "race traitors" to a ten-year-old girl? A-hole!

"June. Roll up your window." My mom's voice is tight, but Dad's already on it. I want to kill that guy for what he said to June, but I swallow my anger.

"Don't poke the bear," Dad says to June.

"What d'ya mean by that?" June has her ready-for-combat look. She knows exactly what Dad means because it's his life philosophy – a "let sleeping dogs lie" worldview. But Dad's from before the napalm of social media ignited everybody into crazy clans. We need to poke the bear because the real bears need saving. Like the one they found sitting in an Ojai stream, unable to walk, paws burnt from a firestorm that tore through his woods at an acre a second. Agony! And now I've choked, allowing little cretins like Stovepipe to win. Giving up on my Plan to save –

"Do you think you'll change that guy's mind by shouting at him?"

Dad asks. "Their last rally here was a riot. Fighting. Pepper spray. People got hurt."

"But he started it," June never backs down. "He called us names."

"They always start it," I chime in, defending June, sounding like a ten-year-old myself.

"Violence isn't the answer," Mom says. "Violence in word or action is never the answer. It just creates more violence."

"Noooooo," June violently disagrees. "Sometimes, violence stops violence. I know that firsthand. I'd like to see a good fight right now. I hate these fools."

"No, June," Mom instructs. "You don't have to like them, but you can't stop loving them. MLK said that. And you can't give up on law and order and politeness."

Cretin is way more about order than law – enforcing the hierarchy. And politeness? Ha.

"'The great stumbling block in the stride toward freedom is not the Ku Klux Klanner but the white moderate who is more devoted to order than to justice.'" I chime in for June. "King wrote that in jail. Everybody loves his 'I have a dream' speech now, but back then, most Americans despised the March on Washington. You could dream but do it out of sight."

"Good one. And what's so wrong about hating evil people?" June neatly sums it up. Damn right – the time for moderation is over.

"'Hate the deed, but always love the person.' That's also King," Mom says, eying me over her shoulder. "It's the only way change happens."

"But Mom," June counters. "The person is the deed."

She's got a point and the car falls silent. As we inch by, a bedlam of babel from Cretin clones following his phony populism. Conned! Santa is your dad. The Tooth Fairy is your mom. Jesus isn't returning. Admit it!

But you'd rather dream about when blacks knew their place and invisible browns picked your food for pennies an hour. Back to when you ruled and America turned away Jews fleeing Nazi death camps, like Cretin does now to the desperate brown asylum seekers at our border. You love that Cretin's only answer to every question is cruelty and –

"Build the wall. Build the wall! BUILD THE WALL!"

Christ, that's rattling the windows. Even June is quiet, stunned by the mob invading this bright day at the beach. Gigi watches, ears forward, alert and calm. But also puzzled. She looks at me as if to say, why are all these humans so mad? Like they have rabies?

"It's okay girl," I say to her, and to myself. These humans <u>are</u> rabid, not even aware that 70 million refugees already wander the planet, 22 million from extreme climate events. Why don't they wake up before it's too late and –

"America First. AMERICA FIRST!" Yeah. Good luck with that. As if there's an America First to the climate.

Immigration paranoia now? Just wait.

I spot a "Rise Above" T-shirt. Figures. Our Nazis are already inside the wall, born and raised here. Will protest, patience, and restraint stop them? No. Cretin, with his commitment to racist fantasy, shares a brain with this Star Trek Borg, conducting their delusional hive mind.

June tries to unroll her locked window as we slide by more protesters screaming directly at us. It might be the Prius – no doubt they drive one of the million Ford F150s sold last year that get a third of the MPG, immune from polluting regulations because it's a "truck." Go USA!

It might be June sticking her tongue out and flipping them off.

"An overactive amygdala makes you emotionally react to anything that looks like a threat, even if it's not," Hale said in class this week. "Like seeing a rope and thinking it's a snake. That's a perceptual disorder. Most people do an experiment and poke the rope to see if it moves. For others, fear rules. They won't even do the experiment. Or believe the results if they did."

As a former soldier using force to deal with high emotions, what would Hale say about this mob, their lizard brains working overtime? Will science and logic clarify their vision of the world? Nope. They see us, a little family in a Prius, and see a dangerous snake. Libtards! Even when they inspect and see it's not a snake, that it's just a family at the beach, or maybe a hardworking Mexican gardener, they still redline. Logic or love doesn't penetrate their hysteria. In their cult, fed nonstop snake oil, the only rope they see is their damn "Day of the Rope." <u>Everything</u> else is a snake.

Do they even know ICE let six refugee kids die in cages last year?

You'd think that would be enough to satisfy their bloodlust.

Progressives supposedly have a bigger Anterior Cingulate, the part of the brain that absorbs abstract information, like a looming disaster...

But we need way more amygdala if you ask me. More emotion, like what June has. You can't reason with people who refuse to see reality. Obama, in all his Spock-like grandeur, tried that and they rolled him like a rug. When the other side is dead wrong, we need to jam reality through, before we're all just dead. We need to act without their permission, like when they stole a Supreme Court seat.

My mind skitters back to the Plan. It keeps popping into my head no matter how much I whack-a-mole it. Can I really watch the mad king pour gasoline around the kingdom as his villagers hold tiki torches because, damn it, they see snakes instead of ropes and maybe only because their neighbors are seeing them? And not even their real neighbors – their Fakebook ones?

Meanwhile, behind these protesters, indifferent to their rage, is a Tsunami of hurricanes, floods, and firestorms – destroying towns, cities, and soon entire countries. And behind that, extinction bearing down. But they don't have a clue. Nobody does. Nobody believes the experts. Over 65% of Americans now think the media spews fake news – truth and science be damned. Like, Climate Chaos is fake news. Like, needing vaccinations is fake news. Reasoning is so antique –

"You know, sometimes violence is the answer," June announces as we finally pass the protest and Mom breathes again. "We have a right to defend ourselves. Why should we always have to 'be better'?"

She sneers the slogan from Cretin's plastic Barbie wife.

Amen, June. Because Cretin's idea of "order" is an amoral Mafioso tyranny, like his fellow kleptocrat Putin. And he only uses the "law" to scare us about fake snakes like immigrants.

But we need to protect ourselves from what's real, the coming climate terrors. We need to guard our planet from Cretin's "Day of the Rope." For everybody, even his own cult protesters.

This irrational mob has changed my mind.

The plan won't quit me.

And I don't think I can quit it.

Today's Headline

"Poachers Have Killed 800 Park Rangers in The Last Ten Years." Hacked to death like Dian Fossey, dying to protect our world heritage. And now they want to drill for oil in Virunga, the last habitat of the world's last 700 mountain gorillas. Cretin would approve, if he ever thought about it.

– NationalGeographic.com

Going Full Hamlet

Midnight. I just read this journal from the freeway fire on.

Note to self, never do that again – what a long list of horrors.

But all these pages do what my writing always does. Clarify. Reading my journal reminds me of my duty and helps me see my truth.

What the hell is it? At its core?

First, I love the planet that existed before man drew lines on it and fought wars over those lines. We have nothing without her health. Like Hale says, Earth is a master algorithm, we'll lose every argument with her physics. And the physics are dire.

Second, I can't just blood-suck the world while the blood-sucking is good. I know too much. I've got a conscience. I can't just live with the Great Sadness and do nothing.

Third, I don't believe half measures will dent those pro-Cretin protesters. This radical moment – our last on the planet – needs radical action to wake people up.

Fourth, the case I make against Cretin is damning. So, as sick as the Plan makes me, I can't just quit. Can I?

"The question is whether any civilization can wage relentless war on life without destroying itself, and without losing the right to be called civilized."

Rachel Carson is my hero, writing about man's war against nature in *Silent Spring*. She said we are a part of nature and so at war with ourselves. Yeah, to the point of falling for our executioner...

Carson also wrote mankind must prove its "maturity and mastery," not of nature, but of itself. Maturity? Mastery? With Cretin in charge?

Ha. He doesn't see humanity's back is against the wall, choked by an indifferent power that will slaughter us without noticing who's rich or poor, white or brown, sinner or saint. The climate doesn't care if you're socialist or capitalist. Or if you "believe" in it. Or if you are just trying to live your life ignoring it. Rachel Carson's nature is as impersonal as the universe itself. We're not its master. We're dependent as slaves.

There's no doubt we're relentlessly destroying ourselves. And we've absolutely lost our right to call ourselves civilized. Is it time for an uncivilized solution?

I don't know – feels like I just don't know anything anymore. Except the Plan is a betrayal of my family. And poor Gigi, who never hurt a fly. What right do I have to destroy their lives? But aren't the stakes so much bigger than one little family? It's terrible, not knowing what to do...

Who is my allegiance to? Mother or Mother Earth?

It's got to be our beautiful planet. Without her, we're dead.

Am I the only one who feels this way? Really? Can't be. But nobody's breaking the Cretin fever. He's traumatized the country – we're in shock. Soon, it'll be time for lobotomies and leg irons.

Going full damn Hamlet here. To kill, or not to kill – for that is the question. Maybe just put one foot in front of the other – put off the final decision. I'll know when I get there. Yeah.

I am dread. Hope. Anger.

The Plan, for now, is back.

Let slip the motherfucking dogs of war.

Today's Headline

"Feds to Open Up 1 Million California Acres to Fracking." Right in my fracking back yard.

– SFChronicle.com

Shock, Future and Present

First real test today for the Plan. I was nervous as I unrolled the print-out of my CAD design, an exploded diagram of every part of a toaster, suspended like shrapnel. Hale gazes at the eighty pieces.

"You sure bit off a mouthful," he says. The toaster is metal, with my 15 ABS plastic gun pieces peppered in. I've grayed the design, so it all looks metal, but I don't like how closely Hale's staring at it.

"Yeah. It'll be a good challenge." I start rolling up the design.

"Hang on," Hale commands, scanning the paper. Uh-oh. Did he spot it? "You going to have time to pull it off?"

"I think so." I say, relieved. All the little pieces are a pain to code, even on Vectory, but making something that takes fewer parts would make it easier to spot the ghost gun. "It'll be fun."

"It'll take some patience," Hale warns. "But you'll have a toaster, so there's that."

He's joshing. I smile, feeling sorry about the shit storm that'll hit him once they find out I printed a gun in his class, under his nose.

"A toaster in my bedroom is my life's dream," I say, making him laugh.

"I'll approve it." Hale takes another long look at the design. "But extra credit for this one is not happening. A lot of work, but not exactly helping mankind, is it?"

"It's helping one member," I joke, quickly rolling up the design. If he only knew.

Luckily the 4.7 gets more undeserved slack. You can be in the middle of a nervous breakdown from planning to kill the president and people assume you're performing the crap out of life. Truth is, I'm not okay. I feel terrible. The collateral damage this brings to people I love, can't even predict how it –

"Everything good, Ben?" Hale breaks in. "You need anything else?"

Damn, I've got to be more careful. Just standing here as this little spiral unravels in my head, thoughts all over my face. Got to pay more attention or he'll catch me for sure. But I'm flooded with an urge to tell Hale everything. He's military. He knows war.

"All good," I say. Hale looks at me carefully. He seems unwilling to let me go.

"Tyler giving you any more trouble?" Is that what he's concerned about? Suddenly, being Hamlet seems dangerous. If the Plan is theoretical, it makes it easier to confide in Hale. Focus!

"No, not really." I can't tell Hale anything. <u>Nothing</u>. "I haven't seen much of him."

"Good. Stay on your own track."

"I'm trying. Hard to know what that is sometimes."

"You're not supposed to know at eighteen. You should be sampling heavy." Hale smiles. Oh, I'm sure doing that, I want to say, but I bite my tongue and change the subject.

"I've got another quote about what we were talking about. Since you like Blake."

"Fire away." Hale leans back, cradling his head in crossed fingers.

"'The tree which moves some to tears of joy is in the eyes of others only a green thing which stands in the way … As a man is, so he sees.' Good one, huh?"

"Yeah. That idea is everywhere, isn't it?" Hale says. "In changing our-selves, how we see, we can change how we experience the world."

"But the balance between accepting the world as it is and trying to change it – hard to know sometimes, isn't it?" Careful – it's just too damn easy to talk to Hale.

"Yep. It can take a lifetime. Points to one of the dichotomies of Eastern and Western thought." Hale glances at his watch. "Got to run. I'll email you the printer password."

"Thanks."

I feel better. Don't know what the future brings. But it's a relief to pause the "to do or not to do" and just start doing <u>something</u>.

Bystander be gone!

Today's Headline

"Sperm Concentration Has Declined 50 Percent in 40 Years in Three Continents." I knew it. In parts of China, it's down to only 18% healthy. Gee, wonder if it has anything to do with their "airpocalypses?"

– WashingtonPost.com

Epic Carelessness

SG was back in school today and tangled hard with Tyler discussing *The Great Gatsby.* The book was a perfect setup:

"They were careless people, Tom and Daisy – they smashed up things and creatures and then retreated back into their money or their vast carelessness or whatever it was that kept them together, and let other people clean up the mess they had made."

What a dead-on description of Cretin, smashing the world.

Tyler, of course, loves Gatsby – all that Old Money versus New Money BS. But what about <u>No Money,</u> as tech will automate half of today's jobs in 10 years? Self-driving trucks alone will disappear four million, destroying guys making a living for families. Going to tell them to "learn to code?" Sorry, you can't – AI will also replace programmers. The future has run us over and is backing up to finish us in a self-driving car.

"Gatsby embodies the American Dream," Tyler rhapsodizes, clueless.

"The American Dream is an illusion," SG shuts him down. "That's what the receding green light is all about. Gatsby can't get what he wants. None of us can."

"And the planet can't take it if we could," I say, backing SG up. But she ignores me.

"How does Gatsby's era affect the meaning of his novel? And how is it like ours?" Mrs. Johnson tries to keep things on track before it devolves into another fight in our class's warfare.

"People were getting rich," Tyler says enthusiastically. "Like now, it was a great time."

"It crashed stock markets," SG says. "A few got wealthy, lots starved."

"Winners and losers." Groans. Tyler always brings it back to Cretin. But so do I these days.

"Who needs a billion dollars?" SG asks. "It's just status."

"The American Dream." Tyler grins malevolently. "Getting baller rich. Like our president."

"He was born rich and he's still sick with affluenza," SG retorts.

The class titters, but it's not a new word. Just an epidemic now, with the McDonald's CEO making 5,000 times his average worker. WTF?

"You SJWs just want to take everybody's money." Ha. Social Justice Warrior is such an Orwellian phrase – like it's so bad to war against injustice and inequality. "You can't take risks with the economy like that."

"Back in the days your president dreams about there was a 90% tax rate after needless wealth. The money went to creating more opportunity – schools, libraries, the GI Bill so white soldiers could get educations, mortgages, and houses," SG rattles off a list. "In Jersey alone, they built a thousand houses a week, for a thousand weeks. Being in it together made us great. For some of us, at least. It built our country. "

"You mean <u>our</u> country," Tyler whispers at SG. WTF? Did he go there? He looks angry that she, a woman, is challenging him – like Cretin gets.

"I was born here." SG's voice is calm and clear, but her eyes narrow with contempt. "Don't pull that White Nationalist crap on me."

"I'm not saying... Just, you're a commie. Like Pocahontas," Tyler sputters. He's such a weird person. Hard-wired wrong. Guess I am too. Are we now two sides of the same sick coin?

"Inequality destroys nations. So, you'll just have to make do," SG scoffs at Tyler, the next generation of psychos plundering the planet. "The heavily taxed rich didn't stop working, they loved what they did. So, go study some history. Philosophy. Maybe learn to be content."

SG twists the knife in Tyler's guts. Furious, he's got no come-back.

Tyler, like Cretin, doesn't know about contentment, the most underrated of feelings. Hungry hoarders, they just want MORE – live like

Gatsby, Earth be damned. Cretin promotes this poverty-stricken wealth, all gold bling with no soul. Guess to people who have nothing, it's a seductive fantasy. On a planet with finite resources, all that consumption is a catastrophe. Live to protect Fitzgerald's "green breast" is what I say.

"Live simply so others may simply live," is what Gandhi said. Yes! Curb your appetite. Fall in love with the simple pleasures – they're enough.

Everything seems so connected – the way we live, what we hold important, our lack of compassion. Sure, capitalism is the clickety-clack-come-on engine – but it needs to go electric. The whole damn world can't be for sale. At least level out luck and give people a ladder up to the playing field. Make it a fair fight. Instead of cutting deductions for teacher's supplies and adding them for private jets, a twofer dreamed up by Cretin – help the rich <u>and</u> pollute the planet.

Do the plutos on those jets know their oysters can't grow shells in acidifying oceans? Nope. They still think the world is their damn oyster –

"Gatsby ends up murdered, showing class tensions similar to ours." Johnson is wrapping it up. "Fitzgerald points out a society can't hold together amidst extreme inequality. As Yeats said, 'Things fall apart; the centre cannot hold.'"

The bell rings before I can comment on Yeats. The center is gone, as blown to pieces as Tyler's humiliated ego.

"Why bother?" I tease SG as Tyler, red-faced, bolts from class.

"Maybe I can't help myself, Mr. Rotten Fruit," she says, before gliding away and joining her friends. She's keeping her distance. Smart.

I'm a lost cause.

Today's Headline

"World's Richest 10% Produce Half of Global Carbon Emissions." While in Europe, the 1% gobbles up 82% of the income. Christ, even serfs did better than that – at least they had clean air.

– TheGuardian.com

Drowning Innocence

Can't sleep, yet again. Tried reading *Hitler's Willing Executioners* about the banality of evil in the Third Reich. Usually, it's NyQuil. But now I can't stop thinking we're them. Makes me feel heavy, like the lubricating part of Benji, the oil in the machine, is coagulating. This Plan, this horrible act, a killing – it forces a deep look inside.

All I see is grinding gears.

"Ardently do today what must be done. For who knows? Tomorrow, death comes." Amen Buddha. Death – fast-tracking for us all, but sooner for me. Each step I take toward killing Cretin, I walk toward my death. Christ. That hits home. Feeling the fragility of me like I'm a magician's balloon, inflating until soon I'll just pop and disappear.

Don't know how to prepare for it.

So, I keep stepping forward, making the gun. Zombie.

The Yeats poem Johnson quoted is one of my favorites, *The Second Coming*, but now I get no enjoyment. It's all too real, *"The best lack all conviction, while the worst are full of passionate intensity."*

Is Yeats talking about me? Or Cretin? Or both?

Am I, in my passionate intensity, going to, *"loose a blood-dimmed tide as the ceremony of innocence is drowned?"*

Maybe like nature itself, I'm both rough beast and innocent? Can't tell. Feels like soon enough I'll be only beast, like Cretin and all he represents, *"His gaze as blank and pitiless as the sun."*

Christ. Am I becoming Cretin to kill him? This is gross. I feel the water rising on my innocence, causing a waterboarding level of anxiety – not drowning, just the panic of it.

"Surely some revelation is at hand Troubles my sight, a waste of desert sand."

There's no sentence that better captures the End Times dread I feel. As China announces it won't hit its modest Paris goal because a drought dried up their hydroelectric this year.

Four in the morning. I can't sleep. Can't read. Can't focus.

I take out the fidget spinner June gave me that was all the rage with kids her age on the verge of a nervous breakdown. I flick the flashing lobes. Soulless as a casino cash register, it spins, round and round, not going anywhere. Perfect. Can't hold it together much longer. When my anxiety level gets up to my nostrils, my mind will drown me. I will screw up and get caught. Got to bear down and speed up. Got to finish my gun and figure out where to use it.

Cretin only visits California for quick photo-ops at fake prototypes of his wall, trolling a state he lost by 4.5 million votes because of "voter fraud." We are a slap in the face of everything he stands for, with our green energy and hardworking immigrants.

He won't come out here. Today he's jabbering it up in Michigan.

"Satan, come to life after twenty centuries of stony sleep."

Bringing hell on Earth. But to kill Satan, I need to go to hell.

Tonight, it feels like I'm already there.

Today's Headline

"There Are 10,000 Lobbyists Working Congress." That's 20 for every corrupt Clown. Cretin's got the demons running wild.

— MotherJones.org

Manginas

Today Tyler punched me, but I got the better of him.

It happened as I was printing my gun.

Monitoring the print by our phones is supposed to give us a longer leash, but I need to remove the small gun pieces as they finish. So, after school, I stick around and think and write and watch the ghost gun get built – grain by grain. As if all was normal. Must appear normal.

If 3D printing is the future, prepare for lots of staring into space.

Hector walks in, startling me as he grabs his toolbox off Hale's desk. He eyes the printer.

"What you making, Benji?" It strikes me Hector is a Buddha. He's got the belly, small and round, over his green pants. And the compassion – always warmly saying to kids he quietly helps, "This too will pass." FTW has that written on the wall with a "shall," and there's a version of it buried in every wise old text, between all the stoning, slavery, and rape –

"Benji?" Hector looks at me. Christ, so tired. Drifting. What do I say? The ABS plastic is printing right in front of him, so I can't say it's a metal toaster. Hector's observant – he knows what's going on in the school more than the teachers. And I hate to lie to him.

"I'm working on a toy for my little sister," I lie to him. There's no way you can tell what I'm making from the one piece of plastic printing, but I feel like he knows I'm lying. It makes me sad. Soon, I'll be the king of all liars –

"A toy?" Hector lingers. "That's cool, what kind of toy?"

"Um. It's a squirt gun. She's almost eleven."

"Good for you." Hector smiles, still not moving.

"Uh, I've got to finish writing this paper while I watch it." The Plan has turned me full A-hole, even lying to the one person who's decent here besides Hale.

"Then I'll leave you to it." Hector nods. "Take care, Benji."

"You too," I say, feeling gross. "We'll catch up later when I'm not so –"

But Hector is already hauling his toolbox out the door as Tyler strides in, passing him like he's invisible. With Dim and Dimmer, Tyler's a baby Cretin with two Clowns.

"I need your time on the printer," Tyler says, on a mission. "I've got a conflict, a trip, and need to get my printing done before I go. Hale said to talk to you because you're hogging it."

"I'm sure he said that," I retort. I don't ask him where he's going – that's what he wants. It'll be the ranch in Sun Valley to kill some animal. Or maybe even Africa on some paid Cecil-the-lion killing "safari." Or a trip to Maui on the family jet. Most of the world is working shit jobs for shit money, while the bloodsuckers living it up off their labor want to tell you about their vacations. "Like, so totally amazing," kids at HWB say after Christmas trips to Aspen. Am I just envious? Maybe. But why not donate all that excess money and save a life somewhere?

"You awake? Anybody home?" Tyler is actually snapping his fingers in my face. I glance at the printer spinning my gun into existence and I suddenly love it as much as a spider loves his web. It really is Robespierre time. Can I get that meme going? It's MAX TIME!

"Hello? I'll pay you a hundo for your slots," Tyler is saying, a douche-bro slipping money to a restaurant host to cut the line ahead of people following the rules of civilization. How long will people put up with it? A long time apparently.

"A hundred bucks?" Tired, I blink and try to focus. No way I'm going to take his son-of-a-bloodsucker money, but that doesn't mean I can't poke the cub. "I think you mean a hundred bucks a slot."

"Look at you, Ginj," Tyler sneers. "A little capitalist when it suits you."

"Yeah. Free market and all that," I say innocently. Tyler will pay up to show his goons everybody's got a price. But a soon-to-be-dead desperado doesn't have a price. I don't need money. All I need is a ticket to wherever Cretin shows his <u>smug</u> next. Today he's in Kentucky –

"Sure. I'll buy all ten slots for a K." Tyler pulls an inch of money from his man bag. It's got to be ten grand. More money than I've seen anywhere but the movies.

"Did I say a hundred a slot?" I take a nice pause, imagining Tyler's clueless head on a spike. "I meant a thousand a slot."

Wonder if ten grand shuts him up. That's a lot of money except for Tyler, who apparently walks around with it. Is the rumor true, is he dealing Adderall? Tyler's eyes slit, pure reptilian.

"Fuck you," he hisses. Ha. I have something he wants. I'm "winning."

"Just price surging, like your favorite company," I retort. Tyler brags about riding free on Uber Alles – his dad invested early, along with the Saudis. "Bend over and take it like John Galt."

"So funny." He's stone-faced – guess the new slack-jaw blankness is only for authorities like teachers.

"Just the free market. Winners and Losers," I say briskly, doing business. "Just think of me like that dirt-bag pharma guy who jacked up cancer meds from thirteen bucks a pill to over seven hundred. What's his name? He's in jail now? Sounds like scrotum? Oh yeah, Shkreli."

How's that for some Onomatopoeia?

Like, I just scraped some Shkreli off my dick.

Tyler stares at me coldly. He has no experience with losing, his whole life is teed up to prevent it. But he doesn't realize there's no winning this game. Just like those people dying for cancer medication couldn't win.

Dim and Dimmer watch him closely. How's their hero gonna play it? Tyler shrugs, but his face is redder than a Canadian tourist visiting LA.

"Whatever." Tyler goes for cool, like the ten grand he tosses on the floor in front of me is nothing. Probably is, what with daddy getting tax breaks to gift Tyler's trust with millions. Guess he thinks I'm going to bend over and pick up the brick, but I don't move.

"Did I say a grand a slot? Meant to say ten grand a slot."

And that's when he punches me in the face. Shit! That came out of nowhere, me forgetting June's rule about letting A-holes in my circle. Damn. Total sucker punch to the jaw. Guess you can only push libertarians so far about the failure of the free market.

"That the best you got?" I say, doing my best Clint as I wipe my lip. It hurts, but for all his roid-rage swoleness, Tyler's no MMA fighter. Dim and Dimmer edge away from him. Punching somebody at HWB is an automatic expulsion.

"Why you such a little bitch, Ginj?" Tyler whines. "I'm trying to be reasonable. Fair."

"Fair? Isn't the free market fair?" Am I the A-hole now? Maybe, but so what? I truly hate this guy. I rub my jaw, feeling the pain now the shock is fading. "Oh, yeah, I forgot. You're on the capitalize-the-wins-but-socialize–the-losses team."

"Fuck you, Ginj." Tyler looks like he might punch me again, which would hurt. Better late than never, I take June's advice and circle away.

"Touch me again and I'll have you expelled," I warn.

"No. You would get expelled for punching me. I'm never gonna get expelled for punching you!" Tyler sputters. "Incel Mangina."

Dim and Dimmer look at each other. They've got no idea what Tyler is talking about. I do – every corner of Discord and all that. But putting them together is stupidly redundant. Mangina is what "Men's Rights Advocates" who have "red-pilled the truth about women" say to call somebody a faggot. MRA websites are full of guys with creepy facial hair – like neck beard child molesters. But Incels hate women because they can't get laid – involuntary celibates. They call women roasties because they think vaginas look like roast beef. No joke. Gee, maybe if you want a girlfriend you shouldn't call vaginas the meat of a poor dead cow? Just an idea. I mean, I'm a virgin, but I don't hate women. If I wasn't so stressed maybe I'd try to Tinder off my virginity before the end, but I guess I'll die unfucked and –

Tyler is snapping his fingers in my face again. Drifting again... into endless spirals. Is something wrong with me?

"Yeah, Mangina," Dim says, catching on. "Tyler's not gonna ever get expelled."

"I didn't see a thing," Dimmer says. I've never heard the lacrosse players speak – it's shocking. Like two sides of a goalpost started a conversation.

"My Dad gave a million bucks to this school," Tyler sneers. "I've got two more brothers coming up. That's two more million. To pay for Manginas like you. Nobody's expelling me."

"I always assumed you paid your way in. Good thing daddy's rich," I can't help goading him. "Because you're a fucking moron, like your president."

Tyler steps forward but Dim grabs him and pulls him away.

"He's not worth it." Dim says.

"Right," Tyler agrees. "Fuck you, Ginj. I'll go buy that printer. Do it on my own schedule."

"Lucky you," I say as he walks out. "We've all got our schedules. I know I've got mine."

Tyler's an A-hole, calling out my scholarship for the 50K yearly HWB tuition. But I won't turn him in – don't need the attention. I've got Cretin to fry and I'm no snitch.

A small piece has finished in the printer. I carefully remove it.

The trigger. Five pieces to go.

One micro-layer at a time, I'll build this gun under everybody's nose.

Today's Quote

"When fascism comes to America, it will be wrapped in the flag and carrying a cross." And spending two billion tax dollars shouting at us teens to "Just Say No" to sex. Single evangelicals my age ignore the message – 80% of them are hooking up. Ha. The Born Agains are no Incels!

– Sinclair Lewis

Bad Execution

Today I went with Mom and June to an environmental protest of all things. Not one of the big feel-good ones around the world, but a small local one. Dad is working on some new network pilot and Mom ambushed me into it.

"You need to get involved in our democracy, Benji. Deep down, I know you care." That's hilarious – our illiberal "democracy" got us Cretin. And Mom would die on the spot if she knew how much I care, as the ball of anxiety in my stomach grows, unseen as the swirl of plastic in the Pacific permanently polluting the planet, larger than Texas, 300 million more tons a year, with shards found in the torn-up stomachs of dead tortoises and seabirds as far away as Fiji –

Christ! Everywhere I look is endless obliteration.

The last thing I need is to get more involved.

But to stockpile a precious day with Mom and June, I start the last piece of my toaster gun and here we are at the People's Climate March, protesting environmental racism. It boils down to all the shitty polluting industries end up in poor neighborhoods – surprise! This protest is against a merger of two refineries to create the biggest oil processing plant on the West Coast. They want to stop the dirty tar sands oil coming here from the Keystone Pipeline, which had three leaks just this year. Gee, who didn't see that coming?

Not Cretin, he just executive ordered a bunch more pipelines.

I stare at a girl June's age holding a sign – "I'm With Her" written with an arrow pointing at a wobbly drawing of Earth, a blue marble glowing against black. A kid's version of what the astronauts saw from the moon.

That's just sad. Does this girl or June have a chance once "Her" convulses into tantrums, today with a monster typhoon in the Philippines –

"'To sin by silence, when we should protest, makes cowards out of men.'" Mom is quoting that poem by Ella Wheeler Wilcox. "I'm glad you're both here. We have to act."

Amen, Mom. But it'll take more than dense speeches from graybeards on top of a big bus. One is shouting about the carcinogenic chemicals polluting the neighborhood and lowering property value. This means less tax money for schools, which means shitty educations, which is how poverty gets entrenched – environmental racism. Why are education dollars tied to home values, so poor people don't have decent schools?

Good question.

Then Robert Kennedy Jr. gets up and shouts in a reedy voice like a crow in a windstorm. Everything he says is insanely optimistic happy talk environmentalism. Do I expect hard science from a guy writing books about vaccines causing autism as measles breaks out everywhere? Nope. Guess denial and BS anti-science magical thinking isn't just a Cretin thing – it's contagious.

The mixed crowd barely listens. There are Hispanic youth groups with signs – Change Starts in The Hood! And little kids on a school outing. And old hippies passing out fliers. But it feels like treading water in front of an oil tanker and expecting it to stop.

June miserably rolls her eyes at me, as the Santa Ana winds bake us in a convection oven. Moms sees it.

"June, pay attention. Change is hard, it starts like this," Mom instructs.

Am I taking the easy way out with the Plan? Skipping the hard work? No. What's easy about the sacrifices I'll make? My death –

"It's a waste of time, Mom. Everybody here already agrees with everybody else." June, as usual, puts her finger right on it.

"Yeah," I jump in. "And even if the world did everything these droners propose, it's like bringing a teaspoon to empty a swimming pool."

"'First they ignore you, then they laugh at you, then they fight you, then you win.'" Mom trots out her favorite Gandhi quote. I looked it up

– turns out he never said it. When I tell her, she shrugs, saying it's still a good quote. Which is true, just not Gandhi's –

"Did you know that 70% of Americans already support restricting emissions on coal-fired plants?" Mom continues. "We just need to let them know what's going on. That's why we're here."

I want to say that "restricting emissions" won't do shit, we need to close the plants. That it doesn't matter what We-The-People want while Cretin pisses on us and calls it rain. That just today, Cretin finalized the purge of all funding for freshwater clean up, from the Great Lakes to the Everglades. Soon we will fight wars over water – animal farming alone uses 56% of our fresh water, 1800 gallons per pound of steak eaten – but all Cretin wants to do is poison our lakes.

Of course, I don't say any of this to Mom. Too afraid I'll never stop talking until I end on, "I'm planning to shoot the A-hole!" And she keels over. Poor Mom. It's so terrible that if I finally screw up my courage, I will bring every horror to my precious family. But the worst will be Mom and Dad losing a child, upsetting the natural order. Is there a bigger nightmare? No. Except seeing your son shot by the Secret Service in front of the world. That's worse.

It's all so gruesome. But what choice do the Grays leave me? What's the point of talking? Hopeful protest, denial, weak environmentalism – it's a joke compared to what we face.

Cretin has turned America into a joke, as we brag about how great we are, even as we drop to 21st on the World Democracy Index, ignoring what We-The-People want.

But hey, we own first place in mass shootings. Go USA!

Between our climate policies and our arms industry, America The Death Star is killing everybody on the damn planet. And Cretin just gifted a 23% increase, 165 BILLION, to the DOD budget. Just that increase is bigger than the entire military budget for China or Russia. Without a war!

I don't know... All empires fade – maybe it's just America's turn, done in by its crazy margins, hollowed out by greed gone mad, spending its fortune on endless unwinnable wars while the country decays into a Roman twilight of decline. And unwilling to give up a damn thing to save itself or the world from the coming storm.

Christ. I knew being here would make it worse in my head, like being exiled in my own country that's suddenly become unrecognizable.

The idea of America was a good one — lousy execution though.

Today's Headline

"Plastic Lasts 1,000 Years In A landfill." Are there support groups for eco-grief? No time for that. And how would I ever stop crying once I started?

— *Telegraph.co.uk*

Torschlusspanik

"Come on, Benji, get me out of here," June whispers. "I'm dying."

I just shrug. Double-teaming Mom is futile. We agreed to come and we're staying, she will say. Just because it's hard doesn't mean we quit.

Then, Jane Fonda magically appears on the bus. Hair perfect, dressed in white, airdropped from Malibu. Dad and I watch her old movies: *Barefoot in the Park. Coming Home. Barbarella.* I've got a crush on her – she's so sexy and free in that 60s way. What happened to that generation's fearlessness? Their wisdom? Why did the boomers make everything so miserably about money? "Woodstock Nation?" Ha. More like would suck their own kid's blood for money.

It all might be futile, but at least Jane is still at it in this industrial part of Long Beach. She's still wise and passionate and the crowd goes quiet. She connects what's happening now to catastrophes to come. She doesn't sugarcoat it, shouting into the punishing wind.

"Who's that old lady?" Even June perks up. Bet she would love *Barbarella.*

"Jane Fonda. She was a huge star." I have a moment as I say this – like we're passing through a cosmic gate, as a country and a species. That as sure as Jane Fonda's star power faded, we will fade, time slipping – irreversible.

When I looked up a bunch of German words, trying to name my weird déjà vu feeling at the dog beach, I had no luck. But I saw one that explains what I feel now – Torschlusspanik – which translates to "Gate-Close-Panic." It's what old men feel when they realize they've got less time in front of them than behind.

But it works for humanity itself, as our time runs out.

And for me – I've got less time than all but the oldest of men. Christ. Ever since the Liberator, it's all become too real as my endgame looms. Will anybody care beyond Mom, Dad, June and Gigi? Doubt it.

In the cold silent universe, everything dies. Everything becomes meaningless. Like the scene in *Blade Runner*, when the dying replicant Roy Batty talks about the wonders he's seen across the Milky Way: *"All those moments will be lost in time, like tears in rain. Time to die."*

Is it our time to die? The universe doesn't care. All we love, the entire history of our species on Carl Sagan's *"mote of dust suspended in a sunbeam,"* is just a blink in the fourteen billion years the universe has been around. A nanosecond when we are here and because of our delusions and stupidity, we are gone. Self-destructing upon our arrival – I mean, we humans just landed! Hard to get any damn perspective on that...

Yesterday, Hale, answering some girl's question, talked about the Fermi Paradox, which asks: If aliens exist, where are they? Why no contact, even though there are 40 billion "Goldilocks" planets in our galaxy alone? One theory is none survive their own technology before runaway CO_2 turns their worlds into wastelands. No time to find another civilization before they all choke themselves out in a "great technological filter."

Hale is chock-full of chilling ideas like that. Good times!

Is that us and we just can't see it? No <u>perspective</u> on our crazy erupting tech – nuclear weapons in the hands of naked apes? Yup...

If the 100,000 years of human history was a 500-minute movie, everything has happened in the <u>last minute</u>. Before minute 500, the last two hundred years, there were only a billion people on the planet. We communicated by letter, not text. Transportation was horse, not space station. We used none of Earth's energy – fossil fuels started on minute 500.

What will happen in the next minute? Will we survive?

Or will we squander the inheritance of the 100 billion people who lived before us? The 10,000 generations that brought us to this point ruined by one generation of idiots! Yeah, that definitely sounds like us...

Here in the hot wind, Jane gets the problem right, but she blows the landing. Sure, she talks about the floods that drove a billion people from their homes in the past decade. She even mentions the "blob," the toxic algae bloom from water warming off the Alaskan coast. Alaska! But Jane ends by saying we must meet the Paris Accord goals and that's when it becomes happy talk. She might as well say you can keep an ice cube frozen with air-conditioning. And so, the Arctic sea ice melts, never again to freeze in the presence of a human being.

Christ, I'm a barrel of laughs today.

But I don't want to be here for just this reason.

Jane finishes. The crowd applauds. It's a rousing speech, but pointless. A feel-good act as deluded as climate deniers – the idea we have time for talk, talk, talk, as we burn, burn, burn.

Paul Watson, a hero of mine, left Greenpeace, which he co-founded, because he couldn't just hold a sign and watch the Japanese illegally kill whales. He couldn't "bear witness" and "protest." He got a fucking boat and uses fire hoses and sheer balls to get between the whalers and the whales. Saving thousands. They made a show about it called *Whale Wars*.

The only choice now is between Greenpeace or The Sea Shepherd – watch or do. Speeches? Nobody's listening. Protest? Nobody cares. Feel-good marches? Ha.

Violence. Only as a last resort. But aren't we here? Torschlusspanik!

Action to save our species before the cosmic gate closes.

It's got to feel better to fight than to bear witness.

Today's Bitter Irony

Before all our CO2, Earth was going into an Ice Age. In 5,000 years, it would have been ice over NYC a mile thick. We blew our cold cushion in Cretin's lifetime. Go USA!

– AMNH.org

Ignorance Meets Futility

"What's with the face?" June punches my shoulder, jolting me out of my dark thoughts. I try to mirror her gap-toothed grin but fail. "Don't make that zombie face. Weirdo."

I stick out my arms and chase her in our zombie routine. She runs, giggling, and for a moment, all is well. June has no clue that my insides are going zombie for real.

The march finally starts, but the crowd bunches up as Native Americans begin a ceremonial dance. Drums and rattles and chanting. They're protesting the Dakota Pipeline through their sacred land and all the dirty oil that ends up here in Long Beach.

The people most affected by the refinery come out of houses with bars on the windows, silently watching. Heat shimmers off the tar road and the scorching wind scrapes us raw.

"I'm hungry," June announces. We didn't bring lunch because usually there are food trucks at protests, but here, they are no-shows.

"Me too. Are you hungry?" Mom asks me. They've started rhythmically clapping and blowing smoke and don't look like they're about to stop.

"Yeah." I sigh, miserably trapped in this endless day and my own nagging thoughts. "We better eat."

Mom checks an app, but there's only a McDonald's near the park. We're in one of those food deserts they talk about in poor neighborhoods. No grab-and-go from Whole Foods here.

"We've got no choice." June's thrilled at the prospect of McDonald's, usually forbidden, enjoying watching Mom and me squirm. "It's Mc-

Donald's or starve!"

"Guess we can get a salad," Mom says, fellow vegan always adjusting to Meat World. I shrug, how can things get worse?

We're the only white people at the McDonald's – everybody is Hispanic. A different world from the gun show crowd. No wonder they're bugging out, even though the people here are way more cheerful.

The one thing the two worlds have in common is everybody's fat. Is the whole country stress eating the food that's killing us? Seems like it because 40% of us are obese. And no wonder – June gets a quarter pounder with cheese, large fries, and a coke. Total calories? 1870. A day's worth of malnutrition. Not that it matters to June – that kid has a hollow leg.

Mom and I order the chicken salad, hold the chicken, and it comes out with pale, limp lettuce. We split fries – salty and cardboard. June's burger looks like they left it in a closet for ten years. Hard to believe this is Cretin's favorite food because he's afraid of getting poisoned. Ha! If I raw-dogged a porn star while my Stepford Wife was pregnant, I'd worry about <u>her</u> poisoning me. And then he gives the porn star $130,000 in hush money. Amazing deal-making, Cretin! You only overpaid for sex by $129,000, you tiny mushroom dick. That's a direct report from the porn star, dick-size wise. Wonder if that's why he's so insecure, bragging all –

"So goooood!" June interrupts my damn Cretin spiral, smacking her lips, secret sauce plopping on her shirt. She knows how to be in the moment, no doubt about that. "And don't you dare lecture me, Benji."

"I won't." I'm enjoying her enjoyment. June still gets excited to get the mail, greeting her friend Lynn, our lesbian mail carrier, at the top of the street. Greedily searching for any response to letters she's written, old-school, to friends. Wish I had a fraction of June's love of life.

When we walk back to the march's starting point it's deserted, with only a few big feathers stuck to the sticky road, as if a coyote killed a turkey. We ask stragglers walking back, done in by the heat, which way to go. They wearily point us toward loud screeches that sound like chimps as they throw shit at you in the zoo – and really, who can blame them? We trudge toward the noise until we see two wild peacocks in a tree.

Wow, a bit of magic in a depressing day.

"What the heck are they?" June asks, squinting up.

"Peacocks." The larger one has his full plumage out, shrieking and rustling his bright blue feathers, really putting on a show. The smaller female is one branch over, ignoring him, which seems smart – the guy's a bit of a demanding dick. But I guess that's where the whole idea of "peacocking" comes from, one source of mankind's demise. Did they escape from a –

"You folks with the march?" Two cops on bikes have silently coasted up. Wearing shorts! Kind of harder to take them seriously –

"Is anything wrong, officer?" Mom tenses slightly. I hate to see that.

"No. But keep moving. We're getting pulled soon and it won't be safe for you here."

I look around the tidy street, slumbering in the heat. Not much action.

"Thank you, officers," Mom says, smiling too brightly.

The cops wheel away but watch us as we plod onward, soon passing rundown houses tossed with graffiti. Shirtless men drink beer on stoops. A rusting pickup collapses next to a lawnmower in a yard, as if its owner drove in years ago, started mowing his lawn, and had a heart attack.

We trudge onto the main drag, passing check cashing and liquor stores until we catch the snake of marchers coiled on a bridge over train tracks. The refinery ignores us, as indifferent as its owners. They don't live here – their kids go to places like HWB, driven there in SUVs.

More speeches, but Jane Fonda's passion is gone. If Paul Watson was here, he would take some direct action – stand in front of a bulldozer like the guy who stood in front of that tank in Tienanmen Square. Like Gigi did on that walk when she jumped in front of a street sweeper, fearlessly protecting me until it came to a shuddering halt, pistons hissing, Gigi trotting back to the sidewalk, feeling so proud – my animal spirit.

It will take that courage now, bodies on the line. That's what starts a revolution, not more words scattered in the scorching wind.

As it finally winds down even Mom has had enough. We silently look at each other and turn for the walk back. I look over the side of the bridge at the trains where hundreds of tankers squat, already unloaded, their oil soon to add tons of carbon into the atmosphere –

"AH HAHAHA!" Two young guys jeer at us and flip us off as they roar by in a pickup. Can't say I blame them. We are ridiculous, with our little signs. But so are they. Ignorance meets futility on a hot street, in a hot city, on a hot planet. All of us trapped in the same burning house while we play stupid games, the doomsday clock ticking down, final buzzer to come.

At the first intersection is a guy with a bullhorn. An organizer.

"Please wait here for the rest of the marchers. It's not safe to cross."

"Are you kidding me?" June snorts. "I'm not waiting for those slow-pokes to catch up."

"Me neither." We look to Mom. Her forehead is shiny and she seems done in, with sweaty protesters backing up behind her. But she's a rule-follower, Mom.

"Hold on, June. Wait." But the light turns and June marches across the street. I follow. And Mom reluctantly follows me as the guy with the bullhorn tries to hold the line.

"Please wait for the rest of the marchers so we can safely cross together in a group. Please." He goes from commanding to imploring, but it makes no sense. A few more tired protesters follow us, then the whole pack.

"You kids are bad news," Mom says, laughing from the small thrill jaywalking provides. She's a gentle person, Mom. She believes in civility and laws and politeness. She's also strong enough to stand up when necessary. "You should have waited."

But civility, laws, and politeness are a memory. Obama, my president since I was eight, took them with him when he left, along with empathy and intelligence. Feels like another century, when we had the freedom not to think about President Porn 24/7 like the Russians think about Putin.

I'm done waiting for permission. Done waiting for society to catch up with reality. Sometimes, you need to go it alone to get the rest to follow.

Wish I could share this with Mom and especially June, but I can't. Can I? No. Going to get too dangerous now. My gun will be finished by the time we get home.

"Why should we wait?" June says. "It's crazy to wait."

Amen, June. Amen.

My wait is over.

Today's Fact

It only takes 3.5% of the population actively participating in protests to move nations. That means 11 million Americans getting off screens and onto streets – every day. Who can wait for that miracle? Not me.

– ScientificAmerican.com

Gun Done!

After the endless day, I went to HWB and brought the last piece of the gun home. I spread the 15 pieces of ABS plastic on my desk.

The barrel of the Liberator is short and stubby, no bigger than my thumb. It doesn't look at all like a gun. The main body is a chunky triangle and the rest of the pieces look like parts of a children's toy.

I try to cue the cool animated video of how to assemble it, but it's gone – some new YouTube policy to stop gun violence. Ha. Maybe because the Liberator was in the news this week, which sucks. Will the Feds be more alert to its threat? Don't know – can't think about it.

I find the video, of all places, on a porn site. Makes sense, "how-to" gun videos migrating to porn, combining our obsessions. Made in America! Guess I've been a customer of both now.

I cue up the video and try to ignore all the tits and dicks.

Monk. Monk. Monk. I am.

The Liberator snaps together with plastic dowels like the endless IQ tests I got as a toddler. The only missing piece is the flathead nail used as a firing pin, which I find in Dad's toolbox. I watch the video and carefully assemble it.

Wow. It's light as a squirt gun. I'm relieved I don't get the power-mad feeling of the gun show Glock. There's forum chatter how useless the Liberator is because it isn't accurate and only fires one bullet at a time.

But I only need one – just need to get close enough so I can't miss.

There's also some talk about the Liberator exploding. It's basic, just a contraption to slam a nail into a bullet and it certainly feels like it could shatter. That's a problem. If it blows up while I practice, I'll get caught – how do I explain ABS plastic shrapnel all over my body? But there's no way I can shoot this gun for the first time at Cretin, surrounded by an army. I need to test it and make sure it works. And then practice. A lot.

You're supposed to use a .38 ACP round, but Discord forums say I can use 9mm. Luckily, I still have Bug Crusher's box of them – fifty rounds. Got to ration them by rehearsing my stance, grip, and draw without firing the gun, another video tip.

Got to get started!

Some gun nutters on 8Chan say you can get a loaded Liberator past metal detectors. But with plastic guns in the news, I don't want to risk it. That means I've got to separately smuggle the nail in with the bullet. So, I need something metal and hollow that I can hide them in. Something that'll obviously set off metal detectors and so go in the basket for cursory inspection. The old buy-something-worthless, shoplift-something-expensive routine.

What does a person have going into a rally? Phone. Wallet. Keys?

I search for metal key chains and find the perfect one – a hollow Statue of Liberty. I can shove a wad of gum in to hold the bullet and nail in place. In a fast security line where they're looking for weapons, nobody will notice the perfect smuggle. Especially from a skinny kid wearing a Cretin hat who's so damn patriotic he's got a Statue of Liberty key ring.

I take apart the Liberator and put it back together again.

Damn. The firing pin nail goes in early, which is a big problem. Means I'll have to take the Liberator into the rally in pieces and assemble it inside. Fast, like the guys on YouTube who can take apart their guns and put them together blindfolded.

I look down the gun's sight, pull the hammer back, and squeeze the trigger. Click. Not very impressive, like a toy gun that shoots rubber bands. Got to test it and –

"What's up, Benji?" June walks in on me as I'm holding the gun. Luckily, she trips on Gigi, who jumps up and shakes herself the way dogs do, cheeks flapping, masters at shaking stuff off. As June staggers to her feet,

I drop the gun in a wastebasket and close my laptop. She misses it all.

"Ack! Sorry, Gigi. You okay, girl?" June exclaims. Gigi, basically indestructible, licks her knees. No harm done, she says with her big brown human eye and wagging tail. June gives her a big hug.

"What you doing, Benji?"

"Just some homework." It's sort of the truth.

"Yeah, right," June scoffs, smoothing her T-shirt that has Nasty Girl printed on it. "Want to finally watch Okja with me?"

"I really don't." I can tell from the Netflix trailer it'll gut me.

"Pleeeease!" June grabs my arm. "I've been bugging you forever. It's supposed to be a great action movie."

I can never resist June and I need to get her the hell out of my room. So, we watch Okja, about a girl and a genetically modified piglet she raises for a Monsanto-like company competition. An action movie ensues as the girl tries to save her soulful pet from a factory farming feedlot.

June loves it, but I can't stand to see animals abused, even CGI ones, so I'm in tears by the end. It doesn't help that Okja looks like Gigi, with the same blue coloring and sashaying ass when she's happy. If we survive, someday we'll look back at how we treat animals the way we look back on slavery.

"I'm sorry, Benji," June says, patting my arm. "But maybe this movie will do some good. Make people see things differently."

"Maybe," I say, now feeling like a total snowflake, getting consoled by June. "Like Paul McCartney said, 'If slaughterhouses had glass walls, everybody would be a vegetarian.'"

"Good one," June nods. But it won't happen while Cretin sets the example, washing down his dead cows with gallons of Diet Coke. If you are what you eat, no wonder he's so toxic – junk food, junk values, endlessly advertised. No sense telling him he might be less angry, less bloated, if he ate better and got some sleep. He wouldn't listen. Cretin believes you're only born with a certain amount of heartbeats, so you shouldn't waste them on exercise. Ha. Wish that was a joke.

Christ. Now I'm OCDing about his damn diet. Pathetic.

"It was hard to watch the end," June acknowledges. "But I'm never gonna eat a burger again. Promise."

"That's huge, June. Beyond Burgers taste freakishly like meat."

"I'm sure it's not as good as McDonald's, but I guess it'll do some good for the planet. Like your girlfriend Greta's always harping about."

I just nod, happy June's got no idea I've blown way past Greta.

Unfortunately, it doesn't look like Cretin's having a heart attack any time soon, no matter how much crap he eats. There's only one thing that will do some good for the planet – my little plastic gun.

Time to test it.

Today's Meat Stat

If Americans cut one burger a week out of our diet, it would be like taking 10 million cars off the road. Christ, how many are we eating? No wonder animal farming takes up 30% of Earth's land.

– ScienceTime.Com

Great White Hunter

It's just before dawn. A mist hangs over the Bitterwood hills like mace.

I hike the Liberator, clamps, string, and the box of rounds up Kenter fire road. The gun's name is cheesy, on the nose as Dad says about bad TV writing, but it's growing on me. It will soon liberate us from Cretin's foul noise and deeds. And me from my endless obsession.

I hustle past a lady walking a chocolate Lab and we nod at each other. In an hour, the dirt road will teem with dog walkers and the cranky old men who hate them. I veer down a deer run to the bottom of the canyon where rocky walls can muffle gunshots.

It's empty of the kids who always smoke weed down here.

Anxious. Medicating. Escaping...

"All of humanity's problems stem from man's inability to sit quietly in a room alone." Pascal said in the 17th century. Maybe. Or maybe BS. Meditating hasn't blown me apart into pure raccoon-loving oneness like Molly. Not yet. Guess I have a long way to go before I see through the illusion of my "false self" and wake up to pure, connected awareness.

And now I won't get there – I'll be dead. I'll miss the only journey worth taking, and the only question worth asking: Who am I?

That's as sad as dying a virgin, but I guess it doesn't matter, dead is dead. Christ. Feels like I'm voluntarily stepping into the concrete boots that mafia bosses use to drown their rats.

Am I just waiting for my concrete to dry? Yup. We all are.

I pass old foundations splotched with graffiti and head to a rocky overhang that's perfect. It's hidden and will muffle the gunshot, bouncing it off the floor of the canyon, making it –

Voices. I freeze.

"Shh! Did you hear something over there?"

It's Tyler. And Dim and Dimmer. What the hell? Did they follow me somehow? At six in the morning? They're trying to be quiet but sound like a herd of moose crunching through the dead leaves. Tyler wears one of those African bush hats with the side curled up and snapped into place.

He's holding a crossbow. WTF?

I slide behind a tree. I really don't want Tyler to shoot me with a goddamn crossbow, so I pick up a rock and toss it behind them – all those Westerns – and it makes a thump. Tyler swivels, raises the crossbow, and pulls the trigger. With a TWANG, the arrow disappears.

"Was it a coyote?" Dim excitedly asks Tyler.

"It was something. But I missed."

Yeah, you missed, you dipshit. Tyler up at dawn hunting coyotes with a crossbow makes me want to test the Liberator right now. It's in my backpack, ready. Just needs a bullet. Surprise! It's not like coyotes aren't an issue in LA – driven by drought, they patrol the alleys from dusk to dawn. They ate two cats on our street and it's horrible, the screaming of the hunted eaten alive. That's nature for you when it comes for a visit. But the coyotes were here first, like the mountain lions that are so rare we give them names like P-45, as they struggle to survive habitat fragmentation and find each other. Guess they too are doomed to die virgins –

"Found it!" Dimmer shouts, scattering animals for a mile as he pulls the gleaming arrow from brush. I step out before Tyler has time to reload.

"Boo!" I shout and they all jump out of their skins. Tyler fumbles as he pulls up his crossbow. A natural reaction, I guess, but it's got no arrow. Comical. And frightening.

"Goddamn it, freak Ginj!" Tyler looks pale for once, the blood seeping from his ruddy face. "What the hell you doing out here?"

I want to say I'm testing a plastic gun made using the 3-D printing slots I didn't sell him to kill something that needs killing a lot more than a coyote. I shrug instead.

"Just hiking. Why you hunting out here?"

"Who says we're hunting? Just doing a little target practice." Tyler smiles without joy. "You'd be a good target."

Tyler pulls back the bow's string with a click and places the arrow, sharp and cold as his eyes. He's trolling. But in his ridiculous Great White Hunter hat and his now locked and loaded crossbow, I'm glad he's not drunk or alone. He'd probably shoot me in the face.

"Yeah, right. Don't shoot your dick off with that thing," I say, echoing Crushed Bug. Guess that's how a meme starts. I turn away.

Even though he's the worst asshole in *Lord of the Flies*, Tyler sees himself starring in *The Most Dangerous Game*, that old movie about hunting humans. Christ. Killing wildlife for LULZ, as he would say. It makes me queasy – his arrows, my bullets. As I hike up the gloomy trail with that sociopath watching, the hair on my neck prickles.

"I'd shoot your dick off if you had one, Mangina," Tyler calls after me. Manginas, again – no winning against the witless.

As I crest the fire road, a young coyote lopes across, spotlighted by the rising sun. His fur is brown and tossed with black splotches. His legs are skinny, but his ears are comically large, waiting for the rest of him to grow in. He pauses and looks at me with calm but wild eyes. A moment. Then, with a sideways glance and that funny coyote grin, like he knows that secret joke all coyotes know, he nods and disappears.

Is he for real? So random!

Like an apparition called forth just to troll Tyler.

Today's Headline

"Interior Secretary Scraps Ban on Lead Bullets." So, without firing a shot Cretin kills 20 million more animals a year as they eat the lead sprayed all over our commons. That's just lazy. In the old days, at least they had to shoot the poor buffalo from the train.

– WashingtonTimes.com

Once We Were Lions

Hiking down, I'm suddenly fuming.

What if Tyler gets lucky and kills a coyote? Or a mountain lion? Like the young lion looking for water that ended up trapped in a gated courtyard in Santa Monica last year. The cops try to do the right thing and dart him, but the lion, contained, starts going wild. And the police shoot him. Blam, Blam, BLAM, before the dart can even work. So, he's as dead as the silverfish I now try to pick up and save in my bathroom – all good intentions gone wrong, as I mush them into dust with my clumsiness.

Did the cops need to shoot that lion? No. They just panicked when faced with an uninvited piece of nature. Instead of awe, they feel afraid. I'm part of that Nature, also uninvited. I feel her force welling up in me now, powering me closer to the point of no return.

Am I nature's Avenging Angel? Ha. Fear me!

But what happens when Nature really freaks out – how scared are we then? What overreaction will we have to Hothouse Earth? What panicked geohacking that just kills what we're trying to save? I mean, what do we really know of our planet when terrifying and irreversible Climate Chaos really gets rolling?

About as much as a cop knows about a young mountain lion who dies – wondering what the hell is going on – with nothing but teeth and claws against guns.

This is how we kill nature all the time. And each other, like that YouTube video of a black guy who police shot while he was following their instructions. Bleeding, he asks the cop who just shot him, "I'm reaching for my wallet like you said, why did you SHOOT ME?"

And the cop, terrified because the whole population is packing, says, "I don't know!"

A moment of raw honesty between them. What did that white cop know about being young and black?

Nothing.

What did the black guy know about the cop's fear, as young blacks trapped in poverty gun each other down faster than *Call of Duty*?

Nothing.

But the young trapped lion was voiceless. No Mountain Lion Lives Matter for him. He depended on humans to protect his habitat and we failed him in every way possible.

I can imagine that juvenile lion, as he lays dying after the cops shoot him, asking, "I'm scared and hurt by the dart. Why did you shoot me?"

And maybe the anguished cop says, "I don't know!"

But that cop would need to take a lot of Molly to see the question in nature's dying eyes, pleading every day, "We are one and I give you everything. Why are you killing us?"

There's no answer that makes a bit of sense – just the madness of Nero butchering his own mom, of Tyler slaughtering animals, of Cretin murdering Mother Earth.

It's just what psychos do.

Today's Headline

"Administration Sees a 7F Rise in Global Temperatures by 2100." Will they do anything as we now pass irreversible tipping points? Nah. Cretin doesn't even know this optimistic prediction will demolish us.

– TheWashingtonPost.com

Anxietyville

When I got back home, everybody was at the breakfast table.

"Where you been, Benji?" June perches on the edge of her seat, slurping Cheerios.

"Hiking," I say, casually tossing the backpack in a corner.

"You? Exercise?" June looks up at me. "In the morning?"

"Bird watching for a project," I improvise. Stupid not to have an alibi, but I didn't expect to be back this soon and find everybody eating breakfast together, something that never happens. Tomorrow I'll go right to school after I test the Liberator – if I still have all my fingers.

"Hiking is a good idea, Ben." Dad always calls me Ben, same as Hale. Guess it's their way of manning me up a bit, using the manly Ben. I like it – Benji is a kid's name, and I'm not a kid anymore. Like in Corinthians, I've put away childish things. The time for magical thinking is over.

"They say nature is a good way to lessen anxiety." Having dispensed that fatherly wisdom, Dad is up, tossing back the last of his coffee. Off to the coal mine – the latest is some comedy called *Bite Me Hard*. Lame.

"Benji's not anxious," Mom pronounces. "It's just the age. Lots of changes happening."

"I never said he was anxious. He's fine. See you all before bedtime." Dad grabs his keys, kisses Mom absently, and takes off. I'm fine? Ha. When did I become such a good fake? Becoming what I study – Cretin.

"Benji's a nervous wreck," June says, smacking her lips. As usual, she's the only one not fooled. I already miss her. And Mom and Dad and Gigi and the garden and everything pure and simple in the world. I'm not depressed or crazy. I don't think the world sucks – just the opposite – I think it's awesome. I'm not in a fugue or deluded. Not under a gray fog and looking for a way to stop the pain, a way to bring relief.

That's not me. But yeah, I'm anxious as hell.

"See?" June says. "Look at his face, like a million miles away in anxiety-ville."

Anxiety-ville. Where I live ever since Cretin came on the scene, the joke that played out so wrong. The punch line after 40 years of Republican setup that destroys humanity.

"Maybe it's because he chose a college. It's real now." Mom throws an arm around my waist. "He'll miss us when he vamooses."

The most mistaken words ever spoken, followed by the truest. Vamooses. Ha. Mom. After I do it, I'm so scared trolls will death threat you into blubbering apologies for my existence. They don't live IRL – can't touch you unless you crawl into their digital basement. Christ, I hope you don't, Mom and Dad. But you'll get doxxed and swatted for sure. They'll drop a dime of lies and an army of cops will bust into our house and rip it apart. Over and over. That terrifies me, your new normal. I want to shout how sorry I am for it all. I want to say please, PLEASE:

- Freeze your credit, or they'll steal your identity.

- Move and conceal your address. Random idiots will show up and hassle you.

- Leave lots more time at airports for when the TSA detains you. Security theater as usual, except now you're the show.

- Just go off-line. Most of it's a conspiracy-filter sewer, anyway.

Of course, I don't say any of this as Mom, unaware, walks back into the kitchen. But June is inspecting me like she knows the real meaning of, "He'll miss us when he vamooses."

How could she? As much as I've wanted to tell her, I've bit my lip.

"What's wrong, Benji?" June asks, with her upturned nose and scraped elbow from scrambling up some wall.

"Nothing." I scrutinize her. Did I screw up, writing this on paper to keep it safe from hackery, but not consider a snooping ten-year-old? I've got to shut her down, disinforstract her.

"You're not sticking your nose where it doesn't belong, are you?" Ugh, gaslighting June.

"What do you mean?"

"You know, my journal." I hold it up. "Off-limits to you."

"As if I'd want to read your boring journal." June is indignant. "How good can it be if you're dribbling in it every minute of the day like every thought is pure genius?"

"Good," I retort, a bit stung. June's so tough.

"What's going on with you? You're acting weirder than usual."

"Nothing," I lie to the human lie detector. Did I just put a target on my journal? I've got to be more careful with June. "I'm fine. Just got a lot on my mind."

"Oh..." She instantly softens. "Are you okay?"

June looks at me with such earnest concern it breaks my heart. She's the best thing about all of us. But I can't leave this journal out of its hiding place above the ceiling panels in my room. If it ever gets discovered, I'm called a sicko, a traitor, a stunted adolescent with an unhinged screed. Before I've even banished Hamlet for good. Before I've worked out the Plan, practiced with the Liberator, made a list, and checked it a million times. Before the Idea and Plan have become irrevocable Action and –

"Benji?" June looks at me, her eyebrows furrowed. "Did you hear me?"

Christ, I'm a colonized zombie brain – all future, no present. It's making me careless. I force my attention a hundred percent on June.

"Don't look at me like that." June laughs.

"Like what, little girl?" I lower my face right in front of hers, intensifying my stare and opening my eyes pried-Clockwork-Orange-open. Flaring my nostrils, I become demonic.

"Oh, no..." June giggles wildly. "Not the Maniac."

She's got me back in this moment, as I snort and growl a low guttural laugh, hunching my shoulders. This just kills June every time. She chokes up with glee as I grab her, giving her a hug that lifts her off the ground.

I shake her like the Maniac always does. Only now, I'm squeezing her tightly as I take a deep breath, smelling her peppermint shampoo, trying to hang onto her essence.

And then I realize it. I'm hugging June goodbye.

"I'm okay," I whisper in her ear. "And so are you."

I release her so she can run away and I can chase her, roaring the maniac's roar.

And hiding the wetness in my eyes.

Ten Beautiful Dreams

This is all getting too real, saying a secret goodbye to June. Crying. What the hell is next?

Have I decided without knowing it? Action is character. Are my actions edging my character closer to an internal border, away from Hamlet? Feels like it. Today I'm even dreaming about what changes after I do it. Nothing? Everything? Ha. Hope really is a habit that dies hard.

But I'm sick of being so doomsday 24/7.

I hope I succeed and don't waste my death. I hope people come together and ACT. Like in this famous presidential speech:

"Mankind. We can't be consumed by our petty differences anymore. We will be united in our common interests. Fighting for our freedom, not from tyranny, oppression, or persecution – but from annihilation. We're fighting for our right to live, to exist, declaring in one voice: We will not go quietly into the night! We will not vanish without a fight! We're going to live on! We're going to survive!"

Of course, it's not Cretin. It's from a movie Dad showed me, Bill Pullman in *Independence Day*, inspiring humanity to come together and save itself from an alien invasion. Ha. We need to ignite that sci-fi imagination right now – Climate Chaos is as dangerous as any alien invasion. We need to creatively attack it!

So today, I feel like daydreaming my moonshot dream of an awesome future after I'm gone. Is it an illusion, a feel-good fantasy? Or is it my closing argument to myself, this list of what might happen, what *must* happen, if I kill Cretin? My last list ever...

1. A WORLDWIDE GREEN NEW DEAL.

Duh. Entire economies redirected the world over. In the same way Gov saved our country during the depression – building freeways, dams, and schools –we need to save and green our planet. NOW. If it takes a million young people camping on the Washington Mall or storming the White House fence to make it happen, then so be it.

2. AN ENVIRONMENTAL MARSHALL PLAN.

Like when we rebuilt Europe after we killed the Nazis. How about declaring a worldwide War on Climate Chaos, starting in the USA? We can do it – Americans love war! We could take defense billions and help a billion people without electricity leapfrog into clean energy, stabilize their countries, and stop mass migrations. Invent financing that makes a pollution-free future painless like Gov did for mortgages. Invest hugely in non-market solutions for a livable planet, like the G.I. Bill – everybody wins, all boats rising!

3. ZERO EMISSIONS IN 10 YEARS.

We have the technology for an awesome future right now. Solar and wind are the cheapest new sources of energy and 70% of Americans want to go 100% renewable – no matter how much Cretin tries to destroy the industry. Solar now employs more people than coal, gas, and oil combined. And is cheaper than Natural Gas. Plus, decarbonizing and converting buildings will create millions of jobs nobody can export.

4. A CARBON CAPTURE MANHATTAN PROJECT.

Zero emissions aren't enough. We need to suck carbon out of the atmosphere. <u>Negative emissions</u> to repair the damage we've done. Let's put the geniuses of the world on a campus to figure it out like the nuclear bombs that ended WW2. Reversing carbon <u>can</u> be done because it <u>has</u> been done – 16th century Euros killed 50 million people in the Americas, same old, same old. But trees grew back in the Amazon, and CO2 levels dropped 7 ppm. Same thing happened during the Black Plague. I'm not saying kill people to reverse CO2... Well, just one.

5. SMART SOLAR HACKING.

Besides massive carbon capture, we need other ways to slow the planet's warming. Green – not the quick-buck BS of spraying sulfur into the atmosphere or pouring iron into acidifying oceans. Nothing that will turn the sky white or create acid rain or poisoned air. But we need to invent something new. Let's go Sci-fi! Orbiting solar umbrellas?

6. WE CAN DO IT BECAUSE WE HAVE DONE IT.

In WW2, in two years we converted our entire economy to kill Hitler. We made no cars. Just ships, tanks, jeeps, and 300,000 bombers – one plane made every hour. Three huge Liberty ships a day built by our own Rosie the Riveters. And companies still got rich, same as defense contractors could now. Bonus? The green economy will provide work for every engineer, scientist, machinist, construction worker, and plumber – every person who knows how to build stuff with their hands IRL. If humans can adapt for war, we can for life. It will be awesome!

7. DESTROY THE INFLUENCE OF THE FOSSIL FUEL INDUSTRY.

Bloodsuckers want to squeeze Gov down to a size where "they can drown it in a bathtub." They don't want Gov to protect our air and water because then it's seen as a force for good. But We-The-People need to restore the idea that Gov's number one job is to protect us. Cops against criminals; army against invading forces; regulators and sheriffs against the rapists of our habitat. Big Gov has done big things like putting men on the moon. We should celebrate its successes. Time to expose Big Oil's propaganda!

8. HEAL THE PLANET, HEAL US.

And guess what? It's fun. It's more than fun – it saves our souls, pulling humans together like the love soldiers feel for their platoon. We need that focus and teamwork, not for death, but for life. Not in the name of nationalism or patriotism or the grotesque machinery of war. But for <u>Earthism</u> – all of us defending our only home.

9. TIME TO GET BUSY BECAUSE THERE IS NO ESCAPE.

We can't build a climate fortress and detain hordes of desperate refugees in concentration camps like an eco-Apartheid, no matter what Cretin wants. It won't save us from failed states. And aren't we a failing state ourselves? A big-fin Cadillac coasting on fumes from abundant times, living off our mythology? Do we really want to be the last people on a dying planet that we are most responsible for killing? We're dope-sick depressed and traumatized now. Imagine the horror and guilt of hiding behind walls, waiting for the last starving cannibal to come knocking at our border, a concept that Climate Chaos will destroy, anyway.

10. THERE IS NO DOWNSIDE.

Even if I'm wrong on the timeline, because who can really know, what's the downside? Clean air and water? Protecting kids like June from dying because she can't breathe? An insurance policy against the worst possible risk? Lessening uncertainty while saving America 89 billion in overall economic costs from air pollution? Millions less dead from that pollution? Preventing pandemics created by torturing and eating animals? A spiritual renewal from working together for the common good? Jobs for people who desperately need them? On and on.

There is no downside.

The upside is we might live. And live happily and healthily!

And if America leads, maybe we can be heroes instead of the laughing stocks we are under Cretin. We can become another "greatest generation" like the one that liberated Europe. But first, we need to own our responsibility for creating the disaster. And then turn it around.

This is my hope.

Is it a dream? Only if Cretin blocks everything on this list. Which he will unless I shock the system – shock everybody out of their denial – defibrillating a corpse back to life like they did for June.

By killing Cretin. Has to be done first.

Today the news said the Climate Chaos we're experiencing is the "new abnormal." Now that's some wishful thinking. We're in so much denial, a guy guzzling a fifth of vodka a day, we can't even SEE the bottom. We're still plummeting. If I don't succeed, it will only get worse.

When the world's breadbaskets fail, starving children will ask their parents, why we didn't prepare for the worst instead of hoping for the best? Why did we stay addicted to oil and increase the amount of CO_2 we pump every year, hoping our wealth and technology will save us down the road? They will accuse us of killing them, and they will be right.

I'm accusing now.

What will you parents, so silent today, say to your children tomorrow?

Whew. My hand is cramping – got to stop.

Maybe it's all a pipe dream. Humans are too addicted to war, too afraid to act together, parasites actively killing our beautiful host. Americans are too selfish. Humanity can't focus. And I'm kidding myself there's still something we can do.

Maybe it's already over.

But we still need to try, don't we? Try to go big instead of spending trillions on Band-Aids and then killing each other over disappearing food. Try to become generous guests, leaving our home better off for all the children to come. Try to fight the disbelief and give ourselves a worldwide values enema that gets shit moving, knowing we might die anyway.

What else can we do? Sit back and get high and just take it? Not me. Not the America Hitler underestimated, saying we were too undisciplined. How'd that turn out, old Adolf?

Christ. Full circle back to Baby Hitler and the birth of the Idea.

It doesn't matter if my last list is a dream or an illusion. I've still got to go – like what the Paris Accord lady said – from <u>possible</u> to <u>probable</u> to <u>likely</u> to <u>DONE</u>. Yeah, Done Dead Cretin. Because impossible isn't a fact, it's an attitude!

Okay, now I sound like an idiot talking in bumper stickers. So be it. Like Mark Twain, who wrote bumper sticker before cars, said, *"You can't depend on your eyes when your imagination is out of focus."*

Cretin's completely out of focus!

But his death is just the spark, the revolution is the fire. Without everybody on the planet dropping everything to push in the same direction, there's zero chance we create a new story for humankind, one based on cooperation and collaboration.

There's zero chance we revolt and survive.

We will die with a whimper, my ten beautiful dreams burnt to ash.

Screw that. Time to get on with it.

Because compared to what's coming, every natural disaster mankind's ever had is a mere tap on the shoulder by Mother Earth.

She's trying to get our attention.

We need to give it to her <u>now</u>.

Today's Headline

"Arctic Temperatures Smash Past Freezing for Third Year in Row." Melting in the dark – fifty degrees above normal. So hot that Sweden and Siberia catch fire.

– TheGuardian.com

Shots Fired!

I'm in the canyon again, tucked in a three-sided cliff. Alone.

Daylight pushes against the dark, compromising into a gray haze. I turn off my flashlight.

"We know the truth, not only by the reason but also by the heart."

Pascal, this week's obsession. Is this act my truth? Yes.

No more reasoning. Just give it straight from my broken heart.

I take out the Liberator – pretentious or great name, still can't decide. And the box of 9mm rounds, a roll of string, and a heavy-duty clamp. I put on swim goggles, a last-minute addition for eye protection, and put a round in the chamber, clamp the gun to a tree, tie the string around the trigger and stare at it.

Gingerly, oh so carefully, I cock it and step back. Don't want it to go off until I'm ten feet away behind a tree. Slowly, I walk in reverse and let the string flow through my fingers, shielding my face with my forearm. I squat, ready. But am I? It feels like a moment here, shooting the gun for the first time. A point of no return?

"Come on. Just do it." I take a deep breath and pull the string and –

CRACK!

It echoes through the canyon, as loud as a regular gun. LOUD.

I rip off my goggles and rush to the Liberator. It's still clamped to the tree branch, intact, with a whiff of gunpowder and a wisp of smoke rising from its stubby barrel.

Holy shit, it works. I feel a rush. What is that? Pride? I built this thing and it works!

I take out another round and repeat the process. Only this time, I spin the gun so it's pointed at the cliff wall. I want to see what the bullet does when it hits. Again, I squat behind a log and pull the string and CRACK! The bullet blasts into the stone cliff, chipping a bit off.

It's so intense!

As if my spirit has left my body – shot from the gun and become the bullet. Blasting past some internal border, the old me gone forever.

Maybe it sparks a revolution that changes everything. Or it tears the country apart. Or I'm snuffed, a useless part of the system I'm trying to destroy. I don't know.

But I know one thing, like Ajax in that old Sophocles play, *"With this knife, cut my life and suffering."*

With this gun, I will cut my suffering. This plastic pistol will execute Cretin for his crimes against humanity.

Finally, I have killed him.

Hamlet is dead.

Today's Facts

Grain production in Europe is down 7.1% in one year because of drought. We have 4 months stored. And 80% of what we eat is a cereal of some sort. Better hoard my Cheerios.

– Nature.org

The Plan

Hamlet gone, I need a plan.

A concrete, how do I do the impossible PLAN.

Online, I force myself to watch a recent Cretin rally in Alabama to see what I'll face. There he is, strutting onto the stage, crowd berserk, chunky pale faces in a vomit of slick red, white, and blue signs. And everybody on phones, recording Cretin, who hulks, preens, and waves his weird rubbery wave. Do they really think they'll go home and watch it again?

Cretin never smiles, that's weak. That's human. He can't even fake a sense of humor, never mind joy, watching the mayhem like a stone-faced dictator. Secret Service is everywhere.

The frenzy of the crowd makes me queasy, acting like Cretin is a damn Nazi Beatle. I've avoided watching rallies, knowing I'll have to enter that mob where everybody's inhibitions evaporate. Where they become stunted and grotesque. Cretin's cult, with the braying meanness of middle school kids, loves Dear Liar. My stomach sinks at its pop star intensity...

How the hell do I kill the most protected man on the planet?

Me, a kid who's just fired his first gun. Who's never even thrown a punch. How do I go from zero violence to infinity? With a plastic pistol I made myself? This won't work –

But then, then... Cretin lumbers onto a catwalk toward the microphone. I can't believe it. The crowd presses right up against the thigh-high catwalk as he takes his time, basking in all the slobbery love, like a contestant in one of his sleazy pageants. No visible SS, just a cop every ten feet. People can touch him if they want. They can even jump up and plug him in the head with a bullet from a plastic gun. Or just shoot him from the floor.

Cretin settles behind the podium, smiling his smug joyless smile – the horrible cartoon man sprung to life. Right behind him in a small grandstand is pure white America – don't they wonder where everybody else is?

How do I get in that grandstand? It's definitely close enough for a headshot. All the gun-nutters say there's a bigger chance of missing, but I've only got one bullet, and it's got to count. Our endless wars have improved the odds of people who get shot, going from dead to permanently maimed. Can't go through all this just to Reagan it.

I turn off the sound and stare at the video. If I can muster my courage and get up against the catwalk, or maybe even right behind him in the grandstand, I can do it. Just need to get there early wearing Cretin memorabilia like gang colors and be his number one fan for the day.

This will take nerves of steel, but it's a plan – finally, a workable plan.

Do I have the balls to do this? No. Not yet. Maybe never.

How the hell do I put myself through the boot camp to be ready?

There's only one way – no thinking. It's got to be pure muscle memory. Like the Tai Chi people at FTW, empty-mind-repetition. Practice for every situation where I could pull the gun, cock it, and fire. Practice putting the Liberator together in under two minutes in some bathroom stall. Practice until I become the Plan and it becomes me.

Bottom line? I've got to brainwash myself.

Like all those Cretin disciples, I too will go full zombie.

Christ. What a thought. But there's no other way. It will be an out-of-body experience at Cretin's rally. It will be like that pro-Cretin demonstration at the dog beach times a thousand. If I had time, I'd go to one just to acclimate to the hysterical atmosphere.

But I don't. He's not coming here. I've got to go to him.

Soon. Before I lose my nerve.

Prep

I watch endless pistol shooting tutorials online.

I learn the grip for lefties – left hand clutching the handle, right hand folded over it in a murderous prayer.

I practice pulling the Liberator out of my belt, where it lurks under a T-shirt. There are videos for that move on YouTube. Oh yeah, right hand yanks up shirt, left hand grabs gun. If parents found out what their kids watch on YouTube – radicalization central – they'd shit themselves.

You can even learn how to prepare for an assassination.

So, I pick up tips on how to "dry fire" train – what the gun nuts call practicing without bullets – stalking the empty house. I'm in a crowded rope line, so I ease the gun out slowly, hiding it with my right hand. Jumping on a stage, so I hop on the couch and draw it. Tackled, so I roll on the floor and spring up, Liberator ready.

Lift shirt. Grab Gun. Cock. Aim. Pull trigger. CLICK. Over and over, until I'm sweaty. I even open the fridge for a snack and whip it out and shoot the milk. Click. Ready for every situation!

I feel like an idiot.

But it's also fun in a Cowboy and Indian little kid way. June would love all the pretend shooting and fake dying. Wish I could at least tell her so I'm not as lonely. But that fantasy died with Hamlet. She'd just want to help and I won't risk her life. No way. An epically bad idea back before the Idea became the Plan. Now, it's happening.

Gigi lies in full crocodile mode, clunky head between paws, brown eye quizzically following me. Why's boy acting so weird?

I take a break, lying with her on the floor for a dog's eye view. Amazing how dogs can be so in tune with humans, even though our faces float way above them. The house looks different from Gigi's level, all weird angles. The ceiling seems far away, as if I've shrunk. Am I shrinking? Inside?

Yeah, the downside of obsession, telescoping the world to one thing.

Gigi tail thumps as she dozes. Her white socks move, dreaming about chasing dogs at the beach. She yips and growls in a world of play only she can see – wish we were there right now! But I let her sleep, it's what you do with dogs and dreams.

Reluctantly, I get up and take the Liberator apart again, hiding pieces in my clothes. Small parts like the trigger go in my pockets. The main triangle – the body? – it goes in my belt at the small of my back. Grip and barrel go in each sock. All invisible to metal detectors.

To prepare, I stand in front of the toilet as if I'm in a bathroom stall. I pull out the pieces to put the gun together and immediately drop the firing pin. The little nail hits the closed toilet and bounces behind it. No seat covers in a convention center restroom. If I don't figure this out, I'll end up fishing Liberator pieces out of a public toilet.

Will a small nail even set off a metal detector? Can't I bring the gun to the rally fully assembled and avoid the trip to the men's room to put it together? Hide just the bullet in my Lady Liberty key chain?

Too risky.

But putting it together standing in a tight bathroom stall is also dangerous, with pieces flying all over the place. I need to put it together fast.

Like a damn Navy Seal.

Today's Headline

"Every Seat on A Cross-Country Flight Equals 3 Square Meters of Arctic Ice Melted." I'll take killing Cretin as my carbon offset when I fly to the rally. He's got to be worth billions of tons.

– TheAtlantic.com

"Winners"

During a break from Liberator practice, I read something so sickening.

A company worth 12 billion dollars, XPO, told Linda Jo Neal they would dock her pay if she went home after complaining of chest pains. She died on the packing floor an hour later. That's not even the worst part – the supervisor "coned" her like she was a fender-bender. He didn't let anybody give her CPR and insisted workers continue packing Nike in the 100-degree heat. She lay there four hours before a worker got up the nerve to call somebody. True story. In America. Today.

Christ, I'm doubting humanity's humanity. Again.

Are we even worth saving?

I try not to obsess about it during another day of dry fire practice.

Draw. Aim. Cock. Click. It's gotten boring, which I guess is good. I turn to assembling the gun. Need to be an octopus to snap the damn thing together. A flat surface would help – one that'll blend in at a rally. Like a campaign sign. I find one of Mom's old *Save The Whales* signs and sit with it on my lap. It takes ten minutes, but I don't drop anything. I do it again and shave off a minute.

Wax on, wax off, I practice. So uncoordinated. Wouldn't last a day slaving in a factory like that Foxconn Apple factory in China where they worked people so hard, they had to put nets under windows to stop suicides. The world's wealthiest company keeps billions offshore to avoid taxes but just can't find the money to make worker's lives bearable. WTF?

I furiously snap and unsnap the Liberator until I fall into the mind-numbing repetition. Slaving, like in the fashion industry – number two polluter behind oil – where they shoot striking workers for wanting over two bucks a day to make all our cheap "fast fashion" clothes that end up in landfills. Great for Cretin, buying his ties overseas while hammering "buy USA" and –

I snap out of it and look down.

My fingers are raw from the hard plastic of the Liberator.

Damn it all, I'm spiraling. But this is where Cretin wants us to live. It's a wonderful life for "winners" and a death camp Potterville for "losers."

And for people who didn't win the birthright lottery and inherit 400 million? The poor people who need to leap from burning countries and crawl a thousand miles to escape violence, poverty, and drought? Earth is their only inheritance. And Cretin casually destroys it.

It never occurs to Cretin it's just a roll of the cosmic dice he's not them – in a sweatshop. Or rioting in Chile over a 4-cent subway increase. Which is bad enough, when daddy gives you all that money and you have no gratitude. But to instead inflict suffering on immigrant families willing to work harder than you can imagine? How much self-loathing must you feel? You piece of shit.

You're a LOSER! And deep down you know it too.

So as boring as this gun practice is, RAGE fuels me.

You think you won't pay the price, Cretin. But you will.

I've got a gun and a plan.

I'm coming for you, motherfucker.

Today's News

In a deal Cretin bragged about, Foxconn announced "Foxbots" will replace 80% of the workers in the factory that Wisconsin bribed them to build. Ha. Conned by Cretin and a company with Con in the name. At least the robots won't jump out the windows.

– Forbes.com

Not A Metaphor

Something horrible happened in STEM today.

Every last word is still ringing in my head as I write it out...

The class is waiting for Hale, who always walks in the door precisely one minute early. Don't know how he does it, considering LA gridlock – probably some military skill set.

"Wish I was there," Dim is saying. "I'd have hit that too."

"Don't be Jelly," Tyler still says Jelly, like a middle-schooler. What a Socio. Dim and Dimmer gather around Tyler's phone, cackling inhuman cackles, creepy as Billy Bush in that "I grab 'em by the pussy" tape with Cretin. Did somebody actually hook up with Tyler?

"That is so lit, my dude," Dimmer chimes in. "She's wasted. Last night's party?"

"Your face is hidden. You should send it around, teach her a lesson."

"Yeah, put it on Pornhub. Virgins." Dim and Dimmer are two cawing crows. Except crows are funny and smart and filled with personality –

"That would be sick. But I'm not risking it on that know-it-all bitch," Tyler sniggers.

"You totally Bukkake'd her drunk off her ass," Dim says. This makes more sense – Tyler jerking off on some unconscious girl like that producer did for a lifetime before he finally ended up in jail. "You should do it."

"It would be cool to take her out." Tyler considers it. "But nobody's eyeballing this."

Who is she? Does she know he taped it? Poor girl must have felt terrible waking up to find Tyler cum all over her. Makes me so sick – I'm suddenly filled with the urge to test the Liberator on Tyler. Work up to Cretin like a dog forced to kill rabbits, then puppies, and then chained, defanged dogs like Gigi. Taste the blood of a weaker human and –

"I'm not gonna lose everything over this mud-ho," Tyler says. WTF? Mud-ho? A horrible thought explodes in my head. SG wasn't in Gov class today. Could it be her? Oh, no! Could it?!! Before I know it, I'm in Tyler's face trying to grab his phone.

"Who was it?" I'm shouting. Tyler shoves me so hard that kids look up from phones.

"What the fuck!" Tyler's eyes narrow. "You want to get punched again?"

"Who was it, asshole?" Feeling crazed, I stare at him.

"What the hell are you looking at?" Tyler's freaked out. I feel like when I held the Glock, flooded with power. I want to kill him. Right now.

"Looking at you." My voice is suddenly a weird whisper. I form my hand into a gun and pull the trigger on Tyler. "Pow. Thinking how good killing you will feel."

The heads of Dim and Dimmer snap in unison to look at me. I can't believe I just said that. Why the fuck did I say that? Holy shit, losing it –

"What did you say?" Tyler sputters loudly.

"You heard me." I match his volume as I say the word. "Rapist."

The class inhales in harmony. Tyler looks ready to charge and I circle away, but he can't attack me in front of everybody. Instead, he instantly covers his ass and deletes the video of him cumming on some poor girl when she's vomit-on-herself passed out.

"I don't know what you're talking about Ginj," Tyler says, smiling, a mask of charm for the class already sliding over his face. "But you just threatened to kill me."

"And you're looking at a video of yourself raping an unconscious girl."

Is it rape? Close enough – not going to explain damn Bukkake in school. The class is silent, like all the air they sucked in on that inhale, they now can't exhale. But my breath is raspy. And my blood pounds in my ears. Was it SG? I want to cry and set Tyler on fire –

"That was just a YouTube of two cows getting it on. Or do you think cows can get raped too?" Tyler smirks at me. "You probably do, don't you, Soy Boy? Right, guys?"

Dim and Dimmer dimly nod, unsure about cow consent. Makes me want to punch those morons –

Was SG his first victim? I know how the appetite grows from eating. Tyler will go from this rape to Frat Boy rape to torturing some poor "electro-slut" with cattle prods to raping us all, as he rises, too rich to be stopped. Rises like President Porn, who's first wife said he raped her, pulling out fistfuls of her hair after his bungled scalp reduction surgery created his bizarre wig. So too, Tyler will rise, attacking dozens of women, the same way Cretin did to all his accusers. Because personal porn always becomes political. Sadism always goes wide if it can. Look at Hitler –

"That was a threat. I'm gonna report you." Tyler presses, sensing his advantage. I don't care. There's a bullet with Tyler's name on it – has this moment been inevitable? How me, a bait dog like Gigi with no taste for blood, becomes a killer of mad kings? Starting with the evil prince who understudies Joffrey in GOT –

"Who you going to report?" Hale strides in with his loose-limbed walk, confident, like an athlete prepped for a competition he knows he'll win. This is going to get bloody.

"Tyler?" Hale looks at Tyler, who doesn't want to get into it but now has no choice. The whole class has heard it and he knows he can't BS his way out of it with Hale.

"Benjamin threatened to kill me." Tyler uses my full name, something nobody does. It's the first time ever he hasn't used one of his insults.

"That right?" Hale looks more amused than concerned. "Why would he say that?"

"You'd have to ask him."

"I'm asking you."

"He… He misunderstood something." Tyler squirms.

"Oh, yeah?" Hale looks at me. No judgment, just assessment. Threat assessment. His face changes slightly – not so jocular. Does he see something in my face?

"What did he misunderstand?" Hale's eyes go a bit flat as he turns back to Tyler.

"He thought I had a video of something, but it wasn't what he thought it was." Tyler's turning red now, trying to avoid saying it.

"Yeah? What did he think it was?" There's that quiet questioning, like an interrogator.

"He threatened me. He said he was gonna kill me."

"I hear that. What did Ben think was on the video?" Like a boxer jabbing an opponent, Hale picks apart Tyler, who is all red-faced desperation and hoping for a haymaker.

"He thought… He thought it was a rape."

Holy shit, this is getting good. But I can't enjoy it because I know my turn is next when Hale shifts his pale blue eyes and sharp questions to me.

"And why would he think that?" All amusement has disappeared from Hale's face.

"I don't know. You'd have to ask him." Hale just stares through Tyler.

"We were… we were just joking around." Tyler turns to Dim and Dimmer, who step away from him like he has Ebola. "Right, guys?"

They nod uncertainly, for all their size, suddenly timid.

"See? Benjamin was eavesdropping and heard a bit and misinterpreted it." Tyler is building up steam now. "He threatened to kill me!"

"Is that right, Ben? Did you threaten to kill Tyler?" And here we go. Hale's eyes are now as flat and gray as winter clouds. I just nod, feeling so out of body.

"Really?" Hale sounds surprised. "Why?"

And this is the riddle of school from when your mommy tells you how much fun you'll have as she sniffles – that should tip you off – and walks you into your first day of preschool. To snitch or not to snitch. But I don't care about a reputation as a snitch. Soon, I'll have bigger reputation problems. And I don't care if Tyler gets punished because I will punish him, removing a cancerous tumor from the body of humankind –

"Ben? Was it a joke?" Hale breaks into my spiral.

"Huh?" I notice my hands are shaking. Adrenaline. God, I hope it wasn't SG. Such a fantastic person to be degraded like that.

"Was it a joke?" Hale repeats, giving me an out – a rope down a well to save me from drowning. But I'm too blasted. My nerves are jangling and I'm not in the mood for it. I suddenly realize I'm free, a superpower gift of the Plan. It'll all be over soon, anyway.

"No joke," I croak. Why am I really doing this? Am I free or do I want to get caught?

"See?" Tyler crows. "I told you. Freak threatened to kill me. As if he ever could."

Tyler is now a boxer I knocked down who improbably gets up and lands a lucky punch after I lower my hands. June wouldn't approve.

"Why did you threaten Tyler?" Hale asks me quietly, almost sympathetically.

"He bragged about raping an unconscious girl. He showed them the video on his phone and laughed. Like it's so funny, raping a drunk or drugged girl. They want to put it online."

That turns the tide – when you don't back down. When you stand and name the evil.

"Liar." Tyler's face flushes red as a dog's dick in heat. His voice cracks as he holds up his iPhone. "Show me. Show me the video."

"He deleted it," I say calmly. "Right after I heard him bragging about raping a girl who we all probably know."

A fan in a computer hums in the silence. Hale blinks as slow as a sigh. But it's not like "he blinked" in some showdown. No. It's the accepting blink of a soldier heading into battle. Sent to death by old draft dodgers for the wrong reasons – knowing that and going anyway. Because not to go violates a no-man-left-behind code I can only guess at. Nobody from HWB will ever see war and –

"Give me the phone." Hale turns the gun barrel of his face on Tyler.

"What about him?" Tyler points at me wildly. "He threatened me. That's a crime."

"So's rape," I spit this out, suddenly enraged, thinking of SG. And what about June when she's a little older? She's not easy pickings. She's smart and tough and even at ten sees the world clearly. But given a roofie or a spiked punch, June could be at the mercy of a Tyler. Who will look out for her? Will one guy have mercy, stand up, and say STOP?

"Tyler." Hale doesn't raise his voice. "Give me your phone."

Tyler stares at him with a look of pure panic. The video's deleted, but is anything ever truly gone in our surveillance society? Nope.

"If you've got nothing to hide, then it's fine," Hale says calmly.

But Tyler has something to hide. Rape, horrible and shameful, that exposes him for who he really is. So, Tyler grabs his bag and bolts out the door. He runs toward Daddy and his money. They will destroy the phone and experts will wipe it from the cloud. Lawyers will threaten and purchase and humiliate SG into silence. And Tyler will learn a lesson straight out of Cretin's handbook – you can get away with anything if you're rich.

As if he doesn't already know it.

Hale looks half tempted to run after Tyler, but walks over to his desk.

"Ben, I'd like to see you after school today," he says mildly. Hale's eyes are pale blue again, as unruffled as robin's eggs in the nest of his tan face.

I nod. But I'm not worried. I think me and Hale are on the same page.

And, like Cretin, Tyler won't get away from me.

No matter how far he runs.

Today's Headline

"Administration Cancels Whale and Sea Turtle Protections" Just another rape from Cretin, his rapey values trickling down to us all. Not me.

– LATimes.com

Pawn Sacrifice

"**I**t's no joke, that kind of threat."

Hale leans back in his chair, stretching his legs, a spring uncoiling after the day's classes. "Was any part of you serious?"

"No more than everybody else," I joke. Hale stares at me, not cracking a smile. I sure don't need the attention, but I don't feel like I-was-just-kidding my way out of the truth. Screw that. And I doubt back-pedaling and lying would work on Hale anyway.

"It's a huge thing, threatening to kill somebody." Hale's taking me seriously. How does he know I am? "Never mind actually taking a life."

"I know," I respond. But do I? Guess I'll find out.

"I commanded men your age after their first kill. I know how it chews on you from the inside," Hale continues. I've got to play this right, so he doesn't turn me in, but I can't help wanting to hear what he has to say about killing.

"I can only imagine. But what if they deserve it?" I try to keep it philosophical, like with Dad. "What if they've got it coming?"

"We've all got it coming, kid."

"Unforgiven." Can't believe he just quoted my favorite new western.

"Yep." Hale nods. Silence as we both welcome the shortcut the movie provides, avoiding so many words.

"You're smart, Ben. The smartest kid I've ever met and not just book smart. You're what they call an old soul. That's your real genius. You see the world beyond your years."

It feels good to hear that, but I stay quiet. I've got no idea where he's going, but it feels like it's going to be deep.

"So, you understand killing somebody is not what you think it'll be. Like the kid discovered." Hale stares at me. "You know the movie, so you know what I'm talking about."

"I know." It keeps me up at night. I've got dark circles under my eyes. Does Hale see them – the anxiety that's eating me up? Can he help me?

"It'll change you, and I'm not talking about the superficial ways, like if you end up in prison. I'm talking about who you are. How you see the world. How you see yourself. You become a different person. Somebody you don't recognize. Somebody you don't even like."

His words land deep and suddenly my eyes flood. WTF?

It's as if he knows <u>everything</u>.

"But what if they're evil? Doing evil in the world? To the world?" This bursts out of me and my eyes now overflow. Fuck. Unexpected. The strain of the Plan, I'm too on edge.

Hale just passes me the box of Kleenex on his desk. I take one and blow my nose and quickly wipe my eyes. Hale studies me without judgment or impatience as I pull myself together.

"When can you take a stand? When is it okay to say enough?" Can he tell I'm not just talking about Tyler? Got to watch myself here. "When you're the only person who sees it, and the whole world is… is paralyzed."

"'If you can keep your head when those about you are losing theirs?'" Hale looks bemused. I know that poem. Kipling. It's like he's read my damn journal.

"Yeah. 'Or watch the things you gave your life to broken…'" I just see the poem in my head, but I feel like a show-off performing monkey, so I cut it short. "I don't want to watch the world broken by assholes."

"So, you want to be judge, jury, and executioner?" It feels weirdly good that Hale thinks I've got it in me. Taking me seriously.

"I don't know. Maybe." I know what he means, but so what? I can't wait for the broken machinery of our system to repair itself. The planet's climate gears will grind us to dust before –

"That's a heavy lift, like a decision to go to war. Got to be sure you're right. And the punishment fits the crime. And you can handle the load. One you'll carry the rest of your life."

"I don't hear don't do it," I say. I can't believe he's willing to have a real discussion. And it's a relief to talk about it. Even though it's not IT.

"I've seen some evil in my life. You sure Tyler's worth it?"

"He's a rapist, a sociopath, and a wild animal killer. And that's just so far. He'll ruin the world just for the hell of it." I spit this out. Hale doesn't respond. What's he thinking? That I'm crazy? Do I misjudge him? Will he turn me in after all? He takes his legs off the desk and leans forward.

"Life takes care of the Tylers of the world, Ben."

"Maybe I am that life." So much for keeping it philosophical, but I can't help it with Hale. I fight the urge to blurt everything out to him. To come clean. To be innocent again on the inside. Confession – I yearn for it, but it's way too late for that now.

"Maybe you are." Hale stares at me, assessing again. Has he read the Virginia Student Threat Assessment Guide? Of course. "But somebody like Tyler, who seems to have everything, seems to get away with every-thing, is missing out on the real meaning of life. It's an unknown, un-known to him. Like a party he doesn't know exists."

"What is? What's the unknown, unknown?" I urgently want to know this myself. A moment as Hale looks at me, measuring some hidden part of my interior landscape.

"It's love, Ben," Hale says it simply. "He doesn't know it, doesn't feel it, just has a hole where it should be. I've seen this in service, which gets all sorts of Tylers running through."

"Boo-hoo for him. Meanwhile, he breaks the world." But his answer surprises me, talking about love. Have I missed out on love because of my obsessions? Missed it with SG?

"The world will break him. It breaks everybody. We're all walking to-wards our coffin," Hale responds. Christ, so true. And much more for me than Hale can imagine.

"But he's… He's baby Hitler in high school."

Hale bursts out laughing and I join, breaking the tension. It sounds ridiculous, like something out of that old Mel Brooks musical *The Producers*. Springtime for Cretin in Germany, it sure is.

"Ben, he's got no internal freedom. He's got no love. He's got no understanding of how to give love. He's got everything and feels nothing. But late at night, when it's just him, he's got a separateness that can't be bridged, an emptiness that can't be filled. Disconnected."

"I get that. I know that. But Tyler chews up the world. They all just chew it up." And what about my separateness late at night? No man is an island. Except now, I am.

"'The poorer we are inwardly, the more we try to enrich ourselves outwardly,'" Hale quotes somebody.

"Who said that? Buddha? Jesus?"

"Bruce Lee." Hale smiles. Can't believe this conversation – I <u>love</u> this guy. He just makes you want to follow him over any hill.

"Let life take care of Tyler. Be the light to his darkness, that's your role." Hale says, wrapping it up. "Promise me you'll leave him alone and this conversation can stay between us."

This is an enormous act of faith. HWB has all sorts of strict rules about reporting disturbed students saying disturbing things. Like threatening to kill somebody.

"You trust I'll tell you the truth?" I ask. Hale nods without hesitation.

"Ben, you have such a great life in front of you – you're not going to waste it on a Tyler. I see how special you are, one of a kind. So yeah, if you tell me something, I'll trust it."

I stare at him, choking up again. He's not just cheerleading like all the endlessly chipper teachers who would rat me out in a second. Nothing Hale says changes my mind about Tyler – the world is instantly a better place without him. But sociopath Tyler still has limited power. Sociopath Cretin is an extinction-level event, already committing daily crimes against humanity. Tyler is a pawn I'll sacrifice so I can go all Jaime Lannister on the mad king.

"Okay. I'll let life deal with Tyler," I say. But what if it was SG? Shouldn't

I right that wrong? Yet another sacrifice to keep my focus on Cretin.

"Good. Because nobody dies on my watch, Ben. Not by cops, not by drunk driving, not by suicide, and not by each other. That's mission-critical for me – for all of you to live through this turbulent time of your lives. Do I have your word?"

"Yes. You have my word." It's the truth, just not the whole truth. I won't kill Tyler – I will kill somebody Hale would never expect. "But what if Tyler reports me?"

"He won't want the attention. And if he does, I won't interpret yours as a 'true threat.'" Hale stands, holding out the gnarled hand missing part of the pinky. I shake the calloused pads of sandpaper. He could crush me, but he's got nothing to prove. "This conversation never happened."

"Thanks, Mr. Hale. I really appreciate it. Your trust."

"Don't mention it, Ben." His robin egg eyes are back and crease as he smiles. I nod and walk out.

Hale spared my life, so I will spare Tyler.

But not Cretin.

Today's Headline

"Prenatal Exposure to Air Pollution Linked to Autism Risk." Guess it wasn't vaccines, after all. Just some good old environmental illness we created for ourselves.

– CNN.com.

Accept Death Freak-out

Three in the morning and I'm lost in a fever dream.

I'm out of time. The whole Tyler meltdown proves I'm losing it. The sand in my internal hourglass running out, each grain dropping like a cannonball on my psyche –

The sand in my internal hourglass? Even my writing is melting down.

I have crossed some line. If I don't do it soon, I'll end up in prison or a psych ward. The idea it never ends well for the Hitlers of history – I get what Hale was saying, but we don't have time for the Arc of Justice. Churchill saved the world from Hitler because he saw the gathering storm early. He knew Hitler couldn't be appeased.

The same way Cretin can't. And the climate absolutely won't.

And if I don't kill Cretin <u>soon</u>, I'm afraid I'll kill Tyler for SG. I mean, he's right here, tempting me every hour.

"Before you embark on a journey of revenge, dig two graves." So said Confucius.

Guess I've been digging mine since I first got the Idea – is that what I'm down to now? Revenge? No, it's still prevention. Today Cretin refused to levy a carbon tax, a small step that would slow CO_2 rise with a stroke of a pen. Some Nobel economist figured out Climate Chaos now costs the world two trillion every year in floods, drought, and fires. If Big Oil paid for the damage they create, then solar would put them out of business. Instead, Fossil Fuel strip-mines world governments for 5 trillion in subsidies a year – 5% of world GDP. Christ.

What if my Ten Beautiful Dreams list is just denial? And love, what

Hale says gets us through the night, fails. What's left?

Maybe it is only revenge.

Tired of thinking about it. And isn't thinking what got us here, losing our connection with our own hearts, with Mother Nature? Trying to solve the problem with the tool that created it, trying not to FEEL our own death approaching. Even as we thrash in our final death throes – clown-walked to extermination.

Two trillion in damages a year – Christ, we are teetering, I THINK.

Ha. My thoughts. What about my feelings?

Denial. Anger. Bargaining. Depression. Acceptance.

My own emotions spin me, as if jumping me into a gang, each taking a vicious shot. Where is my heart? Where is SG? I should find out how she's doing and if it was her in the video. But how? She's not in school. She's become one of the disappeared.

On a wall at FTW is a poster, *"Happiness is reality minus expectations."*

Expect nothing. Accept death. I do.

Not happy, though. Heartsick.

Got to accelerate the Plan NOW. Cretin's doing a rally a week these days, getting his fix. Got to pick one tomorrow and get on with it.

Got to go full zombie. It's the only way.

Wish I could sleep. But zombies never do.

Today's Fact

More than 25% of U.S. oil comes from government land. Our land. A trillion-dollar industry taking cheap loans and other subsidies from the government they hate. Where's my damn check?

– AmericanProgress.org

Final Deadline

*L*ast night was endless, sleepless, and horrible after my Tyler melt-down. But today I totally, TOTALLY, lost it...

Started out fine, searching for the next Cretin circus. And there it is, a rally in Youngstown, Ohio at someplace called the Covelli Centre.

Wow. This Saturday. One week.

Youngstown, Cretin Country, lost 60% of its people after the steel mills closed and NAFTA sucked the rest of the jobs down to Mexico. So, I get why they're open to Cretin's toxic anger. But why's Cretin always so mad? Maybe the silver spoon is chafing his cheeks...

Arizona would be better. It's closer. And ground zero for Cretin nut-tiness with all the white panic border stuff. But I'll fall apart unless I act now. If I don't do it this week, I'll end up blurting the Plan out to any-body. Like, hey Hector or Hale or Guy-On-The-Street, I'm gonna kill the most powerful man in the world. No, really, I am!

It's got to be Youngstown. My brain won't make it any further.

Seven days. Need to practice shooting the Liberator from my hand. Need to put it together in under two minutes and I'm stuck at five – with each minute I spend in a bathroom stall another minute to get discov-ered. Need to fabricate an excuse about why I'm disappearing for a night, then steal Mom's credit card and book a flight. Don't know if I can do it all in a week. But I've got to – anything to relieve the feeling of my brain sloshing in my head.

I register for a Cretin ticket using my real name. It doesn't matter and –

Suddenly I feel hot – like got-the-flu sweltering. My heart throbs in my ears. I'm breathing deeply but in a vacuum. Great, gasping breaths of NOTHING! And now my heart is bursting out of my chest and –

I hit the floor as my computer comes crashing down. WTF!

I curl up and gasp like a fish flopping on a dock. But unlike the fish on the pier, I'm sucking for air and only getting water – drowning on land. Startled, Gigi jumps up and howls, licking my face. That's how June finds me, rushing in after hearing Gigi's rare bark.

"Benji!" June's eyes are wide with fright – I must look like death. She grabs my clammy hands, shaking me. "What's wrong? What happened?"

I can't speak. All I can do is sweat – my stomach trying to explode my guts all over the walls.

"I'll be right back." June rushes out.

Gigi whimpers and licks my face. After hours, but probably seconds, Mom strides in with June and puts her hand on my forehead. It feels cool like that time I touched a python. Am I dying?

And now I hear Mom talking, calm and reassuring, but so far away –

"Benji, you're having a panic attack. I know it seems like forever, but it'll be over soon. I want you to inhale and exhale slowly. Okay? Just inhale four seconds and exhale four seconds."

"Do it, Benji," June sounds close to panic herself. "Please, just do it."

My brain has seized itself, but I concentrate. Inhale four seconds. Exhale four seconds, counting each death-rattle breath.

"There you go, Benji," Mom coaxes me. "Straighten your legs a bit. Keep breathing."

All I can do is shallow pant, a dog left too long in a hot car.

"Keep counting your breath," Mom gently reminds me.

I do – in four breaths, out four breaths. It's come to this. My body slowly unclenches. Could I just uncramp myself? Like with Hale, I suddenly want to confess to June and Mom, then surrender my life to some inpatient vacation. You're only as sick as your secrets –

"Stretch your legs," June commands, grabbing my bent legs and pulling them straight. "You look like a spastic."

"June. Go easy." Mom is calm. "Benji, can you roll on your back?"

I give her a slit lizard side-eye and slowly roll on my back.

"Try straightening your arms, honey." I notice they're curled against my chest, little T-Rex appendages. I unclench my fists and straighten my arms against a great invisible weight. I force my eyes open, blinking. Thump-thump, as Gigi stops whimpering and wags her tail.

"Good. There you are," Mom reassures me I exist. I look up at her face, golden down dusting her high cheekbones, her green eyes filled with love. I can't believe in a week I'll never see this face again. Or June's, a smaller copy of Mom, staring down with heartbreaking concern. My eyes fill.

"Don't be sad, Benji," June says. "It can happen to anybody."

Oh, but June, my sadness is so deep and silent, water at the bottom of a well waiting for me to let go and drown. It's the heartbreak of losing a best friend because they do something so unforgivable you have to walk away, even though you still feel them like an amputated limb –

"Can you sit up?" Mom breaks in, still working on bringing me back.

I feel like a poor dying rat on a glue trap, but I slowly sit up.

And then June is in my arms, giving me a big hug, breath smelling like cinnamon gum. Gigi climbs in, licking my face. Mom hugs June and me, and I wrap my arms around them in a pod of love and warmth, with Gigi wriggling in the heart of it. The blood slowly flows back into my limbs, thawing my insides. My breath is normal, cooling my skin.

I squeeze them for a long moment and then let them go.

I have to. I've got seven days left.

Today's Headline

"Anxiety in Teens Is Rising, What's Going On?" A third of teenagers have an anxiety disorder. What's going on? HAHAHA! Take a guess. As a plague of climate-caused locusts eats through the Horn of Africa, famine to come. Locusts! So end times biblical.

– NIH.gov

Six Days – Lie and Lie

I'm not exactly Jason Bourne – might have a heart attack before I get close to Cretin. So I'm glad to have my date chosen. Less than a week.

Just as bad was the aftermath of concern – discussions about what caused it, and whether I need to see a doctor, or take some medication, or maybe even see Nichols again. Christ. But it also gave me an excuse to get out of town, which I brought up at our endless family meeting.

"Like I keep saying, it was a one-time thing. I was a little stressed, but I'm okay now."

"You looked like a dead fish," June curls her arms and starts gasping, doing a cutting imitation of me.

"Won't happen again," I say breezily, hoping like hell it's true.

"It was scary, and a first," Mom scrutinizes me. "We'd really like you to see Nichols. Just for a tune-up."

"Okay, okay. I'm happy to see her." I've got to make some concessions. "And I understand how scary it was, scary for me too."

"Good. So, what else will you do?" Dad asks, all mild, hiding his fear and desire to take me to the hospital right NOW.

"It turns out there's a cognitive behavioral therapy clinic for panic attacks," I lie and lie. "They've got a weekend program for teenagers. Next one starts on Friday."

"Really?" Mom asks. She looks at Dad, pleased. He nods slightly. They are a united front – playing one against the other is impossible.

"Where is it?" Dad pulls out his phone to tap in notes.

They're not irresponsible. They'll check and find a real program in Ojai that specializes in helping distressed teens. It starts Friday and goes for three days – pure luck. But unlike some parents who act like their kids are property, they won't tell me what to do. Right, Mom and Dad? You aren't "my way or the highway." You support me unconditionally and don't feel I owe you anything. You don't care what other people think. You never judge, living that line about kids being of you, but not yours. You allow me to follow my interests and discover who I am – a liar and a killer. Christ...

"Ben?" Dad interrupts my thoughts, looking at me with his thick glasses and owl eyes, his brow now furrowed with worry. My love and sadness for them floods me. Is this part of saying goodbye and – stop spiraling! Focus or fall apart and get caught.

"It's in Ojai. I can take the bus. It's called The Moment."

"The moment?" June sneers. "That sounds sooo stupid."

"I don't remember asking you." I mean, it does sound stupid and pretentious, but it's the same meditation stuff they teach at FTW. And it's not like I'm going.

"Family meeting, family rules." June sticks out her tongue with just her face.

But I'm watching Mom and Dad, who look at each other and nod. You like that I'm taking responsibility for myself, something you've taught us from our free-range childhood. I feel a brutal stab of guilt as you agree to the lie that sends me away forever. Manipulating your loving and supportive parenting style – oh, Mom and Dad, I'm so sorry...

"We'll think about it, but it sounds good," Mom says. This means yes. "I'll drive you."

"And I'll come too. Road trip!" June pipes up, looking at me way too sweetly. Damn. She knows I'm lying about something. "We can check out the fire burn."

I've thought of this contingency. June has been talking about the latest *Wonder Woman* for months and how she can't wait to see Gal Gadot kick some ass. That's how she puts it. Don't know why female empowerment always involves skinny models beating up four guys twice her size, but there you go. At least Wonder Woman is a god –

"Benji?" Now, it's Mom interrupting my thoughts. My mind is a dog off its leash. I've tried to train it to sit, but it's gone feral, possessed by a force of nature I can't control. "Where are you right now?"

"Sorry. I'm here. I'm fine," I say, pulling myself together. "A road trip sounds like fun. But I have a surprise for you and June. Two tickets to the all-girls advanced screening of *Wonder Woman*. It's Friday afternoon at the Aero, with the director and Gal Gadot."

"You got us tickets to that?" June screeches. "How? So cool!"

June rushes me and jumps into my arms. She's as solid as Gigi and I squeeze her tight. Grabbing hugs and goodbyes wherever I can.

"Very thoughtful," Dad chimes in. Perfect. I can count on him being at work.

"Yeah, too bad you'll have to miss it," I put it out there casually. I scored the last two seats available and not next to each other. Luckily, June likes to sit in the front row, her head leaning so far back it's like she's taken a head punch, stunned –

"Benji, you're just gonna have to take yourself to the nuthouse," June declares. "Okay?"

I burst out laughing. June always cracks me up. And it's exactly the response I need.

"Sure. I can take the bus to Ojai. It's the easiest thing in the world."

"Really?" Mom hovers between suspicion and concern. "This doesn't feel right."

"Maybe I can take the day off," Dad muses. Uh-oh. This is serious – he never takes a day off.

"First of all, it's not a nuthouse," I say. "It's just more mindfulness training like at Face the Wave but designed for panic attacks. I don't really need to go, but it sounds nice. And they take insurance."

"See Mom?" June implores. "He'll be fine."

"I'm fine," I repeat. Who's the better fiction writer now, Cretin or me?

"We'll think about it," Mom says as Dad nods slightly.

"Okay." I know that means yes.

"Great!" June says. "Thanks for the tickets, Benji."

"My pleasure."

And that's my alibi. I can buy a ticket to Youngstown the day before and charge their card. Nobody will know until it becomes evidence…

Wow. I just choked up, writing that. Mom and Dad, you don't deserve these lies. You are all about the truth. You always try to really see me, the greatest gift a parent can give a child. From my first words, which were, "I'll do it myself."

And you let me try, fail, succeed – over and over. That must've been so damn hard. I love you and –

"So, you'll see Nichols?" Mom asks, looking at me, worried again. Damn my spiraling mind.

"Sure." It's a waste of time and Nichols won't help, but so what? I'm out of here in six days. I'll have to deal with any more panic attacks on my own. I know how – slow down and pay more attention – back to the ever portable breath.

I'll do it myself. A beautiful and tragic line from a two-year-old.

Still true. A man threatens our planet and it needs help. I'll do it my-self. As alone as a butterfly in its cocoon.

Six days to metamorphosis.

Today's Headline

"Reports Paint Dire Climate Picture, Change Few Republican Minds." I'm shocked, *shocked* – that they're too in love with Cretin's tax cuts and racist border BS to give a damn.

– *NYTimes.com*

Five Days – Abnormal to Normal

I'm in the canyon again.

Gentle light filters across the treetops, the sun too low in the sky to do much more than stake a claim on today's heat.

I grip the loaded Liberator. Proven reliable, I'm finally ready to fire the first shot from my hand. The plastic gun is hard and wet with my sweat, the opposite of everything I see, which is soft and green – the difference between organic life and man-made murder.

I have a moment of pure self-loathing. I am Thanatos, death itself. How did I get on the wrong side of all I believe?

A twig SNAPS and I whirl. Tyler again?

No. It's a mule deer and its fawn, eating shrubbery, moving toward me. The fawn is a light chocolate brown with cotton balls on her back. She's got spindly legs and fuzzy ears as big as her head. The deer looks right at me, nose twitching – mom on the alert. I hold my breath, frozen to be invisible, as they continue their delicate steps toward me. The fawn gazes with an open, innocent face like Bambi, not seeing the statue of me.

We are still beyond our bodies, dipping into the vast quiet of creation.

It's another hushed communion with nature I never want to end.

The fawn sees me and is close enough to touch. I slowly reach out and feel the impossible velvet of her ear. Unafraid, she allows it. We are one.

Suddenly, Mom's ears spring forward. She sniffs the air as if she got a whiff of the death in my hand and they become cartoon characters bounding over logs. Crashing and bouncing and gone. I'm so happy Tyler isn't here to create an orphan. Or tempt me to kill him.

I put on my swim goggles and stand in the silence, with only chirping birds bustling the bushes. I aim at my target, a head-shaped piece of bark on a log about five feet away. Carefully cocking the gun, clenching the handle, I try to slow my breath as my hands drip sweat.

It feels like holding a lit firecracker. What if it explodes now? What if it only has a few good shots and I already used them with my other tests? What if the nail hits wrong? What if –

I push the thoughts out of my head. Aim. Exhale like they say in all the videos. And now, don't pull, but <u>squeeze</u> the –

CRACK!

The morning silence shatters as bark flies off the log. It's LOUD. So much louder than when I'm ten feet away holding a string. I can't see the birds flying but hear their fluttering wings. And then a profound silence, every living being frozen. Not in the peaceful stillness of the deer, but in protection. I feel shame as I walk to the log, the sound of crunching leaves crashing the quiet. The dull lead is splatted in the wood – the color of the water at the bottom of the polluted well into which I endlessly fall.

I can do this.

I reload the Liberator and step back, cocking it. I aim and squeeze the trigger. CRACK. And again, I check my wood target – only a bit off. For a toy gun printed by a computer, it's accurate enough.

I go again. And again. Each time reloading, moving further away, but getting more accurate, pulling it from my hoody pocket – aiming, cocking, firing.

CRACK. CRACK. CRACK. CRACK. CRACK. CRACK.

Each time, the gun sounds a little less loud, feels a little less surprising. My hands sweat less until now they're dry. Is this what happens? You get a little more desensitized until the abnormal is routine? Is this what Cretin does to us all?

The Sierra Club says schools of cod used to stall tall ships mid-ocean and salmon swamped the canoes of Pacific explorers a mere two hundred years ago. Born into Eden, do we accept the world we create because it's all we know? It's our normal... Soon, we'll look with wonder at elephants the way we now look at Mastodons – in books and cartoons.

Never. I refuse to give in to that abnormal any more than Cretin's. So, I'm glad the gunfire is starting to feel normal to me now. It has to.

The sun is up. I need to stop making a racket. And conserve bullets – 32 left. I dry fire my draw, aim, cock, squeeze – CLICK.

The pockets in my hoody are perfect, wide enough to quickly pull the Liberator. And it's long enough to hide gun pieces in my pants pockets as I go through security. In Youngstown I can buy a Cretin hoody to fit in.

I dry fire some more.

As I draw, I hold the gun with my trigger finger straight along the barrel like the videos teach. I don't want to shoot myself like that black basketball player who accidentally shot himself. They sent him to jail – shooting while black in America. Meanwhile, that old VP Cheney drunk-shot a guy in the face while hunting tame birds. And the guy apologized!

Shooting while white in America.

What's it like to shoot somebody in the face? Guess I'll find out.

Over and over, I practice my draw, aim, cock, squeeze – CLICK.

Until it's totally normal.

Today's Quote

Cretin is *"The worst president for the environment our nation has ever had,"* the director of the Sierra Club announces today. Ha. Not just our nation.

– Michael Brune

Four Days – Ready. Aim...

Another day, another 110 million TONS of carbon dumped into the atmosphere.

Another day, another 34,520 people dead in the world, just from air and water pollution. Thirteen million people a year – a number so huge it's meaningless. Unless it's your kid who suffocates in front of you from an asthma attack. Or your sister.

Another day, another 14 million acres of wild public lands sold to oil and gas prospectors. Claims that are permanent, even after Cretin and his cronies are long dead. Precious sites like Bears Ears National Monument cut in size by 85%, our beloved commons looted.

Just another day for Cretin, who makes the illegal legal, like *The Purge*. Where up is down, stupid is smart, and the seas retreat instead of rise.

As he shoves us into his demented reality, another million words are written about his daily desecrations. They still call him Mr. President, this tiny man, while he destroys everything pure, sacred, and powerless.

But I am not powerless. I am not disinforstracted.

So, it's another day of target practice and assembling the Liberator, looking down so long my neck burns.

Align. Push. Snap. Slide. Squeeze. Shove. Pull. Click. Load.

Disassemble. Again.

Ingraining it into muscle memory until I'm under three minutes. I am beyond thought. Beyond fear. Beyond doubt. Fast as kids whipping through Rubik's Cubes after memorizing the pattern to impress people.

I go to classes, eat, listen – but I'm not there. Nobody notices as I prepare for war, a diver submerging away from the light as the pressure increases, squeezing my head.

I even practice at night, the house silent except for Gigi's snores. I dry fire constantly, making the Liberator a part of me like the grunts in old army movies. I would sleep with it – Mongol warriors slept with their bows to keep them from freezing and cracking. But I'm afraid I might roll over and snap off a plastic piece like a mom suffocating her baby in bed.

For a moment, during the early morning hikes to the canyon, the pressure eases. The soothing light, the crunch of my Converse on the rocky fire road, the smell of Jasmine – it bathes my jangled nervous system.

But as soon as the CRACK of the Liberator breaks the morning silence, I'm right back in, diving deeper and deeper into darkness.

Most of my practice is the draw, aim, cock, squeeze, CLICK of an empty plastic gun pulled from a hoody. But I also fire rounds and the click becomes a CRACK. Twenty bullets left.

I practice shooting up in case I can't step onto the stage. I practice running, drawing, and shooting. I practice every way I can imagine it going down until I can hit the head-shaped stump ten out of ten times from twenty feet away. Until I can draw the Liberator and shoot it in less than a second. Until, if it's already in my hand, shooting through my hoody, I can instantly kill.

I am down to three rounds. I hide two in my room in case I lose the one bullet with Cretin's name on it. Today is not just another day.

Today I am full zombie.

I am heaven. I am hell. I am the big bang.

I will change everything.

I am.

READY.

Four Days - Soy Girl

I went looking for SG. I didn't know if she was the person in Tyler's video, but I wanted to see her one more time and maybe find out. Comfort her if I can. Also, to silently say goodbye to another precious person who doesn't know I'm leaving. It didn't go the way I pictured it...

Getting her address is easy enough. Between Insta-Lie, Fakebook, and Maps, in no time at all I'm standing in front of a modern home in Santa Monica. The front doors are ancient, with intricate Indian carvings, warming up the house's stark white exterior.

I ring the doorbell and hear a few sitar cords inside. It stops. I wait a minute and press again – the same sitar. Beautiful, but it brings forth no life, just plaintive notes echoing in the empty house. I can't stay and wait for SG to show. Of all things, I've got to see Nichols. Christ...

I barely make it on time. We spend the whole hour discussing why I want to quit therapy and in the end, I agree to return. Ha. After wasting that hour, one of my last on the planet, I slip out the door designed to keep Nichols' victims from running into each other in the waiting room.

I walk down Therapist Row toward the elevator and press the button. The door opens, and like a magic trick I conjured, there's SG. I'm so shocked, I stumble back a step.

"Am I a ghost?" SG smiles, but her almond eyes aren't shining like usual.

"No. I mean, yes. You've ghosted school," I blurt out. "I was just at your house."

"Stalking me again. Not a good look, Rotten Fruit." She's teasing, but her smile is tired.

"My specialty." I recover a bit. "I wanted to see if um … if everything is okay."

"With me? Oh, fine." She looks at her feet. "My Mom's been sick, so I'm taking a few weeks off school, working independently from home."

"I'm sorry to hear that," I say. Silence falls between us. Unlike with the cow a million years ago, it's uneasy. Another gate closed. I try to open it without prying.

"Guess you heard I threatened to kill Tyler. It was a scene. Of course, I won't."

"Pity." The word falls from her mouth, a drop of acid. Her face sets.

Shit... It <u>was</u> her in the video. I'm too stunned to say anything as SG glances at her watch. Late for an appointment. With Nichols? I hope not.

"I'm late for the dentist. See you around, Benji." She smiles too brightly, teeth perfect. My heart breaks into furious pieces.

"Yeah... " I find my voice as she turns. "You'll know why soon."

"Why what?" She circles toward me, hovering. Close as the fawn, but I can't bring myself to reach out and touch her.

"Why I can't kill Tyler for you."

That does it – laying the truth out. She blinks, releasing one tear.

For a long moment, we connect in silence as the world whirls.

Was that a messed-up way to say I love you? Yeah. I wish with all my heart I could slaughter Tyler and lay him at your feet like a sacrifice. I want to hug you and tell you I love you and maybe even kiss you, but don't dare as you wipe your eyes clear.

"Thank you. But Tyler's not your job. He's mine." She walks away. "Bye, Benji."

"Bye, Adra," I say as she turns a corner without looking back.

I feel sad. It's the last time I'll ever see her. And stupid. She can handle Tyler without my fatal fantasy.

And isn't one fatal fantasy enough?

Three Days - Empty Cup

It's Wednesday. I leave Friday. The rally is Saturday. Holy shit.

June and I are in Ye Olde King's Head, a British shop that sells Smarties and plates with the queen stenciled on them. Tourist junk. I'm looking for a metal Lady Liberty key chain to hide the bullet that will blow Cretin's head off. I like Lady Liberty helping me out – she's #metoo with Mother Earth and all the huddled masses yearning to be free of him.

I find the perfect one, coppery green, with a hollow metal base to hide the bullet and nail. A piece of gum can stick them in place and nobody will notice a thing. They'll be too busy looking for guns and knives, not tiny nails and one bullet, a drop against the ocean of their security. But it will only take one well-placed drop to dissolve the whole nightmare...

June waits impatiently with a big box of Smarties, the reason we're here as far as she knows. Just want to spend one of my last days with –

"Come on, Benjeeeeee."

June rattles the Smarties, waiting for me to pay so she can greedily inhale them, one handful after another. To me, they're just M&Ms. But to June they're perfection – less sweet, better chocolate, with a thinner hard candy coating. I've got no idea how she discovers them, imported from countries with subtler taste. I pay the cashier.

"What the heck's that?" June wrinkles her nose at my kitschy keychain.

"Keychain. It's a gag gift."

"For who?" She opens her Smarties, takes one out, and puts it on her tongue. She always does this for a couple, letting the hard candy melt in her mouth until the chocolate oozes through. But soon it'll be too much and she'll start eating them like popcorn.

"Hale," I improvise. "It's a joke."

"Suck-up move," June pronounces. I wish it was true.

I feel terrible about Hale, the best teacher at HWB because of how he makes kids think about life. What else will they remember from school? Not much. Hope he doesn't blame himself, there's no way for him to know about the Liberator. I've just turned into too good a liar. It'll be a mortal embarrassment for HWB, but if they have any spine at all, they won't fire him. Not hopeful about that. Will Hale understand you can't wait for the world to take care of –

"Benji," June breaks up my rambling thoughts. "Come on, snap out of it."

"Sorry," I mumble and turn away so she can't see my face as I stumble out into the Santa Monica sun. I'm too emotional. Everything is way too raw. The closer to I get to Cretin, the less control I have. Control I need to pull the trigger –

"What are you thinking about all the time?" June is right behind me.

"Just, you know. Like I said. Some writing I'm working on –"

"The same project? What is it? You're, like, possessed. Always scribbling like a maniac."

"Private thoughts," I say, a bit short with her. She's seen me write journals her whole life. Damn. Need to destroy them all. And my hard drives. There's no reason to help the Feds build their profile. They'll go into every Internet search I've ever done as if curiosity was a crime. But I'm not a mystery, like the nature anorexic who killed 60 people in Vegas for –

"I thought we were hanging out together," June breaks in again, tugging on my sleeve. "What's the point if you're just stuck in your head?"

"June!" I snap, right on the street in downtown Santa Monica. "You're bugging me."

June's mouth hangs open, mid-chew, chocolate tongue flecked with garish chips of green, red, and blue. Her eyes widen at my intensity as people stare, mostly at me, with "what an A-hole" written on their faces.

"What's wrong?" June squints. "You're not having another panic attack, are you?"

"No. Sorry. Just… tired. It's not you." I muster a smile, but June squints harder. Maybe it's because I never yell at her – kids and animals, just not right to yell at innocence – so she knows I'm lying. "Sorry."

"It's okay. Just don't get used to it," June warns me airily. "Yelling at each other in public. We don't want to be those people."

I laugh. That's so you, June, generous and tough, at age eleven in a month. I want to scoop you up and squeeze you for that instant forgiveness and warning, but I'm afraid I might lose it. More than anybody, I do this for you, June. Old people have gulped life, leaving youngsters the dregs. And I've at least sipped from the cup of the world. But you're at the beginning of the beginning. You deserve more than an empty mug, carelessly spilled –

"Benji?" June's voice is soft, like she's gently waking me from a nightmare. Is she trying to? "Are you really okay?"

I stare at her worried upturned face as another gate closes – another chance to come clean. I yearn with all my heart to tell her, but there's no way I can. No way. Never.

"I'm okay. Sorry." I want to tell her I love her, but that would be too suspicious, so I shut it down. Shutting down parts of myself left and –

"It's okay, Benji." June is patting me on the shoulder.

"You're right." I try to put her at ease. "We don't want to be the kind of people who argue in the street. Let's do something fun. What do you want to do? Anything."

"You know, Benji." I do – go play air hockey on the pier. June is impossible to beat and the arcade noise is an icepick to my brain, but right now, I'd do anything for her.

"Okay. Let's go."

"Really?" June grins her gap-tooth grin. "I'm gonna destroy you."

And she does. Every point results in a victory dance, an arm pump, and a loud "YES!" Highly entertaining how she lives life. Damn, I'm going to miss her birthday. Miss her whole life, who she becomes…

Don't go there.

Gradually, my world narrows down to the floating, flying puck.

I focus on it totally and give myself a break from the fear in my belly.

Now that I've got everything I need for the mission, I'm terrified.

Today's Quote

"The Ogre does what ogres can, Deeds quite impossible for Man, But one prize is beyond his reach, The Ogre cannot master Speech: About a subjugated plain, Among its desperate and slain, The Ogre stalks with hands on hips, While drivel gushes from his lips."

– W.H. Auden

Wow. Drivel. How come the classics keep nailing Cretin?

Three Days - Killing Coffins

Wednesday night we did the usual hump day family thing: news, nachos with fake cheese, and a movie. Another last thing I do with them, maybe <u>the</u> last –

"So boring. I'd rather watch a Fox show. At least it's funny." June is balking at tonight's lottery winner, a recorded 60 Minutes. "Let's redraw just this once."

"The box has spoken," Dad comically intones, putting away the shoebox holding Ping-Pong balls with news shows written on them. He cues the DVR. "Time to leave your bubble."

"Can't we go right to *Mission Impossible*?" June proposes, wanting to bail on the news without missing nachos and the movie – a bundled deal. Been watching since I was five and –

I stop listening – the first story is about the guy the Bernie Bro shot.

Oh, for crap's sake. Shot Guy's getting a puff job about his heroic recovery and gold-plated Gov physical therapy. No mention of his David Duke connection, his A+ rating from the NRA, or the gay, black female cop who saved his ass. And no mention of his devotion to Cretin, voting lockstep on every environmental rollback. This isn't even on Cretin State TV. Tools. Nobody has any shame anymore.

Have I become heartless? About a guy who got shot?

Christ. Guess I've become what I hate.

"That was so fun." June chisels a chunk of fake cheese off the plate. "What's next, their usual story about some general in a war they love?"

June is such a wise-ass. And wise.

Only one day until I leave. I've got a lot to do after everybody falls asleep, but I try to enjoy this last moment of family coziness. It's hopeless. My palms sweat as if *Mission Impossible* is a horror movie where a madman creeps up the stairs, knife drawn to slaughter an innocent family. Only it's me who's on an impossible mission, about to slaughter my own family. Christ. Don't think about it that way. Don't think!

After the movie, I do some Liberator assembly practice in my room until the house goes silent. I need to destroy my journals. Tomorrow I'll crush my computer after booking my flight. As I stand from my watchmaker stoop, Gigi gets up, wagging her tail, groggy but game.

"It's okay, girl." She lies on the floor, chin between her white boots, her eye slit just wide enough to watch me pull the trunk from under my bed.

I unlock it, revealing hundreds of spiral notebooks, each with a date on the front. I open one and flip through the narrow lined pages crammed with my jagged handwriting on both sides. I drag out the first one on the bottom of the first pile, dated January 1, 2008. And open to page one.

"My name is Benji and this is my life."

I stare at that first sentence, with its crooked child handwriting. Wow. So innocent. I feel sudden sadness about throwing out these journals, stacked like paper coffins, each one holding the body of my life – hours, days, years. Destroying them is killing how I became me.

Maybe I can bury them in the yard? I almost laugh at that idea. I don't come back from this. And they'll bring in dogs to look for evidence. My life is none of their business.

I know I'm a sentimental person. But I've got to lose it like other parts of myself – kindness, patience, tolerance – seats thrown from a plane that's going down.

I shove the notebooks in my old duffel from camp. It's four feet tall, the size of me as a child, and I fill it like a murderer getting rid of a corpse.

I hoist the duffel over my shoulder and quietly open my door. Gigi follows on my heel, always ready to go out. I slide through the house, but her tapping toenails obliterate my stealth. Everybody will just assume Gigi needs to pee – dogs are excellent cover for midnight rambling.

I open the front door and stagger up the driveway, hauling the heavy duffel like a demented Santa. I can dump them in different trash bins four blocks away. Feels wrong not to recycle. But who knows how long they will end up stored, waiting to be found?

Gigi's toenails tap on the road as we walk the dark street. Comforting.

"That should be your nickname – Gigi Toenails. Like a mob boss," I say to her. "Like Whitey Bulger, that mob killer they found living right in Santa Monica. Dangerous old men everywhere these days, Gigi."

Gigi grunts in agreement. When I get to the first trash bin, I rip the spines out of each notebook. It takes an hour and my hands are sore afterwards, but nobody will get curious about the thousands of jumbled pages I dump. All my writing, just garbage now.

When I get back to the house, I ease my way in through the front door and back to bed, exhausted, one thing crossed off the list. A whole life erased – all my obsessions and thoughts and endless daily recording. Destroying the body of myself could feel liberating, but I'm just numb.

It's so horrible, this hardening in me.

I just want it to end. I'm sick of my obsession. Sick of writing about the end of the world. Sick of focusing on what Cretin does to our beautiful planet. Sick of this endless call to arms to myself.

Sick to death of DEATH. Sick at heart, ready for action.

My name is Benji. Is this the end of my life?

Today's Cretin Tweet

"Global Warming has been proven to be a canard repeatedly over and over again. The left needs a dose of reality." Ha. Canard. Good one. Figures Cretin knows every word for a lie, like an Eskimo does for snow.

56 Hours – More Secret Goodbyes

It's Thursday, the morning before I leave for Youngstown. Writing this, the tendons in my wrists jangle, guitar strings wound too tight.

Nerves. Or too much Liberator practice.

Mom bought my bus ticket to Ojai for the panic attack cognitive therapy program. It sounds perfect – wish I was going. I "leave" for Ojai tomorrow on the 8:30 bus from Santa Monica. It's a four-hour ride instead of 90-minutes in a car and Mom is having second thoughts.

"I think June should see *Wonder Woman* with a friend. It doesn't feel right to be sending you up there to… to check into this program by yourself."

"I know what you mean." I knew this was coming. I put both hands on Mom's shoulders and look down at her worried face. "But it's like four hours of driving there and back for a minute of saying goodbye. I'll be fine. I can do some writing on the bus."

"Are you sure?"

"Mom, I'm an adult now. I got this." She suddenly hugs me, impulsive and uncontrolled. Does she suspect anything? Mom intuition kicking in – she just knows without knowing.

"I guess I'm just worried," she confirms. "About the panic attack."

"I know, but I probably won't ever have another."

I'm amazed I've only had one. I just keep putting one task after another without thinking. Now shoot the Liberator. Now ditch my journals. Now talk to Mom. No past, no future. An endless stream of now-now-now – like they teach at FTW – until NOW I pull the trigger. Turns out, the path to kill the ultimate environmental terrorist is the same to waking up –

"Benji?" Mom's concerned face looks up at mine, interrupting my spiral. "Are you sure? You seem distracted. And it's just a dumb movie. Not like we can't see it any other day."

"And disappoint June? No. I'll text you when I get there. I can send you a selfie before they make us turn our phones off." I've already photo-shopped myself standing in front of the sign for the retreat center. I can send it to Mom tomorrow when I land in Youngstown.

"Okay," Mom concedes, searching my face.

I try to smile. You always know the right move, Mom. Usually, you let me keep my independence, so different from a snowplow parent. You sense something is off, but let it go. I hope you don't regret that decision. Like people obsess about the last thing they said to somebody before they die. Replaying it over and over like I did when Bubbe died. Feeling sorry for months that I blew off a promised visit on her last day alive...

Suddenly, I'm fiercely hugging Mom, lifting her right off the ground.

"Whoa," she laughs. And I can see June in her, the humor, and the strength. I release her – another secret goodbye. "Are you really okay, Benji?"

"All good, Mom."

Today's Quote

"Power concedes nothing without a demand. It never did and never will." Damn right. Bottom line. Fight the power!

– *Frederick Douglas*

Fifty Hours – Game Theory

I didn't want to go to school today. Pointless. But they'd notify Mom and Dad if I didn't, and I'd just have to produce more depressing lies. Going turned out much worse. I got caught. And now might be screwed...

Starts normal enough except HWB seems smaller – maybe because it's my last day. Or maybe I'm already gone. I've packed my emotional luggage and shipped it to a far-off land with foreign ideas and values and vocabulary. Body to follow tomorrow. Hope I can blend in at a Cretin rally long enough to do the job.

Should be able to – plenty of practice hiding in plain sight at HWB.

No different today, as I ghost the halls. Kids with their heads down in phones gently jostle like salmon swimming upstream, ignoring the contact. Our last moments of carefree life and we digitally pin them, dead butterflies to a corkboard of misery and comparison. What will happen to my generation as we bury our heads in bytes of sand to avoid the horrors that are coming? I want to shout, "The end is here! Go outside! Watch a butterfly flitter IRL before they're all gone. And don't take a damn selfie, just be in it –"

The end is here. Ha. It's come to this – I'm a crazy street prophet.

On the bright side of all this checking out, nobody notices I'm phoning it in too. Except Tyler, who, with Dim and Dimmer, leans on the wall outside STEM. They give me the sideways look of lizards on a fire road and then Tyler blows a mock kiss at me. Dim and Dimmer do their weird tittering. Hale says life will take care of Tyler. I don't believe it, but as much I want to avenge SG, I don't break my promise to leave him be.

"I know that feel, my-dude-brah," I say, aping Tyler-talk.

"Mangina," Tyler scoffs.

"Rapist." I can't resist. Christ, I hate his guts. What happened between him and Hale? Anything? Nothing? Can't dwell on it. Got to stay focused. At least it's the last time I'll ever see Tyler – somebody else's problem now.

Poor SG. How will she handle him?

"Gentlemen." Hale nods at us as he strides into class, one minute early. We follow him in and watch as he examines an array of projects, including my toaster.

"Phones down." Hale doesn't mean down, he means off and out of sight. Now. Tyler lingers on his new phone, the latest one that costs a thousand dollars –

"Tyler." You get one call-out before Hale takes your phone for the day. For kids who sleep with it, who would literally rather lose a finger than give up their phone, that's death. Tyler slips his phone into his pocket.

Hale flicks on the screen and takes my toaster out of the lineup, placing it on his desk. It came out great, my toaster. Not as useful as the Liberator but –

Holy shit! On screen is the CAD of the toaster, including the Liberator's 15 pieces! I glance around at everybody staring blankly at the screen. Surely somebody notices certain pieces make no sense. Like the gun barrel – what's a stubby tube doing in a toaster?

"This was the most ambitious of your projects," Hale says. I'm weirdly disappointed he didn't notice the gun. "It has the most parts and required the most coding. It gives you a glimpse of what's possible with 3D printing, even if it's not exactly changing the world. Well done."

A "well done" from Hale is rare. It means an A-plus, and racking them up in every AP class is how you get to 4.7. The other nerds glance at me with a mix of envy and puzzlement, but you might as well hate me for being left-handed. I stare at the screen, waiting for it to come down before my luck runs out. But Hale leaves it up the whole time and nobody notices the gun in the toaster.

As class ends and kids grab their iPhones, Hale looks at me.

"Ben. Got a minute?" It's not a question. Shit. Did he see it? To not report a kid 3D printing a gun is negligent and Hale is the opposite of that. Can I stall him one more day? So close!

"Ben?" Hale is staring. I can't come up with a lie quick enough and I don't want to lie to him. I like and respect Hale, even though I feel like pulling a Tyler and bolting out of the room.

"Um… sure." I wait as the class files out. A few kids glance at me, no doubt thinking something good is happening – more kudos and opportunities. From the look on Hale's face as he closes the door, I know better.

"Anything you want to tell me?" He starts out friendly enough.

"About what, Mr. Hale?" If he didn't find the gun, I'm not going to offer it up.

"Really?" He asks, less friendly. I just nod, dumb as a bobblehead.

Hale taps his computer and my CAD pops up with the 15 pieces of the Liberator now circled in red. Oh, no, no, no!

"Took a while to see it after I spotted the barrel, but that's a gun. Why are you printing a gun in my class?"

Hale stares at me and I suddenly desperately want to unload. What a relief to turn over the gun and file the Plan under "A Supposedly Fun Thing I'll Never Do Again." Write a funny essay about how my senior project in high school was to kill the president with a plastic gun, an homage to DFW. Not that his writing kept him alive any more than this writing will keep me alive. But it's a moment here, the last chance to bail and lead a regular life. Ignore Climageddon and go to college. Enjoy a couple of years before joining the hunger games –

"What's it for?" Hale punctuates my spiral – the last temptation passes.

"Just to see if I could do it," I shrug, trying to feign nonchalance.

"You knew you could do it. Your toaster is more complicated."

"You did say I'd only have a toaster. So, I took your advice to make something useful." Hale ignores my lame joke, scrutinizing me like a map, looking for hidden terrain.

"You threatened to kill Tyler, then made a gun in my class. Nothing funny about this," Hale's friendly tone has evaporated.

"Oh, no. It's not for Tyler." It feels good to tell one truth. "I gave you my word."

"Why then? Because you're not a make-a-gun-for-the-hell-of-it kind of person."

"No. I'm not. That's true." Silence falls between us like a broiled bat falling from the Australian skies – abrupt and horrible.

"One last time, Ben. What's it for?" Hale looks at me with more concern than accusation.

"I'm not going school shooter if that's what you mean," I venture.

"Not with one bullet and a plastic gun," Hale says ruefully. Does he know most school shooters try to kill themselves first, an early warning sign? Probably. "I'm worried about you."

"Really?" I'm surprised he puts it right out there – suicide. But why waste your life on that when you can use it to take out a bloodsucker? And doesn't suicide come from wanting to stop the pain? Dying to end the loneliness, anxiety, or helplessness? Okay, I've got those for sure. But if you don't feel this way now then you're an idiot. Of course, I'm anxious. Maybe that's what Hale sees. But am I depressed? Guess I could be. Not gay-dad-in-a-van-trying-to-blow-a-teenager-to-forget-your-life depressed – that's dismal. Wonder how Crushed Bug is doing –

"Yeah, really," Hale breaks in again. "What should I think? You seem spaced out. You made a gun that fires one bullet. In my class."

"It's just a cool project. I knew you wouldn't, the school wouldn't let me do it, so I just did it on my own. It's no big deal. I'm sure not going to use it, especially not on myself."

"Do you have any bullets?"

"Of course not." The lies slip out so quickly now. Is this how Cretin became Cretin, one lie at a time? Is it true you become whatever you put your energy into and –

"So, you built a gun but don't have any bullets." Hale is full-on interrogating a hostile witness now. "Why are you bullshitting me? I thought we were on the same page."

"No BS, I don't have any bullets. Where would I even get them?"

"In America?" We both smile at that, our mutual understanding relieving a bit of the tension. "What's going on, Ben? You don't seem yourself. If I didn't know better, I'd say you were on drugs."

"That's funny. Guess I'm just a bit tired." Blasted! But I only need to stall him 48 hours. And keep everybody from finding out I'm not at a cognitive-behavioral mindfulness retreat to reduce panic. A panic I feel rising hot in my throat. I take a deep breath. Keep it together –

"Why am I always having to trust you?" Hale asks.

"Because I'm trustworthy?" I try to keep it light, but Hale doesn't crack a smile.

"You've put us in an impossible position," Hales says wearily.

"Sorry to cause you concern, but it was just a goof," I improvise. "I'll toss it when I get home."

Hale shakes his head, not buying my BS. And why should he? A student made a damn gun in his class. He blinks that slow blink and his eyes flatten. Uh-oh.

"They'll expel me, right? I won't graduate? Or go to college?" I toss the victim chip out, trying to finesse some faux vulnerability. "This ruins my life, right? For one mistake?"

Hale nods, makes a face, like, yep – you're screwed. I start talking fast.

"Tomorrow morning I'm going out of town with my family. Some meditation retreat in Ojai – I can send you my admission form. So, I won't be alone for the whole weekend. First thing Monday I'll bring in the gun. Disassembled."

Hale considers this torrent and shakes his head.

"I'm not waiting until Monday. You need to go home and get it right now. I'll give you an hour. Then maybe we can keep this between us."

"That's generous. But I've got a mid-term in half an hour."

"Listen up, Ben." Hale is instantly crisp like he's talking to a soldier. "You just got too sick to take a test. Go. Now. I'd take you myself, but I've got a class and then a presentation I can't cancel. If it were just the class, you and I would already be in the car."

Christ. If I don't agree to get it will Hale ruin my life? Maybe. But if I agree and don't show up with the gun in an hour will he then ruin my life? Definitely. Because I broke his trust and everything else I say becomes BS. Just have to take a chance here.

"Mr. Hale, I respect you. And I respect you trusting me to make it right. But I can't warp the space-time continuum. I can't get home and back in rush hour traffic in an hour. Just trust me on this. I won't hurt myself or anybody else with that gun. It was just a dumb experiment and I'll bring it in Monday. Promise."

I'm talking way too much. I try to let the silence sit there as Hale appraises me, a commander assessing a soldier. HWB encourages independent thinking and honor system trust. Ha, failure. But I'm sure the Navy Seals do the same. You need flexibility to survive and adapt, which is what I'm doing. Adapt or die. You don't get more adaptable than going from bookworm to assassin –

"Okay, Ben. If that's your decision." I can't read him, but it sounds like, if that's how you want to play it, you idiot. I feel like I've lost a round of game theory but what can I do? There's no other way to play it. I hope he knows when an angry kid says or does something stupid only 1% become violent. So, I stick to my guns. My gun.

"I'm sorry to put you in this position," I continue my pitch. "I know you have your code of duty. I respect that."

"Don't be a suck-up. You're no good at it." Hale smiles slightly. My head feels like it's been in a vise for days, but I muster a smile back.

I can only hope Hale doesn't tell the school because he doesn't want to ruin my life. And hope he doesn't call my parents tomorrow as I'm traveling out to Youngstown. And hope to Christ he doesn't show up at my house tonight. This clusterfuck is all coming down to a lot of hope.

But don't all lonely crusades of conscience?

"Listen." Hale pauses, then sighs as if exhaling a lifetime of pain. "When I was your age, I did something stupid, something that almost got me killed. And killed somebody else."

"Really?" I've got no idea what to say. What the hell did he do that killed somebody when he was my age? Was he in the military when it happened? Is that how he lost his finger?

"It's taken a lifetime of work to get over it. And you never do," Hale's voice is low and steady. "When I finally faced it, many years later, I changed my life and became a teacher. So, I know what it's like to be your age and confused. To have something you can't talk about to anybody. To make one unwise decision before your brain is fully booted that rides you forever. Remember, getting you all out of high school alive is mission-critical for me."

"I'm sorry that happened to you," I say lamely. There's that phrase again – mission-critical. But if keeping me alive is mission-critical, then doesn't Hale have to turn me in as a potentially suicidal student? Who made a gun in his class after threatening to kill another student? It's so messed up. I don't know ANYTHING anymore –

"I only bring it up because I've been you," Hale continues. "The only reason I didn't end up in jail is I got lucky. Somebody took a big risk in helping me out."

Hale pauses a moment, considering me. I appreciate him for being so honest. Is he going to repeat the favor and give me a pass here? That would be a tremendous risk –

"Here's what I'll do. I'll trust you until I can't. And hope I'm not making the second biggest mistake of my life. Bring it in on Monday."

"Wow. Thanks, Mr. Hale." He's such a good guy. And I've become such an A-hole.

"You got it." Hale pulls his phone and shuttles through his contacts. My text dings.

"That's my cell. Use it if you need it. For anything, any time."

Wow. I get an instant lump in my throat. To have a guy like Hale in my corner offering that amount of trust and help – I don't deserve it. If I try to speak, I'm afraid I'll burst into tears. It's all too much. Luckily, the door opens and kids trickle in for his next class.

"Thanks Mr. Hale," I manage to croak before I nod and hustle out.

What the hell did he do when he was my age?

Will he keep his promise? I hope so – nothing to do but march on.

Hope for the best.

Wish I'd cut school today.

Today's Quote

"The secret of freedom lies in educating people, whereas the secret of tyranny is in keeping them ignorant." Hale is a real-life educator. Have his seeds of wisdom fallen on fallow ground? With me, yeah.

– Maximilien Robespierre

48 Hours – The Other Side

I can't believe I leave tomorrow morning.

And in 48 hours I kill Cretin.

I've got a lot to do. Swipe credit card from Mom's purse. Buy plane ticket. Destroy computer drive.

The front door opens and Dad trudges in – 8 PM, an early night.

"Hey, Dad."

"Hey, Ben." He looks solemn. "Just the person I want to see."

Uh-oh. Did Hale renege already? I search his face, but Dad's mild as ever.

"You ready for tomorrow?" He asks, opening the fridge to pull out a beer. My mind goes to the mission – automatic – but then I realize he's talking about the retreat I'm not going on.

"Oh, yeah. All set. Should be good." I allow myself to think about a mindfulness retreat in Ojai. A bath for my jangled brain.

"Great. How'd calculus go?" He already knows the answer to that, but I humor him.

"No problem."

"Nice." He pulls a beer stein out of the freezer where it's been for 24 hours since last night. He pops a Hoegaarden, expensive, and pours it perfectly, like a commercial. Dad never drinks beer out of a can or bottle. He likes to say it's carbonated and you should pour it – like, you don't drink champagne from the bottle. And that it's not about the beer, it's the ritual, taking a moment to appreciate and mark the end of another day.

I feel a surge of love for Dad. Bitterwood is full of charmers who hyp-notize with their charm. Who don't have real talent but have <u>that</u> talent. Mean bloodsuckers like Cretin, who would stab you in the back for five bucks. Not Mom and Dad – I won the lottery with them. I just needed to run down the tracks they laid out for me. Instead, I'm going off the rails.

"So, I want to chat with you about something." Dad takes a sip of his beer and sighs with satisfaction at the small daily luxury, the only one he allows himself. "How to be with the police."

WTF? About what? But he's not upset – it's not about the Liberator. He's just getting ready to give me one of his Dad Talks.

"The police?" I ask, settling in.

"Yes. Now that you finally have your license, you have a much higher chance of intersecting with the police. Driving. Traffic stops."

"Yeah. If I break the law."

"Well, everybody gets stopped eventually. Gets a ticket. Or has an accident. Even me, right?" Guess he means our Big Bear car crash. "The thing is not to get shot in some kind of mix-up. And the way to avoid that is to do exactly what the officer tells you."

"Shot for a traffic ticket?" I ask. What am I, black? The sour joke slouches through my tired brain but thankfully doesn't make it to my mouth. Gallows humor about cop shootings isn't funny in our family, which is why this talk is even happening. Thirty years later and they're still traumatized because a cop shot Dad's black roommate at Cornell during a traffic stop, with Mom in the back seat. So, they have a healthy fear of the police and how terrible things can go –

"It happens." Dad takes another sip of beer. "And not just to minori-ties, even though blacks are killed at three times the rate per population."

Dad trails off. It's painful and I wait for him to continue.

"Look at that drunk guy who just got shot in a hotel hallway. He was white. They already had him on the floor, arms spread out, screaming orders at him. But he was too drunk and terrified to comply. He goes to pull up his sweatpants and they shot him dead. A moment of confusion or panic. It can happen to anybody."

Dad gulps his beer. I stay silent as he gathers his emotions.

"You'll be in upstate New York. Lots of guns, so the police are on high alert. And now they've got the opioid problem. People on the edge, dying from deaths of despair. So, it's a stressful job. And the way you lessen police stress is to do exactly what they say with a 'yes officer.' Even if you think you're right, you don't work that out with the cop. That's for court. Make sense?"

"Don't worry. I'll be careful, Dad." That's all he wants to hear. Poor Dad, worrying about traffic stops and I'm off to kill the president. How funny/sad is that?

"Okay. Good. You'll be fine – you won't go driving drunk or something stupid."

Dad is glad to end this conversation, like the "sex" and "how you treat women" conversations, for which we watched *When Harry Met Sally*. It doesn't come naturally for Dad. I'm surprised we didn't watch a movie first, but I love him so much for trying –

"One more thing I'll say about it. If you get pulled over, keep your hands at ten and two on the steering wheel so the cops can see them." He demonstrates, almost spilling some beer. "That will lower any officer's blood pressure as he approaches the car."

"Good idea," I reassure him again, patting his arm. "But I don't even have a car."

"You will someday." Dad allows himself a brief smile. "The police are just human. They're scared, and that's when over-reactions happen."

"Don't worry, I'll be careful." Why is he still going on about this? Does he somehow sense something, like Mom? Some hidden danger to me? Have I not been as good a liar as I thought?

"We just don't want to… to lose you to a –"

The front door opens and saves Dad, who's upset, thinking back to his dead friend as he tries to protect me from the same fate. Oh, Dad. I want to hug him, but in saunters Mom and June, both giggling. Dad looks relieved, swapping smiles with Mom.

"So, Ben." Dad shifts gears and relaxes. "We think you need a bit of independence."

"Yeah." June grins her Cheshire cat grin, eyes slits of merriment. She rips off her scarf and dramatically swirls it, a magician prepping a trick.

"We have a surprise for you," Mom chimes in.

"But first, I'm gonna cover your eyes!" June rushes forward and hops on a stool. She puts the scarf on me more like I'm a hostage than a volunteer at a magic show.

"Take my hand," June commands. "And follow me."

June grabs my palm with her baby chimp grip. Hands fall on my shoulders, one small and delicate – Mom's. The other heavier and firm – Dad's. They guide me around furniture as Gigi's tail thumps against my leg, always the barometer for how we all feel...

Then, fresh air and the smell of jasmine, gifting us their delicate scent. Sightless, I hear the light snap on as we walk up to the carport.

June rips the scarf off my head, revealing a gleaming new Volt hybrid with a bow on top.

"This is for me?" I'm stunned. Now the Dad Talk makes sense.

"It's for you, Ben. So, you can stop taking the bus." Dad is beaming.

"And I can stop driving you," Mom jokes.

"And you can drive me everywhere!" June declares, not joking.

They all laugh, thrilled to be in on such a memorable moment of generosity. The best people, Mom and Dad – so big-hearted, teaching me the joy of giving, the joy of generosity.

"What do you think?" June snaps her gum. "Are ya surprised?"

"I'm blown away. It's so generous."

"Well, it came out of part of your college fund. But since you got that fellowship and all," Dad clarifies, always a stickler for the truth. "I thought next fall we could drive it to Cornell together, take our time, see the country."

"That sounds amazing." I allow myself a moment of happiness at this thought, a father and son road trip, off to college in that rite of passage, cruising on the new car smell – a fresh start in a place where nobody knows me. Then the Plan tornadoes in, whirling me down like Icarus. All I can see is this car sitting as a forlorn totem after I'm gone, rebuking this happy moment. I flash on all the electric vehicles left after the humans disappear, too little too late, rusting underwater like something out of a *Planet of The Apes* movie.

Suddenly, I've got tears in my eyes. It's okay – I can play them off as tears of joy, which is the truth too. This is such a big gesture for naturally thrifty people. I grab Dad, hugging him, and wrap my arms around Mom, and June scoots in too.

I pull them tight in a group hug and I'm crying as this is the <u>last</u> goodbye. Gigi, sensing the love, thwacks her tail against the car as I hold them all for a long moment. I know I've got to say something to put their minds at ease that these are tears of joy and not the beginning of another panic attack, but I don't want to let them go –

I never want to let you go, Mom, Dad, June, and Gigi.

But I've got no choice. I'm locked in, every decision and thought and experience leading me to a terrible sacrifice. Tomorrow!

"I'm just so… Can't believe it." I'm suddenly sputtering with emotion. "Thank you so much. It's amazing."

I let them go. It's hard to believe this is the last time I feel the solidity of their bodies.

"You're welcome, Benji," Mom says. "It's our pleasure."

I drink them in, with their big grins and shining eyes, enjoying my enjoyment as they miss what my tears mask – that I'm a beggar at Christmas, nose pressed against a toy store, watching a happy family through a window. So far from them – alienated, lonely, and poor – a husk, a shell, a pretender. Far inside myself now. Learning to die. Christ, I don't want to die –

"It's okay, Benji," June says. "We all know you're a big crybaby."

"Yeah," I swallow my tears. "A real snowflake."

Everybody laughs at the insult turned into a family joke.

"Thank you so much. I love it. So generous." I already miss them, as I watch now from the dark side – here, but not here.

Already gone.

Today's Headline

"Benji Done with Headlines, Quotes, and Facts." No more talking to myself when nobody's listening. They'll all be hearing from me soon enough.

46 Hours - Packing Heat

Before bed, we sat around eating chocolate chip cookies Mom made. Lots of chips, dark chocolate, just the way I like them. Dad proposed I drive the new car to Ojai, but I begged off…

"But that's the whole point of the car," June says. "You don't have to take the bus."

"I know. But I don't want to take it on a road trip the first time I drive it." And no way do I want to drive to the airport and leave it there for them to find. That's just too terrible.

"You need to live a little," June proclaims. She thinks I should jump in the car and drive cross-country with the windows open and music blaring. She thinks my lie is ridiculous. She's right.

"I'm excited to drive it. Just not on a long trip right after I got my license." Then a perfect manipulation I loathe using. "I don't want to get pulled over for something stupid."

"Wise thinking, Ben," Dad says, pleased his Dad Talk made such an impression.

"Whatever you think is best." Mom nods. Lying – it's the new me.

"What an idiot," June pronounces with an eye roll. I miss that eye roll already. But I need to wrap it up so I don't start crying again. I give everybody many more thanks, say I'm off to pack for the retreat, and head to my room. Everybody goes to bed.

I can't carry the Liberator on the airplane. Even in pieces it will show up in X-ray machines and body scanners, so I need to put it through checked luggage.

I wrap each piece in socks and T-shirts, like when I protected glass trinkets from our Mexican vacation so long ago. I allow myself a moment to drift back to when a school of fish swam up to my snorkel mask, looking at me with alert curiosity – who is this ungainly creature that can't even swim? Then, moving as one, like a flock of birds, they dart away, forever changing my mind about eating them...

A memory from a different life, not my own.

I stare at the stubby gun barrel. Then wrap it.

I buy my airline ticket and a room at a Comfort Suites with Mom's credit card. Print a paper boarding pass to avoid email notifications. Last-minute, so it's expensive, but I can't help it. At least it's a one-way ticket. The ultimate one-way ticket.

Reformatting the hard drive on my computer isn't enough for the Feds, so I take a T7 screwdriver and dismantle the laptop, pulling the drive.

On the way out, I slip Mom's credit card back in the same slot in her purse, behind several others, too many others – Mom juggling interest rates and bills and somehow coming up with Turning Point money for June every semester.

I grab a hammer – time to go medieval on my hard drive.

Gigi faithfully follows me out the door, nuzzling my leg.

45 Hours – Stalling with Gigi

I'm gutted. This is Gigi's last call, in every sense of the word.

Going a little crazy, smashing the hard drive with the hammer.

Maybe I'm paranoid with all this cloak and dagger stuff, but the first thing Cretin did after his inauguration was demand the records of people registered to anti-Cretin protest sites. This is where he wants to go — enemy lists fed to neo-Nazis, who do all the terrorism in America now. Cretin doesn't care that he's playing with fire. Or even know the only time Americans killed 700,000 other Americans was in a Civil War that white nationalists now won't even say was about slavery. Ha.

Cretin thinks there were good people on both sides of WW2.

So, I'm worried about Mom, Dad, and June. Mom's right that non-violence is the best way to battle racists, but their reaction to me will be violent. So, I obliterate another part of myself, smashing the drive as Gigi watches, cocking her big head as I toss the pieces. No need to give trolls my life as ammunition.

We walk to the trailhead and sit in the moonlight.

Gigi leans against my shoulder and I put my arm around her in a classic "boy and his dog" silhouette, her squat solidity a comfort. She puts her clunky head on my knee and I can smell her musky smell. Gigi's so beautiful — what they call a Blue.

Wow. I have to say goodbye to her and now is the time.

But not yet. Just a few minutes longer in the canyon's peace, LA twinkling below. City of Angels, so ugly on its surface, so charming in its hidden pockets, so precariously pushed up to the sea by desert. Constantly under threat from earthquakes and its success, sucking in too many people with its magnetic appeal. It's the power of American showbiz – Universal Studios and Hollywood Blvd – all that shimmering junk looks good from a distance...

Still, looking at it now, I appreciate my hometown. She doesn't lay it all out, but LA's beauty is there if you take the energy to find its charming neighborhoods and mountain trails and hidden beaches. Work to get beyond the deadly traffic and surface ugliness –

Now I'm just stalling. Stuck in my head to avoid my breaking heart.

"'Put your thoughts to sleep, do not let them cast a shadow over the moon of your heart. Let go of thinking,'" I say this to Gigi, who doesn't need to hear it. Rumi sums up what I can never do, but what I must do to feel this moment.

I turn to face my best friend. Her white barrel chest and boots shimmer in the moonlight. The rest of her is the same blue velvet that's between the twinkling lights of LA. I lean in and she licks my face with a sneaky little lick.

"Kisses, eh, girl?"

I take her clunky head in my hands and scratch her heavy jowls and she grunts in appreciation. Although I can't fully see her face, I know it's filled with the same calm trust it always is.

This is impossible, saying goodbye to Gigi.

"Good girl. Good girl." She grunts again, nuzzling my face with her bristly whiskers, her breath soft on my cheek. "I love you, Gigi. You're a good girl. Such a good girl."

My eyes fill, and I'm relieved to let the tears flow without hiding them from the world. Gigi licks them off my face, her grunts intensifying. She's got no idea I'm worse than Brutus, betraying her trust, maybe even her very life once Cretin activates his trolls.

"You take care of them, Gigi," I sob to her. "I'm sorry, but I've got to go away."

I clunk heads with her again.

We hold that way, foreheads touching – dog to man.

"You love them good, eh, Gigi?" I'm bawling now and I just let it go. Need to get every tear out of me tonight – the last cry. Tomorrow, I need to be dry as a milk bone. Tomorrow, a mask goes on and it can't crack. Tomorrow, I need to become one of those toxic alt-right pinheads.

And I better be Tiki-torch convincing or they'll sniff me out.

Tonight, here, now, I let myself blubber until the tears slick my face.

Gigi sits calmly and takes it all in. She doesn't know what's happening, but she knows I'm sad in the way animals know. They feel you. I pull her in close for a hug. At least I can say goodbye to her and honestly cry it out, all my secrets safe in her trusting muteness. Unlike with humans, I can stop hiding and just be myself.

"I'm sorry, Gigi, but this is goodbye. I love you always, but this is goodbye forever."

I cry and cry as the jewels of lost angels twinkle below.

37 Hours – End of Normal

Friday morning. D-day.

Feel like the flu, head filled with cotton, veins filled with dread.

I try to keep it routine. Get up. Have breakfast. Make small talk about the weekend retreat. Take Gigi out for her morning business. Wagging her tail, she has no idea this is the last time. I pause and clunk heads with her one final moment and stare into her human brown eye.

"You take care of them, Gigi," I say. Then I quickly stand. Even one tear would bring the flood, an avalanche unfrozen. I walk in with Gigi and hug Mom and June goodbye.

"See you Sunday," I say.

"Smell ya later," June shoots back.

"By honey. Text me when you get there. Let me know how it's going." Mom hugs me.

"Okay. But they collect phones once it starts. To get me, you'll have to call the office." Mom nods. Why wouldn't she believe me? Usually, I never lie. But I'm powerless over it now.

"All set?" Dad's missioning toward work. I nod, grab my bag, and follow him out. Know I shouldn't look back, but like Lot's wife, I can't help myself.

It's just a typical morning – no pillars of salt as punishment.

Gigi lies in her living room bed by the front door, her head resting on the floor, jowls spilled out as usual. Mom bustles the kitchen, clearing breakfast plates. June speeds through homework like she's filling out a mandatory survey, annoyed and bored. I want to stand there forever and soak up the normality of it all, but turn and walk to the car.

Dad and I say little as he drives into Santa Monica. He's prepping himself for work, no doubt. I'm glad for the comfortable silence he allows, but as we pull up, he breaks it.

"You know, if you're not enjoying it, or it's not what you want to do, just call and I'll come to get you tomorrow. We can go hiking up there instead."

I nod. That would be a good offer if I were going to Ojai. "Thanks, Dad. I'll be fine."

We do that awkward car hug people do when sitting side by side. I get out and grab my bag from the back seat.

"Bye, Dad."

"See you Sunday, Ben. Love you, son."

"Love you too, Dad."

It's true every time you say goodbye to somebody can be the last time. But it's a whole other thing to know it. Watching Dad drive away, oblivious, I quickly turn away to avoid tears. I'm done crying. I'm in downtown Santa Monica and I've got to get to the airport. No Lyft for me. Got to pay cash.

I walk away from the bus stop and call a cab.

It begins.

36 Hours – Pack Behavior

*L*incoln slides by in a dream. No wonder people think LA. is gross if this boulevard of used car lots, homeless tents, and check-cashing joints is their entrance.

At LAX, I get in line for Spirit Air and check my bag, paying the extra 25 bucks. Mom always complains how back in the day you got free food, free checked bags, and way more legroom. How nowadays it's worse than a bus because you can't just pull a cord and get off.

Good one, Mom.

My bag with the Liberator pieces rumbles down the conveyor belt. Life pared down to the essentials to get the job done. As the airport bowels swallow the bag, I have a moment of panic that it gets lost. So much of life comes down to luck, which includes not getting unlucky. But there's nothing I can do now. If luck is preparation meets opportunity, I've done my best.

The bullet and nail are in a pocket, hidden in Lady Liberty. But with the airport's X-rays and full-body scans, I feel like an arrow is pointing at me. What if the X-ray can see the bullet inside the metal of Lady Liberty? Should I have put the round in my checked bag, even though they have dogs down there sniffing for explosives? Don't know. Today just seems to come down to making a less wrong choice.

Kicking off my Converse, I try to calm myself by remembering how many knives and even guns make it past TSA. Thousands. Still, my palms sweat as I put Lady Liberty in the plastic bin. The bored TSA guy motions me into the full body scanner and I step in.

A long moment as the machine whirs.

Another agent motions me out. No problem.

But the TSA woman looking at the X-rays is way more alert, stopping the conveyor for every bin and scrutinizing them. Damn. Where's my stuff? What's she doing? An hour ticks by as the woman squints at an image. I'm the only person waiting. It's my bin –

She glances at me. In her mid-fifties, with dyed blond hair and wrinkles around her mouth like a smoker, she is all business. I try to stay calm and breathe. Try not to gulp or fake smile like the Maniac. What does she see? I hope an innocent high school student. She nods curtly and turns back to the screen. Christ. Why didn't I get in the bald guy's line, him joking around and barely glancing at his screen? Hours pass.

Finally, my plastic bin bump-rolls out of the X-ray hood.

I exhale and casually grab Lady Liberty and shove her in my pocket with my phone. I snag my sneaks and walk over to a bench to put them on. Home free – TSA is on to the next traveler.

Getting through airport security and an actual X-ray machine with a bullet is a good sign. The rally's metal detectors will be a piece of cake. I stand and walk toward the terminal –

That's when a beautiful black lab trots out of an office, ten feet away.

Any time I see a dog, I catch their eyes and swear they wink at me without blinking. There's a kind of recognition. Are you in my pack? Open-eyed wink and dog grin. Not in my pack? See ya.

But I'm not happy to see this dog. Don't want to be in his pack. He's checking me out. Shit! I force a smile that reaches my eyes, as if I can fake out a dog. Impossible.

I'm frozen between TSA behind and the dog in front, blocking the terminal's entrance. Are you working yet? Or always working? Christ.

How terrible if a dog does me in.

The gunpowder is in the cartridge shell, sealed by a molded piece of June's cinnamon gum and stuck in Lady Liberty. It's in my pocket and I'm ten feet away from the dog, with lots of people milling around. Still, that's a piece of cake for dogs. They can sniff gunpowder in a bullet buried 40 feet underground. Or a trillionth of a gram of material masked by layers of stronger smells. My only hope is they trained this dog for drugs, not explosives.

The black lab looks at me again and yawns, a sign of stress in canines –

Are you alerting on me? Shit! Come on, buddy, give me a break.

Then his trainer gives him a slight tug and they move off into the terminal. Whew! I exhale and watch him trot away.

The dog looks back at me and winks without closing his eyes.

Maybe I'm losing it, but I swear that pooch just gave me a pass.

29 Hours – Ohio

E ndless day, lots of writing...

Landed in Youngstown's Warren Regional Airport after a quick lay-over in Cleveland. The airport was two strips of asphalt surrounded by woods...

"Thank you for flying Spirit Airlines. Please take any trash with you. It will help our crew on a tight turnaround." This comes over the intercom. The plane is one of those cheapo "buses with wings" Mom complains about. Except these seats are harder, don't recline, and my knees bump the person in front of me. No water. No pretzels. Nothing.

More like "Dispirit Airlines" if you ask me.

Aw, that's a Mom-joke she'd love.

"Why don't you ask us to clean the bathroom on the way out and you can eliminate that job too," the guy next to me mutters. That's funny and sums up the country's economic situation. Makes me like Youngstown already – why do they fall so hard for Cretin?

We stand waiting for the door to open, the aisle barely wide enough for the super-sized travelers crowded into it. Nobody's this big in LA – everybody's too vain. Maybe it's the "classic" restaurants I saw online that serve raspberry barbecue ribs with a corner-to-corner tray of fries and a lonely cup of slaw. Enough food for two days. Feel bad getting OCD about all this fat, but isn't it weird how 40% of Americans are obese as a billion people starve?

Shuffle off the plane onto the tarmac and insta-sweat in humidity that smells like fresh-cut grass. Walk into the terminal, with a low ceiling and no food – nothing but a bathroom. Wait for my bag next to a bony woman and a small boy who runs around the luggage carousel shouting. She wears jean shorts and a tank top and is fed up with her son. As the boy runs by, she clotheslines him so hard he falls on his ass and immediately starts bawling, all blond hair and red face. What would Mom do?

Something. But I've got to stay under the radar, so I turn away.

Where the hell is my bag? Did it make the connection? I try to calm down and text Mom the doctored selfie of me standing in front of the retreat center sign: "Here. Good trip. Call you Sunday."

Her return is immediate: "OK, honey. At movie. June's excited! Talk Sunday."

I text back a thumbs up and the smiley face. No emotion required. Just send emojis to do my job of pretending to be happy, pretending to tell the truth, pretending all is fine. What a relief after having to act for weeks on end.

Should destroy the phone, but I might have to deal with texts from Mom. And it doesn't matter. If Hale calls Mom and Dad, or the retreat center calls wondering where I am, the credit card will point right to the Comfort Suites. The first question will be, why am I in Youngstown with a plastic gun? Oh, Cretin is bloviating there?

Busted.

I disable the find-my-phone app to stall them a bit if they try the obvious. I glance at the TV, silently playing in the corner of the baggage claim. CNN blankets another shooting. A whole lot of kids shot by another kid with an assault rifle he legally buys because he's eighteen. WTF? He can't buy a beer but can buy an AR15? They should just sell grenade launchers, way more efficient. Sickening...

And terrible news for me. What are you doing, Hale? Will you give me until Monday now with another school shooting all over the news? Or did you already turn me in? If you rat me out on the day of a mass shooting, HWB will call Mom and Dad – too much liability, blah, blah, blah – instant expulsion.

And then begins the frantic search to find me.

Do I even want Hale's trust in me to hold? Or do I secretly want him to save me from myself? No. Cancel that thought – that's some BS Nichols would say. No self-sabotage! Hale knows it would ruin my life. He won't report my gun.

My bag rolls out. At least I got lucky with that. I grab it and walk out into the heavy air, passing Doric columns, an obvious afterthought to the airport entrance. Wow, I'm here!

Maybe Hale reports me or maybe he does me a solid. Either way, I can't control his reaction to another awful school shooting.

So, onward I march.

Gun-crazed country is making it hard to pull off an assassination.

28 Hours – Ground Control

eel cold and disembodied, like I'm watching myself on a security camera, which I am – in the lobby of the Comfort Suites. I'm looking for some comfort, but that would be like finding spirit on Spirit Air.

Feel so disconnected. My breathing sounds like an astronaut walking on the moon. Major Tom to ground control. No, stay on this planet – pay attention to <u>this</u> world right now. Focus!

I smile into the camera and watch myself on the screen behind the check-in desk. Freak. Keep it together.

I usually like hotel lobbies, with their excitement of arrival, people suspended from their reality for a night. That feeling of, if I'm not home, and if the people that define me aren't around, then I can be anybody I want to be – even an assassin.

Booth, Oswald, Hinckley, and me. Christ, what lousy company.

There's zero excitement at Comfort Suites. Just a worn-out feeling like the day after a party when you clean up cigarettes and alcohol spills and realize everybody treated your house like a toilet. Or so I imagine, having never thrown a party. Who would I invite?

I don't expect Internationals like the ones who visit the fancy Santa Monica hotels where I sometimes write in the lobby and watch Italian tourists check-in – slim women in sundresses and wide-brimmed hats and men wearing linen and loafers with no socks. They look like old-fashioned movie stars. And the kids look nothing like American kids – all wiry and tan and not buried in screens, just horsing around with each other, having fun.

Nobody's having fun at the Comfort Suites. Everybody wears T-shirts and shorts, revealing piano legs bleached white. Their faces are soft and dull, with eyes that glitter like hard candy on cupcakes. I suddenly understand what Hale meant by "stateside" when I first met him. The Indian man at the front desk is so unfailingly gracious and alert, with dancing warm eyes and a face so filled with sympathy, he seems like a damn holy man in comparison to the natives in front of him.

"Enjoy your stay at Comfort Suites," he says with a lilting accent to the two in front of him, as if welcoming them to the Taj Mahal. "Please let me know if I can help you in any way."

The couple doesn't acknowledge him with even a grunt before lumbering away. He's a damn Comfort Suites Sadhu, but they treat him like a slave.

On my way to a killing – killing time in line with judgmental thoughts!

"Comparison is the thief of joy," said Teddy Roosevelt, progressive president, winner of the Nobel peace prize, creator of America's national parks, protector of the little guy and our environment – so different from Cretin in every way possible.

Am I stealing my joy by judging everything and everybody?

Yeah. Mind won't stop, even here on the mission. Can't remember the last time I felt real joy. Maybe with June and Gigi at the beach.

Guess it goes with the journey I'm on. But what journey are these people taking that makes them all so mean and miserable? Cynical and hostile? It's not money, they have enough. It's just… they're lacking a sense of relaxation and connection to the world. Of enjoying life and knowing if they get cancer, they won't end up bankrupt on the streets. Maybe it's as simple as not living with <u>that</u> stress.

Or maybe it's like Thoreau said, *"The price of anything is the amount of life you exchange for it."*

And Americans exchange a lot, working 50 hours a week, for 50 weeks a year, for 40 years – swapping 80,000 hours of their precious life for the stuff in their house. Are they happy, as they keep pushing the Amazon button for more? As they ignore the environmental bottom-line that all that stuff turns everybody into a furnace, cooking the planet?

I don't know. I've only had a couple of jobs, but it seems like a bad trade. Am I too idealistic? I'm a teen, so my insula, the brain part for empathy, is on hyper-drive. But hey – Zoomer to Boomer – maybe you all need an insula reboot so you can really feel what's happening in the world. That all that consumerism, 70% of our economy, is killing us.

Why am I spiraling about this? Got to stop or it'll be a long 24 hours, which isn't the worst thing, considering where I'm ending up.

Christ – just stop. Focus! Here and now.

Next up are two couples that laugh at everything they say to each other. They all wear red T-shirts with Cretin's slogan, in town for the rally. Just like me, but drunk.

"I'd like a quiet room, Amigo," a beefy guy orders, pulling his wallet out. No idea why he calls the Indian clerk Amigo – guess it's his brown skin. "I'll come back down here and kick up a fuss if I don't get one."

The group giggles like that's the funniest thing in the world.

"But of course," the elegant clerk says, unruffled as he processes Beefy's credit card. Damn. Do I need Mom's credit card to check-in?

"Enjoy your stay at Comfort Suites." The clerk passes the keys to Beefy. "Please let me know if I can help you in any way."

"You can count on it," Beefy growls, looking like he wants to punch the clerk. Instead, he grabs the cart piled high with their stuff, as if they were on a world tour, and shoves it forward. A bag falls, sending them all into gales of laughter. So funny, that falling bag.

"Good evening," the beaming clerk says to me as I step up to the counter.

"Hi." I give him a smile to make up for all the casual rudeness he's gotten in the last five minutes. Also, I don't have Mom's credit card and need to finesse some slack. "My name is Benji Wallace. I have a reservation."

"Certainly, sir." Nobody's ever called me "sir" and it feels like Dad is behind me with a credit card. "I'll just need an ID and the credit card with which you booked the room."

"Um, here's my ID." I pull out my brand-new driver's license. "But my Mom booked the room on her card and I don't have it with me."

"I see." The clerk is unperturbed. "Can you confirm the number I have on file?"

I recite it in a rattle. The slender clerk raises an eyebrow at the feat. Damn. Just gave him a reason to remember me. Guess it doesn't matter now.

"Excellent, sir." The clerk slides a key card over the counter with a smile. "Enjoy your stay at Comfort Suites. Please let me know if I can help you in any way."

Same exact words, but somehow it doesn't feel canned. He smiles with eyes that are glowing and warm. Pulled into the moment, I can't help but smile back.

It's a bit of relief for an astronaut hurtling through cold silent space.

27 Hours – Cold Comfort

My comfort suite is reneging on its name.

It could be the air-con is blasting and it's freezing, with a weird chlorine smell. Could be the carpet is shit brown, with what I guess are leaf-like patterns. Wouldn't want to put ultra-violet lights on it like they do in all those cop shows where everybody in America is a murderer.

The two rooms that put the "suite" in "comfort" are connected by a little kitchenette with a coffeemaker. It's right across from the plastic bathroom, so you can take a crap and reach over to make coffee at the same time.

Or hang yourself from the showerhead. Christ. But it's that bleak.

The enormity of where I am suddenly sinks in. Maybe because I'm not putting one foot in front of the other to reach this place – I'm HERE.

It doesn't help to think somebody else passed through last night and slept in this bed. Took a dump in this toilet. How gross is that? And there are a hundred rooms in this motel, identical down to the little bar of soap wrapped in plastic.

The conformity suddenly makes me clammy and claustrophobic. It's like all of America is this motel. Wherever you land, it's the same rooms and box stores and fast food joints where they lay out everything the same so you can find it quickly until the whole damn country is just a pinball machine with the same flippers every two blocks to nudge you to spend your money – your life – more efficiently because you've got to make room for the next person so just hurry up and die until the whole system collapses –

I'm losing it.

Alone in Youngstown, Ohio, with a plastic gun, to kill a man surrounded by an army. The enormity of it crushes me. I'm not brave – I'm scared. I'm not ready to die – I love my little life. I'm not cool and calm – I'm flush and afraid. The way I was before my panic attack and holy shit I need to get out of here and feel real air and walk by real trees, not the plastic fern in the corner, before I'm curled up in the fetal –

The phone rings. Not the motel phone. Mine. And it doesn't ring because the ringer is off. It vibrates in my pocket. Insistent.

I pull it out. An unknown number. Filled with dread, I swipe.

"Hello?"

"Ben?" It's a familiar voice, but for a second, I go blank.

"Yeah?"

"It's Mr. Hale." Holy shit! Why is he calling?

"Hi?" I feel stunned.

"Just checking in. Where are you?"

I try to focus on the lie I told him.

"I'm in Ojai at this… retreat." The silence on the other line pulls words out of me like a vacuum. "Remember? I had a kind of panic attack and I'm at this mindfulness retreat to help get control of my thoughts and that's why I wasn't in school today to, um, to give you the gun."

I stop as the word gun hangs in the dead space of the connection.

Can't help but fill it.

"Actually, I've got to go because phones aren't allowed on account of –"

"Wait. You never mentioned you had a panic attack."

"Um, yeah." Shit. Concentrate, Benji! But it's hard, yanked from one reality into another. Dematerializing like in the transporters on Star Trek, only to materialize in an unfamiliar land fraught with weird alien danger, soon to face the Borg.

"Ben? Are you there? You were talking about a panic attack?"

"Yeah. It's no big deal, but this program is supposed to help."

"Why didn't you tell me about it?" Uh, oh. There's that interrogator voice creeping in.

"I don't know, guess I forgot." Lame.

"You forgot." He's not buying it – I don't forget anything.

"I mean, I didn't forget. But I didn't think it was a big deal."

"And yet there you are, on a family retreat to address your panic attack." Why's he checking in? Can he smell something's up with me?

"It doesn't have anything to do with the gun." Please, Benji, stop saying gun.

"It has to do with us trusting each other. I'm trusting you to tell me the truth, which also means not lying by omission." Hale sounds suspicious and even a bit irritated, which is unusual. Got to switch tacks, finesse for some sympathy.

"Guess I was maybe too embarrassed to mention it." Yuck.

"Nothing to be embarrassed about." Hale softens his tone a bit. "You said you would email me the admission to that retreat."

"I'm sorry, Mr. Hale. That one I totally forgot. I'll send it to you right now. Hang on." I work my phone like mad to send him my registration.

"Put your mom on the phone."

"What?" The hum from the bathroom light is like water torture on my chemical brain.

"Your mom or dad. Put one on the phone." That's right, I'm here with them.

"They're, uh, on a hike right now. A mindfulness walk – really slow."

Really slow? Christ. How do I not see this coming? Is a guy like Hale going to let this go without a follow-up? A kid makes a gun in his class and he'll ignore it with a massive school shooting today? No way. The line is quiet except for the whoosh of my outgoing mail.

"Mr. Hale?"

"I'm here."

"Just sent it. I should get going."

"Got it. Hold on," Hale commands. "I don't see your parents on it."

"I, uh, got a separate admission because I'm eighteen."

"So, if I call this center, I can talk to them?"

No. I never even canceled the retreat, so who knows what they'll say. Trying to avoid refund notifications going into Mom's email, but was that the right choice? What if they call Mom asking where I am? Impossible to know every right move –

"Ben? You there?"

"Yeah, I don't know. It's a private retreat. I don't think they'll give that information out." I'm just spinning now, spinning a web of BS, trying to catch a much stronger insect.

"Where's the gun?"

"The gun? It's home. Not assembled or anything. No bullets. Just hunks of plastic." Will he let it go? "First thing Monday morning. I'll bring it in."

A long silence. It takes everything I have not to fill it.

"How do you feel, Ben?"

"How do I feel?" I don't expect Hale's question. I feel numb. And under that I feel terrible for too many reasons to list. "I'm okay. Here in Ojai at this beautiful center. Mom, Dad, and June are here. Doing cognitive-behavioral therapy, aka mindfulness."

"Remember, call me if you feel anything out of the ordinary. No matter what the time."

"I will." I feel a rush – Hale's kindness overwhelms me. He doesn't want to ruin my life and in that risks everything. No other teacher, hell, no other person besides Mom and Dad would do this. And in return, I demolish his world –

"Ben? Do I have your promise to do that, to call me?" Hale sounds unsure about the risk he's taking – like I'm no longer a good bet.

"I promise. And I really appreciate you trusting me. But don't worry, I'm not doing anything rash. Far from it." And I'm not. Killing Cretin isn't a rash decision. This journal is living proof of that. "It's so beautiful and peaceful up here. I completely forgot about the gun."

Gun again. Come on, stop saying it.

"Okay, Ben," Hale seems reluctant to go. "When you see your parents, have them call me."

"I will. I think we go into silence pretty soon, but I'll have them call you, maybe tomorrow." Should I ask why? Wouldn't that be what I would do if I were telling the truth? It's impossible to know.

"Okay. I'll take your word on it."

"You got it, Mr. Hale." I feel such deep shame. LIAR. "I should get going."

"One last thing. It's not what happens to you, it's how you react that matters. So do the mindfulness part. Observe your thoughts carefully. They're an illusion. They're not even you. Remember, 'some of the worst things in my life never even happened.'"

"Mark Twain," I say, feeling such a connection to Hale. Like we share a brain. We could have been such good friends. "I'll remember that. Bye, Mr. Hale."

. "Bye, Ben. See you Monday. Bring that gun."

"For sure. And… thanks. For everything." I want to talk more, thank him for being such a great guy, but I need to get the hell off the phone before I snitch on myself.

"No problem," Hales says and my phone goes dead.

I stare at the sad little room and turn off the air conditioning.

I miss Gigi and June and Mom and Dad – they seem like a dream. And Hale. Is he the last person I talk to from my life? The last person I betray? What a thought. But yeah, probably.

The worst thing in both our lives is definitely happening.

Got to go check out the Covelli Centre.

Got to get the hell out of this room.

26 Hours – Covelli Centre

Walking. One foot in front of the other. Back to this.

"Use the moment as a life raft in the turbulent sea of thought."

I say this to myself out loud, keeping myself company. It's a good one, from a dharma book in the little FTW library. I try to anchor in the moment because my mind is a hurricane right now. Whenever I think about tomorrow, I focus on the foot I plant in front of me. Every time I think about Hale and whether he calls my parents, or worse yet, comes to his senses and notifies HWB, I drop a foot.

I destroy Hale for helping me out. Foot.

I kill a human being in 24 hours. Foot.

I never see Gigi or Mom or Dad or June again. Foot.

They catch me, a fool on a fool's errand. Foot.

I die tomorrow. FOOT.

"Having no destination, I am never lost." Comforting myself with aphorisms, this one from Ikkyu, I try to observe my skittering thoughts and land in the moment. Just a walk – nothing to see here, folks. Keep it moving.

With each step, my blood gradually warms until I'm finally <u>here</u>, sweating in the humidity, back in my body, thoughts dissolving in the <u>now</u> setting sun, as I foot my way toward the Covelli Centre. I cross a bridge over some railroad tracks and suddenly, there it is.

Holy shit, I'm HERE.

The Covelli Centre is smaller than it looks online. Guess spelling

"Centre" like the Centre not holding in the Yeats poem is to add some class, like the Doric columns at the airport. But it just looks like a big high school gym in the middle of nowhere, surrounded by a huge parking lot. And I'm talking free parking, not like LA.

An old guy in a folding lounge chair with torn webbing reclines at the entrance. First in line? Must be. Metal sawhorses are out and several police cars crouch around the perimeter. Men with dogs move from an 18-wheeler into the Centre. They wear earpieces with curly white cords trailing up their necks like gang tattoos. SS. The dogs are the type Special Forces use, Belgian Malinois. No dog winks from them – not even a glance from their handlers.

The man stretched out in the rickety lounge is the opposite of the brisk men around him. He wears a worn Cretin hat with a Vietnam Vet POW pin in it, and a red, white, and blue vest. His scuffed cowboy boots point straight up like tombstones and his skin is leathery, with sunspots and veins looking like the desert I flew over today. Beside him are a cooler, a dented thermos, and a blanket, all within arm's reach. Is this old man spending the night?

I snake through the sawhorses. Nobody pays any attention to me as they focus on securing the inside. Plus, I'm just a kid. What can I do against an empire? Funny you should ask, Mr. Vader –

"Howdy, son," the man in the armchair drawls. What kind of accent is that? He sounds like a grizzled cowboy in a movie. "You here for the rally?"

"Sure am. Are you spending the night?"

"Yep. Wanna be first." He smiles, showing a missing upper incisor like Gigi. Is this just some crazy? Or do people really line up a day early to hear Cretin?

"Where you from?" I ask, making conversation before I fish for information.

"Texarkana. Drove the whole way. I got a brother that lives up here."

"Where's Texarkana?" I've honestly never heard of it.

"Border of Texas and Arkansas, but on the Texas side. Which is the side you wanna be on, believe you me."

"You think there'll be many people here early?" I ask. It's hard to imagine people coming so early to hear a liar lie – Cretin's thousands of whoppers for what feels like decades now. But I've got to get into a different mindset. And find out how early I need to –

"It's always packed. And after the run he's had, people are gonna wanna see him."

"The run he's had?"

"Yeah. Peachment. The fake news piling on him every day. Not giving him any credit for cutting our taxes and building the wall. Or millions of new jobs. The draining of the swamp, getting rid of all those crooks in Washington." He drawls out Washing-tuuune. I bite my tongue – he's my people now. I'm in his tribe and he's in mine. "You hear what I'm sayin'?"

"Sure do. But this is my first rally."

"Yer first rally?" Texarkana crows in disbelief. "Yer in for a treat. It's a good ole time."

"You think it'll be crowded?" I ask again and he squints at me like I'm stupid.

"Son, ain't you been listening? They gonna turn out for him. And all the protesters and the Communist News Network, they gonna turn up too. It's a wild show."

"What time do I need to be here to get a spot in the front?"

"Right in front of him?"

"Yeah, like, along the stage. Or the ramp going up to the stage."

"Oh… well, then you need to be in the first fifty. And they still might not choose you," Texarkana drawls. "I'd spend the night. Or get here way before dawn."

"Before dawn?" Fifty people aren't showing up here before dawn for an 8 pm rally. No way. And that's when an old lady with a helmet of curls plastered in place walks up with her husband, hauling matching folding chairs. Is this grandma – what the hell?

"Are you spending the night out here too?" I blurt out. She looks at me like I'm nuts.

"No, thank you very much," she minces off her words. "We have an RV. We'll be spending the night in that, like civilized people."

Grandma, unaware she just insulted Texarkana, points with pride across the parking lot to one of those RVs the size of a bus with the expandable sides. The husband pops open their chairs next to the old man's lounge.

"To hold our place." Grandpa's wearing a neatly pressed button-down shirt and chinos, with the buzzed hair of a marine. "We'll be in them at zero six hundred."

It's not a question. Texarkana, who's ratty-near-homeless compared to this guy, nods.

"I'll keep an eye on them for ya." He lazily salutes, a disgruntled grunt to an iron pressed officer.

"Aren't you thoughtful," Grandma says. "I'll bring you some coffee."

Texarkana pats the thermos on his cooler. "Oh, I'm all set. What I might ask is to use your bathroom in the morning, if they don't have the Porta Potties unlocked."

Stepford Grandma looks at the ancient cowboy and smiles thinly, picturing this oddball taking a dump in her perfect RV, which I just know has doilies and pictures of grandchildren.

"If they don't have them set up, you're welcome to it. But they usually do," she says in a tone that hopes to hell the Porta Potties are ready.

"Thank you kindly," Texarkana says, sweet as can be.

"Well, I've got chili in the crock-pot. Ready, Steve?" He nods and they walk back to the RV.

"So, anybody can hold a spot? Like, can I hold a spot?" I ask Tex.

"You got a chair?"

"Um, no."

"Well, you need a chair." It makes sense. Damn! Should've thought of this. Do I need to spend the night here? No sleep, but I don't expect to sleep anyway. Need to go back and get the Liberator —

"Where you from, son?"

I don't have a lie prepared, so I just tell him the truth. "California."

"Oh. Now I know why you're a bit slow on the uptake. Yer IQ drops as soon as you cross the border from Nevada." Texarkana laughs and finishes with a cough. I smile, not knowing what to say as he lights up a Marlboro with an old Zippo, snapping it shut.

"You out here by yerself?" He expertly blows a couple of smoke rings.

"Yeah. I uh, really want to see him before he gets impeached again."

"Nah… Don't drink that California Kool-Aid. There's a snowball's chance in hell they're gonna convict him, that bunch of crooked pussies in congress. They don't have the balls and he ain't done nothing wrong."

"Well, that's good. I'm excited to be here."

"Tell you what, son. I can lend you my cooler 'til seven in the a.m." Texarkana pushes his cooler further away, knocking over the RV couple's chairs, which have stencils of the Grand Canyon on them. I slide them down and set them upright to avoid a chair war.

"Don't mind them chairs," Texarkana drawls. "You see how she looked at me like I was a goddamn Mexican when I asked about the crapper?"

I'm surprised he noticed Grandma's reaction, but I guess you couldn't really miss it. Still, I need to be careful with old Tex. He's harmless – like a rattlesnake stretched out sunning itself on a California fire road – if you're not a "goddamn Mexican." But what if he coils up?

"Are you sure about holding my spot? Because I'd love to be up close."

"You have my word." He leans forward and holds up his hand. "Name's Hank."

"Thank you, Hank. My name's Ben." That's so weird. I just called myself Ben.

"Pleased to make your acquaintance, Ben." I shake Hank's outstretched hand, which feels rough and dry, not unlike that rattlesnake.

"Thanks for helping me out. Are you sure it's okay?"

"We just shook on it, didn't we?" With that, I know Hank will keep his promise or die trying. A lucky break – because spending a night out here on the concrete with zero sleep would severely impact my focus tomorrow.

"Yes, we did." I nod at Hank.

"Well, there you have it. My word is my bond."

"Thanks again. I can't, um, spend the night here. I've got to get to my uncle's house." Hank's word is his bond. My lies flow like water. "But I'll see you tomorrow at seven."

"Yer uncle's not coming?"

"Nah. He's a Democrat." I shake my head sadly, getting into my role.

"Now that's a goddamn shame," Hank says. "But the future's in young fellas like yerself anyhow. Taking the country back."

"Can I bring you anything?" I ask, caught up in the neighborliness of it all.

"Nah, I'm good. Unless ya got a Porta Potty. Cause that old bitch ain't gonna come through." I laugh with him at that. So true. Can't help but like this veteran from a different world, dreaming about a mythic time that never was, swallowing Cretin's fantasies whole.

"No, probably not. See you tomorrow morning, Hank. Thanks again."

"Sleep tight, Ben. Yer in for a real treat." Hank blows a series of smoke rings, torpedoing out of his mouth in perfect round intervals. "What you kids call a troll? Well, the president's the biggest troll with the biggest balls you'll ever see. He ain't gonna roll over, that's for sure."

I nod. No, he won't.

Not until I make him.

24 Hours – Only Do

riting this with the motel TV on Hank's Communist News Network. They're blanketing the school shooting.

Some girl who survived just called Cretin a piece of shit in a tweet. Finally, somebody who calls it like it is, "respect for the office" be damned. Why do the media treat him like he makes a bit of sense? Could it be his madness is money for both sides? Yup.

Ignored in the scroll is the fact it was 124 degrees in Phoenix today, too hot for planes to fly. As we kill each other, Mother Earth's getting ready to shake us off like a dog does fleas –

Are these my last written words? Wow. They have to be. Christ…

This is bad – how will I live through my last 24 hours on the planet? I owe my life to writing. I would never survive, never mind get to this comfortless room, without writing myself here. Out of my head onto paper, floating down a rapturous river, words effortlessly rising like foam on water, keeping me company, keeping me <u>sane</u>. But now my connection to the vast silence that chooses the next word, like meditating all day, will break forever and –

Fuck. Once I stop this journal, I'll be alone with my terrible mind.

There will be no mystical communion with cosmic reality. I won't be able to connect to myself as I take the final steps, staying, like Ray Bradbury said, "drunk on writing so reality can't destroy me." I'll be locked in, trapped with my relentless grinding gear brain, unable to write myself out of my head. Reality will crush me!

And now, the astronaut feeling returns. Only I'm not in the spaceship anymore. I'm floating outside the goddamn can Musky dreams of living in, drifting further and further away. Untethered. Disconnected from life, breaking even this stringy scrawl of ink, my last feeble lifeline. In a nightmare of loneliness as our beautiful blue planet recedes –

I'm losing it again!

How can I quit a lifelong, lifesaving, writing habit in the most intense moment of my life? But what else can I do? Can't be recording it all, squeezing it in like I usually do –

But I can literally record it.

Everybody has a phone out taping Cretin's vile bile as if he's a cult leader they'll watch over and over. Having one out with EarPods won't attract a bit of attention. So, I can talk myself through the day, a verbal journal instead of a written one. Not as good as writing, but it might keep me connected. Keep me on the planet long enough for word to graduate to action. And my final act to obliterate all words –

Which means after I stop writing tonight, I need to toss this journal.

I flip through the pages, everything that's happened since the 405 fire a million years ago. Every thought that got me here – a massive dose of truth. Wow. I don't want to throw this journal away. It's all my reasons for killing Cretin. It's the truth.

My truth… Is it even true? Will it make a difference?

Guess tomorrow my actions will have to speak louder than my words.

But don't Mom, Dad, and June deserve to know what happened to me? Why I suddenly "went crazy" and killed the president? Of course. I don't want them to wonder forever.

Why the hell haven't I thought about this until now? Head up my ass, that's why. I've got to mail this journal to them.

Some of it's so weird. Embarrassing. Whatever…

Sorry, Mom, Dad, and June. No time to edit it. It's more important you don't blame yourselves. And you don't believe all the lies people will tell about why I'm doing this.

I can mail it in the morning, so this written part is on the way, while the verbal recording keeps me company and bucks me up through to-morrow.

How weird to finish this journal, not by writing, but by talking to my-self to my end. This way, I'm not so lonely – it helps me survive the day. It gives me courage, coaxing my way there. Hope it works.

Until no more talk, only the act itself.

Only do.

20 Hours – Last Words

Midnight. No chance of sleep. Last practice with the Liberator. Align. Push. Snap. Slide. Squeeze. Shove. Pull. Click. Load. Deconstruct. Again.

Tomorrow is – don't know what it is. Loud. Stressful. INSANE. When I kill Cretin, will it break the trance, waking everybody up? Hope everybody understands! How can they not –

Because they won't know. HOLY SHIT!

They won't understand why I'm doing it because I've been talking to myself the whole time. The lists, the facts, the planetary crisis Cretin's creating, my desperate plan to stop him. Reasoning it all out. To me.

HAHAHA! Talk about a tree silently falling in the woods.

How dumb is that? If I don't say something as I do it, I'll just be another deranged shooter. Only Mom, Dad, and June will know my reasons after they read this journal and they won't share it with anybody.

Christ, how did I not think of this until now?

Maybe because it's finally real, it's happening in a few hours. Can't believe it... But stopping him isn't enough. People need to understand why I'm doing it. I need to say something as I pull the trigger.

What the hell do I shout to the world? Save the planet! For the environment! Stop extinction! For all humankind!

Lame. Melodramatic.

Too bad John Wilkes Booth used "Sic Semper Tyrannis." Good one. Say what you will about that guy, he was hardcore, refusing to come out of a burning barn and surrender, choosing to be burnt alive and then shot for good measure.

Hope I can hold my nerve as well as him. Thus always to tyrants! No shit. But I can't use that. He was on the wrong side of everything.

What about... for all animals? Yeah. For all the poor dying animals. For all the voiceless species winking out. And for all us human animals, soon to be on the list.

FOR ALL ANIMALS!

Stopping our extinction, every other disaster a warning shot.

FOR ALL ANIMALS!

To circle away from the knock-out punch.

FOR ALL ANIMALS!

To stop Cretin's murderous rampage.

I've got to bug that Indian guru for an envelope and a bunch of stamps so I can mail this journal to June. She'll get it first from Lynn.

Need to write a note to send with it. Final goodbyes. Last apologies. Warn them about the shit storm heading their way. Christ.

Then maybe get some sleep. Doubtful.

Last written words. The period at the end of my sentence.

For all animals...

What else is there to say?

5:03 AM

Phone in pocket. Pods in ears.

Zero sleep. Wrote a poem about Gigi instead – so worried about her. And my note to Mom, Dad, June – what a gut punch. Sealed with the journal in a manila envelope with stamps from that nice Indian Guru.

Cretin speaks at eight. Fifteen hours. Going to be a long day.

Talking this out is so much easier. If I spoke my journals, they'd turn into a million transcribed pages. Not as private, the mic will record sounds, people talking, the insanity of it all – an immersion into the mob. But it sure is faster.

Testing, testing.

(Inaudible.)

Plays back great, even whispers. Not that it matters. Going to delete it right before. Too brutal for Mom, Dad, and June to hear what happens today. So painful what I'll bring down on their heads.

But it's all out of my control now. Just surfing the wave. What a relief.

Feel kinda crazy, talking to myself like a schizophrenic wandering around my room, but this wire in my ear grounds me to me. I hope it's enough to get me through the day. Keep me from losing it. Guess I should try to limit recording – can't get caught talking to myself about killing the president. Christ, what a weird thing to say.

Final check. Liberator pieces in socks, pockets, hoody. Each bit will do its job, the whole greater than the sum of its parts. The whole that makes a hole. Lame. Way too blasted –

(Inaudible.)

Double-lacing Converse. Lady Liberty with the bullet and nail in my front pocket. I've got it all. Ready.

Walking out the door of my sad little room. Feels so good to leave this room. Feels so bad to leave this room. But it's finally happening, this moment I've been dreading. Dead man walking.

I've really got nothing. One bullet. In a plastic gun. Against an entire system. Hope I'm not Don Quixote tilting at windmills. Or attacking bad guys in a puppet show, thinking they're real –

Stop it, Ben. No more doubt.

Cretin is a living, breathing planet killer. Remember that.

Christ. Finally, down to this – nothing.

"Sometimes, nothing can be a real cool hand." That was such a great movie, watching it with Dad. Wish I was home doing that right now –

(Inaudible.)

EarPods hit the ground – gonna have to watch that.

6:07 AM

Dawn. Empty road. Phone in pocket, pods in ears. Glad for them. Feeling so out of body. Need a mailbox and –

(Inaudible.)

Already humid. Sweaty hands staining the manila envelope. Fingerprints. Doesn't matter. Mail this journal and life as I know it ends no matter what happens today –

(Inaudible.)

Freeway underpass. Noisy. Two homeless Burners on their haunches up embankment –

(Inaudible.)

Shit! Strung out jackals on the move –

"Yo, yo, man!"

"Whatyougotfaggot?"

"Nothing! Just school stuff."

"Give it here."

"You got a wallet? Gimme that phone!"

"Get off me!"

"Where you think you're goin?"

"Here, take it! Keep the bag. My wallet's in it."

"What's in the bag?"

"His wallet and some shit."

"Gimme your phone."

"FUCK! GET OFF ME!!"
(Chaotic panting. Inaudible.)
"AH!"
"Grab him!"
"FUCK YOU! I GOT A GUN!"
(Scuffling, heavy breathing.)
"Get that skinny motherfucker's phone."
"You get it. I ain't chasing —"
"FUCK!"

6:20 AM

Shit!

(Inaudible, heavy breathing.)

They got the backpack. Wallet. And, damn, punched me solid.

Shit. Could be worse. Lucky they're high and stumbly. Didn't get the phone. Or journal. Or the hundred bucks in my sock with Cretin ticket –

The Liberator!

(Inaudible.)

– Oh, so lucky. Still got all fifteen pieces. And Lady fucking liberty – we got mugged!

(Wild laughter.)

Okay. Okay. Shit. That sucked. Could have fucked up the whole plan. Stopped me cold.

Assholes! Could be worse. I'm okay. I'm okay. Shit!

Swearing a lot. Talking instead of writing. Makes it easier.

6:40 AM

Eye hurts. Random bad luck, the future showing up to punch me in the face.

Mailbox. Pick up at 9 am. Good. In the system when I pull the trigger.

Feds will search mailboxes for evidence. Will they bury the journal if they find it? Nothing to see here – just another screwed up kid shooter...

That would suck. My real reasons buried with me. Should have left this journal at home for Mom, Dad, and June.

Can't think of everything. Like June says, everybody's got a plan until they get punched in the face. Didn't think I'd literally get punched. Circled out of a couple – June would be proud. Missing you so much right now.

Screw it. Just got to trust the postal service. Through rain, snow, and assassination. Hope June gets it from Lynn at the top of the street before anybody else.

(Metal creaking. Slamming sound.)

No turning back now.

7:05 AM

Covelli Centre. Already steamy enough to cook broccoli.

Wow. Like a hundred people in line. Media trucks setting up. Lots of action twelve hours out. Good news is no news from Mom, Dad, Hale.

Hank – in his lawn chair drinking from his thermos. Jeez, looks the same, not like some old guy who slept outside all night. A couple big dudes with buzz-cut hair on the sides and the top flopped over like Tyler's are next to the chairs for the RV couple. Rude Boys or Alt-righters. Both wear Cretin Ts with "2020, Fuck Your Feelings" on them. Christ.

Need to get a MAGA hoodie. But won't it look suspicious in the heat? Damn, another thing I didn't think about –

"Hey, Ben – you talking to yourself?"

"Hey, Hank. Yeah. Just want to record my first rally. My impressions. Like a journal."

"You kids, recording everything. I just like to live it. What happened to your eye?"

"Ran into some trouble."

"I can see that. Have a seat on the cooler."

"Thanks. Thanks again for saving my spot."

"Sure. Here's something for your recording. Yer gonna have a shiner pretty soon."

"Yeah, kind of got mugged – you don't have to lean in Hank. The mic's getting it."

"Mexicans?"

"What? No."

"Dude, you can't jump the line like that."

"He's not jumping it. He was here last night while you were sucking yer thumb in bed."

"Okay, old man. Keep your pants on."

"Were they protesters, Ben?"

"No, just some guys… burner types."

"Tell us where they are. We'll go fuck those Antifa faggots up."

"No, not Antifa. I got away. I'm okay."

"What's a burner type?"

"Um, kind of, you know, Hank. A druggy drifter."

"Oh, yeah. We should collect 'em all and put 'em in jail. Dry 'em out."

"They don't wanna get dried out, old man. Just like they don't wanna work. They need to go to one of Sheriff Joe's camps with some pink underwear. Like what the beaners got."

"He's running for Senate again."

"Good. I'll vote for Joe. We need law and order. And arresting beaners for riding bikes on the wrong side of the road is a good start. Sends a strong message."

"I guess. Can you hear, Ben? With those damn things in yer ears?"

"Yeah. I can hear it all, Hank. But I'll take them out."

"Keep 'em in if ya want. Record yerself. Record me. I don't care. Gotta go lay some pipe."

"In the RV?"

"Hehe. Good one. Nah, they got the Porta Potties unlocked."

"I'll watch your stuff."

"See you later. Hey, reach in and grab some ice for that eye."

"Thanks."

"Don't mention it."

"Hey. Kid. You watch our chairs too?"

"Um, sure."

"Okay. Cool. Come on, Eddie, let's get a breakfast beaner burrito."

"Good idea. You want one, kid?"

"No, I'm good. Thanks."

"Okay, back in ten."

Beaner burrito? Concentration Camp Joe – the racist who killed 157 Hispanics in tents so hot their Nikes melted? Killed their unborn babies with rat-infested food, all before a trial?

Christ. How am I going to make it through this day?

$$\text{10:30 AM}$$

Phone vibrating. Mom. Early in LA. Got to call her back.

"Taking a break?"

"Yeah, Hank, going to go stretch my legs."

"Hold your breath in them Porta Potties!"

"Will do. See you soon."

(Inaudible.)

Need a break from Hank, the RV Oldsters and the drivel they drool. The big guys are the worst – "nigger this, beaner that" – all morning long, just as casual as can be. Immigrants are welfare lazy or stealing American jobs – they can't seem to decide. Total shit show. Even Military Grandpa told them to zip it. Zip it! Gotta love the old school lingo.

Mom must have been checking in. Got to listen to her message and text her. Just need to walk to the end of this parking lot and be alone for a bit. Pee. Only ten and tropical as a sauna – already sweating through my shirt.

A text from Mom: "Where are you?"

What? Why's she texting that? Did the meditation center call her?

A text from Dad: "Here with Mr. Hale. Where are you?"

No, no, SHIT. NO! Hale. At our house first thing Saturday morning? Why?!!!

Then Hale himself: "Ben, whatever you're doing, it's not too late to reconsider."

No no, no! What happened? How did he find out? Fuck! Did they find the flight on the credit card? Mom and Dad don't go to cards right away, but Hale? For sure. This is what he does –

Dad again: "Ben, call us right now. Please!"

No no, no! Hale told them. Did they put it all together yet – the gun, the rally, the whole plan? How did this –

(Inaudible.)

– you believe it, Mom and Dad? Only a matter of time, then what do you do? Call the FBI? Secret Service? Or do you worry about me getting shot? Mom and Dad, you're paranoid about that for sure. Does it stop you from calling it in? Make you pause? But what about Hale? And what about getting shot while killing the president and –

Phone vibrating nonstop. Can't check the messages.

Can't hear the fear and desperation.

Walking in circles at the far end of the parking lot. Dizzy. Got to piss like crazy. How did they find out? Doesn't matter. Delete messages and forward calls to voicemail. Turn off text. Shut down cellular. Just a recorder now.

What a clusterfuck. Must've been Hale. Followed his hunch and checked in with Mom and Dad. Or called the retreat center...

Ten hours to Cretin. Will they cancel the rally? After they find out a kid with a plastic gun flew across the country to be here? Definitely.

But will Mom and Dad call it in? So confusing. What do you worry about most? Me shot dead. Your worst nightmare. So ashamed to put you through this. Your son, a killer. So terrible. And Hale, you must hate me –

(Inaudible. Sniffling.)

Mom and Dad, do you fly out yourselves? Try to keep it in the family? Try to save the remains of my life, which ends the second you call the Feds? Still time if you catch a flight.

What about you, Hale? Can Mom and Dad talk you into not reporting it? Does your no-man-left-behind code apply to me? Will you help them with your military skill set?

What a bunch of wishful BS.

Need to listen to your messages to figure out what you're doing. But I can't – it would gut me. Your hysteria would stop me cold. Wait. Wait –

(Gasping, then deep breathing.)

Feel panicky. Sick. Got to get a grip.

Nothing to do but keep going. Hope for the best. Just talk it into this box and zombie it out. Can't abort. They know I'm here. Journal mailed. Life wrecked.

Nothing changes. Get this done or die trying.

One foot after another. No other way.

12:03 PM

Talking to myself in a damn Porta Potty. Like a Greek hidden in his Trojan Horse, ready to sneak out and ransack Troy.

No more Cassandra – I'm a Porta Potty Trojan assassin!

Losing it – so hot in here. Feel sick. Stomach a bucket of acid. Head on an acid trip.

Mom and Dad. June. Hale. What are you feeling? Doing?

Makes me so sad.

Need to eat something. Need to buy a baseball cap to hide face and a hoody to fit in. Then back in line to bite my tongue at the casual racism and bottomless ignorance – hidden before Cretin made it okay to let everybody's freak flag fly.

So far, they buy my act. But feeling bruised and disoriented, like choking myself from the inside. What will change this madness and –

(Banging sound.)

"You talking to yourself in the crapper?"

"On the phone."

"Oh, that makes it okay. People got to go and you're hogging it on the phone –"

"Sorry. Important call."

12:30 PM

"Um...you have veggie dogs?"

"Veggie dogs? No man. We don't have no veggie dogs. We sell hot dogs and pizza."

"Okay. A slice of pizza."

"Five bucks."

"For a slice?"

"You heard of supply and demand, right Dog? I mean, Veggie Dog?"

(Laughter, inaudible.)

Christ. Feel like a Mexican on the inside and everybody has X-ray vision. Ridiculous. Paranoid. I totally fit in this sea of white identity – pale as a human can be. But can they smell it under my blue eyes and pasty skin? Pure animal instinct telling them I'm not in the pack?

Asking for a damn veggie dog doesn't help.

Tastes good, this greasy slice. No longer a vegan. Doesn't matter now. Keep it together. Just a bit longer and this endless journey will end.

What the hell are Mom, Dad, and Hale doing?

Wow, hundreds more people showing up in Cretin red –

(Inaudible.)

"Bumper stickers. T-shirts. caps."

"How much for a cap?"

"Ten bucks. T-shirts are twenty. Thirty for the 'Fuck Your Feelings' one."

"Uh. You have any hoodies?"

"Yep. Gonna be hot, though."

"Yeah, it's for back home. A hoodie and a T-shirt. And a cap."

"What size on the hoodie and T?"

"Uh, medium?"

"Okay. Eighty bucks."

"Thanks."

"MAGA."

(Inaudible.)

Fuck Your Feelings! On caps, shirts, mugs. Onesies. Ha. Toxic swag. Got to put mine on. Blend in like somebody who stayed up all night to see Cretin spout the truth. Everybody's truth feels like BS today. Mine too? Cancel that. No doubts!

(Inaudible, several minutes.)

"Hey, look at you. Getting in the spirit."

"Oh, yeah. Not as much as you, Hank, but you can't find these in California."

"That where you're from, little man?"

"Yeah. Los Angeles."

"Smell-A. We been there once. Right, Bob?"

"Wetback city. Already more browns in California than whites."

"Everywhere you go, there they are, working away."

"Don't worry, the president's got you. Get that wall built. Round 'em all up, stick 'em in camps for a long time and send 'em home. Make 'em think twice about coming back."

"Sure. Makes like, total sense. Especially the kids."

"Anchor babies. All those jobs need to go to Americans."

"Did you hear about the school shooting? Terrible. We're praying for the children, aren't we Steve?"

"Always, dear."

"So now we gotta listen to Libtards at the Jew York Times who don't know the difference between an assault rifle and a BB gun —"

"You watch it in the RV?"

"Yes, we've got TV and everything in there."

"And a bathroom too."

"Well, you should have just knocked on the door this morning if you needed to."

"Didn't wanna wake you up."

4:20 PM

The blacktop is melting licorice.

Walking perimeter again – away from the camp of crazies. Never imagined a crowd this bad. Self-selecting. But damn, pure idiocracy. Hard to keep biting my tongue.

And still the mob grows, waiting for the show to start. Cheerful, like a festival. No sign it's canceled because a kid travels cross-country with a plastic gun. Why the hell not?

Mom and Dad, what are you doing? What about you, Hale? No man left behind? Or did you call it in and the Feds are already searching? Christ. Hang tough. Four more hours – that's all. Then it's over.

(Shouts, horns blowing.)

Protesters. Chanting. Penned up away from the entrance. Handmade signs and blow-ups of Earth. No Antifa, with their faces covered. Just hundreds of people sweating to make a change. Way too little, way too late, but you got to love them.

"Fascist Nazi!"

"No KKK. No Fascist USA"

"What you gonna do, shoot us? Where's your gun?"

"Gun? What gun? Why you pointing at me?"

(Inaudible.)

"You're so young. Think about what you're doing!"

It's the Cretin Gear, dressed like a kid on Halloween –

"Yo, ginger, don't you care about climate change?"

Ha. Talk about a nightmare – like going to school dressed as a Nazi.

Wow, National Guard soldiers wearing green camo and carrying assault rifles. Only shit – they have beards and wear Oath Keepers patches.

"Are you Oath Keepers?"

"Yep."

"What're you guys doing here?"

"First amendment. Here to protect free speech. Your right to assemble."

"But you're not police or military."

"Former and current military. Law enforcement. Here to keep the peace. Neutral. Like in the constitution."

"But isn't that what the police are for? Aren't they the 'well-regulated militia for the security of a free state' the Second Amendment talks about?"

"We're here just in case. We got your back. One of those Antifa black block scum might get hold of you and stomp you. Looks like you already got stomped by one."

"Yeah. But no. Just criminals. Thanks."

"Be free and speak your mind. Glad you know your constitution."

(Inaudible.)

It's all so jumbled. Nothing what it seems. The cops don't look twice at the armed radicals. Probably know them. And white, so they can open carry AR-15s all day long –

Holy fuck, is that MMA Ears? Shit, shit! Dressed up like an Oath keeper? Is that him –

(Heavy breathing, running.)

What the fuck? Was it? No way that's him. Is it? Can't tell. Are these his people? Christ. Am I losing it? Got the spins – so thirsty. Cottonmouth and –

(Inaudible, several minutes.)

"– much is the water?"

"Five bucks."

"I'll take one."

"Here you go. MAGA."

MAGA. The new Heil Hitler? Is my hat a Swastika?

All too terrible. Got to get past the RVs out into that field. Find some silence. A bit of nature. Escape the carnival.

Fucking MMA Ears. Was that him? On a job? Following me? Maybe. Got to watch out. What if he's killing Cretin? Disguised as an Oath Keeper? Or maybe he is one and this is just how he spends his weekends.

Or is lack of sleep making me paranoid? Seeing things? So random.

Tall grass feels nice... feeling faint. Got to lie down in this field. So tired.

"Out beyond ideas of wrongdoing and rightdoing there is a field. I'll meet you there. When the souls lie down in the grass and the world is too full to talk about."

Rumi. So beautiful. Want to go to that field. No wrong. No right. No dogma. Away from all this madness. Guess I am going...

I'm ready. My heart, too full to talk about.

(Ambient nature sounds, nine minutes.)

Shit! Did I fall asleep? Okay. Okay. Wow. Weird.

Keel over like a corpse, why don't you?

Miss the whole damn thing.

5:05 PM

"You're back."

"Yeah. Just needed to stretch my legs."

"I hear ya. Might do that myself. You want a water?"

"I'm good, thanks, Hank. I'll watch your stuff if you need a break."

"Holy shit, isn't that Amber? That hottie from Right Side Broadcasting?"

"It is. Damn, Eddie. Look at her."

"Hey, Amber. OVER HERE!"

"Hey guys, you keeping cool?"

"With you here? No way."

(Laughter.)

"We watch you all the time. And Fox. Big fans."

"Why, thank you very much. You guys are the die-hards, right at the front of the line. Do you mind if we show you on camera? We're streaming Facebook live."

"No problem."

"Okay, thanks. I always gotta check. Where you guys from?"

"Mesa, Arizona."

"Hot out there?"

"Yep. Makes today feel air-conditioned."

"Libtards gonna blame the weather on Global Warming. Hashtag Fake News."

"Totally. So, you guys excited to see the president?"

(Whisper): Totally? This is too painful –

"Hell, yeah."

"Great. It's a good crowd. Only about twenty protesters on the other side."

(Whisper): More like two hundred –

"They know better than to mess with us."

"What do you two hope the president talks about tonight?"

"The wall."

"Taking our country back. So, yeah. Immigration. We been waiting for somebody like him a long time. Get rid of the criminals and rapists coming here illegally."

(Whisper): Immigrants that have lower crime rates than Amer –

"You boys just wait. He's just getting started. Don't forget to vote. Four more years."

"Absolutely! Then send em all home. Get rid of DACA. And those kids separated in detention, what's the big deal? They get three hots and a cot. School. Medical. Lots of Americans would love that deal. And the law is the law."

(Whisper): Three hots and a cot? Prison for toddlers?

"You boys are right. Illegal is illegal. What about you? Where are you from?"

"He's from Smell-A."

"Do you mind if we show your face?"

"Better not. My family doesn't know I'm here."

"Totally understand that. What do you hope the president talks about?"

"I don't know. Maybe everything he's done already."

"Like what?"

"Uh. Well. Like, getting rid of environmental regulations that protect water and air, but kill jobs. Pulls back on that bill that protects people's money – we don't need big Gov protection from banks. He's tough on crime, so that's good – once minorities get a conviction, they can't vote with the Libtards. And if you're a minority, you're five times more likely to get arrested for pot smoking than whites. Which is good for us. Oh, and he's smart. He talked Fox News into being his own, like, state-run media channel. And he uses Republicans to crack and pack congress districts with gerrymandering – beating those sore losers crying about democracy. And I'm excited how his trillion-dollar tax cut to the richest people in the world is gonna trickle down to me. Strong on security too, giving billions to the military, so we're bigger than the next eight militaries combined – kicking ass and keeping us safe from Canada. And he's protecting all the beautiful monuments celebrating the confederacy. Sure, they fought for slavery, but it's not like they're statues of Hitler, right? But mainly it's the climate regulations he repeals to unleash the power of capitalism. We need four more years to lock those in. We don't need elitists telling us the world is ending – so-called experts. Like with guns, not allowing mentally ill people to buy them. Who's to say who's mentally ill? Some people say the president is –"

"Wow, you really know your stuff. Lamestream media likes to portray his supporters as uninformed."

"Low information voters, the president loves them. But I try to stay informed. You really help."

"Thank you. We do our best. And you two, where are you from?"

"Texas. Drove the RV up. Not Houston, thank Jesus. We'd need a boat for that."

(Whisper): And why would that be?

"So, what do you hope the president talks about tonight?"

"Pro-life. Which, as Christians, is the most important thing to us – all those poor babies. Despite all the negativity in the Fake News, there's a method to his madness. Right, Steve?"

(Whisper): No method, just madness.

"Right. Look at the stock market. That's our retirement. Lowered taxes. And like the young man just said, he's patriotic, pumping money for the military. Plus draining the swamp."

(Whisper): He is the swamp.

"Did you want to say something more?"

"No, sorry. Just keeping a verbal recording of the day. I want to re-member everything."

"That's an excellent idea. What about you, Sir? What's your name?"

"Hank."

"Really liking your outfit, Hank. Very patriotic."

"I've been to twelve rallies from way back early on. He's the real deal."

"Sure is. And what do you want the president to talk about tonight?"

"Doesn't matter what he talks about. They gonna misportray him anyhow. They gonna insult him — they gonna insult us. But we know the truth, don't we young lady?"

"We sure do, Hank. We sure do."

(Whisper): Et tu, Hank?

6:03 PM

Oh, goddamn it. Oh! Christ, just awful.

(Vomiting. Spitting.)

The bowels of hell. Ugh. Sweating so hard. Porta Potty shit sauna.

(Groaning.)

Wired. The surreal slack of this endless day – am I really going to die in a couple of hours? All alone in front of this crowd? Can't think about it – oh, shit, here we go –

(Vomiting. Spitting.)

Oh, fuck. Terrible. Oh – no, no, no.

(Groaning.)

Oh, Christ, hope that's it. Note to self: never eat cheese before an assassination again. Got to get out of here. Got to get back. No toilet paper. Perfect. Going to have to use a sock.

(Wild laughter.)

No big symbolic reason the shooter wears one sock, just no damn toilet paper.

Christ. Feel Mad Cow sick. Shaking like Gigi at the vet.

6:30 PM

Empty inside. Hollow. Gotta take a sec here... sit in this field again.

Ninety more minutes left behind enemy lines. Will I make it?

Everybody's the guy in *Alien*. Eating dinner until out rips a screaming alien from his stomach. The humans here look normal until they open their mouths and out pours pure alien gibberish –

(Coughing.)

"Homo sum, humani nihil a me alienum puto."

Nothing human is alien to me. Used to think so. Not anymore, surrounded by pure inhumanity

Where's MMA Ears? Did I hallucinate him?

Or do all those guys just look alike?

It's not too late to reconsider… Christ, Hale, get out of my head. Way too late – gate's closed. Life over. What the hell's going on, Mom and Dad? Why's it not canceled?

Where are you?

(Inaudible.)

– this drunken cult. Just want it to end.

Autopilot, build gun, pull trigger.

Before an alien bursts out of my damn stomach.

6:40 PM

"Gosh darn it, Ben, you didn't leave me much time to stow my gear."

"Sorry Hank. I had to take a break in that field. Not feeling good."

"Okay, we still got time. Be back in ten minutes. We'll get our spots inside and I can take a leak then."

"Okay."

"You don't look right. Sweating like a sheep shearer in August. Maybe take off that sweatshirt. Unless you got a fever. You got a fever?"

"Yeah, maybe. Feel bad. Just… You go put your stuff in the car."

"Okay. The RV folks are putting their chairs back. And the two big guys – I don't know where the hell those good ole boys are. Hold their spots. See you in ten."

"Okay, Hank."

The good old boys don't buy my act. Got to watch them – they're big and could grab me quick. Got to be more MAGA convincing.

(Inaudible, several minutes.)

Still on? Thought it was off. Wasting battery. Oh, here comes Hank. Limping. Feel bad for him. Right or wrong, Cretin is his hero. An insult to Cretin is an insult to Hank and –

"You recording again? You young folk and yer selfies and whatnots. Surprised you haven't taken a selfie with me."

"Nah, just keeping a journal. Not into all that Instagram junk."

"You don't wanna take a picture with me, Ben? I'm offended."

361

"Okay, Hank. Let's take a selfie."

"I haven't had too many selfies before."

"Me neither. Just, get in close… Okay. Ready?"

"Ready. Wait. Should I take off my hat?"

"No. It's good. Here we go."

"Thank you, young man. A pleasure to meet you."

"You're welcome, Hank. Pleasure to meet you too."

"Hey, somebody's inside. They're going to open the door. Come on, honey, hurry up."

"I'm right behind you, Steve."

"You ready for this, Ben?"

"Ready as I'll ever be."

"Okay, folks. No pushing, no running. Step on inside to the metal detectors."

"They got this part worked out pretty good. Only takes a second."

"That's good."

"Air-conditioning!"

"Everything metal goes in the plastic bins. Cellphones, keys, belts. Shoes stay on. Keep the line moving."

"Sir, you need to remove your hat because the pin has metal in it."

"I know. Not my first rodeo, son."

"Thank you for your service, sir. Step on through."

"I'll wait for you, Ben. We can go up together."

"Okay. Thanks."

"Next. Everything metal in the tray. People have your METAL OBJECTS out and ready to place in the tray. Cellphones, keys, belts. Shoes stay on — what's this?"

"Statue of Liberty."

"I see that. But what is it?"

"Keychain."

"For one key?"

"Yeah, um. I don't drive yet."

"Okay, keep it moving."

"Thanks."

"Have your METAL OBJECTS out and ready to place in the tray. Cell-phones, keys, belts. Shoes stay on."

Damn. Close one. Should have put more keys on Lady Liberty.

7:01 PM

Holy shit. Loud! Rock-and-roll in the belly of the beast.

(Journey: Don't Stop Believing.)

"Stop fiddling with yer damn phone and give me a hand."

"Sorry, Hank."

"Just step lively. Maybe we can stand right behind the president."

"You think we can?"

"We'll find out. This way —"

"Hi. Can you hold up? What about them, Tom? The old guy's a regular."

"Okay. Sneak them into the clutch, make sure Service doesn't see you."

"Are they a good on-camera mix?"

"What can be better than a grandfather and his grandson? And I'm a veteran. Drove all the way from Texarkana to hear the president."

"We're at zero hour with two cancels. They're fine."

"Okay, follow me, gentlemen."

"Uh… Can I grab one of those signs?"

"Sure. You certainly look like fans of the president. What happened to your eye?"

"Um, ran into a tree branch. You can't see it with my hat down low."

"Waited all night to be first in line, young lady."

"Well, we had two vetted no-shows, so today's your lucky day. Would you be willing to take off the vest but keep everything else?"

364

"I'd be willing to hop up there stark naked."

"No need for that, sir. Okay then, here's your stamp. Sam here will take you two up."

"Alright. This is real exciting. Now, can I come and go? Cuz I gotta go."

"You'll be able to for the next 45 minutes, then we'll lock it down."

"Thank you, young lady."

"Thank you for your support."

(Inaudible.)

"Can you believe it? Been trying to get back here every rally and they never let me back. It's cuz of you, Ben. You're my lucky charm. Look at this… He's gonna stand right there in front of us. We're gonna be able to reach out and touch him!"

"Okay, grandpa."

"Got us up here, didn't it?"

"It sure did."

"Thanks for playing along. Okay. I got to go. Don't let nobody take my spot, you hear?"

"Okay, Hank. But don't be long. Got to go too. Bad."

"Back in a jiffy. We're gonna be on TV, Ben!"

Like a rock concert, everybody waiting for the headliner.

(Lynyrd Skynyrd: Sweet Home Alabama.)

Squished in this mob. My worst nightmare, feeling panicky. Only twenty minutes. Where's the damn bathroom?

One. Two. Three. Four. One – counting is BS tonight. Feel sick again.

Come on. One step at a time. Almost there. Cap low, hide face. Just keep going. Need to do it the minute he starts talking. In case they're looking for –

"Heads up, buddy."

"Sorry. Sorry."

"Take it easy. It's okay."

Damn! So loud in here. The white tribe has gathered. A cult, a religious fever dream. True believers dug in. Like a crazy church having an oldies rock and roll party – is MMA Ears here? Where's the fucking bathroom? Oh, there –

(Inaudible, crowd noise.)

– even matter what Cretin spouts? After I do it, they'll tear me limb from limb. Gonna die a horrible death that changes nobody's mind and –

"Excuse me."

"No problem."

Just shut up. Basics. Carry sign. Get to bathroom, one foot at a time. Automatic. Build the gun. Like being on Molly, that's how sharp everything is. Bright. Loud!

(Inaudible, general din.)

Bathroom. Christ, the smell –

"Dude, you live-streaming your dump?"

"Oh, hey, guys. You get good seats?"

"Not as good as you and the old man. Right behind him. You're gonna be able to touch his hair."

"Might just do that. See if it's real."

"Don't drown him in your flop sweat."

(Laughter.)

"We're down in front."

"Cool. Well. See you out there."

"Take a picture if it's a big old floater."

(Raucous laughter.)

Idiots.

In a stall. Finally, end of the line –

(Inaudible whispering.)

Liberator pieces on the sign. Bullet and nail out.

One last time: Align. Push. Snap. Slide –

What the hell? Are you for real? Wow, look at you – hitched a ride from that field? Aw, floating up off the hoody – so delicate. Are you a messenger? But what's the message, Miss Ladybug? Go ahead, land on the sign. Am I tripping? No. You're here for real. A chip off the block of nature. Like with Gigi and hummingbirds and butterflies and bees in the garden. So different from the death in my hand and the death to come. My death to come.

(Sniffling.)

No, no, no – goddamn it. No crying. No pity-party. Just auto-zombie finish. Squeeze. Shove. Pull. Click. Load. Done –

(Inaudible.)

– really ready to do this?

(Heavy breathing.)

Gun in hoody. Locked and loaded. Ready.

But what about you? Crawling Cretin's crappy sign – watch the puddle of tears. Can't let you die in this putrid bathroom. Come on, little lady, you can do it. Just crawl onto my hoody. That's it, climb up there. Good. There you go. Okay. Angel on my shoulder. Keep me company – then fly away to a better place.

(Toilet flushing.)

Here we go. Easy does it, hang on – I got you. Glad you're here – remind me who I was. Christ. What have I have become?

(Rolling Stones: Brown Sugar)

Phone over face. Hat low. Oh, Christ. Freaking out. Easy now. Stay calm. Breath. Walk. Breath. Walk. One foot. Other foot.

For sure, it's on. SS everywhere, but nobody gives me a second look. Just another true believer. Why is it still on? Mom? Dad? Where are you? Damn, my phone is almost out of juice. Need to save –

"Sir, do you have a stamp?"

"Yes."

"Okay. The president will be on time and starting shortly. If you leave the stand, you won't be able to get back up."

"Nothing could make me leave."

"Okay. Enjoy the speech."

"Thanks."

(Inaudible. Crowd roar.)

"SO LOUD! Who's that, Hank?"

"Some warm-up guy. How's yer stomach? You gonna make it?"

"Hope so."

"Can't shit yourself right behind the president in front of a billion people."

"Hope not."

"Goddamn, look at this. What a view. Can you believe it?"

"No. Impossible to believe. Crazy."

"Hey, you got a bug on ya."

"Yeah, she's a little lady –"

"Got him."

"Yeah. You did. You got her."

Cretin for real. Oh, shit. Here we go –

(Lee Greenwood: Proud to Be an American)

FOUR MORE YEARS! FOUR MORE YEARS!

Looks fake. So old. Can I really Baby Hitler this dotard?

(Inaudible. Crowd ROAR.)

"Thank you, Ohio. My fellow patriots. Thank you! My favorite state! Tonight, together, we gather to share our customs, traditions – values. We love our country. Don't let the lying press tell you otherwise. Look at them back there, enemies of the people."

(CROWD ROARS.)

Hand on Liberator. Now. Come on – come on!

"We celebrate our troops. We embrace our freedom. We respect *our flag. We are proud of our culture. Nobody. Nobody's gonna take our Christian culture away, believe you me."*

USA! USA! USA!

Christ. He's pathetic. Got to –

"We cherish our Constitution, especially the Second Amendment."

Can't delete this – Fuck it. Do it! Mom, Dad, June, I –

(Inaudible.)

"USA! USA! USA!"

"FOR ALL ANIMALS!"

"What – please! NO!"

"You stupid old man –"
"BEN, NO!"
(GUNSHOT. SCREAMS.)
"Get him!"
"Got him!"
"MOVE! MOVE! MO –"
(Recording stops.)

As I Lay Dying with Gigi

The garden is dark.
No hummingbirds zip between buds on the orange tree.
No laughing bees buzz.
No insects march on their important duties.
Even earthworms sleep off a long day of eating dirt.
Inside, Gigi dozes by door, head resting on white boots.
All day Gigi licks many faces — girl with wet face.
Not boy. Boy, not home.
Gigi waits. Boy, come home.
Boy loves Gigi.
And Gigi loves boy.
Suddenly — pain.
A heart pain so sharp Gigi stands and howls.
Where is boy?
Gone.

Epilogue – Day One
The New York Times

Teenager Aims Homemade Gun at President, Kills Self at Rally
By DAVID BAKKER, THOMAS SHAEN

YOUNGSTOWN, OH – Moments into the president's speech last night, Benjamin Wallace, 18, jumped on the stage of the Covelli Centre and pointed a homemade plastic gun at the president before turning it on himself and pulling the trigger. The Secret Service rushed the president unharmed from the stage. Wallace died instantly from a bullet to the temple.

According to a short statement by Secret Service spokesperson Anthony Berman, the gun, self-made by Mr. Wallace, was a rudimentary 3D printed pistol called the Liberator, the design of which is available online and has recently stoked controversy. Because the gun is plastic, it was undetectable to metal detectors, although it remains unclear how Mr. Wallace smuggled in the single bullet. Mr. Berman said the Secret Service is reviewing all protocols.

Mr. John Hale, 43, Wallace's science teacher, identified him at the scene as being from Brentwood, California. Hale, who is also a security and technology consultant, flew on a client's private jet to Youngstown after learning his student had traveled to the rally with a 3D plastic gun printed in his class. It took five Secret Service members to subdue the Navy Seal veteran as he vaulted onto the stage, perhaps trying to stop his student. The FBI is holding Hale for questioning.

Benjamin Wallace, with a 4.7 GPA, was the top-ranked student at the prestigious Harvard Westbridge School in wealthy Brentwood, California. He had perfect scores for both the SAT and ACT. According to Hale, besides being a brilliant student with a photographic memory, Wallace had a burgeoning interest in moral philosophy.

Several witnesses confirmed Wallace waited in line all day to secure a spot in the stand behind the president. The crowd was thundering a "USA" chant after the president said, in one of his signature partisan lines, that they all cherish a shared culture, especially the Second Amendment. At this moment, Wallace jumped on the stage, pulled the gun from a MAGA hoody, and aimed it at the president. Wallace's intent seemed to be to assassinate him and a look of stunned disbelief swept the president's face as the young man shouted, "For all animals!"

"What – please! NO!" the president cried, cowering in front of Wallace, who instantly turned the gun on himself. It doesn't appear that Wallace saw or heard his teacher screaming out, "Ben, no!" as he rushed the stage. Because of the crowd noise, only nearby witnesses recording the president's speech on their phones heard the frantic appeal. The young man's suicide, recorded by thousands in the arena, is now the most viewed in world history.

Pandemonium reigned after Wallace shot himself. The Secret Service swarmed the stage. There were screams in the audience and confusion for a moment as the "USA" chant continued. Then the crowd, after realizing they witnessed the suicide of a young man, grew silent as the Secret Service hustled the president from the stage. Videos have surfaced online that show a wet stain around the president's groin. Several agents initially jumped Mr. Wallace, but he was already dead. Doctors at the scene called the time of death at 8:09 pm.

Some people sobbed as the lights came on. Others stood around, blinking with shock. Security locked the arena down for an hour before they allowed people to leave, at which point the president's supporters silently filed out. The Secret Service detained and interviewed everybody near Wallace, confiscating cellphones.

Wallace was standing directly behind the president before he jumped on the stage. How he ended up in a customarily vetted spot is under review. Local news footage clearly shows him talking into his EarPods, perhaps recording himself. Secret Service confirmed they recovered an iPhone belonging to the young man. They haven't released the phone's contents, or even confirmed if a recording exists. Facebook executives have quashed initial rumors that this was the first Facebook Live streaming of a presidential assassination attempt.

An hour later, in Brentwood, California, at 6:08 pm PST, a Los Angeles SWAT team stormed the home of the shooter, encountering the family dog, a pit bull. The police shot and killed the dog after it lunged at them.

Authorities are questioning Peter and Hannah Wallace. Why neither parent nor Mr. Hale called law enforcement upon learning Benjamin Wallace printed a 3D gun and traveled to Youngstown, is unknown.

Although he shouted, "For all animals," pointing to a possible environmental motive, no concrete reason has surfaced for the young man's actions. Authorities have not mentioned a note. It is also unclear whether Wallace initially planned to kill the president and changed his mind, or just wanted to scare him before committing a premeditated suicide.

Right Side Broadcasting posted an interview with Wallace on their site. In it, Wallace both praises and excoriates the president in a spontaneous satire of Republican policies, making a veiled political statement.

According to David Marks, 56, postmaster general for Youngstown, the FBI searched mailboxes for evidence, to no avail. Unusually, for a teenager, Mr. Wallace has no presence on social media.

Hank Smith, 68, from Texarkana, who waited in line with the young man and was beside him on the stage, expressed shock at the suicide. The two became acquainted during the long hot day. Initially, there was some confusion about their relationship, which Smith cleared up by saying they just, "Pretended to be kin to have a better chance of being close to the president." The Secret Service has not implicated Smith in the shooting.

"He seemed normal to me. Bit green, but he was young. Hell, I didn't know anything when I was young either. I liked him." Mr. Smith said, growing emotional. "Don't know what would possess him to go do a thing like that. Sorry, got something in my eye. Sorry, got to go."

Others who met Wallace have different opinions. Two men, Eddie Jones, 23, and Bob O'Keeffe, 24, from Mesa Arizona, were also near Mr. Wallace in line.

"He was a show-off," according to Mr. Jones. "Plus, he was from LA. So, fake."

"Probably wanted to kill the president but chickened out," Mr. O'Keeffe added.

Mr. Steve McCabe, 73, and his wife, Susan, 70, presidential fans who traveled to the rally in their RV, were also next to Mr. Wallace in line.

"Like so many young men his age, he was confused," said Mrs. McCabe. "And his grandfather, or whatever, was just not our kind of people."

"Damn shame, though, to kill yourself at that age," Mr. McCabe added. "It points to a lack of purpose in our young people."

Mr. Guatam Anand, 29, the hotel clerk at the Comfort Suites where Mr. Wallace stayed the night before, had yet another opinion. A recent immigrant from Lucknow, India, Mr. Anand said, "The young man was very polite and lively. Very unusual in that he recited his mother's credit card number from memory. We spoke for several minutes late at night when he needed stamps and an envelope. I feel it is a very great loss to lose such a quality human being."

The president tweeted early this morning about the young man's suicide, "Stared evil in its pimply face and evil blinked. LOSER! Spilled water on me. Thanks for love and support. Still Alive! As is agenda. MAGA!"

Day Three
The New York Times

Suicidal Shooter's Recording Leaked, Details Assassination Plot
By DAVID BAKKER

BENJAMIN WALLACE, the 18-year-old who killed himself at a rally for the president on Saturday, originally intended to assassinate the president, according to a recording made on Wallace's iPhone. Leaked on Reddit, it chronicles his last day and references a long-planned plot to kill "Cretin," as he dubbed the president. While he called the president a "planet killer," pointing to possible environmental motives, most of the recording is an extemporaneous monologue revealing his thoughts and feelings, a self-professed way to "stay grounded."

On that front, it didn't work – the recording viscerally captures Wallace's fear while waiting to assassinate the president. At one point, Wallace vomited into a Porta Potty. On his way to assembling the plastic gun, smuggled in pieces into the rally, Wallace fought a panic attack. He cried when rescuing a ladybug, pointing to an unraveling or overly sensitive nature, although he was stoic when Hank Smith, who stood with Wallace, heedlessly crushed the insect.

The recording also captures Mr. Wallace getting mugged as he walked to the Covelli Centre. And him mailing a journal to his family, expressing worries the government would intercept the document, preventing his family from knowing his "true reasons."

Intensely personal, alternately chatty and grim, Wallace gave no sign he was considering suicide. But he also seemed uncertain; was his assassination plot just tilting at windmills? Would his teacher or parents rescue him? Would a vague environmental reference in shouting, "For all Animals!" as he shot the president change anything? Questions, but no real answers as to why the young man chose martyrdom over murder in the last moments of his life.

Whatever his motives, Wallace was clearly uncomfortable at the rally, calling it a cult, with the president acting as the head of a prosperity-type church of true believers. Also recorded were snippets of conversation, much of it profane, some of it racist, of the crowd in which he waited. Although he seemed to like Hank Smith, who waited in line with him, bonding in the heat, Wallace talked about feeling surrounded by humans spouting "alien gibberish."

Peter and Hannah Wallace, the young man's parents, along with Mr. John Hale, his teacher who jumped on stage to stop him, desperately tried to contact Wallace throughout the day. He ignored their calls and texts, apparently hoping his parent's fear of the police killing him would delay their decision to turn in their son. Ultimately, Wallace was correct in thinking they would try to stop him themselves to "save his life."

Although they had no legal duty to report a threatened future crime, authorities are questioning both parents and Mr. Hale on their failure to report the plot.

Day Four

CNN

Suicidal Shooter Accused of Drug Addiction, Motives Endlessly Debated

By MARY ZANE

(CNN) - He was 18 and gifted. He killed himself in the most public way possible. This much we know about Benjamin Wallace. Everything else is a cause for furious debate and speculation, as the recording of his last day has gone viral.

Wallace's family has remained in seclusion since the death of their son, only spotted once in their garden, burying their dog Gigi, killed by SWAT team members upon entering the house searching for bombs, accomplices, and motives.

That his intent remains murky hasn't stopped fans and foes alike from seizing on Mr. Wallace as either hero or bogeyman. Was he a principled young man protesting the president's environmental policies, or an assassin who lost his nerve? Was he a deliberate martyr, or a confused teen? On a mission, or depressed? The answers are falling on typically partisan lines.

According to teachers, Benjamin Wallace was a gifted student with a photographic memory, who, despite his academic achievements, kept a low profile. Described by his Government teacher, Samuel Baxter, 51, as a "gentle person" and "a genius," he seemed an unlikely assassin. But some who knew him at Harvard Westbridge, the elite school Wallace attended, have strongly negative opinions about Mr. Wallace.

Classmate Tyler Kincaid, 18, captain of the lacrosse team, said, "He was a weird little snowflake with a school shooter vibe. A total liar. And a druggie. Not surprised he went off the deep end."

Friends of Mr. Kincaid, John Dickerson, 18, and Alex Drack, 18, both also on the lacrosse team, confirmed Wallace's drug use.

"There's a famous video of him puking on a girl, high on drugs," said Mr. Drack. "No wonder he lost it,"

"Hard to keep the thread when you're buzzed all the time," added Mr. Dickerson.

Mr. Hector Cortez, 53, a school custodian at Harvard Westbridge, said he saw the video of Wallace vomiting on a girl at a party but didn't think it was typical. According to Mr. Cortez, "Benji was a sweet kid bullied by some kids jealous of his abilities."

The one thing all the interviewed students agreed upon was that Mr. Wallace liked to keep to himself.

"He was always writing, scribbling in his journal," said Alice Edsall, 18. "Even in class. He never seemed to have to study or pay attention. So lucky."

"He was definitely a loner. I used to see him walking his massive pit bull. That dog was scary. I used to cross the street," commented Willow Pirelli, 18, a resident of Brentwood, California, where Wallace lived.

Mr. John Hale, Benjamin Wallace's STEM teacher, is on an unpaid leave of absence while the FBI and Secret Service investigate him for not turning in Wallace. A technology security specialist and a retired member of the Navy Seals, Hale has remained silent about his student. The Secret Service has cleared him of direct involvement in Wallace's actions.

While no definitive motive has surfaced, environmental groups are seeing it as a protest, like David Buckel, a prominent Brooklyn lawyer who set himself on fire as an environmental protest.

The consensus on social media seems to be that Mr. Wallace was a brilliant but confused teenager, prone to anxiety and depression, perhaps brought on by drug use. Or maybe, upset by the president's policies, he went off the deep end. But all this is speculation.

When asked by reporters about motives and the existence of a journal that might explain them, FBI spokesperson Jason McCall said, "It's all under investigation. According to the recording, his admitted plan was to assassinate the president. Beyond that, we don't know why he instead committed suicide. We have not found the journal mentioned in the recording. The family denies receiving it."

All attempts to contact the family have been rebuffed.

Day Six

Associated Press

Benjamin Wallace's Sister, June, Breaks Family Silence, Releases Brother's Journal

By JANE LANSCOMB

JUNE WALLACE, 10, standing with her parents outside their Brentwood home, held a brief press conference today. She read the following statement:

"First off, thank you to all the people who send us support in this sad time. My brother's death has gutted us. The world's reaction to it is overwhelming. We are in shock. But I'm also mad as hell at how the media has portrayed Benji.

"My brother was a kind person – he cried when he watched Okja. He loved animals and nature. And our dog Gigi, gentle as a lamb, killed in cold blood no matter what the liar cops say. Guess I need a video, huh?

"Sorry... I might cry during this and I never cry. I hate crying. But jerks like Tyler Kincaid who're saying Benji was a drug addict and mentally sick, you can just suck it. Benji wasn't a crazy loner or a school shooter type – that's the real fake news. Tyler Kincaid is just saying all that because Benji accused him of being a pervert.

"The reason my brother killed himself was to draw attention to our climate catastrophe. He mailed us his journal and my friend Lynn gave it to me after she saw all the suits at the post office. Nice try, FBI. I kept it hidden, even from my parents. It makes Benji's motivation clear.

"Benji wasn't a fighter. He was a thinker, a reader, and a writer, always writing something. I should have paid more attention because he was writing about Climate Chaos. He wrote that we face an extinction-level crisis and that our so-called president isn't just ignoring it like everybody else. He's throwing gas on the fire. Benji's facts and headlines and lists about what this demento is doing are accurate. I checked. So, I released his journal and then told my parents.

"Benji would kill me if he knew I put his journal on Reddit and sent a copy to the New York Times. But I'm sick of all the lies. His writing will tell you who he was and what was important to him. I even put a copy of the note he sent us with the journal, warning us to take care of ourselves. And a poem he wrote about Gigi, imagining what she might feel as he died. Benji knew what was at stake. He wanted us to protect Gigi, but we failed at that."

At this point, Wallace struggled with her emotions for a moment, wiping away tears. She then soldiered on as her parents comforted her.

"My brother died to draw attention to our planetary crisis. He was planning to kill the person who is the worst of the corrupt climate criminals. I think he was too gentle to do it. And he saw what might happen if he did – maybe a civil war that would distract us all from the battle for our survival as a species.

"But don't be, as he would say, disinforstracted. They want you to be disinforstracted!

"I believe what Benji wrote, all of his facts and science. #ItsAllTrue. Once you read my brother's journal, you'll know why he did what he did. And how special he was. Thank you."

With that, the family retreated into their house, asking for privacy.

Day Seven
CNN

John Hale, Benjamin Wallace's Teacher, Fired
By MARY ZANE

(**CNN**) - Upon the release of Benjamin Wallace's journal, Harvard Westbridge fired Mr. John Hale, 43, a former Navy Seal and Wallace's teacher, from the elite prep school.

Richard Silkon, the school's president, read a short statement, "Benjamin Wallace's suicide greatly saddens us. We are deeply disappointed that Mr. Hale, a new teacher, took matters into his own hands rather than follow school protocol to report a struggling student's behavior. Harvard Westbridge takes the safety of its students seriously and cannot allow this conduct to stand."

Many of the journal's conversations reveal a close relationship between the student and his teacher. The most consequential discussion happened after Hale discovered his student had 3D printed a gun in his class. In a fatal misjudgment, Hale trusted Wallace when he insisted that he only made the gun as an experiment and would turn it in.

Mr. Silkon responded "no comment" when asked about Wallace's accusation that Tyler Kincaid, the scion of billionaire Jonathan Kincaid, committed a sexual assault. Wallace's journal negatively features Tyler Kincaid and recorded many verbatim confrontations with him, perhaps aided by Wallace's photographic memory. The most severe came after Wallace accused Kincaid of videotaping a sexual assault of an unconscious girl. Wallace threatened to kill Kincaid, pointing to a violent and impulsive temperament.

In another fatal misjudgment, instead of reporting Wallace, Hale talked him out of retribution, telling him he must be "the light" to Kincaid's darkness.

Hale still hasn't revealed how he discovered his student went to the rally with the homemade weapon, but he did break his overall silence in a short statement this afternoon after he was fired.

"Ben Wallace was a gifted and thoughtful young man whose gifts extended into the moral and political realm. A spiritual seeker, he cared deeply about the world. I'm not surprised he turned the gun on himself rather than take a life. Ben was a kind person and his parents feared for his safety if we called the authorities. I went there to save him, to stop him from making a mistake that would ruin his life and a one-of-a-kind mind. I promised his parents I could save him, but I failed in my mission. And for that, I'll be sorry for the rest of my time on the planet."

During three tours in Iraq and Afghanistan, Hale received a silver star, two bronze stars, and a purple heart for losing a finger in a classified raid. He left Seal Team 5 with an honorable discharge in 2015 and worked as a security consultant before transitioning to becoming a teacher.

According to Wallace's journal, Hale mentions an incident to Mr. Wallace in which Hale almost died and which cost the life of a friend. There is no criminal or military record of it.

Despite the president's twitter tirades about him, prosecutors have not filed charges against Mr. Hale.

Day Eight
The Atlantic

Benjamin Wallace's Journal: A Manifesto for our Times?
By CHRIS JACKSON

JUNE WALLACE, 10, sent her brother's original handwritten journal to The New York Times, matching a copy posted on Reddit. It details Wallace's meticulous plan to defeat the world's most sophisticated security and kill the president.

The environmental protest group Extinction Rebellion has combined the note, poem, journal, and leaked cellphone recording, transcribing it into one document that's gone viral. Facebook groups have formed to translate it into different languages. Journalists are calling it a manifesto. However, unlike mass shooter manifestos, it's being widely read. But should the media disseminate such a radical and provocative document?

Wallace's sister, who released it to combat "fake news" about her brother, says yes. And that while the fact-laden journal is a personal look into the mind of her brilliant brother and why he wanted to assassinate the president, the reasoning behind it is far more critical. Namely, as June Wallace said, "It draws attention to our impending climate catastrophe."

Still, the document details how Wallace made the plastic gun in his 3D printing class at Harvard Westbridge, a highly competitive high school in Brentwood, California. It chronicles his self-training to prepare for a political assassination.

Isn't this, at the very least, inflammatory?

Some argue no, because he didn't go through with it. Others say yes, because it's a realistic plan. The extreme reactions fall along America's partisan divide. The family, under police protection, has been deluged by death threats. But also, by people traveling to leave flowers in front of their house in a makeshift shrine. Meanwhile, responding to the president's exhortations, the Attorney General vows he will prosecute Wallace's teacher, Mr. John Hale, for criminal negligence.

While it's true Wallace obsessed in the book-length journal about his reasons for wanting to assassinate the president, whom he called "Cretin," what's struck a chord is his anxiety at the threat of "Climate Chaos," an emergency "needing drastic action to avoid human extinction."

The California wildfire that almost reached Wallace's house, and the near-death of his sister from a related asthma attack, appear to have radicalized him. Wallace characterized his planned assassination as an act of "planetary self-defense," carefully outlining his reasoning in lists and in each journal entry, where he tallied the president's daily attacks on "Mother Earth."

Although he expressed doubts about "his mission" throughout the journal, which is also peppered with thoughts on suicide, why he turned the gun on himself at the last moment is ultimately a mystery. Perhaps he realized self-sacrifice might be a more powerful act against an entire system. Indeed, his suicide has electrified people the world over. As has his journal, in which he routinely wrote to process his feelings and harness a powerful but anxious intelligence.

While much of his writing is about "climate chaos," he devotes equal time to spiritual and philosophical musings about his warm family life, his crush on a girl, and his struggles with a bully. And his fears about executing "the Plan."

Wallace also describes many poetic interludes in nature, including one high on ecstasy. And several with his beloved dog Gigi, in the garden or at the beach. Besides the science he meticulously detailed as a justification for his actions, Wallace also cataloged California's homeless crisis and criticized America's gun culture, depicting a dismal visit to a gun show. He pulled many strands together in describing the effects of runaway capitalism on the environment.

But mainly, Wallace excoriated climate deniers, relentlessly attacking the president's policies. He had nothing but contempt for the Republican congress, calling them climate criminals "raping Mother Earth" for profit. He also went after the elite moneyed class who quietly support the president, calling the hedge-funders and libertarians selfish "bloodsuckers." He called for a revolution to save the planet.

But he also criticized the "happy talk" of optimistic environmentalists, whom Wallace thought are in denial about the tipping points for irreversible climate destabilization – underestimating the "speed, scope and severity" of the emergency. He constantly reiterated that nothing matters except dodging the coming "extinction bullet." He tried to practice meditation to cope with his anxiety.

Quoting from Whitman to Sophocles, the well-read teen also wrestled with himself about the ethics, morality, and ultimate effectiveness of his planned assassination, and its effect on his loved ones. Alternately hopeful and pessimistic, naive and wise, sarcastic and pedantic, the self-aware young man saw climate chaos as an opportunity for the world to put down its arms and come together to face the challenge, while healing humanity's problems.

A movie buff, Wallace quoted them liberally, including a speech from *Armageddon,* in which a fictional president exhorts humanity to unite against a common enemy. Wallace called this enemy, referencing Winston Churchill, the gathering environmental storm. He envisioned an environmental Marshall Plan to zero out carbon emissions in ten years and a Manhattan Project to research and create carbon capture programs. He also feared there was too much corruption from "Big Oil" and that it was already too late; the gate has closed on saving ourselves.

Wallace coined the term "disinforstraction," a portmanteau for the combination of distraction and disinformation that prevents humanity from acting to save itself. Many journalists are now referring to the president's tweets as the "daily disinforstraction."

Although he chose martyrdom over murder, Wallace never explicitly mentioned killing himself in the journal, even denying it as his intention during a conversation with Hale, his concerned teacher. But there are also many hints left by the self-described "political junkie," including references to Thich Quang Duc and Norman Morrison, both men who self-immolated as a protest in the 1960s. This form of deadly protest was where the sensitive teen ended, perhaps impulsively, after all his careful thought.

The president, when asked if the growing reaction to the journal would change his policies on climate change, laughed and said, "We're not killing jobs because an unstable loser killed himself."

The president also stated, that along with the Kincaid Group, he plans to sue the "failing New York Times" for slander. And investigate the "terrible traitors" in the "deep state" who leaked the recording Wallace made of his last day. The case will be a First Amendment test, as the president persists in his war against the press.

And so, Mr. Wallace's journal and suicide joins the battle over what's real and what's contrived. Perhaps it is a manifesto for our times.

Day Nine
CNN

Sexual Assault Victim Comes Forward
By MARY ZANE

(CNN) - ADRA BHARADWAJ, 18, a classmate crush of Benjamin Wallace and featured in his journal, stepped forward with a bombshell in front of the Santa Monica police department. In a statement read with her parents and lawyers present, she accused classmate Tyler Kincaid, son of billionaire libertarian Jonathan Kincaid, of sexual assault.

"My name is Adra Bharadwaj and Benji Wallace was my friend. I am SG in Benji's journal. Today, because of Benji's description of Tyler bragging about attacking me, I am accusing Tyler Kincaid of drugging and sexually assaulting me. Tyler Kincaid is a sadist, a bully, and a liar. He relentlessly picked on Benji. And after I spoke my mind to him, Tyler planned and carried out this humiliating assault. But unlike what Benji worried about in his journal, they will not buy me off, silence, or bully me. I have DNA evidence. Somewhere there is a video. Everybody will know the truth. Tyler Kincaid will go to jail to spare future women. Thank you."

With that, she broke down as her parents comforted her.

A spokesperson for the Santa Monica police said they have issued a warrant for Tyler Kincaid's arrest. A lawyer for the Kincaid Group released a statement that Tyler Kincaid is innocent, the sex was consensual, and that he looks forward to his day in court. The statement also said Tyler Kincaid is currently out of the country.

Despite several attempts, CNN could not reach the Kincaid family for comment.

Day Ten
Slate

Hacker Group Anonymous Claims Video of Tyler Kincaid's Sexual Assault
By MINDY MARQUEZ

The lengthy manifesto written by Benjamin Wallace, 18, who committed the most public suicide ever recorded, continues to reverberate in unintended ways.

The hacking group Anonymous announced it has retrieved the video of Tyler Kincaid, 18, of sexually assaulting Adra Bharadwaj, also 18. Several more students have come forward, confirming the dramatic Manifesto account of the classroom confrontation between Benjamin Wallace and Tyler Kincaid about the assault. Wallace, upset by the attack, threatened to kill Kincaid. In his Manifesto, Mr. Wallace, an admitted former hardcore porn addict, famously compared the environmental ethos of the current administration to a "gang rape of Mother Earth."

While the video doesn't reveal the male's face, Anonymous says they can match the audio recording to Mr. Kincaid because he "slut-shames" the unconscious and drugged girl while masturbating on her, calling her a "stupid bitch" and a "stuck-up whore."

Anonymous also claims to have "cybercased" the event to the Kincaid compound during a party Tyler threw. The hacking group, "disgusted by Mr. Kincaid's smear campaign" against Mr. Wallace and Ms. Bharadwaj, claims Kincaid premeditated the assault because he set up his phone to record it. Anonymous will not release the video but has offered it to Ms. Bharadwaj to use in court, both civil and criminal.

The "Times Up" Legal Defense Fund has pledged to cover all legal expenses for Bharadwaj. The #Metoo movement is calling for a boycott of all Kincaid Manufacturing consumer products. Kincaid manufacturing is a subsidiary of the Kincaid Group.

Wallace's Manifesto is also attracting other young activists from around the country, including Emma Gonzalez, 18, one of the student activists of Marjory Stoneman Douglas High, in Parkland, Florida, who started the "Never Again" movement. In a short statement, she pledged to incorporate Wallace's climate platform into their anti-gun crusade.

"Back when slavery existed nobody thought it was possible to get rid of it," Ms. Gonzalez said in a CNN interview. "Or enact equal rights for women. Gay marriage. But look at where we are now. We can change. We're seeing everything must change to fix this world screwed up by old adults. And it has to change fast. We're on the clock."

The president, whom Mr. Wallace compared to Nero fiddling while the world burns, lashed out in response to growing ridicule of his environmental policies, tweeting, "Benjamin Wallace – loser. Climate change – HOAX. I have best people in EPA. NO job-killing enviro regs!"

The president also said he would sue Wallace's parents "back to the stone age" for their son's "endlessly libelous" document. The ACLU has vowed to defend the family for free.

Day Eleven
The New York Times

Shooter's Suicide and Viral Manifesto Provoke
A Rash of Copycats
By DAVID BAKKER

BENJAMIN WALLACE'S journal has broken records for downloads. Fan clubs have sprung up, citing the young man's intelligence, idealism, and sensitivity. T-shirt companies are printing shirts with the president's face under the word "Disinforstraction." But a dark and unintended consequence of the fact-laden Manifesto is it has inspired a series of suicides.

While it's difficult to separate the epidemic of depression and anxiety plaguing teenagers, at least nine suicides specifically named the Manifesto, which environmentalists are touting as a howling doomsday alarm. Susan Daly, 48, a volunteer at a hotline in San Francisco, said their suicide hotlines are receiving "a staggering amount of calls."

Several of the suicides were public, including plummets off school roofs during school hours. A few of the suicide notes are mini-manifestos, citing the current administration and the indifference of corporations to the catastrophic effects of what Wallace called, "extinction-level climate chaos." But some are simple, like one on Instagram, written by Karen Bransfield, 15, which said, "Why live when the greedy boomers are killing us all?"

The epidemic of suicides have created panic in some school districts, causing many schools to suspend classes, including Benjamin Wallace's high school, Harvard Westbridge, where one suicide occurred. Other communities have approached the crisis by bringing in counselors for school-wide assemblies and small encounter groups, encouraging young people to talk about their fears raised by Mr. Wallace's Manifesto.

But while some youth are falling into hopelessness, young anti-gun activists from the group, Never Again, citing the Manifesto's anti-gun stance, are calling for a merging of the environmental and gun control movements sweeping the country. The talk is revolutionary.

"Times up on this generation that's destroying our future." David Hogg, 18, said in a statement. "We need a government that cares about us. We view Benji as a martyr and his Manifesto as the truth. It's young people who are inheriting a burning planet from the most selfish and short-sighted generation to ever live. Like Benji said, no more talk. Time for action."

But where some people see a martyr, others see a disturbed loner goading vulnerable young people to suicide. Right wing outlets like Breitbart and Fox News have attacked Mr. Wallace and questioned his motives, respectively labeling him a "lunatic fringe communist" and an "unhinged polemicist." Fox News has relentlessly attacked Mr. Wallace, possibly because Wallace referenced them as a State News "lie factory" in the Manifesto. Sean Hannity is under fire for labeling the suicide victims "snowflakes that are part of a generation that needs to toughen up."

Other right wing agitators, including Rush Limbaugh and Alex Jones, have claimed that older and more experienced "agitators" wrote the fact-laden document. But an analysis of the Manifesto sent to The New York Times, when compared with school essays written by Mr. Wallace, shows that the handwriting matches.

Anti-Semitic attacks have also increased after neo-Nazi Richard Spencer tweeted that Mr. Wallace is, "a Jew because his mother is Jew." The neo-Nazi website Daily Stormer wrote a slew of anti-Semitic articles, saying that George Soros is behind the Manifesto.

Mr. Wallace was a self-described "obsessive" about Hitler and declared "climate chaos" an existential threat worse than WW2. Wallace wrote that only a revolution of our values and policies could save humanity, tying together racism, inequality, gun control and climate change. He also called out ways in which the president mirrors Hitler's early rise.

Despite the right wing backlash, a wave of young people, the first generation without expectations of doing as well as their parents, is stepping forward and saying they identify with Mr. Wallace's fears about a looming environmental catastrophe. The trending hashtags on Twitter are #WeThePeople and #Itsalltrue, both lines from the Manifesto. Ironically, Mr. Wallace was a critic of social media, the leaders of which he called "pathological liars," singling out Mark Zuckerberg, who was testifying (and apologizing) yet again on Capitol Hill today.

In interviewing students in Marin County, which saw 120 people die in wildfires, one student, Paula Westfield, 17, of Napa, California, said, "Our whole neighborhood burnt down. My best friend died. It was hell on Earth and it's like all the old people don't even care. Ben was right. Look at Paradise. It's happening over and over, and nothing's changing. Nobody's doing anything. And our stupid Cretin president and the clown congress is responsible."

Marin High School had one suicide, Tim Janks, 16, who used a hose to pump carbon dioxide exhaust into his parent's Mercedes. The Manifesto was in his lap.

On the cover was a five-word suicide note, "It will only get worse."

Day Thirteen

Washington Post

Benjamin Wallace's Sister June Calls for Action, Not Suicide

By MARY ZANE

BRENTWOOD, CA – After two weeks of worldwide media frenzy caused by the suicide of Benjamin Wallace, the release of his dense manifesto, and the subsequent copycat suicides, June Wallace, 10, today stood outside her Brentwood home with her parents. Wearing a black T-shirt with a white snowflake stenciled on it, June read the following statement, calling for action instead of hopelessness:

"First off, thank you to all those people who send us support in this sad time. My brother's death and the world's reaction to it – we are still in shock.

"My brother killed himself to draw attention to our climate catastrophe. I believe what he wrote in his Manifesto and so should you. We are in a crisis. But my brother was a gentle person, so there's no way he would want other kids to kill themselves. That would horrify Benji. So please, please, stop jumping off buildings. Talk to each other instead.

"Benji wasn't a fighter, but I am. I love fighting. And I'm mad as a boxer who got his ear bit off. And you should be too. Everybody needs to get up off the damn couch and fight hard for Mother Earth. We are in a war for our very survival as a species. #ItsAllTrue. But killing ourselves is not the answer. It's already what the old people are doing to us.

"So, this is what I'm doing with my parents, who, no matter what all you haters say, didn't release Benji's Manifesto. I did. We're going to camp in front of the White House on the mall between Cretin and the Clown

Cult Congress, as my brother called those Republican flying monkeys. We will stay until this president is gone. It's time to get real and look our opponent in the face for the fight of our lives. It will take sacrifice and hard work. But I say bring it.

"We are not going next week. We are leaving tomorrow. And we are not just marching and going home. No! We will do what my brother said and stay as long as necessary. We are going to start a revolution – a kid's coup. And take it worldwide to politicians, including the ones that talk a good game and do nothing.

"And I don't care if your dad is a right wing nut like the haters sending us death threats. Or if your Mom is a tree-hugger who talks a lot but does nothing. Like Benji said, the climate doesn't care – the rain and fire fall on everybody, even the rich people in our neighborhood. And to the people that call us snowflakes. Fine. We will stick together like snowflakes until we create an avalanche of change. If we don't, the planet will melt faster than a snowball in August. The Sunrise Movement is joining us. Greta, I hope you join us too.

"So, stop jumping off school roofs and come to Washington. Bring your parents. And prepare to stay awhile – we're selling our house. We can't live here anymore, pretending everything's fine. You're right to be scared, but you're not alone. Join us until this defect of a president and all his crooked clowns are history.

"I'm still sad, but I'm done crying. I'm doing Camp for Climate to save our planet. And for Benji. If we have to, we'll climb the White House fence. And if they don't like it, what are they going to do? Kill a bunch of kids? Well, I'm not leaving Washington until every sleazy, money-grubbing climate denier is gone. Like my brother said: We are out of time! Everything must change! Everything else is disinforstraction!

"We leave tomorrow. Join us. #CampForClimate. #It'sAllTrue."

The speech has gone viral. Flights to Washington, DC, immediately sold out. World leaders, including Angela Merkel of Germany and Emmanuel Macron of France, have called for the United States to join Europe in the race to battle climate change.

While scientists debate the exact time-frame presented in the Mani-

festo, they acknowledge their predictions have consistently been too optimistic. And almost none deny that humanity is at a tipping point, as the
"global weirding" of record rainfalls, droughts, and fires from Sydney to
California demonstrate.

"This year, nearly half of our energy is renewable," Mrs. Merkel said.
"The United States only has 14%. Surely we can all do better after the
planet's hottest year ever recorded."

Swedish climate activist Greta Thunberg, 17, immediately threw her
support behind June Wallace's statement. "I have read the Manifesto and
agree with its urgency. Humanity is out of time. The tipping point is now.
I will lead the Camp for Climate siege in Stockholm. It is an outrage that
children must lead the way. But lead, we must."

The British environmental group Extinction Rebellion has also put its
weight behind the Manifesto and the Camp for Climate idea, releasing a
statement, "We are in a battle for our very survival, with a hard-out time-
frame. Wallace's sense of panic is right on point. Those committing the
worst violence against humanity are counting on your fear of conflict to
cow you into silence. Don't be afraid. Join the rebellion!"

Justin Trudeau said zero emissions in ten years is achievable if national
priorities and economies shift from warmongering to saving the planet.
He pledges Canada's support to reach this goal, echoing the Manifesto,
and the world's top trending hashtag, by saying, "It's all true."

Alexandria Ocasio-Cortez has also gotten behind the Manifesto, vow-
ing to make its "Ten Beautiful Dreams" come true. No Republicans have
stepped forward.

Paul Watson, of the Sea Shepherd Foundation, whom Mr. Wallace
cites in the manifesto as one of his heroes, vowed to bring one of his
smaller Sea Shepherd boats up the Potomac. He said he will use fire hoses
to spray bridges and block the daily commute of congress from rich Arlington suburbs.

Said the typically blunt Mr. Watson, "Ben Wallace is right. The situation is way past dire. If the oceans die, we die. And they are dying now.
I'm honored to join his fight."

Week Three – Headlines

Thousands Converge, Camping on Washington Mall

— Washington Post

SWAT Body Cam Reveals Wallace Family Dog Wagging Tail When Shot
— LA Times

Manifesto Science Challenged

— Breitbart

Benjamin Wallace's Father and the Police Shooting that Shaped Him
— Vanity Fair

"Camp for Climate" Goes Worldwide

— The Guardian

Tyler Kincaid Arrested for Sexual Assault, Extradited from London
— Los Angeles Times

The Birth of a Manifesto

— New York Magazine

Benji Wallace: Untreated OCD, Asperger, ADHD or Depression?
— Buzzfeed

The Manifesto is Pornographic

— South Texas Catholic

Alex Jones Says "Suicide Shooter a Government Actor, not Dead"
— Media Watch

Camp for Climate Protests Threaten Chinese Regime

— The Guardian

Macron and Trudeau Visit Climate Campers, Vow to Take Up Crusade

– Le Monde

Heeding the Manifesto – The Only Way to Slow 6th Extinction

– Global Animal

Camp for Climate, Real or the Next Occupy?

– Wall Street Journal

Jonathan Kincaid Accused of Bribing his Kids into Harvard Westbridge

– LA Times

Zero Emissions Now, How We Get There

– Rolling Stone Magazine

Manifesto Written by Hilary Clinton and Al Gore

– Washington Times

U.N. Chief Again Warns of 2020 Tipping Point on Climate

– New York Times

Benjamin Wallace, a Victim of Adolescent Brain Syndrome?

– Psychology Today

Massive Camp for Climate Protests in European Capitals, Moscow

– The Guardian

How the Republican Party Locked in Climate Change Forty Years Ago

– Washington Post

10 Ways Benjamin Wallace was a Traitor

– New York Post

Anonymous Leaks Emails Detailing Exxon Pay-offs to Administration

– Vox

Administration Hardens Attack on Climate Science

– New York Times

What the Manifesto Got Wrong About Guns

– American Rifleman

Birth of a Symbol for a Burning Planet: The Melting Snowflake

– Vogue

Did Benjamin Wallace Achieve Satori Right Before Death?
— The Buddhist Review

Wallace's Free-range Childhood, Negligent or Not?
— Parenting Magazine

Over 40 Million Refugees on the move from Bangladesh Floods
— The Guardian

10,000 Children Surround White House, Singing, Holding Hands
— Washington Post

Was Benjamin Wallace a Communist?
— Forbes

90 Australian Towns Considering Abandonment due to Fire and Drought
— The Guardian

President Tweets, "I'll Never Change, Never Step Down"
— Washington Post

June Wallace and 100 Children Arrested Climbing White House Fence
— New York Times